Kingdom of
MOONLIGHT

Also by Josie Litton
in Large Print:

Castles in the Mist
Dream Island

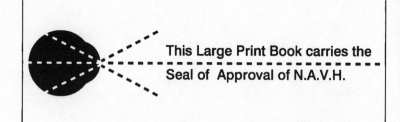

Kingdom of
MOONLIGHT

Josie Litton

WHEELER
PUBLISHING

Published in 2003 by arrangement with The Bantam Dell Publishing Group, a division of Random House, Inc.

Wheeler Large Print Softcover Series.

The text of this Large Print edition is unabridged.
Other aspects of the book may vary from the original edition.

Set in 16 pt. Plantin by Ramona A. Watson.

Printed in the United States on permanent paper.

Library of Congress Cataloging-in-Publication Data

Litton, Josie.
    Kingdom of moonlight / Josie Litton.
      p. cm.
    ISBN 1-58724-479-9 (lg. print : sc : alk. paper)
    1. London (England) — Fiction.   2. Princesses — Fiction.
   3. Large type books.   I. Title.
PS3612.I885K56 2003
   813'.6—dc21   2003052500

This book is dedicated to readers.
You have been incredible in your
support and encouragement, and
I cannot thank you enough.

National Association for Visually Handicapped
-------------------------- *serving the partially seeing*

As the Founder/CEO of NAVH, the only national health agency solely devoted to those who, although not totally blind, have an eye disease which could lead to serious visual impairment, I am pleased to recognize Thorndike Press* as one of the leading publishers in the large print field.

Founded in 1954 in San Francisco to prepare large print textbooks for partially seeing children, NAVH became the pioneer and standard setting agency in the preparation of large type.

Today, those publishers who meet our standards carry the prestigious "Seal of Approval" indicating high quality large print. We are delighted that Thorndike Press is one of the publishers whose titles meet these standards. We are also pleased to recognize the significant contribution Thorndike Press is making in this important and growing field.

Lorraine H. Marchi, L.H.D.
Founder/CEO
NAVH

* Thorndike Press encompasses the following imprints: Thorndike, Wheeler, Walker and Large Pr int Press.

THE BLESSINGS OF WATER

"The water is greatly valued," Kassandra said. "Even today, we bring ewers of it to the temples for blessings." Bending, she cupped her palm, caught sparkling drops of water and drank.

As Royce bent to catch the water in his hand, Kassandra almost reached out to stop him but drew back at the last moment. He was a strong man; it would still be his choice. The water was merely . . . encouragement.

Or so legend said. From time immemorial, Akoran husbands and wives had enjoyed a goblet of the water taken from the buried temple on their wedding night. Years later, old couples basking in the sun would remember it fondly and share secret looks of tender passion.

She stared at Royce as he drank, watching the ripple of the water ease down his throat. He was such a beautiful man, so perfectly formed in body and mind. The memory of him riding horseback wearing only a kilt, his powerful muscles flexing as he threw the javelin, haunted her dreams.

Ever since then, she had been living in a nightmare. The attack on her brother, the danger brewing in Akora, her desperate desire to save both her family and home — all seemed to close around her until she could scarcely breathe.

Until the moment when she emerged from her desperate, futile quest for vision to see in Royce's beloved face the future for which she yearned with all her heart.

A future that in all likelihood was impossible.

Chapter
ONE

Royce walked alone in the gardens of his ancestral home. The sun was setting, gilding every leaf and blade of grass with its last gifts of the day. As he watched night seep over the land, he looked out toward the sea, following the silver trail of the risen moon. In the stillness of the moment, there rose from deep within him the sense that he stood on the edge of something shadowy and undefined, yet momentous. Indeed, so powerful was the sensation that without thought, he raised a hand as though to seize it. The day had been long and he was tired, and thus perhaps it was that as he stood there with hand outstretched, breathing in the fragrance of stone and sea, he thought, just thought, he caught the scent of lemons . . .

Drifting on the night air, mingling with the jasmine, thyme and oleander to weave the fragrance she had known all her life here in Akora, home and prison both. How she longed to leave it, how she would miss it when she did. Kassandra sighed and laid her head on folded arms, gazing out beyond the high windows of the palace to the sea turned silver by the risen moon. Moon that cast the ribbon of a road leading . . . where? Into which of all the futures lying just beyond the next breath, the next moment? For once, she could not see it, could only feel. In the feeling, she reached out her hand and for just an instant, touched another's.

London * April 1812

Through the thin soles of her silk slippers, she felt the thickness of the Persian rugs varying with the smoothness of the polished floors over which she passed as she made her way along the corridor from her bedroom to the stairs. The curving banister was slick and cool beneath her palm. The house smelled of lemon oil, dried roses, the lavender water used to scent the linens, and faintly of vinegar, for all the drains had been cleaned the day before, as they were weekly.

The dove-gray light of morning softened every edge, blurring color that would emerge only in the full glare of day to withdraw again into shadow when night came and the lamps were lit. One night she had been there, one glorious night since setting foot on the quay at Southwark. Her first glimpse of London seen from the great river had exposed the limits of her fantasies, paltry when compared to the stunning reality. So, too, the ride through the crowded streets, brimming with people, smells not entirely or even mainly pleasant, and a din so impressive that the keeners for the dead would fall silent with envy. Never had she imagined such a place, for all that she had imagined a great deal, dreaming there in Ilius of the journey she longed to make.

Was making. She was here, glorious here, and the enormity of that had kept her wide-eyed and wakeful as all around her the house slept. Until she could bear it no longer and having dressed herself, an awkward process for all that she had practiced before arriving, came tip-toeing down to pause in the hushed hall and . . .

 . . . listen. She could hear the city, only faintly to be sure, for the house was surrounded by generous lawns and gardens, and further sheltered by a high stone wall. But beyond the twittering of birds already darting after worms, the whisper of a breeze in the fragile spring leaves, and the occasional murmur of voices from the distant kitchen, she could just make out the creak of wagon wheels and the clop of hooves ringing on cobblestone streets. Delight jolted her. The sounds were proof that the city really did exist and she was really in it. She did not merely dream of following the silver ribbon of the moon road over the sea, as she had on so many nights lingering at the palace windows when she should have been abed. As she would be now but for the excitement that thrummed within her.

She laughed and twirled, the jonquil-yellow of her skirt belling out around her, her arms flung wide to embrace the new day in so wondrous a place.

So Royce first saw her. Through the high windows near the front door, the sight shimmering behind the veil of the breeze-wafted muslin curtains, the Lord of Hawkforte stopped and stared.

Kassandra, Princess of Akora — the fortress kingdom beyond the Pillars of Hercules — daughter of the royal house of Atreides, bearer of a name out of bloody legend, dancing as though round the maypole in the giddy flush of fairest spring.

He knew her at once. Had he not been aware of her arrival, he would still have guessed her name, for there was an air of the exotic in the tumble of ebony curls down her back and the sun-kissed blush of her skin. She bore a faint, highly feminized resemblance to his brother-in-law, understandably enough, as Alex was her own brother. They were both half-British through their father, but just then and despite the fashionable garb she wore, he thought her the embodiment of the mystery that had fascinated him since boyhood.

Akora. For a long time men had called it a myth yet gone in search of it all the same. Those who returned did so disappointed. Others, perhaps cursed with better luck, were never seen again. Stories abounded: Akora was a fortress island, the dwelling place of fierce warriors who slew any foreigner unfortunate enough to near their shores; it was the last refuge and ultimate glory of the selfsame race that had stormed the walls of fabled Troy; it sheltered wealth and wisdom beyond calculation; it would emerge one day from the realms of legend to challenge the world.

Little had been known about Akora except that it truly did exist. Sheltered behind impregnable cliffs, guarded by warriors who were indeed among the fiercest on earth, Akora remained inviolate. Or nearly so. In the library at Hawkforte, Royce's ancestral home, was a collection of artifacts believed sent from Akora by a younger son who had stumbled across the place about the time of the First Crusade. It was even said that for some years thereafter contact had been maintained between the Fortress Kingdom and Royce's own ancestors.

Contact that had been renewed the previous year with the marriage of Alexandros, the Prince of Akora who was also Marquess of Boswick, and the Lady Joanna Hawkforte, herself the daughter of a house more ancient than any other in England. The union had thrilled the *ton*, which for months had seemed unable to talk of anything else. Had they known the true circumstances attending the wedding, they would have chattered even more. But only a select few suspected the truth, and even they could not be sure.

Such obscurity suited Royce perfectly. He preferred to work in the shadows. Yet just then

13

he stood revealed in sunlight, a figure of such masculine perfection that, catching sight of him, Kassandra stopped suddenly and stared over her shoulder, half turned away, half turning to him, suspended between one and the other.

Hawkforte. She knew him at once though she had seen him only once. No, not true, seen him only once in person and then only a glimpse. Hawkforte yet not Hawkforte, the man she recalled who had survived a captivity the previous year that would have killed most anyone else. He looked . . . like the sun, she decided, entrancing yet dangerous to gaze at directly. His hair was golden, untainted by powder, and thick, just brushing the collar of his morning coat. His features were compelling, powerful and unrelenting. He was as tall as her brother, which was tall indeed, and he had the same broad sweep of shoulders and torso. He stood with the easy grace of a warrior, likely unaware of the perfect balance of his body. But he was aware in other ways . . . of her and, she saw just then, of them both caught in that moment.

She was a young, unmarried woman alone in the hall of a house not her own, confronted at an unfashionably early hour by the arrival of a man to whom she had never been introduced. She might reasonably withdraw and summon a servant to deal with him. Indeed, Royce expected her to do exactly that.

She turned fully toward him, regarding him

14

through the muslin curtains. Her skirt still swung slightly with her exuberance. A faint smile touched her mouth. Without hesitation, she walked across the marble floor and opened the door to him.

He was a sensible man, but just then sense seemed to be deserting him. In the back of his mind he made note not to expect the Princess Kassandra to do the expected.

"Good morning, Your Highness. My apologies for disturbing you at such an hour. I am Lord Royce Hawkforte, Joanna's brother."

She offered her hand. He bent over it as she said, "Let us not stand on formality, my lord. After all, we are family. Please call me Kassandra."

He straightened and she saw the surprise in his hazel eyes. "Oh, dear," she said, "is that too forward? Should I not have asked you to call me by my given name? It is just that we do not put so much store in ceremony on Akora."

"No, it's fine," he assured her. "And please call me Royce. For all that I spent several months on Akora" — he discreetly avoided mention of the unpleasant nature of that stay — "I know little of it, but I tend to find formality tiresome and am glad to know it is not so much the custom there."

He released her but reluctantly, and promptly clasped both his hands behind him as though preventing himself from reaching out for her again.

15

A pleasing, female awareness stirred within Kassandra. She knew what that signified, of course, for no young woman growing up in the sensual atmosphere of Akora could possibly not know. Yet she was startled all the same, for no such awareness had ever come upon her before. It made her look at the Englishman warily.

Unless she was mistaken, the same surprised caution lingered in his eyes. Already they had something in common.

"What amuses you?" he asked as she smiled.

She laughed, a little flustered — she who had never been flustered in her life — and shook her head. "Nothing. I am just very excited to be here."

"Joanna and Alex were both delighted when word came that you would be allowed to visit."

"No more delighted than I was myself, I am certain. I have dreamed of such a trip for years. My eldest brother, Atreus, is a wise and good leader but he does tend to be quite protective. At any rate, it is very rare for anyone to leave Akora."

"So I understand. May I ask what persuaded the Vanax Atreus to allow you to come?"

"He has complete trust in Alex and Joanna, of course, and they are expecting their first child. It was only natural that I should wish to be with them at such a time. Besides, conditions seem to be calmer than they were a few months ago."

"They do seem that way," Royce agreed, but doubt showed in his eyes.

Her eyebrows rose. "You have not come at such an hour with some dire news, have you? Has Napoleon suddenly launched a fleet toward England's shores? Are we about to be invaded? No, wait, I know! It is that fellow, what is his name, Byron? The one who wrote the poem of which everyone is speaking. He has forsworn poetry and vows to never write another line. Is that it?"

Royce shook his head in masculine befuddlement. Her speech was quicksilver, her mind seemingly the same. She challenged him to keep up with her.

"How can you possibly know about Byron? That poem of his was only published a few weeks ago and you have scarcely arrived."

"Ah, but Joanna sent me a copy with the clothes she so kindly arranged. I read it on the voyage here."

"I see, and what did you think of it?"

"He is being hailed as the poet of the age, is he not?"

"I suppose. At any rate, all society is agog. But you have not told me, what is your opinion of the work itself?"

"It is very . . . vivid."

"It is that."

"And romantic. People are saying it is romantic, are they not, and Byron the man as well?"

"People say all sorts of things. What do you think of it?"

"I think the poet rather taken with himself, if you must know. But as I am looking forward to going about in society, I shall probably refrain from announcing that to all and sundry."

"A diplomat," Royce said with a grin.

"Do I perceive you are no more enamored of Lord Byron than I?"

"In time, should he ever emerge from his absorption with himself, he might produce something worth reading."

"I shall not wait with bated breath. At any rate, it is good to know I am not alone in my view of him. But come, I am rude to keep you standing in the hall. The servants are awake, I heard them in the kitchens. Perhaps we can beg tea."

"A princess beg?"

"Beseech? Entreat? Courteously request? Is none of that the done thing?" She sighed, anticipating his answer. "I have so much to learn."

"No," Royce murmured, looking at the play of light over the fullness of her mouth. "I rather think you don't." All gallantry, he offered his arm.

They were seated in the morning room overlooking the gardens when Alex found them. Royce stood as his brother-in-law entered. "I hope you will forgive me for coming round so early but we need to talk."

Dressed casually in trousers and a white

cambric shirt left loose at the neck and with the cuffs rolled up, Alex looked at ease but his eyes were as perceptive as ever. He missed nothing, as Kassandra reminded herself.

"Of course, Royce, you are always welcome. I see you have met Kassandra."

"We introduced ourselves," she said blithely. "No doubt a dreadful breach of protocol but somehow we've survived. How is Joanna?"

"Fine, or so she claims, and I have to admit, she looks it. She is awake. I'm sure she would welcome your company."

That was rather pointed but she supposed it meant Royce's early arrival really did signify something of importance. Much as she would have liked to linger, Kassandra was far too schooled in the ways of men to do other than nod demurely. She stood, smoothing her skirt. "I will take tea with her and we will chatter about all sorts of suitably female matters, nothing too serious or substantial, of course, for that would tax our brains."

Alex kissed her cheek lightly and said, "Behave yourself, scamp." He led her to the door. She stopped, glancing back over her shoulder at Royce, who still stood, watching her.

"Very nice to meet you, Lord Hawkforte."

Her effort at propriety made him grin despite himself. But she knew even before the door closed behind her that his amusement was likely to be fleeting. Something was wrong in this England to which she had come. Alex and

Royce both might be intent on keeping such knowledge from her, no doubt for the best of male motives, but they would not succeed. She would discover it and probably sooner rather than later. After all, to do otherwise would betray her purpose in being there. Her own purpose, to be sure, and no one else's, but one she intended to see to completion no matter what the risk or difficulty. That, too, was of importance.

Joanna was sitting up in bed when Kassandra entered. Her sister-in-law did indeed look very fit despite the advanced state of her pregnancy. Her hair, of a shade akin to honey, was in its usual wild disarray but slightly tamed by silk ribbons that matched her lacy bedgown. She was leafing through a silver basket filled with invitations.

"Oh, lord, Lady Melbourne already," Joanna said. She held up the envelope, peering at it warily. "You were barely off the dock yesterday when she sent this round. It is likely an invitation and you may have no choice but to go."

"Why would I wish not to?" Kassandra asked as she sat down beside the bed.

"Lady Melbourne is known as 'the Spider.' She is said to despise anyone's happiness and to take no greater pleasure than in destroying it. Yet for all that, she is a power to be reckoned with. Perhaps better to just go and be done with it."

"Is it not better yet to avoid spiders altogether?"

"Not in this case, alas. Lady Melbourne is a hostess of rare renown, mistress of the fine art of bringing people together in such ways that they frequently find themselves obligated to her. Mistress also, in her youth, of more than a few men of great power with whom she has maintained the most cordial relations. She is therefore a power in her own right and cannot be ignored without penalty. On the more positive side, she counts it a great coup whenever Alex or Royce appears in her drawing room. To capture you, even for a few hours, might well make her positively congenial."

"Oh, lord . . ."

"Exactly. Well, how are you today? Did you sleep?"

"Not a wink," Kassandra admitted, her natural good cheer returning. "It is all far too wonderful for that. I met Royce just now."

"Royce? He has called already?" Joanna made to rise but Kassandra stopped her.

"Don't bother, he and Alex want to talk alone. I was sent up here."

"The gall. Never mind, we'll amuse ourselves and find out later why he's come. Ring for Mulridge, will you? Oh, here she is."

The tall, black-garbed woman who entered with a tray gazed down the sharp beak of her nose at Kassandra and nodded. "Princess, you rise early."

"I hope I did not disturb anyone?"

"Not at all. Early rising is a virtue. Here, my lady, I've brought your tea and another cup for the Princess."

Joanna sat up farther and peered at the tray. "You've brought warm scones, as well. Bless you, Mulridge."

Mulridge sniffed and withdrew, but not without a pleased look. Having buttered one of the scones, Joanna handed it to Kassandra. "Be kind and do not let me eat alone. I swear, these days I am hungry every hour."

"But that is to the good. In these last weeks, the baby must gain sufficient weight to be strong when she is born."

About to bite into her scone, Joanna looked at her sister-in-law instead. "She?"

Kassandra bought herself a moment as she chewed and swallowed. "Did I say she?"

"Don't toy . . . oh, no, do. I do not truly want to know . . . I think."

Another would have been hard-pressed to take her meaning but Kassandra understood perfectly. "Joanna," she said softly, "you know that I do not always see."

"I know, of course I do, and I would never ask. It is only that —" Her fingers plucked at the sheet of fine Holland linen fringed with lace. "My mother bore two children safely but she lost her first at birth."

"I did not know that." After a moment, Kassandra added, "Does Alex?"

"No, and have no thought to tell him. He worries enough as it is."

"But Elena says you are very fit. She assured me of that yesterday."

Alex had summoned the renowned Akoran healer almost as soon as he learned of Joanna's pregnancy. Kassandra had hoped to travel with her but Atreus had withheld his permission, concerned by civil unrest in England. The Vanax had not allowed his sister to depart until the situation had calmed.

"Elena is wonderful," Joanna said. "I felt terribly guilty about her having to leave Akora but she told me she always wanted to travel and is delighted to be here. So is her niece, Brianna, who accompanied her. Elena also says my pregnancy is completely normal; I am the picture of health and all will be well."

"Yet still Alex worries . . . as do you."

Joanna touched her belly lightly. "The child moves. I feel his" — she looked at Kassandra — "or her strength and eagerness. To come so close to knowing the world yet be snatched away —"

Kassandra covered her sister-in-law's hand with her own. In truth, she had seen, but only faintly, months before when Joanna and Alex visited Akora with the news that they were to be blessed with a child. Then she had gone into the temple beneath the palace to pray and meditate. There the pathways of possible futures opened to her vision as they had for her name-

23

sake long ago in doomed Troy. She never knew what she would see, good or evil, horror or joy. Often, the experience left her drained and sick. But on that occasion, what she sought had proved gentle yet elusive. She had gleaned only a little — the laughter of a child, a flashing smile, and Joanna's own voice, loving if exasperated, calling, "Melly!" Just that and happiness like a rush of golden warmth through her. It was kinder by far than most of her visions, and enough. She had gone straightaway to select the birth gift, as yet unpacked.

Now, her hand on Joanna's and both theirs resting near the child, Kassandra needed almost no effort at all. Scarcely had she begun to reach out than she knew, simply and utterly knew. Joanna's fears, though understandable, were misplaced.

"You are not your mother," she said softly. "The tragedy of a first babe lost will not be yours."

Joanna blinked back quick tears of relief. "Thank you, Kassandra, with all my heart, thank you." She laughed a little shakily. "Oh my, I did not realize how deeply that fear had taken hold of me until you rooted it out."

That which was called her gift, and which as often seemed a curse, did not allow for many such moments of unfettered joy. Kassandra laughed and hugged her sister of the spirit. The two women chatted a little longer, sipping tea and eating scones, before Joanna rose to dress.

"We have given the men long enough," she declared.

Together they went down to the morning room, but Alex and Royce were no longer there. They had gone out to the stables, where the women found them in conversation with a short, shaggy-haired fellow whose black brows, thick as caterpillars, were drawn tightly together.

"Good morning, Bolkum," Joanna said. "Lovely day." She smiled at her husband and brother. "Going riding?"

Bolkum cleared his throat and glanced away.

"Not at the moment," Alex replied with a quick glance at his brother-in-law.

"Just having a chat with Bolkum here," Royce said.

"What about?"

She asked with such cheerful innocence, Kassandra thought, that they could hardly refuse to reply. Yet they did try.

"Nothing in particular," Alex said.

"The weather," Royce ventured. "Warmer than expected."

Joanna shrugged. "I'll ask Mulridge. She'll know."

Stroking his beard, Bolkum said, "Best see to . . . uh . . . what we were discussing." He nodded to the women and departed, vanishing round a corner of the stable.

Joanna waited, still smiling. Kassandra looked at Royce and found him looking back.

Time passed. Off in the distance, stableboys called out to each other.

"For heaven's sake," Alex muttered. "I suppose there's no point trying to keep anything from you even for your own benefit."

"None at all," Joanna agreed.

"You know," Alex said, "that I have asked you to leave London. You could choose our estate at Boswick, which you have given every indication of enjoying, or, if you prefer, go to Hawkforte. It matters not to me whether our child is born at one or the other so long as you are comfortable and safe."

"And you know," she replied, "that I have said I will do so gladly provided you accompany me."

"Which I cannot do yet given the situation." Alex turned to his sister. "Now that Kassandra is here, I hoped you would be more inclined to do what anyone with an ounce of sense . . ." He broke off, visibly fighting for patience. "That is to say, what I am certain you realize is best for you."

Kassandra pressed her lips together tightly. Having reached London at last, she was reluctant to leave it. Yet she could not deny a certain sympathy for her brother. Magnificent though the city was, it was also crowded, noisy and dirty. That he would wish for his wife to give birth in calmer, gentler circumstances was understandable enough. Beyond that, the sight of Alex cast in the role of a harried husband unable to compel his wife's obedience was so diverting that it almost made up for the possibility of being sent to rusticate in the countryside. Although she loved her brother dearly and thought him among the best of men, she knew he had been prey to the typical arrogance of the male, leading him to believe that women and marriage were vastly simpler than he had since discovered.

His wife went to him and placed a hand gently on his arm. "Our child and I will be safe wherever you are. Now will you tell me what has happened?"

He looked to Royce, who answered reluctantly. "There is trouble in Yorkshire. It appears 'General Ludd's' army has returned. They are back to smashing looms and threaten to kill any who oppose them."

Kassandra struggled to conceal her shock. She knew all too well that it was the uprising the previous autumn by workers who called themselves Luddites that had caused Atreus to delay granting permission for her to visit England. Only recently, when it appeared the danger was passed, had he relented. Now he would regret that and might even insist on her return to Akora.

"I don't understand," she said. "There really isn't any General Ludd, is there?"

"Apparently not," Royce replied. "But the workers who are seeing their wages cut by the new industrial machines have taken shelter be-

hind the myth of him. They swear oaths of se-
crecy, wear masks when they launch their
attacks, and are protected by numerous sympa-
thizers."

"They are also risking their lives," Joanna
said. "Parliament passed that dreadful law
making the smashing of such machines punish-
able by death."

"Death for breaking a machine?" Kassandra
asked. Surely, she had misunderstood. For
years she had studied England, albeit from a
distance, savoring every book and anecdote
Alex brought back from there, examining every
object and dreaming of the day she would be
able to go there herself. She thought it a
country of — to quote the title of her favorite
novel — sense and sensibility.

"It was an overreaction," Royce acknowledged. "To give credit where it is due, that poet
fellow, Byron, spoke out against it in the Lords.
He was actually rather eloquent. I was probably
less so but I did try, unfortunately to no avail.
The bill passed into law but now seems to have
failed in its objective. Far from being suppressed, the Luddites appear more determined
than ever."

"And potentially more dangerous," Alex said.
He looked at his wife. "Are you truly bent on
staying here?"

Joanna touched his arm gently, her hand lingering as she said, "I am bent on staying with
you, my lord."

He was, Kassandra realized, a man torn: still concerned for his wife's safety yet cherishing of the love that made her so reluctant to leave his side. He also knew how to give in, if not gladly, at least gracefully. "In that case, Royce and I have agreed to bring men up to London from both Boswick and Hawkforte. Bolkum is arranging for tents to be set up for them behind the stables. They will patrol the grounds night and day, and you" — his gaze moved to include Kassandra — "neither of you will leave here without an armed escort. Is that clear?"

"You don't really expect trouble from the Luddites here, do you?" Joanna asked.

"If I did," her husband informed her, "the choice to remain here or go would not be yours. As it is, I think them likely to be all too well occupied elsewhere, but I prefer to be prepared all the same. And in that light, I have your word you will go nowhere without escort?"

Both women assured him that he did. Kassandra was sufficiently relieved to be remaining in London that she suspected she would have agreed to virtually anything. Even so, the irony of the situation did not escape her. On Akora, the kingdom where warriors were said to rule while women merely served, she had gone anywhere she wished without concern. But here in supposedly more advanced England, she could not venture beyond the door without the company of armed men.

Progress, it seemed, was a two-edged sword.

"Speaking of going," Joanna said. She drew an envelope from her pocket. "Lady Melbourne has wasted no time."

The men groaned. "You understand," Alex said quickly, "with the situation so unsettled, I will be occupied at all hours —"

"Strenuously occupied," Royce added. "We both will be. The very thought of socializing when there is so much else to do —"

"The very thought of not," Joanna interjected, "is worse. You know perfectly well that most of real importance will be said in the drawing rooms."

Alex scowled but did not disagree. All the same, he declared, "You cannot be thinking of going near her, not in your condition. Who knows what such exposure would do to our unborn child?"

"I am hardly likely to let Kassandra go alone." On a hopeful note, she added, "But perhaps this invitation is for tonight or tomorrow, and we will have a ready excuse."

"What would that be?" Kassandra asked.

"It's a bit complicated," Joanna replied. "We could discuss it over breakfast."

Despite their avowals of pressing business, the men agreed readily. The morning being so pleasant, they adjourned to the stone terrace overlooking the gardens. Mulridge brought them more tea and scones, muffins flavored with cinnamon, crisp bacon, coddled eggs in little blue-and-white china pots, and hothouse strawberries. They ate and talked as the sun rose farther and the day warmed.

"You know," Alex said to his sister, "that there are two political parties here in England?"

Kassandra nodded. "The Whigs, who are reformers, and the Tories, who are not. The Whigs wish to sue for peace with Napoleon, the Tories are intent on continuing the war to total victory for Britain."

Royce, who had already been looking at her, as he could seem to do little else, was surprised. "I wouldn't have expected you to be informed about British politics." Belatedly, he remembered his resolution to expect the unexpected.

She bestowed upon him a glance of supreme female patience and understanding cast from beneath the thick fringe of her lashes and lit by the golden shards that transformed her eyes from a rich, dark brown to something more. Extraordinary eyes really, windows on a soul that seemed to be growing more . . . amused by the moment as he continued to stare at her like a green boy.

Alex cleared his throat. "Kassandra likes to read. I've kept her supplied with books from England as well as various periodicals, some of which cover the political news. At any rate, the Whigs suffered a grave disappointment earlier this year when the Prince Regent, whom they had always considered their friend, decided to keep the Tories in power."

"The result," Joanna added, "is that the *ton* has separated into two camps: the Tories flock round the Prince Regent, while his former Whig friends shun him. It's very tiresome for everyone, of course, and can't possibly be kept up. Too many people are missing too many parties."

"But in the meantime," Royce told Kassandra, "you cannot be seen to socialize with the Whigs, particularly the formidable Lady Melbourne, before paying your respects to the Prince Regent."

"Of course not," she agreed. "His Highness must take precedence. To which party do you belong?"

Royce answered smoothly, "I occupy that uncomfortable ground in the middle, agreeing with the Whigs on the need for reform but with the Tories on the wisdom of accepting nothing less than victory in the war with Napoleon."

He glanced at the invitation from Lady Melbourne still lying unopened on the table. "Perhaps we should see what the Spider wants."

Alex grimaced but took the missive and, with the edge of his knife, slashed it open. He removed a single sheet of paper and read. "We are invited to Melbourne House on Tuesday next for a supper" — he shot Royce a wry glance — "in honor of that fellow, Byron."

"Oh, lord," Joanna murmured and drove the spoon into her coddled egg.

The men took themselves off a short time

later. Kassandra was just considering whether she might attempt a nap, when the brass knocker on the front door sounded loudly. Joanna jumped, then looked guilty for having done so.

"I had forgotten the time," she said.

"Are you expecting someone?"

"I'm afraid so . . . that is, not afraid precisely, just regretful, although of course, there is no avoiding it."

Kassandra stared at her, observing the sight of her sensible sister-in-law looking rather anxious.

"No avoiding at all," Joanna said and stood up. "Come and say hello to Madame Duprès."

Chapter
TWO

Torture. Plain, unmitigated torture. To have to stand still for hours being poked, prodded and worse yet, pinned. To listen to the chattering and deflect the questions of a woman who never seemed to pause for breath. And then, after all that, to be told this was only the beginning.

Kassandra let out a huge sigh and slumped in her bath. From her perch on the bed where she was keeping her sister-in-law company, Joanna asked, "Is something wrong?"

"No, no, everything is fine. I'm just a bit tired, that's all."

"Madame Duprès can be exhausting but she is the most renowned dressmaker in England at the moment. Who knows how many clients she is disappointing in order to see to the needs of the Princess of Akora."

"I was thinking about that," Kassandra said. "Wouldn't it be more appropriate for me to appear in Akoran dress?" The far simpler, vastly more comfortable Akoran dress.

"I thought you were tired of all that virginal

white. At least here you can wear different colors."

"White really isn't all that bad."

Joanna tossed a towel to her. "Come out before you're all pruney or fall asleep. Besides, the worst is over. A few more fittings and you'll be done."

"How many is a few?" Kassandra asked.

"Mmmmf."

"What was that?"

"A few, that's all. Daydresses are straightforward enough. It's the ball gowns that take more effort."

"I could skip the balls," Kassandra said, drying herself off. She exchanged the towel for a sleeveless chemise that stopped a few inches above her ankles. It, at least, was comfortable. "We could say it is an Akoran custom to go to bed early. Mulridge would approve of that."

"Royce is a wonderful dancer."

Seated at the dressing table, Kassandra watched her sister-in-law in the gilt-framed mirror. Joanna looked entirely innocent, if one discounted the gleam in her eye.

"Does he waltz?" Kassandra asked before she could stop herself. "I confess, I long to waltz."

Joanna put a hand to her heart and pretended to swoon. "I am shocked, utterly shocked. Don't you know the waltz is considered much too 'fast'? Why, it's banned from Almack's."

"Am I going to Almack's?"

"Only if you want to. The proprietresses would admit you, without doubt, but I cannot see there would be much purpose in your being there."

"Why is that?" Kassandra asked as she took up a silver-backed brush and began working it through her hair.

"Because Almack's is the Marriage Mart, that's why. I hardly think you would have any interest in such a place . . ." She let the comment trail off, not quite a question.

"Of course I don't," Kassandra said very firmly.

"Still, I seem to remember on Akora last year, you had some concerns about marriage. What did you say? Oh, yes, something about marriage to an Akoran warrior being too restrictive for you. That it was unlikely such a husband would indulge your wish to travel. Of course, an English husband would see things differently."

"Not necessarily. Of late, I have been thinking I might be wiser not to marry at all."

Joanna said something that sounded like "pshaw" and jumped up from the bed. She was surprisingly agile for someone very pregnant. Taking the brush from Kassandra, she assumed the task of untangling her hair. The motion was undeniably soothing. Within minutes, Kassandra's eyes were drooping.

"To bed with you," Joanna said. "Tonight you will sleep and tomorrow we will go over everything. Before you set foot in Carlton House or anywhere else, I will describe to you all the players. You will know their intrigues and their ambitions, their secrets and their scandals. In short, you will not go unarmed."

"Secrets," Kassandra murmured. "Everyone has them."

"I suppose." Joanna led her over to the bed, pulling back the cool sheet and urging her beneath it.

"Even me," Kassandra said, or perhaps she only imagined she did, for it seemed she was speaking not to Joanna but to Royce, who nodded gravely as though he understood. He took her hand as he had in the hall that morning and drew her attention to where they stood, on a hillside overlooking sparkling water, and nearby, proud stone towers rising to the sun.

"Hawkforte," a voice said in her dream, and the name wrapped round her as though in ancient welcome.

The feeling of that still lingered when she woke to morning and the clink of china. Mulridge set down the tray and opened the windows wider. "Good morning, Princess. A fair day."

Reality flooded back with a jolt. "Is Madame Duprès here yet?"

"No, but she will be shortly." Mulridge ruffled her black bombazine, tilted her head to one side and regarded the tray. "Don't let the scones get cold."

Kassandra did not, for she very much feared they might be the last food she got for some time. After another exhausting day in the clutches of Madame Duprès and her minions, Kassandra had begun to entertain fantasies of swimming back to Akora, when the dressmaker suddenly exclaimed, "There, done and perfect, if I may say." She rubbed her hands with glee, perhaps already counting the coin she would receive.

Rousing to faint hope, Kassandra said, "Done? All of it? Really?"

"How amusing, Your Highness. The gown for this evening's soirée at Carlton House is completed. There are still many, many other garments. My little assistants sew their fingers to the bone but then —" Whether or not she was actually French, she had mastered the Gaelic shrug. "That is their job. So, it is beautiful, *non?*"

Kassandra looked at herself in the large mirror one of the little assistants rolled forward. Madame Duprès might be a gossiping harridan but she had the soul of an artist. The gown of amber silk with an overskirt of gold lace perfectly complemented Kassandra's coloring. The high waist and small puff sleeves were deceptively simple, preserving the elegant flow of the fabric. There was a short, easily managed train that added a note of regalness.

While the garment was heavier and more constricting than what she was accustomed to on Akora, it made her feel armored to meet whatever might lie in wait for her at Carlton House.

"It is perfect," Kassandra admitted.

Madame Duprès nodded in agreement. Modesty, it seemed, was not her strong suit. She gestured brusquely to her assistants. "We will leave you to prepare for this evening, Your Highness, but I will return tomorrow for more fittings."

Kassandra blanched slightly but she was of an ancient and fierce house; she could survive this.

Joanna had been lying down to rest, Alex having insisted that she do so if she had any thought of attending Carlton House that evening. She joined Kassandra and, true to her promise, provided a quick, startling summary of the *ton*, their feuds, foibles and fancies. Most particularly, she explained the social arrangements that drew the polite fig leaf of the family name over children of decidedly varied parentage.

"Lady Melbourne, the Spider herself," Joanna explained, "had six children in the bloom of her youth, of which at least two are not generally thought to have been fathered by Lord Melbourne. She is hardly unique."

"I don't think of myself as naïve," Kassandra said, "but I have to admit that I am shocked. Does no one sleep in his or her own bed?"

"As little as possible, so it seems. Morality

as you and I know it is nonexistent. The only rule is discretion, which applies only to women and then only haphazardly. Men do as they please."

"Does it really please them, any of them? Are they happy?"

"Not as far as I can tell. They know that on some level, I think. Remember what the Romans used to say: Enjoy today, trusting little in tomorrow. I think that sums up the *ton*."

"It would also make them rather dangerous, wouldn't it?"

"They can be, to themselves and to others. But to be fair, there is another side. Whatever else they are, they cannot be accused of hypocrisy, and they have a tremendous sense of style. It infuses everything — clothes, music, books, but also buildings and entire neighborhoods, even cities. They are transforming their world."

"They? You do not count yourself one of them?"

"No, and neither does Alex or Royce. We move among them because that is the surest route to influencing events but we are not really a part of them. Their values, such as they have, are not ours, nor are their concerns. Alex, being a prince of Akora, has always stood apart, but so has Royce in a different way. He is Hawkforte and as Hawkforte has always done, he serves England, or perhaps I should say he serves what he believes England can be."

Kassandra, who knew something about visions of what could be and the service they demanded, nodded.

The ladies had joined Alex in the drawing room. Kassandra was still adjusting to seeing her brother in British garb. During his visits to Akora, he was strictly and entirely a prince of the house of Atreides, but here he bore a different identity, that of Lord Alex Haverston Darcourt, Marquess of Boswick, Earl of Letham, Baron Dedham, the titles that were his through their British father. He looked the part in a perfectly tailored swallow-tailed coat, white shirt and cravat, and pantaloons. Although he explained this was not court dress, the evening being unofficial and therefore less formal, Kassandra thought he appeared most impressive, at least until Royce arrived and she found herself unable to think of much at all.

He was attired similarly to her brother except his coat was of a dark hunter green rather than the charcoal gray Alex favored. The thick mane of his golden hair was brushed back from his forehead. His eyes, when they rested on her, lit with male approval she could not possibly mistake.

"Ladies," he said, without taking his gaze from Kassandra, "you both look lovely."

"I'm over here, Royce," Joanna said and gave him a little wave.

He flushed but only for a moment before his natural self-possession returned. With good humor, he said, "So you are, but are you sure you should venture into the crush tonight?"

"I expect I shall be dreadfully well protected," she replied with a nod to Alex. "Besides, my delicate condition assures we will not be expected to tarry into the wee hours."

A short time later, Alex called for the carriage. Drawn by four horses in two matched pairs, the landau comfortably accommodated both couples while keeping them sheltered from the cooling spring air. Outriders proceeded and followed the carriage, evidence of increased security. Both the men had also brought along walking sticks, which Kassandra immediately suspected concealed swords. She had read of such things and saw no other reason why two very fit men would require walking sticks to attend a social evening. She thought the notion fascinating and could not put off staring at the polished wood canes. Seeing her interest, Royce finally laughed and raised the tip of his just enough for her to see that her suspicion was correct.

"I knew it," Kassandra exclaimed. "But why don't you just wear swords and be done with it?"

"They've fallen out of fashion," Royce said with evident regret. "Even dress swords aren't seen anymore. The best we can do are these things."

The carriage proceeded on to Pall Mall and shortly joined the line of vehicles dispensing guests before the Prince Regent's residence.

Alex and Royce stepped down first and assisted the ladies. Gazing at the elaborate Corinthian portico, Kassandra shook her head in amazement. "There is so much of the Greek influence. Is the Prince attempting to re-create Athens?"

"He would be flattered by the notion," Royce replied as he escorted her inside.

At once, heads swung in their direction, and as swiftly bent close together. The sudden hum of whispers reminded Kassandra of a hive of insects. She thought of what Joanna had told her of "the Spider" and wondered how many other malevolent creatures she would encounter. Just so long as she did not become a snack for them.

To escape that unpleasant thought, she glanced around and was struck immediately by the opulence of her surroundings. The spacious interior was, she quickly calculated, in the shape of an octagon, all eight sides framed by columns of red-veined marble. The walls, themselves ornately decorated, rose to an elaborately carved ceiling. Every surface was embellished in some way. The sheer excess was dizzying.

"Not to your taste?" Royce inquired.

"It's not what I'm accustomed to," she admitted. "On Akora, our public rooms are extensive but not so elaborate."

They were passing into a very large room done entirely in blue and gray, from the lush carpeting and wall coverings to the exquisitely crafted furnishings. Those hues were reflected back by the brilliant facets of an immense three-tiered chandelier fringed in gold. Beneath it, the Prince Regent stood to receive his guests. Kassandra saw a rather tall man with a soft, plump figure, fine brown hair and features that might have been handsome had they not borne the stamp of dissipation. He was elegantly dressed in garments similar to those worn by Alex and Royce, and carried himself well despite his weight.

His face lit when he saw the foursome approaching. Immediately, those ahead of them made way as the Prince Regent gestured them forward.

"Darcourt, Hawkforte, delighted, so glad you could come this evening. And Lady Joanna, radiant as always." His gaze focused on Kassandra with warmth that gave every appearance of being genuine. "This must be . . ."

Thus prompted, Alex said, "Your Highness, may I present my sister, the Princess Kassandra of Akora?"

The Prince Regent took both her hands in his and beamed in pleasure. "You are most welcome, my dear. We have all been looking forward to your arrival. How very good of His Majesty, your brother, to allow you to come. We do hope to make his acquaintance ourselves when the opportunity arises."

Kassandra looked into the gray eyes that

were badly bloodshot, felt the slight tremor of the hands holding hers and smiled. With instinct born of blood royal when England was young, she said, "I am sure the Vanax would welcome such an opportunity, Your Highness, should circumstances ever favor it."

She chatted a little longer with the Prince Regent before moving off to be introduced to the dozens of ladies and gentlemen eager to meet her. Thanks to Joanna's coaching, she managed to put faces, names and reputations together fairly well but one gentleman in particular commanded her attention with no difficulty, this despite his small stature and dour expression. He was presented to her as Spencer Perceval, the Prime Minister of England. Kassandra stiffened as he bent over her hand. Mercifully, he released her swiftly but then proceeded to speak with exaggerated enunciation as though he presumed "foreign" and "slow" were synonymous.

"I do hope your stay will be pleasant, Your Highness."

"Thank you, Prime Minister, I am quite assured that it will be. England is a delightful conjunction of seeming conflicts and contradictions, don't you think?"

Perceval frowned, taken by surprise and unsure how to respond. "Well, as to that —"

"After all, the culture that has produced that astonishing novel *Sense and Sensibility* and Lord Byron's . . . ummm . . . affecting work within

45

the space of just a few short months can hardly be considered *merely* a self-aggrandizing island with delusions of empire, can it?"

"I suppose not; that is to say —"

"Do excuse us, Prime Minister," Alex interjected smoothly. "I am sure you will understand there are so many waiting to meet Her Highness."

As he guided her toward the next eager greeter, Alex murmured, "Pray do try to remember we are not actually attempting to incite war with England."

Kassandra shrugged, feeling better since she had set down the vile Perceval. "Didn't you suspect the Prime Minister of plotting an invasion of Akora just last year?"

Her brother cast her a sharp look. "You weren't supposed to know about that."

"For pity's sake . . ."

"All right, yes I did, but he was soundly discouraged by the Prince Regent himself. There is no reason to have any further concern in that regard."

Kassandra did not answer. She had her own thoughts on the subject and was not yet ready to share them.

The introductions continued. Too soon, her head throbbed and the small of her back ached, but she kept her smile firmly in place. When the gong sounded for dinner, she resisted the urge to sag with relief.

The party that evening being comparatively

small and the night air cool, supper was served in the circular dining room. The chamber was done entirely in mirrors and silver. The reflection of one in the other created an opalescent glow that gave Kassandra the sensation she was dining inside the coiled shell of a nautilus. Joanna had warned her the meal would be elaborate and she was glad of the caution. Before it was done, she had lost count of the dishes trotted out but had eaten only a little, for she found the food overly sauced and so minced, mashed and manipulated as to make the individual ingredients unrecognizable. She had drunk even less, preferring to keep a clear head.

With Royce seated to her right and Alex on her left, she was effectively insulated from the more curious, who clearly would have liked to have conversation with her. For this, too, she was grateful. Royce proved an easy and engaging dinner partner, inquiring as to what she looked forward to doing during her stay in England and drawing her out to talk of Akora. She was a bit reluctant to speak of the latter out of consideration for the unpleasantness of his captivity there, but he quickly gave her to understand she should not concern herself with that. Soon she found herself telling him of home, of the light on the Inland Sea at dawn, the scent of the lemon groves, the flower-draped road leading up from the harbor of Ilius to the palace that had stood for more than three thousand years. As she spoke, her throat grew unexpectedly tight. After dreaming for so long of leaving Akora, the discovery that she could be so homesick was a surprise. She was relieved when the Prince Regent rose, indicating that supper was over.

They adjourned to a spacious drawing room where the colors were rose and gold. The effect was rather that of a gaudy blossom likely to be short-lived. The Prince Regent's majordomo, a small man tense as a drawn bow, was waiting for them at the entrance to the room. He offered a jerky bow and led them to a settee positioned near one end. Kassandra and Joanna took seats there but Royce and Alex preferred to stand, doing so directly behind them. Kassandra rather thought they had the better of it, for she had already noticed that the furnishings were astoundingly uncomfortable. The settee, for one, was nothing more than a long, flat board lightly covered with stiff upholstery she suspected concealed a layer of horsehair that felt like pounded rock. There was no back against which to rest, therefore no choice but to keep the spine rigidly upright. It was all wonderful for the posture but exhausting. With a sigh for the pillow-strewn furnishings of Akora, she watched the rest of the guests as they filed in, finding seats as best they could. The Prince Regent had already mounted a small dais nearby. He was joined there by two other men. They consulted with one another in low voices.

"A musical evening," Royce murmured.

"Is His Highness musical?" Kassandra inquired over her shoulder. She wanted to know just how bad this was likely to be.

"He's quite skilled with the pianoforte and the cello," Royce replied. "He also has a creditable voice. Unfortunately, he is not at his best right now, but this should still be tolerable enough."

At a signal from the Prince Regent, the majordomo thumped one end of his black enameled staff against the floor. Silence fell.

"Glorious Apollo from on high he hailed us
Wanting to find a temple for his praise . . ."

The unaccompanied voices rose, gathering in strength. Kassandra had never heard anything of the like, yet found the song pleasant enough as it continued.

"Thus in combining heads and hearts joining
Sing us in harmony Apollo's praise . . .
Long may continue our unity and joy
Our unity and joy . . .
Our unity and joy . . ."

"A rather ironic selection for this evening, wouldn't you say?" Kassandra murmured as she joined the other guests in applauding. "There appears to be no unity and as little joy."

As she spoke, she turned to look at Royce,

who nodded. "Perhaps Apollo will hear them and take pity."

"We know the messenger god on Akora but he is not trusted, nor any of his ilk."

"But you have a religion . . ."

"Very old, different from yours in some ways, not in others."

"I would like to learn more about that."

She hesitated, staring into the green-gold depths of his eyes, remembering the towers beside the sparkling sea. "Perhaps one day you will."

Several more similar songs were offered, including one that seemed to be a tribute to the god of drink, Bacchus. By the time the singers stood down to tumultuous applause, it appeared most guests were themselves eager for a drink or, better yet, several.

Liveried waiters hurried to accommodate them. As they did so, Alex offered a hand to Joanna to help her rise. "Time for us to be going," he said.

Kassandra also stood, glad to be leaving. She had enjoyed the evening up to a point but had no desire to extend it. They made their farewells to the Prince Regent, who was graciously understanding. He really did have beautiful manners, Kassandra thought. Such a shame the consideration he could show to a favored few did not extend to his people in general.

In the carriage, Royce asked, "What did you think of it all?"

Kassandra hesitated. She was, after all, a guest in England and although her visit was entirely unofficial, she did represent Akora in an informal sense.

"Carlton House is unlike anything I have ever seen," she said.

Royce laughed and shot her a look she felt to her toes. "This is going to be a repeat of the Byron business, isn't it?"

"What Byron business?" Alex asked.

"Trying to get your sister to tell me what she really thinks of Byron was surpassingly difficult. She is far too diplomatic."

From his seat on the facing side of the carriage, Alex looked at them both. "I hadn't realized you were at the point of discussing poetry."

Joanna stuck an elbow in his side. "Don't tease them."

He looked affronted by the mere notion. "I am not teasing them. I am simply pointing out that I wasn't aware they knew each other well enough to be discussing much of anything."

"If I might just . . ." Kassandra offered soothingly. "I found the evening fascinating. I longed to travel in order to see new places and encounter new ways of thinking. On that score, this trip is already a great success."

"And the Prince Regent?" Royce prompted. "What did you think of him?"

"I will admit he surprises me but you must understand, the only leaders of a nation I have

51

ever known were my grandfather, and since his death, my brother Atreus. The Vanax is simply . . . different from your Prince, that's all."

"Not inclined to get up in front of audiences and sing?"

"Does Atreus sing, Alex?" Kassandra asked.

"On occasion, among a few good friends. A very few, I might add. You must remember," he told his sister, "the Prince Regent holds a hereditary position."

"Doesn't the Vanax?" Royce inquired.

Alex shook his head. "Atreus did not become Vanax simply because he was the eldest Akoran male of our family following our grandfather's death. To be Vanax is to be chosen."

"By whom?"

"Not whom," Kassandra corrected softly. "What. Atreus underwent the trial of selection. It is an ancient Akoran ritual. I hope you will not be offended that we do not discuss it."

"No, of course not," Royce assured her. They were approaching the double iron gates in front of Alex and Joanna's Mayfair residence. Two men stood on watch there. They carried cudgels and had pistols tucked into their wide belts. As the carriage passed through the gates, Kassandra could see other men on patrol along the walls.

"Keep the carriage," Alex said to Royce as he alit in front of the house and helped the women down.

"For scarcely a quarter mile?" Royce asked.

"I still bear the scar of an ill-advised stroll in civilized England." Before Royce could object further, Alex closed the carriage door behind him.

The wheels were just beginning to roll when Joanna called out, "Oh, Royce, Kassandra will need dancing lessons. Do come by tomorrow and show her how to waltz."

"Waltz?" Alex said. "I see no reason why Kassandra should need to know how to —"

The rasp of metal on stone provided Royce with the convenient fiction that he could not hear his friend. He rested the back of his head against the leather seat and contemplated the strange lightness of heart that had overtaken him sometime in the past few hours.

Kassandra was . . . beautiful, of course, no one could fail to notice that, but she was also unexpectedly . . . worldly? No, that wasn't precisely right. There was a naturalness and spontaneity about her far removed from the studied mannerisms to which he was accustomed. Yet she had a seriousness of purpose he would not expect to find in one so young and sheltered.

But then he really knew nothing at all about her upbringing. Or much else about Akora for that matter. A prison cell held very little in the way of diversion, and starvation left little strength for curiosity.

There were still times when he had to remind himself that it was over.

Perhaps tonight he would sleep inside. And

tomorrow . . . The idea of teaching her to waltz had undeniable appeal.

Thus in combining heads and hearts joining . . .

He caught himself humming and stopped abruptly, but the music lingered in his mind long after the carriage deposited him at his door.

Chapter
THREE

As it happened, Royce was delayed before he could return to his sister and brother-in-law's London residence. He went instead to Carlton House, summoned there the following morning by a message from the Prince Regent, a startlingly early hour for a man inclined to sleep most of the day away, the better to enjoy the night. Even more surprising was the lack of the Prince's customary elegance. He still had on the trousers and shirt he had worn the previous evening, now severely wrinkled and stained. His hair looked as though he had worried it repeatedly. Taking in all this as well as the puffy face and the tremor around the mouth, Royce spoke softly.

"You wanted to see me, Your Highness?"

The Prince Regent stared blankly for a moment, as though he could not remember summoning him. He blinked rheumy eyes, reached for the brandy at his side, and downed it with the grimace of a man taking his medicine.

"Yes, yes, of course." Abruptly, he waved away the hovering servants. "Do let us be. Always about, never of any particular use." He rambled on as Royce stood patiently, taking his usual, careful note of the man now charged with ruling England. Since injuring his right ankle the previous fall while demonstrating a Highland fling, the Prince Regent had deteriorated alarmingly. He had taken to his bed, refusing to stir from there for several months while complaining of violent pain and berating his doctors for failing to help him. Already corpulent, he had gained yet more flesh while also indulging in even more drink than had been his habit. Perhaps of most concern, he had taken to dosing himself with ever-increasing quantities of laudanum. His temper had suffered and with it, his reason.

"Damn Luddites," the Prince Regent said. "Been up all night trying to think what to do. My responsibility and all that. Can't have what happened in France going on here." He shuddered and reached for the brandy again.

This was an old fear, one Royce was well accustomed to dealing with. "Your Highness, the Reign of Terror took place almost twenty years ago. Surely, if something similar were going to happen in Great Britain, it would have occurred by now."

"During my father's rule? He would never have stood for it. Wouldn't stand for most things, come to that. But now it's all up to me." He started to rise, reconsidered and slumped back down. "Thought Perceval's new law would put a stop to them. What sane man wants to die for smashing a loom? But here they are, back at it."

"They are desperate," Royce said quietly.

"Then they must work harder to improve their situation, mustn't they? Going about smashing things, that's hardly the way, what?"

"Desperate men don't always behave rationally, Your Highness."

"Suppose not . . . there it is, then." The Prince Regent rubbed a hand wearily over his face.

"If I may say so, you should rest."

"Gawd, yes, what I'd give for a proper night's sleep. Weight of the office and all, probably never know peace again. Look though, called you here for a reason."

All in all, it had taken less time for the Prince Regent to get round to whatever he had in mind than Royce had expected when he first walked into the room. That was just as well since at the rate brandy was sliding down the royal throat, it was doubtful he would be conscious much longer.

Prinny peered up at him. "Always thought you were smarter than the rest, and your father before you. Perhaps it's your family being so old, inclines you to take the long view."

"I would say that is accurate, Your Highness."

"Still think we have to stand up to old Boney?"

"Absolutely. The negotiation of any sort of peace with Napoleon will severely weaken Great Britain's position in the world now and for a very long time to come."

The Prince Regent laughed harshly. "Wish to Gawd Grey and the others understood that. Damn Whigs can't see what it would mean to have England second best to France, if that."

"However, as I believe you know, my views regarding reform put me in agreement with those same Whigs."

"Yes, yes, no point going into that now. Can't see how you imagine reform can be carried out in such uncertain times, but there it is. What matters is you're known to both sides and I dare say, being the man you are, you're trusted by both."

Or by neither, Royce thought, but kept that observation to himself. "That is very kind of you, Your Highness —"

"Not kind at all, just sensible. I need a man like you, someone who can move between both sides. Want you to see what can be done to smooth the way, put things back as they ought to be."

Royce had a sudden memory of the children's rhyme: *Humpty Dumpty sat on a wall, Humpty Dumpty had a great fall; threescore men and threescore more cannot place Humpty Dumpty as he was before.*

Bloated and bleary-eyed, the Prince Regent made an all too unfortunate Humpty Dumpty.

Even so, Royce said, "I will do my best, Your Highness."

He left a short time later, his passage duly noted by the usual hangers-on who gained from him no more than a curt nod in response to their eager greetings. Having reached the street in front of the royal residence, he stopped, turned his face to the sun, and stole a moment for himself. What the Prince Regent was asking was impossible but it never did any good to tell royalty that. Standing there with the clatter of London traffic about him, he found himself wishing, not for the first time, that some alternative to hereditary monarchy might be found. England, at least, had given considerable power to the Parliament but not enough, in Royce's view. France had replaced a king with an emperor — no improvement there. As for the Americans, they were attempting an extraordinary experiment in republicanism that might — or might not — succeed. England would simply have to find its own way as best it could.

He thought briefly of dropping by one of his clubs but he would scarcely have a foot in the door before there would be the usual attempts to draw him into conversation, preferably of the sort worthy of being repeated later for avid ears. His patience having been expended on the Prince Regent, he decided against such activity and instead began walking in the direction of the Strand. He had no particular objective in mind but was not surprised to find himself in front of Rudolph Ackermann's print shop.

Mister A, as he encouraged his patrons to call him, had built a tidy business exploiting the public's seemingly insatiable appetite for political caricatures. The newest of these were customarily displayed in the front window before which Royce now stood. He expected to see the usual offerings lampooning the Prince Regent, leading members of the *ton*, or perhaps a wealthy *cit*. He had yet to see a version of himself in the window and had commented to Mister A once to that effect. The publisher had replied that there actually were people in London he respected and left it at that.

But on this particular morning, the window was strangely bare. Only a single drawing held pride of place on a small easel set in the very center and surrounded by an elegant draping of silk. A single drawing, not remotely a caricature, of a young woman with dark hair cascading in curls down her back, her lovely mouth curved in a smile and her eyes warm with intelligence and interest.

Kassandra.

He was surprised and not. Her foray into Carlton House had commanded not only the attention of the *ton* but of the public that tended to make instant celebrities of society beauties. She was that, as the drawing clearly showed. Who had created it? A clever employee of Madame Duprès' possibly working at the dressmaker's own direction? A servant at Carlton House supplementing his meager wages? Or just as likely, a member of the *ton* not averse to shoring up an income likely battered by gambling and drink.

Not that it mattered. Whoever the artist was, the drawing was excellent. The more he stared at it, the more Royce realized how well it captured the light that seemed to shine within Kassandra: her humor and naturalness, her enthusiasm for all life had to offer. Not to mention the exquisite fullness of her mouth, the slender line of her throat and there, just above the suggestion of a gown at the bottom of the drawing, the curve of her breasts.

The shop door banged behind him as he entered and went directly to the mahogany counter where Mister A appeared to be awaiting him.

"Thought that was you, my lord," the publisher said. "Lovely drawing, isn't it? Of course, you know she's the Princess of Akora? Why certainly you would." As though the thought had just occurred to him, he said, "She's your sister-in-law, isn't she? Imagine that."

"Care to tell me who did the drawing?"

"Ah, well, as to that, the artist prefers to remain anonymous." He shrugged, one man of the world to another. "You know how it is."

He did indeed. "How much?"

For once in his clever life, Mister A looked startled. "My lord — ?"

"How much for the drawing?"

To his credit, Mister A recovered quickly. He named a price a sane man would have laughed at. Royce agreed immediately. The publisher frowned, clearly having anticipated a pleasant session of bargaining.

"My lord, it is only a drawing . . ."

"Take the money, Rudolph."

The use of his first name, imbued as it was with the sense of their long acquaintance, clearly took the publisher aback. Slowly, he said, "I am an honorable man, my lord. My conscience will trouble me."

Royce laughed, suddenly terribly amused by the whole business. "Then donate the money to some worthy cause. God knows, London abounds with them."

"Perhaps starving artists . . ."

"There you are, just the thing. The drawing . . ."

"Is yours, my lord." It was placed in his hands scant moments later.

Royce left the shop well pleased. He had decided not to question his extraordinary action. For once in his life, he had acted on impulse. Somehow, the world would survive.

But as to the drawing, he resisted the urge to look at it again before he returned to his own residence. Only then, secluded in his office, did he remove it from the crisp blue paper and white string in which Mister A had insisted on wrapping it. For a long time, Royce stared at what he had paid for so dearly. It really was an extraordinarily good likeness. But no substitute for the original.

None at all.

Mister A had insisted on including the pretty little easel. Royce found a place for it on the bookshelves that ran from floor to ceiling all round the room. He set the drawing so that he could see it from his desk, and absolutely refused to question why.

"He sends his regrets," Joanna said as she perused the note from Royce. "He is summoned to Carlton House and does not know when he will be free."

Staring at herself in the mirror, Kassandra managed not to sigh. "How unfortunate, but I quite understand."

As she folded the paper, Joanna said, "The Prince Regent seems to need a great deal of tending these days. I fear he is not doing terribly well."

"It is inevitable that the pressures of his position would weigh heavily on him."

Joanna went very still. Quietly she asked, "Are you saying that because of what you see?"

"No," Kassandra said, surprised by the notion. "It is merely common sense. A son overshadowed by a domineering father, thrust into power not by the father's death, which at least would be normal, but by a mysterious incapacity that renders the father mad. If your Shakespeare were alive, he would write it."

"Perhaps some poet will capture this moment."

"Byron," Kassandra said with a laugh. "I can just see him, rising up out of his carapace like a reborn insect and discovering the world beyond himself."

Joanna grimaced. "That sounds rather nasty."

"Yes, I suppose it does, but don't misunderstand me. This is an astounding world, so much younger and more unpredictable than Akora. I am delighted to be here."

"I am so glad," Joanna said and hugged her. Without warning to either of them, she said, "The child my mother lost was a girl. I suppose I shouldn't know that but I do. I have always wondered what it would be like to have a sister."

Kassandra stepped back a little and looked at her. "On Akora, every summer all the girls born that year are brought to the temples to be blessed. There is another, different rite for the boys but this one is only for the girls. When there is an older sister, she officiates at the blessing, touching the sacred oil to her sister's brow. If you go to this, you can see the very young girls, sometimes not more than two or three years old, solemnly carrying out their duties for their baby sisters."

There were tears in Joanna's eyes. Kassandra wiped them away with the tip of a finger. "You know, in your heart, that your sister lives. She is not of this world but she is still a child of Creation."

"There is a difference?"

"Oh, yes," Kassandra said and smiled. "In Creation, all things are possible and all things exist. It is only in this one little world that we experience limits."

Joanna looked deeply into her eyes with sight Kassandra could not ignore. She reminded herself that her sister-in-law, too, bore a gift: that of finding what was lost. In her own way, she, too, could see. "You sense those other possibilities, don't you?" Joanna asked.

"Sometimes, some of them. Have you ever positioned two mirrors so that you can see one reflected in the other?"

"I have seen that at dressmakers'."

"You can see yourself going on forever, reflected over and over until it is impossible to count how many of you there are."

"That is only mirrors."

"No," Kassandra said, "that is truth. But enough, we will set our heads to aching. So Royce cannot come today. However will we amuse ourselves?"

"I hesitate to mention it but Madame Duprès . . ." Joanna began.

"I have a favor to ask."

"Of course, anything."

"You have a maid here, her name is Sarah. We are of the same height and similar in form. I would like to engage her to take my place with Madame."

"What an excellent idea! Then we would be free to —"

"Do as we like. However, no woman should have to suffer so without recompense. Sarah has a fondness for a young man hereabouts. I thought a pretty new gown for her —"

"Perfect. I shall inform Mulridge, who will grumble but see to it. Now, tell me what you have most longed to do and we will go there."

"Anything and everything," Kassandra declared. Quickly, she added, "But you must not tire yourself."

"I shall be fine, especially if we stop by Gunter's —"

"For an ice? Oh, I would love that!"

And so they went, walking because it was not far and they both wanted the exercise, ignoring as best they could the sharp-eyed protectors who followed on their heels, their presence a silent warning to any who might be so foolish as to disturb the ladies' pleasure in the day.

In Berkeley Square, they made their way to the famed confectionery shop where they quickly agreed to be very bad indeed, each indulging in a paper twist filled with candied fruits, marzipans, nougats, pastilles and toffees. They purchased the same and flavored ices as well for their guards, who accepted them with abashed pleasure.

Thus fortified, they strolled toward the

Strand, where they were surprised to find the window at Ackermann's only just being set up with a new selection of caricatures. "It is usually done much earlier in the day," Joanna remarked as they continued on, arm-in-arm, to visit the shops along Bond Street. There they were mainly content to browse, although Joanna found a delicate infant's cap embroidered with tiny violets that she could not resist.

They returned to the Mayfair residence in mid-afternoon, entering the house to the clash of swords.

The white linen shirts of the two men clung damply to the broad sweep of their shoulders and chests. The supple fabric of their trousers outlined lean hips and muscled thighs. They stood, each with one arm aloft, curved in a posture so elegant it might have belonged to a dancer. For a heartbeat, they seemed frozen in the light swirling through the clerestory windows near the high ceiling of the long gallery and falling on the portraits that lined the walls, revealing the ancestors imperturbably observing the struggle playing out before them.

Then Royce tossed back the thick mane of his hair and attacked.

Steel met steel as Alex responded in kind. Down the length of the gallery, they feinted, thrust and parried, neither giving any quarter, neither expecting it.

"Not bad," Alex grunted as he blocked

Royce's foil with his own. "Just not quite good enough."

"Think not? What about this?"

The clash of blades rang out again. Back and forth they went along the sweep of the gallery in a deadly dance that fascinated Kassandra as much as it made her fear for the men's safety. She and Joanna watched from a small balcony set above the long hall, a place for musicians to play when the gallery was used for a different sort of dancing.

"Do they do this often?" Kassandra asked, unable to draw her eyes from the men.

"Often enough," Joanna replied softly. "They are superb, are they not?"

Kassandra watched a little longer before she nodded. "It is as well they are not enemies."

The men locked swords just as Royce happened to be facing the balcony. The moment he saw the women, he stepped away, disengaging with a quick word to Alex, who turned and looked up.

"You are back," Alex said as he joined Royce in lowering his sword. "How was Gunter's?"

"Sticky," Joanna replied. "We were very bad. Are you done?"

"Yes, of course," Royce said. "I hope we didn't disturb you." He looked to Kassandra as he spoke. She returned his scrutiny calmly despite the sudden, rapid beating of her heart. With difficulty, she dragged her gaze away and followed Joanna down the steps from the balcony.

As the women emerged into the gallery, Joanna said, "Why ever would I be disturbed by the sight of my husband and my brother seemingly intent on skewering each other?"

"You know it is only play," Alex said, a touch defensively. "It relaxes us."

"I would hate to see how you fight when you are not relaxed," Joanna rejoined, but tenderly. Between these two flowed a love and understanding so absolute that Kassandra felt compelled to look away lest she trespass even inadvertently in a realm where only they belonged.

Royce must have felt the same, for after a quick glance, he turned his attention to Kassandra. "And what did you think of your excursion?"

"It was wonderful. Everything was as I imagined, only more so."

"You will make enthusiasm the fashion."

"Will I?" she asked, scarcely aware of what she said, for awareness of him overwhelmed all else. He stood, sword in hand, the damp fabric of his shirt revealing the powerful, sculpted muscles of his chest and arms. He looked, she thought, uncannily like the warriors she and every other young Akoran girl had peeked at during illicit visits to the training fields, giggling behind their hands even as they goggled appreciatively. Yet he was British from the top of his golden head to the bottom of his brilliantly polished boots.

A British lord who had almost died in an Akoran prison. Since then, his sister had married into the royal family of Akora seemingly with his wholehearted approval. Kassandra's own brother had accepted him as a trusted friend. Desperately, she wanted to believe Alex was right and Royce as honorable and forthright as he seemed. Yet the stakes were so high — her country . . . her people . . . truly life or death for all she held most dear. And, too, her own feelings rising so unexpectedly to complicate matters already complex enough.

"Is something wrong?" Royce asked. He reached out to steady her but she stepped back just swiftly enough to avoid his touch. He frowned, as did Alex who witnessed the exchange.

"Kassandra . . . ?" her brother began.

"Forgive me," she said, and tried to cover her discomfort with a small laugh. "I have had a wonderful day but I fear the excitement is catching up with me." That was such an obvious falsehood, at least to her, that she half-expected Alex to call her on it, but instead he looked concerned, as did Joanna.

"How thoughtless of me," her sister-in-law said. "Of course, you must rest." Deeply chagrined at having falsely claimed a need that should more properly belong to Joanna, who was, after all, heavy with child, Kassandra nonetheless allowed her sister-in-law to draw her upstairs. While rest was furthest from her mind, she did want time to order her thoughts. Never in her life had she gone mooning after a man. She did not intend to start now, no matter how disturbingly attractive Royce Hawkforte might be.

"It's not the sweets, is it?" Joanna asked when they had reached Kassandra's bedroom. "If your stomach is upset, Mulridge can bring you something or Elena can see to you, if you prefer."

"Oh, no," Kassandra said hastily. "I'll be fine."

"If you're sure —"

"Absolutely, don't give me another thought. Besides, shouldn't you be resting?"

"I suppose," Joanna acknowledged. "But if you need anything —"

"I will ring and one of your extraordinarily efficient servants will come."

Satisfied, Joanna departed. Scarcely had she done so than Kassandra kicked off her shoes — nasty things with pointed toes and wedge-shaped heels! — and flung herself backward onto the bed, emitting a great sigh in the process.

She was not proud of herself, definitely not. Truth be told, she had fled from Royce Hawkforte rather than face him and the yearning he provoked. Now she was virtually hiding in her bedroom, trying to get control of her wayward self before she had to be in his presence again. That was hardly the behavior of a princess of Akora.

A good stern talking-to, self-administered, followed by a refreshing bath did much to improve her state of mind. As she descended the stairs again, the clock on the landing chimed the hour of four. She was just in time for tea.

Joanna was seated on the settee in the family parlor, a silver tea set in front of her. Royce and Alex stood nearby. Neither man showed any sign of their earlier exertions but Kassandra was not fooled. She reminded herself that Royce, like her brother, possessed the heart of a warrior. She would be wise not to forget that. Taking her place beside Joanna, she responded to queries about her well-being with assurances that she could not be better.

"Just as well," Joanna said, handing her a delicate Meissen cup of Earl Grey accompanied by a sliver of lemon cake. "Monsieur Maurice is due at any moment."

"Monsieur Maurice?"

"The dancing instructor." Joanna shrugged apologetically. "I'm afraid there's no way round it. Many social events are such crushes that dancing is impossible, but sooner or later you will want to dance, so it's best you learn the steps now."

"Why is it," Kassandra mused, "that in the midst of a very long and bloody war with France, the British seem obsessed with all things French? French fashion, French wine, French dancing. Is there anything French that fails to draw rhapsodies of delight from the

British? Aside from Napoleon, of course."

"I suppose it shows us to be a contrary lot," Royce said as he accepted a cup from his sister. "Although to be fair, there are more than a few English people with scant patience for anything French."

For the first time since entering the parlor, Kassandra looked at him directly, only to be struck by the intensity with which he returned her regard. He seemed to see into her far too deeply. Determinedly, she mustered a smile.

"I take it such folk do not come to Court?"

"Generally not. Joanna tells me Akora is very different. There, everyone goes to the palace."

"Yes, that is true. In fact, we have a saying: If you want to see someone, wait at the palace because they are bound to come by eventually."

Taking firm hold of her courage, she added, "It is regrettable that you were not able to remain on Akora for a time after you were freed. Although I can certainly understand your eagerness to return home, I fear you had little opportunity to get to know us as we really are and that you were therefore left with the worst possible impression."

Distantly, she was aware of Alex and Joanna's surprise that she would bring up so sensitive a matter, but it was upon Royce's reaction that her attention focused. He set his cup on the nearby mantel before matching her directness.

"I left quickly because I believed at the time that your brother the Vanax Atreus was responsible for my captivity. However, I have long since realized that was not the case."

In for a penny, Kassandra thought, and drove the point home. "Then you bear no ill feeling toward Akora?"

Joanna shifted uneasily in her seat even as Alex frowned. He was about to speak when Royce said quietly, "I bear considerable ill feeling toward the opponents of your brother since they were the ones actually responsible for what I experienced. However, as their leader appears to have drowned last year and their movement seems to have perished with him, I have little hope of satisfaction from that quarter." His smile, coming without warning, sent a frisson of pleasure through her. "Does that reassure you sufficiently, Princess?"

It would have to, she supposed, although she was very far from being reassured about the man who affected her so powerfully. Best to take refuge in evasion. "I thought we had settled on Kassandra?"

"So we did, my apologies. And now, if you would not mind, I have a request." She had confronted him bluntly and therefore owed him some amends.

"Of course," she said, and remembered to breathe.

"I believe you wish instruction in the waltz."

Her limbs felt unaccountably heavy. Surely, that was not because of the challenge of his gaze. "I have expressed an interest in it."

"Allow me, in all modesty, to suggest I would be an adequate partner."

"Alas, we lack music."

But they did not, for just then Monsieur Maurice arrived, accompanied by fully half-a-dozen musicians who promptly set up shop in the vast ballroom, and Royce offered Kassandra his arm. Joanna sat in a chair near the tall windows overlooking the garden and appeared inclined to smile fondly. Alex stood beside her, one hand resting lightly on her shoulder in a gesture both proprietary and comforting. He looked thoughtfully at his sister and the Englishman with whom she danced.

And danced and danced and danced as Monsieur Maurice — who perhaps truly was a Frenchman, for he seemed to have a proper regard for incipient *amour* — called out his instruction with increasing infrequency and concentrated his efforts on cooing encouragement.

Of a sort she hardly needed, for Kassandra was gone, lost in the warm, strong grip of his hand holding hers and his other hand on her waist, a proper amount of air between them, yet their bodies seemed to glide as one, round and round the ballroom in the London of her dreams.

Chapter
FOUR

Alex was alone in the breakfast room reading the *Times* when Kassandra came down the following morning. He set the paper aside, rose and pulled out a chair for her.

"Did you sleep well?" he asked.

"Very well, thank you. How is Joanna?"

"Not yet awake. She had a restless night."

Which meant, of course, that so had Alex as he would have remained awake to watch over his wife. Yet, Kassandra thought, his lean features showed no sign of weariness. The discipline of warrior training allowed for none.

"You will be a father soon," she said, and smiled at the prospect.

His face softened and she saw suddenly how he would look when he gazed upon his child. "Joanna told me of your reassurance. Thank you."

"Sometimes the 'gift' I bear truly is that."

Resuming his seat, Alex waited until the maid had brought Kassandra's tea and received her request for coddled eggs — new to her and already a favorite. When they were alone again, he said gently, "Sometimes it is not gift but curse. You bear it bravely but you do not have to bear it alone."

She had expected this, was even relieved by it. Of course, the brother who knew her so well would realize she was holding something back, especially after observing her conversation with Royce the previous day. All the same, it was hard to speak even a little of what she had kept so deeply buried within herself.

She toyed with the tea before she said, "Alex . . . you realize almost anything I see is only one possible future out of many?"

He nodded patiently. "Yes, I understand that."

"Nothing is written. We can be the masters of our own fate. We simply have to choose the right paths."

"And deter others from following paths that will harm us."

"Yes, exactly. Last year, when I had visions of a British invasion and conquest of Akora, you and Atreus wasted no time acting to prevent it."

"That is true, and Royce joined us in that endeavor." He spoke quietly but his hand, lying on the damask tablecloth, tightened into a fist as though he already sensed what she had to tell him.

She took a breath, willing calm. "The visions have returned. I can't explain how or why because that has never happened before. But for some reason, the path to that particular future has appeared again."

"You haven't told Atreus this?"

"No, he was reluctant enough to let me come here. If he knew we might still face danger from the British, he would never have agreed."

"It is not like you to presume your judgment is above that of our brother who, I remind you, is also our Vanax."

She took the reprimand in stride, knowing it to be deserved but knowing also that she could not have done otherwise. "I would never have withheld information from Atreus unless I believed it vital that I be allowed to leave Akora."

"Why? What can you do in England that I cannot?"

"I don't know. In the few days I have been here, I hoped I would discover that but I have not. I only know that I had to come here."

Alex was silent for several moments before he said, "All right, I think I can understand why you did as you have but we must consider carefully what this means."

As she had done little else since the visions' return, Kassandra did not hesitate. "It means Deilos may not be dead."

At once, Alex demanded, "You have seen him in your visions?"

"No, not at all, but last year he was trying to bring about a British invasion of Akora because he believed it would lead our people to repudiate Atreus and make Deilos himself Vanax.

Apparently, he assumed he would be able to defeat the British, but he was terribly wrong."

"For such treason, he drowned."

"So we believe but his body was never found," Kassandra pointed out.

"There has been no sign that the movement Deilos led to stop Atreus from bringing the changes that are needed on Akora still lives, whether the man himself does or not."

"I know, but Deilos and his followers managed to keep Royce captive for nine months with no one even suspecting a British nobleman was on Akora. Had they succeeded in using him to prompt British rage at such treatment of one of their own, you and I would not be here now."

"That is true," Alex said slowly.

"Besides, even if Deilos is dead and his movement to stop change dead with him, there are still those on the other side who believe Atreus is not bringing change quickly enough. Of late, the rebels have been active in the capital. So far, it is only small demonstrations, signs and slogans demanding change, but they have stirred talk among the people and more may come. Either faction could be responsible for what I have seen."

"Atreus cannot be left in ignorance of this."

"I know, but now that I am here, surely our brother will see the wisdom of allowing me to remain at least until we have a better sense of what is happening."

Alex's look was not unsympathetic but he

held out no false hope. "I would not count on that if I were you."

"Atreus respects your judgment above that of anyone else. You can convince him."

The maid entered just then with the eggs Kassandra had requested. When the young woman had left again, Alex said, "I will send word to Atreus today. It will be several weeks before we know his response. You understand that if he orders your immediate return to Akora, there will be no question but that you obey?"

Kassandra stared at the little blue-and-white china pot. She had lost her appetite. "Yes, of course, but will you at least encourage him to let me remain?"

He looked torn, caught between his love for her and his natural inclination to keep her safe. "Frankly, if I followed my instincts, I would send you to Akora on the next tide and Joanna with you. Matters are far too unsettled here in England."

"They would be far more unsettled in your own household if you attempted to dispense with your wife at this point."

He sighed. "I suspect you are right. At any rate, you must promise me that you will take the greatest care."

"I would you do the same."

She put her hand over his. They sat together in silence as all around them the great house and the city beyond went about its unknowing business.

"Royce will be back by Tuesday," Joanna said later in the morning. She had emerged from sleep but not yet from bed. A great yawn engulfed her. "He won't let us go to the Spider's without him."

"Where has he gone?" Kassandra asked. She sat in a chair beside the bed, her stockinged feet propped on the white counterpane.

"Hawkforte. New irrigation equipment is being installed. With such a lure to draw him, he could not possibly stay away." She smiled fondly. "Hawkforte holds his heart."

"Do you miss it?"

"From time to time," Joanna admitted. She rested a hand on her greatly swollen belly. Overnight, she appeared to have grown larger. "But it seems part of another life."

"I dreamt of Hawkforte."

"Did you? How remarkable."

"The first night I was here. Odd since I have never seen it."

"Was it a vision?"

"No, not at all, just a dream. I think . . ."

Joanna made a show of eating one of the scones Mulridge had brought but she set it aside quickly, intent on more important matters. "You and Royce waltzed wonderfully well together."

Kassandra laughed and shook her head, the better to conceal her sudden self-consciousness. "Could you be more obvious?"

81

"I doubt it," Joanna acknowledged cheerfully. "Pregnancy has robbed me of whatever subtlety I possessed, which probably was not much. I would love to see my brother well settled with a truly wonderful woman, and nothing would give me greater pleasure than if you were she. Is that so terrible?"

"No, not terrible, but you must understand, I did not come to England seeking a husband."

"But you like Royce?"

"Yes, of course —"

"Even if you do think it is possible he contemplates Akora's downfall."

"I do not! Oh, all right, I had concerns when I did not know him, but he has resolved them."

Dragging herself more upright against the pillows, Joanna said, "I should hope so. He is the most honorable of men, along with Alex, of course."

"He suffered greatly through months of starvation and isolation. Very few men could endure that."

"He has recovered," Joanna said firmly. "He even sleeps inside again . . . from time to time. Besides, as he said, if he wanted vengeance against anyone, it would be Deilos."

"Deilos who drowned while trying to kidnap you."

"I saw him go into the water myself." A moment passed before Joanna asked, "You do not believe he is dead?"

"I have no reason to think him otherwise,"

Kassandra replied. Nor did she have any intention of confiding in Joanna as she had Alex. It was enough that he knew the true reason for her presence in England. His heavily pregnant wife soon to face the travails of childbirth did not need to be similarly informed.

Her decision was quickly confirmed a few moments later when there was a knock at the bedroom door.

"Come in," Joanna called.

The woman who entered was in her middle years or perhaps somewhat beyond. It was hard to tell for she was tall, sturdily built, and carried herself with graceful strength. Her broad face was lightly tanned, her eyes bright blue and surrounded by lines that revealed her customary good humor. Snow-white hair twined in a neat braid around her head before tumbling halfway down her back. She was dressed in a loosely flowing robe in the Akoran style.

"Good morning, Lady Joanna," Elena said. "I am pleased to see you remain in bed."

"I would scarcely dare to do otherwise," Joanna replied with a grin, "considering your instructions." She extended her smile to the young woman who accompanied Elena. "Kassandra, do you know Elena's niece, Brianna?"

Kassandra had risen from beside the bed when the Akoran women entered. So great was her respect for the healer that she could not possibly have remained seated in her presence. Of the younger woman, she knew nothing,

83

which in itself was surprising. She would have thought she had met everyone associated in any way with the palace, if only through a relative.

"I am pleased to know you." Brianna recited the customary acknowledgment of a new acquaintance. She was a little taller than Kassandra, closer to Joanna's height, with fiery hair that was the perfect foil for her fair skin and delicate features. Her eyes were a deep green flecked by gold. Intelligence shone from them, but also something else Kassandra could not identify immediately — caution perhaps, or was it merely shyness?

"I am sorry not to have been able to greet you when you arrived, Princess, but I have been in bed with a cold. Until I was well again, I did not wish to risk infecting anyone."

"I fear our English spring has not agreed with Brianna," Joanna said kindly.

"The habit of staying up to all hours reading in your library might be more responsible than the weather," Elena declared. "I promised my sister I would look after Brianna when it was arranged she would come with me as my assistant. To date, I fear I have done a poor job."

"The blame is entirely my own," Brianna insisted. "My family has a farm on Leios," she said, naming the westernmost of the two main islands that with three other small ones made up Akora. "It is rare for any of us other than my father and eldest brother to make the journey to the royal city of Ilius. I myself have not been to the palace since I was a small child, taken there so that my adoption could be recorded. The excitement of being so far from home has quite overwhelmed me." She did not look overwhelmed so much as quietly pleased, as though the experience was proving to be everything she had hoped.

Kassandra had known, of course, as soon as she saw her that Brianna had likely not been born on Akora. Her coloring was very different from that of most native Akorans, who, like Kassandra herself, tended to have dark hair and honey-toned skin.

"You were *xenos?*" she asked softly.

Brianna nodded, unoffended by the use of the word that denoted strangers, as well she might be, for the *xenos* lay at the heart of one of Akora's most deeply cherished secrets.

"I was found after a great storm that destroyed the ship I was on. Unfortunately, there were no other survivors."

"Your parents — ?"

"Were lost. It was clear as soon as I regained consciousness that I was English, for I spoke in that language. Inquiries were made to discover if I had family here but no one was found."

"Do you hope to find someone now, while you are here?"

A flicker moved behind the young woman's eyes — wistfulness? yearning? But she said only, "It seems pointless to seek what I have no reason to believe exists. Besides, I am Akoran now."

And that, Kassandra thought, was really all that needed to be said. While Akora presented an inhospitable face to the rest of the world, accepting contact only on its own very limited terms, the *xenos* who did reach the Fortress Kingdom found a warm welcome from a people who had realized long ago that their survival and well-being lay in encouraging diversity. Once settled, none wished to leave. They became, as had Brianna, Akoran.

But how, Kassandra wondered, would they and indeed all Akorans feel if they knew how tenuous the peace and security of the Fortress Kingdom truly might be?

Careful not to reveal any hint of the dark shadow hanging over her, Kassandra said, "Now that you are recovered, perhaps we can see something of London together? There is so much I am longing to see and I suspect Elena will disapprove if I try to coax Joanna to accompany me everywhere."

"Regardless of whether I approved or not," Elena replied, "the *kyril* Alexandros most certainly would not." She used Alex's Akoran name and title as though to emphasize his authority. "The Lady Joanna is very healthy but she needs to preserve her strength."

"Especially if I am to continue any part of the social round," Joanna said. "Remember, we have but two days until we are expected in the Spider's web."

"You don't have to go to Lady Melbourne's,"

Kassandra suggested. "I'll be perfectly all right."

"Oh, I'm sure you would be, but the truth is, I have a horrible fascination with her. When you see her, perhaps you will understand." She mustered a brave smile. "In the meanwhile, you and Brianna go, amuse yourselves; I'll be fine."

"With only a devoted husband to dance attendance on you," Kassandra teased.

Joanna looked less than dismayed by the prospect. Kassandra was halfway out the bedroom door when she called after her, "If you go to Gunter's, bring back some of the little raspberry candies. Oh, and the orange slices as well, don't forget those!"

Or the honey drops and toffees, butterscotch and caramels, nougats and pastilles, Turkish delights and taffies — all the assorted sticky indulgences that flowed in paper cones into Joanna's nest over the next several days. She delighted in them yet ate very few, for she had entered the final time of waiting from which she would rouse herself only to call upon the Spider.

"Magnifique," Madame Duprès declared. Pointedly, she added, "Especially when one considers that it was completed under such adverse circumstances."

"I would hardly say that having Sarah stand for the fittings was adverse," Kassandra replied cheerfully as she turned this way and that, looking at herself in the mirror. The gown was no less lovely than that which she had worn to Carlton House, but it was very different. Silk the hue of a spring forest dipped over her breasts to fall from a high waist, ending in a broad hem embroidered with pearls, which also adorned the short, puffy sleeves and the curve of the bodice. When she moved, the fabric rippled around her as though blown by a gentle breeze. While the gown was modest in comparison to many she had seen, it was also exquisitely feminine. Demanding, Madame Duprès might be, but she earned the right to be so.

"Sarah is the very model of patience," Kassandra said. And owed another dress for herself, if she was any judge of what the maid had endured at the exacting dressmaker's hands.

"Even so, it would have been so much better if Your Highness had been present. I really cannot take responsibility —"

"But you can take credit surely? The gown is exquisite, everything I could have hoped. You have outdone yourself."

Thus mollified, Madame Duprès went away. Kassandra emitted a sigh of relief and accepted the glass of lemonade Joanna poured for her.

"It is warm for the start of May, don't you think?" Joanna remarked as she fanned herself. They were seated in the master bedroom, high enough amid the trees to enjoy both shade and whatever air might stir. The windows were thrown open but only faint sounds reached them from the street beyond the lawns and walls. Even mighty London slowed when the temperature climbed.

"Not for Akora, but I suppose for England. Are you all right?"

"I am perfection itself and if you breathe a word otherwise to that dear brother of yours, I will personally wring your lovely neck."

"Has he been that awful?"

"I cannot blink — I am truly serious — not *blink* without him assuming I have gone into labor."

"He means well."

"He will drive me mad. It is fortunate I love him to distraction. Do try to remind me of that in the days ahead."

"I will mention it at frequent intervals," Kassandra promised solemnly. "Are you still determined to go with us this evening?"

"Nothing short of this baby arriving would stop me."

Given how close Joanna was to her time, Kassandra did not dismiss the possibility that the evening's plans would have to be changed until they were actually in the carriage and on the way to Melbourne House.

Royce had joined them shortly before they set out. He arrived sun-burnished and smelling very faintly of the sea, having sailed up from Hawkforte. Kassandra stifled her envy of the freedom of such a voyage, sternly repressed the quickening of her heart at first sight of him, and determined to concentrate on the event at hand. This was made slightly more difficult by the fact that their knees kept brushing as they sat on facing seats in the carriage. And because each time she tried to move away, he smiled.

Melbourne House stood within sight of St. James's Park. Indeed, Kassandra guessed that the swans swimming languidly on the park lake would be visible from the upper windows of the house. She had passed the residence several times in recent days and taken due note of its impressive façade. Now she was curious to see the inside.

The rotunda was framed by a series of reception rooms, high-ceilinged, gilded, and already crowded. Beyond them, tiers of steep stairs rose to the floors above. Kassandra thought the stairs rather odd but understood they were a distinctive feature of the house. Apparently, the family tolerated them well enough to leave them in place. Or perhaps the younger members simply appreciated a climb that would discourage Lady Melbourne, who would not see sixty again and was said to prefer the comforts of her cozy, ground floor salon.

At the moment, she was holding court in the largest and most extravagantly decorated of the reception rooms. The vestiges of the beauty that had made her the most renowned hostess of the *ton* decades before and drawn some of the most powerful men of the age to her still haunted the visage of a woman well past her prime. But it was the shrewd intelligence of her gaze that drew Kassandra's attention. She had heard so much about Elizabeth Milbanke, Lady Melbourne, not in the least her dreadful nickname, that she was prepared to meet a virago. But as Joanna had warned, the Spider was capable of disarming charm.

"Dear Princess Kassandra," Lady Melbourne said with a brilliant smile that revealed she had kept her own teeth and apparently cared for them well, "how delightful to see you." Despite her age, she stood and began to curtsey.

"Please," Kassandra said quickly, "I would prefer we did not stand on ceremony. After all, my visit to England is purely private."

"And how wise of you to make it so, my dear," Lady Melbourne said as she resumed her seat. She patted the settee beside her in invitation. "I have so looked forward to meeting you. You have not gone about much since your arrival." The observation was offered a bit archly, Lady Melbourne no doubt being fully aware of Kassandra's visit to Carlton House down to the precise details of what she wore, everyone she spoke with, what was said, how long she stayed, and what people said about her after she left.

Kassandra chose not to restrain a smile of amusement. Rather to her surprise, she found she was enjoying herself.

Taking the offered seat, she said, "Ah, but

you know my sister-in-law, Lady Joanna, is *enceinte*. Indeed, that is why I have come to England. I am dreadfully concerned, though, that my presence may prompt her to overdo."

"Yes, I see," Lady Melbourne said thoughtfully. She eyed Joanna, who sat a judicious distance away, talking with Royce. Alex remained close to his wife, clearly watchful of her. His own greeting to their hostess had been less than warm.

"Lady Joanna is so very . . . conscientious," the Spider murmured. "To think, only a year ago she was considered quite the country mouse."

Kassandra laughed as though Lady Melbourne had made a joke. In fact, she knew very well such was not her hostess's intention. Joanna had warned her that Lady Melbourne disliked her intensely, although she was not so foolish as to show it.

"She cannot bear anyone's happiness" was how Joanna had put it. "People say it is because she was so dreadfully hurt by Peniston Milbanke, Lord Melbourne. She was sixteen when they wed, and wildly in love. A few months later, all the world knew he had taken a new mistress. Heartbroken, she was reborn a cynic, perhaps the supreme one of our age. She has made power her Grail and never looked back."

Keeping in mind her hostess's antipathy to romantic happiness and the reason behind it,

Kassandra said, "A mouse could hardly have captured my brother's heart."

"She does seem to have done that, doesn't she? Quite remarkable, really. One would never have thought it of Darcourt. But enough, I cannot hope to keep you to myself much longer. Do tell me of your plans while you are in England."

"I have none, save to be of help to my family, of course."

"How noble of you. Tell me, is it true what I hear, that on Akora warriors rule and women serve? Is that the way it is?"

"So I believe it is said," Kassandra replied. Lady Melbourne was clever, darting in a probing question without warning, but Kassandra had grown up in the royal court. She was more than capable of managing such forays.

"Ah, but is it true? Anything at all can be said without there being a fig of truth in it."

"Akora is a very old society, older by far than is England. There are many complexities of meaning."

"Really? How fascinating. But you are English as well, are you not?"

"Strictly speaking, I am."

"Only strictly? Do you not feel even the littlest bit English?"

"I do when I am reading Jane Austen," Kassandra admitted.

"Austen? Oh, that country woman who

writes. My dear niece, Annabella, adores her. I really must introduce you."

Even as she spoke, Lady Melbourne beckoned to a young lady standing not very far away. Kassandra thought her to be about her own age and most remarkable for being quite thoroughly round, not in the sense of fat although she was not what could be described as slim. No, Annabella Milbanke was simply *round*, of eye and cheek, bosom and everywhere else. She had the sort of figure no doubt many men admired. If her expression was anything to judge by, she also had a sensible appreciation of her aunt's authority. At once, she broke off her conversation with another guest and came to stand before Lady Melbourne.

"Yes, Aunt Elizabeth?"

"I wish to make you known to Her Highness, the Princess Kassandra of Akora, dear girl! Whyever else would I summon you over here? You would do well to spend less time with your head in a book and more time taking notice of the world around you."

Having delivered what gave every appearance of being an oft-heard chastisement, Lady Melbourne returned her attention to Kassandra. "Annabella is quite brilliant, if I do say so myself. She has a particular gift for mathematics, which must be discouraged, of course, as it is considered unfeminine. Annabella, the Princess is also a devotee of your Miss Austen."

"Hardly mine, Aunt, but a delight all the

same." Turning to Kassandra, she asked, "Have you truly read her?"

"Oh, yes, or at least the single book I have been able to find. Is there another?"

"No, only rumors, but I fear we shall see nothing for another year at least. However did you discover her?"

"My brother was kind enough to bring her book back from one of his visits to England last year."

"How very thoughtful. Tell me, who else do you read?"

"Oh, everything really, I am quite indiscriminate."

"Are you familiar with Lord Byron? His poem has caused quite a stir."

"Yes," Kassandra said carefully. "It is quite . . . evocative."

"It has made him the object of universal attention. I confess myself quite smitten." Hastily, she added, "With the work, of course. Of the man, I know very little."

"But you have met him?"

"Oh, yes, but do not think I sought the introduction."

As Kassandra had been of no opinion whatsoever about the matter, she found this admonishment rather odd. But only a short time later, as she continued chatting with Lady Annabella Milbanke, she began to understand better why the young woman had denied any personal interest in the "object of universal attention."

A stir through the crowd, a sudden breathless attentiveness, a swift clustering near the entrance to the reception room and shortly, the news flew to them. George Gordon, Lord Byron, had arrived.

Kassandra could not deny that she was curious about the man, but she felt no impulse whatsoever to join the crush of people who instantly surrounded him, all vying for his attention. Nor it seemed did Annabella, who remained beside her. However, a quick glance at the young woman revealed that her apple cheeks had paled and there was a look in her eyes somewhere between yearning and alarm, as though she warred within herself.

The cause of all this excitement, as Kassandra shortly saw, was a man in his early twenties, a little taller than herself, quite thin and rather oddly dressed. While all the rest of the men present wore dark breeches, long-tailed coats and unadorned shirts, Byron sported billowing white linen pantaloons so wide as to be mistaken for a skirt, a shirt of equally unusual design, an embroidered waistcoat and to complete his appearance, a heavy gold chain strung round his neck. The overall effect was at once masculine and feminine, as though he combined both within his person. So, too, was the same impression conveyed by his features — his large gray eyes fringed by thick dark lashes were the envy of any woman, while his oversized and very firm chin was entirely male.

As he came forward to greet Lady Melbourne, Kassandra saw that he dragged his right leg, making her wonder at first if he had suffered a recent injury. Only when she looked further did she realize that he was burdened on that side by a shoe with a thick, high sole, presumably to compensate for what must be a deformity to his right foot.

How odd that a man so bent on flamboyant grace should be in so essential a manner graceless. Swift assessment led her to conclude that this "object of universal attention" was the embodiment of contradictions.

"Lady Melbourne," he said, bowing with a flourish over their hostess's hand even as his gaze darted to Kassandra. "How very kind of you to invite me."

"Nonsense, dear boy," the Spider said with indulgent warmth she had not shown her niece. "We are always delighted to see you. I do hope you are taking better care of yourself, as we discussed. Have you eaten today? These diets of yours take their toll."

"One tries, but it is so very difficult . . . there are so many demands. However, that is of no matter." He smiled courteously at Annabella, although his eyes did not meet hers, for already they were moving to Kassandra. In an aside, he gestured languidly to his hostess. "If you would be so kind —"

"Yes, of course. Your Highness, may I make known to you George Gordon, Lord Byron, of whom you undoubtedly have already heard so much?"

The hand that took hers was cool and smooth. He did not allow his lips to touch her skin but came close enough that she felt his breath, by contrast warm, even hot. The poet seemed to burn with an inner flame so bright she wondered that it did not consume him.

"Lord Byron, how pleasant to make your acquaintance."

For a moment, he did not respond but merely continued to stare at her. When he did speak, he stammered slightly but recovered after scarcely a syllable. It was enough, however, to make her realize that within the seemingly worldly artiste who had society at his feet was a rather self-conscious young man.

"P-princess, you are too kind. Indeed, I marvel that anyone takes note of my own poor self now that you have arrived. I confess that all things to do with Akora fascinate me. If it would be possible for us to talk —"

"No doubt there will be many such opportunities for us to do so," Kassandra said noncommittally. She had absolutely no intention of granting him the private meeting she sensed he sought.

"You intend, then, to go about in society?"

"As circumstances permit." From the corner of her eye, she saw Royce approach, and breathed a little sigh of relief. "You will understand I am in England for family reasons."

"Ah, yes," Byron murmured vaguely, "family." His eyes left her to settle on Royce, from whom it seemed he could not look away. The contrast between the two men could not have been greater. Whereas Byron cultivated a languid, even fragile air, Royce radiated strength and purpose. Nor was there any blurring of sexuality in the latter, who could not possibly have been mistaken for other than thoroughly male.

"Lord Hawkforte," the poet said. "We see you too rarely at these affairs."

"Matters of a more serious nature call me elsewhere." Royce spoke curtly, on the fine edge of discourtesy, but his response did not seem to discourage Byron, who replied, "I marvel at what you find to occupy yourself. We live in such empty times."

"Empty?" Royce inquired. Instinctively, Kassandra laid her hand lightly on his arm in a gesture meant to soothe. Any Akoran woman would have done the same. And, she realized with a start, any Akoran man might well respond exactly as Royce did. At once, he covered her hand with his in a gesture both protective and possessive.

The significance of that did not escape Byron, who frowned. "Yes," he said defensively, "quite empty, arid of meaning or purpose. Of course, there are those among us who fool themselves into thinking otherwise."

"Unlike you, who do understand the true nature of reality?" Royce inquired. He had relaxed somewhat and was even smiling, albeit mockingly. "I find, Lord Byron, that reality does not place us at the center of all things no matter how much vanity might wish it so. Reality is far larger and to grasp it, we must broaden our perspective."

"That is one view," Lady Annabella interjected. She had remained silent thus far, as well as ignored by Byron, but now she rose to his defense. "You are not an artist, Lord Hawkforte. That is not to disparage you in any way, for I am certain you have many abilities. All the same, Lord Byron's vision of the world is bound to be entirely different from your own."

This earned her a startled glance from the poet, who seemed to take notice of her for the first time. But it was Lady Melbourne's response that drew Kassandra's attention. The Spider studied the poet and her niece, looking from one to the other, with the avidity her namesake would have awarded a nice, juicy fly.

Whatever stratagem their hostess might have been weaving was interrupted by the sudden appearance of a young woman. She arrived as though blown in by a great gust of wind, darting up to them seemingly on wings rather than feet. Indeed, so small and slight was she that Kassandra would have been scarcely surprised to see actual wings sprout from her narrow back. Her face was heart-shaped, her eyes immense, her hair cropped startlingly short and let loose in a riot of curls. She was dressed, so far as that could be said, in a gown that appeared nearly diaphanous, stopping just short of revealing all. She was also quite annoyed.

"I did not know you were here!" she exclaimed, addressing Byron. "Why did no one tell me?"

"For pity's sake," the poet muttered and turned to Lady Melbourne as though for help.

In an instant, Kassandra realized the ill-clad sprite was Lady Caroline Melbourne, her hostess's daughter-in-law and the other half, with Byron, of a love affair scant weeks old but already exploded into full-blown scandal. Joanna had provided her with the details, which had shocked her thoroughly, not in the least because the scandal came not from the fact of infidelity but from the public spectacle of it Caro Lamb insisted on making. And apparently intended to make now.

"You thaid nothing to me of coming today," she continued, speaking with the slight lisp affected by some among the *ton*. "I might have gone out. Indeed, I almost did! Really, this ith too bad of you!"

"Lower your voice, Caro," Lady Melbourne snapped. "If George did not inform you that he was coming here today, it was because he did not feel any pressing need to see you at this precise moment. Really, you expect to hang

101

about him like a limpet. That is no way to keep a man's attentions."

Hearing this, Kassandra only just prevented her mouth from dropping open. Did she understand correctly? Was Lady Melbourne advising her daughter-in-law, the *wife* of her own son, how to continue her affair with Byron rather than taking her to task for indulging in it in the first place? Had Lady Melbourne no thought for her son's honor? Or did her own licentious behavior in the past — bearing six children with an assortment of fathers — dispose her to regard such behavior as normal?

"Oh, be quiet!" Lady Caroline hurled at her mother-in-law. "It ith positively dreadful how you encourage George to confide in you, then twist everything to drive a wedge between uth. Annabella," she appealed to her cousin, "you understand, do you not? We have ever been the dearest friends since you came to London. You know the content of my heart."

"I know you are overwrought," Annabella replied. If she felt any sympathy for the woman Kassandra suspected was her unknowing rival for the poet's affections, she kept it well hidden. "You should go and lie down."

"Not you ath well, turned against me!" Lady Caroline cried out. She clasped her hands to her bosom and rolled her eyes back, as though she was about to faint. "I cannot bear it!"

Lady Melbourne got to her feet. She glared at her daughter-in-law and raised a hand, summoning two footmen. "Then fail to bear it somewhere else!"

To the titillation of the avidly watching crowd, Lady Caroline was escorted from the reception room sobbing copiously and bewailing the cruel circumstances of her life.

Scarcely had she gone than conversation resumed as though nothing whatsoever had happened. Byron stood chatting with Annabella and Lady Melbourne while all around them the guests looked well satisfied by the entertainment they had witnessed.

Only Kassandra was left quite thoroughly stunned. "Have you seen enough?" Royce asked, *sotto voce*.

"That and more," she replied in kind.

A short while later, they were back in the carriage with Joanna and Alex. To their great relief, Melbourne House vanished into the night.

Chapter
FIVE

"Your Highness . . ." The soft voice accompanied by a light touch on Kassandra's shoulder drew her from sleep.

Turning over in the bed, she murmured, "What is it?"

"I am sorry to disturb you," the maid, Sarah, said, "but Mistress Elena told me to fetch you."

Instantly, the remnants of sleep dissolved. Kassandra sat up and tossed back the light cover, all she needed on a balmy night. "What time is it?"

"Not gone five, Your Highness. Lady Joanna is awake, as is his lordship. I think something's stirring." She spoke with suppressed excitement, sharing as she did the anticipation of all the household looking forward to the baby's arrival.

"Is everything all right?" Kassandra asked as she rose hastily and looked around for her wrap.

"I think so, leastways Mistress Elena doesn't seem concerned."

"Has she called for water?"

"She just told me now to get it boiling as soon as the fires are lit."

"There's time, then. I'll dress."

Sarah nodded and hurried off about her tasks. Kassandra washed quickly before donning a simple morning gown. A few swipes of a brush through her hair and she was done. Outside in the hall the house remained very quiet, although she did hear the faint sounds of activity in the kitchens. Hurrying to the master bedroom, she knocked on the door.

"Come in," Alex called.

She stepped inside to find her brother standing at one of the open windows overlooking the garden, looking unaccustomedly harried as he attempted to reason with his wife, who also stood there, clad in a nightrobe that ballooned over her distended belly, her hands bracing the small of her back.

"I really think you would do better to be in bed," Alex was saying.

"I need to be up! I need to move! Oh, Kassandra, thank heavens, will you explain to your brother that a woman in labor is still capable of standing on her own two feet?"

"Indeed she is," Kassandra said quickly. She took in the situation with a glance, suppressed a smile of sympathy for Alex, and hurried to Joanna's side. "Until, of course, she isn't, but I suspect you will know when that is the case. How are you feeling?"

Joanna grimaced. "As though I am about to lay an immense egg."

"That's as good a description as I've heard,"

Elena said as she joined them. She had gone to fetch her medical chest and had Brianna in tow. Mulridge followed hard on their heels, her arms filled with fresh linens. She chuckled at Joanna's description.

"Isn't there something that can be done?" Alex asked. He ran a hand through thick black hair that was already mussed and looked from one woman to the other in search of an answer.

"We can wait," Elena said, "for Nature to take its course, which it will in due order. In the meantime, *kyril*, I respectfully suggest you do whatever it is you would be doing this morning; but pray, do not go far from this house. I will send word when it is time for you to attend your wife."

"Go on," Joanna said quickly before Alex could object. "Absolutely nothing is going to happen for hours, much as I wish otherwise. You will simply be anxious on no regard."

"I would still prefer to be with you," he insisted.

"And I would prefer you still feel that way several hours from now when I will have true need of your company." Her voice softening, Joanna added, "Please, dearest, indulge me."

Alex's face lightened just a little. "When do I not?"

Kassandra followed him to the bedroom door. On impulse, she said, "Send word to Royce. He will want to be here and you, too, should have some support."

106

They both knew that at home on Akora, a man would never be left to face the rigors of impending fatherhood alone. His brothers, if he had them, and his closest friends from the years of warrior training would be with him, especially those who were already fathers. Here in England, it seemed everything was different, but Royce would understand. Somehow, Kassandra was convinced of that.

"He, too, will worry," Alex said.

"You can worry together but everything will be fine, truly."

He nodded, but not before she saw in his eyes the desperate need to believe her.

How complex was love, she thought after he had gone. So great a source of strength and joy, yet it made hostages of all. Loving, no man or woman was ever truly free again.

The thought lingered in her mind as she returned to Joanna but it was quickly submerged beneath the irresistible wave of feminine practicality.

The women talked. As Joanna paced, pausing occasionally to flatten her palms against the wall and brace herself, they chatted about everything and nothing, leaping from topic to topic, never speaking of childbirth itself but laughing over the antics of children and men, men and children, of loved ones departed and cherished in memory, of the marvels of London and the vagaries of the weather, and even of the twittering of birds in the twining vines just beyond the window.

"Good year for starlings," Mulridge observed. "Not so much for pigeons."

"Ebb and flow," Elena said. "You see it everywhere. Five years ago on Akora we had an explosion of rabbits. Take a step beyond Ilius or the larger villages and they were everywhere, bounding across the roads, peering out of every hedge. Each year after that there were fewer until now we seem back to normal, for the moment."

"The deer at Hawkforte are like that," Joanna murmured, clearly trying to concentrate on what was being said but pulled away by yet another deep contraction that swept over and through her.

"Easy," Elena said gently, "you're doing very well."

"I'm just not sure," Joanna said, "how much longer I can keep on doing it."

"Long enough," the Akoran healer reassured her. "This is a strong baby eager to be born. Just think, this is the day on which he or she will see light for the first time, breathe for the first time, know your touch for the first time."

"She," Joanna said with a gasp as another contraction seized her. She bent over, clinging to Elena. On a note of wonder, she murmured, "My daughter is coming."

"You have seen her?" Brianna asked, coming closer to assist her aunt, as together they enabled Joanna to stay on her feet so that gravity could help the baby make her descent into the world.

Joanna nodded. "A few nights ago. I thought it only a dream but it wasn't . . . she is real . . . my daughter . . . *God, that hurts!*"

"Breathe," Elena said. "Good . . . very good." She motioned to Brianna, who gently wiped the sweat from Joanna's brow. Kassandra put her hands to Joanna's back, rubbing firmly as she said, "Many women see their children in dreams before they are born. I have heard that said even of mothers who have not given birth to a child but become mother to it after it is born. They, too, have visions."

"She wasn't a baby," Joanna said through the pain. "I saw a little girl playing with a golden ball in a garden . . . on Akora, I think . . . Aaaahhhhh!"

Elena gestured to Mulridge. "Tell the *kyril* it is time for him to be here."

Moments later, it seemed, the door flew open as Alex hurried in. He went directly to his wife and embraced her despite her bulk and the tension of her body straining through another contraction.

"Beloved . . ." he murmured.

She looked up into his face and managed a faint laugh. "Don't look so grim. We are about to become parents."

We, Kassandra thought, the word encompassing Alex and Joanna as well as the child about to join them. A small family, part of two much larger families, part of two nations, two worlds, and yet one future. A future that waited, itself as yet unborn, for the right choices to be made.

"You are in pain." The very words seemed to hurt him.

"Not for much longer," Elena said briskly and gestured to the birthing chair brought specially from Akora. "My lady, please to sit now."

Joanna might have managed the maneuver on her own but there was no need. Alex lifted her, bulging belly and all, with ease and deposited her so gently and carefully that Kassandra's heart tightened. He was her brother and she loved him dearly but he was also, she realized, a man desperately worried about his wife even as he was about to assume the awesome responsibility of parenthood. If he looked a little gray beneath his usual tan, he had the right.

Everything happened very quickly then, or at least so it seemed to Kassandra. She and Mulridge stayed back, letting Elena and Brianna do what was needed. In truth, Joanna did most of it as Alex held her, murmuring encouragement and praise.

Toward the end, Joanna screamed and Kassandra felt the sound clear through herself where it struck some ancient chord, not of memory, for she as yet had none, but of deeply rooted knowledge present and waiting for the day when that would happen. The sound still reverberated even as it was joined by another, the robust and clearly irate bellow of a new-born babe.

"A daughter!" Elena proclaimed and held up the pink-flushed, shining creature who flailed her arms and legs while continuing to make herself known with all her might.

"A strong, healthy daughter," Elena added with a chuckle as she handed the babe to Brianna, who quickly cleaned and wrapped her.

"A daughter," Alex repeated just a bit dazedly. He looked at the squalling infant with shock already giving way to adoration.

"Give her here," Joanna directed as soon as she, too, was fully done and cleaned. Alex had carried her over to the bed where she sat, propped up on heaps of pillows, demanding her due, which was placed in her arms by a beaming Elena who said with simple honesty, "You did well, my lady."

Joanna nodded, but only absently, for all her attention was on her daughter. Alex sat beside them, torn in wonder between the woman and the child she had so miraculously produced.

It was, Kassandra thought, a moment to be immortalized, for no matter how many times it had occurred and would occur again, it was always precious and unique.

And yet, there was one person missing.

"Joanna," she said softly, not wishing to intrude, "do you think Royce — ?"

"Oh, yes," the new mother said at once. "For

heaven's sake, someone get him. He will be worried."

He was, in fact, just outside in the hallway where he looked pale and grim. When Kassandra threw open the door, he demanded, "Why has it gotten so quiet?"

She looked at him, really looked, seeing a man of such grace and strength as to make her feel the deep yearning pull of need, a man she had feared might be an enemy but seemed instead a friend and more. A man who loved his sister and, she realized, would adore his niece.

"You are an uncle," she said, and grinned at his look of utter stupefaction. Quickly, she tugged at his arm, drawing him into the room. "Come and meet her. She is wonderful, of course, and Joanna . . . let us just say I have a new heroine."

"Enough of that," Joanna said with a laugh and gestured to her brother. "What do you think of her?"

He stared down at the baby, visible now as only a small form swaddled in linen, hidden save for her face and a few tendrils of silken hair that looked to be the same honey hue as her mother's.

"She sounded very fierce," Royce said.

Alex laughed, the release of a man riding the crest of vast relief. "She is Akoran. Of course she is fierce."

"And English," Royce reminded him. "Boswick and Hawkforte together, a good heritage. Look at that! She opened her eyes."

"She's very intelligent," Alex said confidently, as though that proved it.

Royce nodded in agreement. "Have you a name for her?"

The new parents looked at one another. Softly, Alex said, "Amelia, for your mother."

"Only," Joanna said, "if you are quite certain your mother will not mind. I would not hurt Phaedra for the world."

"My mother will be far too ecstatic over having been made a grandmother to care what we name this child. But she will understand the wish to honor yours who is gone from this world."

Joanna squeezed her husband's hand in thanks and looked down into the face of their daughter. "Then Amelia it is. Welcome, Amelia."

The baby blinked, prompting a new burst of admiration from her adoring audience.

A little while later, Mulridge fluttered off to spread the glad tidings. Shortly thereafter, hearty cheers resounded through the house. Amelia, rousing herself, indicated she expected to be fed. As Elena offered instruction, Kassandra and Royce tiptoed away, leaving the little family to its privacy.

At the foot of the stairs in the central hall, Kassandra paused for a moment. She felt unexpectedly light-headed and put out a hand to steady herself against the wall. Instantly, Royce

113

was there with a strong arm around her waist.

"What's wrong?" he demanded.

She shook her head in surprise, partly at the sudden dizziness but more at his nearness and the flood of feelings it unleashed. "Nothing. I imagine it was just all the excitement. I'm fine."

She expected him to step back but instead his arm tightened, making her vividly aware of his strength kept so carefully leashed. She looked up into the depths of his hazel eyes lit through with shards of gold such as might be found in a summer forest, cool, welcoming, concealing unknown pleasures. "Royce . . ."

"Damn it, Kassandra." On that note, scarcely romantic but imbued with frustration she understood all too well, he kissed her.

His lips were warm and firm, not hard, enticing rather than demanding, tempting, teasing . . . He pulled gently on her lower lip, coaxing her mouth open so adroitly that she had no warning, only a melting sensation that, paradoxically, curled her toes even as it turned much of the rest of her to pure molten need.

The man was dangerous. Delightfully, deliciously, definitely dangerous.

And just what was it that made danger so appealing?

But that was a thought, and thinking was something she was far too preoccupied to do.

Oh, my . . . Oh!

Her arms were twined around his neck and

she was pressed close against the hard length of his body before Kassandra was next aware. She had no idea how she had gotten that way but it felt too right to be concerned about.

Royce drew a deep, shuddering breath and put his hands over hers, drawing her arms down.

"Kassandra . . ."

"Hmmm?"

"We . . . that is, I shouldn't have done this."

Abruptly recalled to herself, she looked up at him. "Why not?"

"Why not?" Belatedly, he released her hands and stepped back. "Because you are my sister-in-law —"

"No blood relation," she broke in hastily. "We are not *apodos*."

Royce looked bewildered, not to say shocked. "*Apodos?* . . . We are not . . . excrement?"

She, too, stared at him before breaking into surprised laughter. "Oh, dear! I gather that word has various meanings and yet, I suppose in some way, they are connected. On Akora, *apodos* means 'forbidden,' but in a special way, having to do with going away from life into death."

"And if people who are blood relatives do as we did . . ."

"That is *apodos* because the children born of such inbreedings are likely to be sickly."

"Which is why Akora actually welcomes outsiders who happen to arrive there."

"As you have discovered, but that is not something we shout to all the world. Akora is very special and precious. We must take care to protect what is best there."

"Of course, I understand. What I meant was that as my sister-in-law you are also under my protection. It is wrong for me to take advantage in any way."

He was serious, she realized. He truly thought that kissing her had been wrong. This must have to do with the English morality she had heard about, yet it seemed sharply at odds with the licentious behavior of the *ton.*

"You did not enjoy it?" she asked, knowing the question was provocative but suddenly not caring. For just the space of these few minutes, she wanted to be free of the terrible concerns that haunted her, free to flirt and laugh . . . and kiss. To just be blessedly ordinary.

"Of course I did! Good God, if I'd enjoyed it any more, we'd be . . . Never mind. I only meant you are a young girl and . . ."

"Woman."

"What's that?"

"I am a young woman. That is different from a young girl, is it not?"

"Well, yes, I suppose so but my point is . . ."

"That you should not have kissed me?"

"Yes, precisely."

"Why not?"

Taken aback, he said, "It's not right, that's why not. You can't just go around kissing people."

"You are not people. You are Royce."

"Yes, but . . ." He stopped, staring at her as the significance of what she had just said reached him.

"You have nothing to apologize for," Kassandra said. She shook out her skirt, which was rumpled after the long day, and walked across the hall. Over her shoulder, she said, "If I had not wanted you to kiss me, I would have stopped you."

He followed, as she had been quite certain he would. "Indeed?" he asked as they stepped into the family parlor. "How would you have done that?"

She smiled, well aware that she had pricked his male vanity. "You don't really want to know."

"Of course I do. I'm fascinated. Here I thought only men on Akora received warrior training."

He spoke humorously but Kassandra responded with complete seriousness. "Why would you think that?"

"Because men are the warriors?"

"Let an invader come to Akora and he will discover that women can fight as fiercely as any man. We are no one's victims. The education of any Akoran girl is complex and exacting. We learn a great deal about all sorts of subjects, including the workings of the human body." She looked at him deliberately. "On Akora, no one confuses innocence with ignorance."

"I see —" He did not, she suspected, but the implications were beginning to sink in.

"Did you know there are pressure points all over the body that, used correctly, can render any man unconscious?"

"I've heard that."

"Would you like a demonstration?"

"No," he said hastily and surrendered with a graceful smile. "Actually, what I would like is a pot of tea."

"An excellent idea, and perhaps some breakfast? No, it is much too late for that. Ah, Sarah, Lord Royce and I are in need of sustenance."

"I should think so, Your Highness," the maid said with a smile, "since it's not a morsel any of you has had since last night. Tea, sir?"

"Hot, strong and lots of it, if you please," Royce replied.

"And perhaps some of those little sandwiches Cook does so well," Kassandra suggested.

"There's a quite nice apple tart," Sarah volunteered.

Kassandra's stomach rumbled. "Excellent. You might want to take something upstairs for the new parents, as well."

"Already on its way, mum. Isn't it wonderful? A baby girl. I'm sure she's going to be a perfect little lady."

"Good lord, I hope not," Royce murmured when the maid had left. "If she is, she'll be insufferable."

"You aren't supposed to think that," Kassandra

admonished. "You're supposed to be all in favor of ladies, especially perfect ones."

"Am I? Just where are you getting all these 'supposeds' from?"

"I just assumed. You seemed quite busy with your own 'supposeds' a few minutes ago."

"You mean not supposed to kiss you? I suppose I was but you've got me thinking about that."

"Really? You do understand I never kissed anyone before?"

"Good lord."

"What does that mean?"

"Only that you did it very well for someone who never had before."

"Oh, thank you. As I said, innocence isn't . . ."

"Ignorance. So I understand. Look, if it's all the same to you, I think we should change the subject."

"If you like, but would you mind telling me why?"

"Because you kiss the way you do, only you never had before, and I'm under your brother's roof and —"

"Supposeds."

"They do rather complicate things, don't they?"

"Hmmm. Ah, here's tea." And rather more importantly from her stomach's point of view, nourishment.

They ate and when hunger was satisfied, they

talked. He was very easy to talk with, Kassandra thought. Perhaps that came from his having a sister and respecting that she had a mind.

"What was Joanna like when she was little?" Kassandra asked after a bit.

Royce laughed affectionately. "A hellion." His smile faded. "At least before our parents died. After that she was very quiet for a long time. It wasn't until she met Alex that she really came back into herself."

"They are so in love."

"They are, aren't they?" he said with some wonder.

"Don't you believe in love?"

"Actually, I do. My parents loved each other deeply. I was old enough to understand that and I still remember it."

"My parents, as well. My mother loved her first husband, Atreus's father, too. I know she grieved deeply when he was killed in a hunting accident. But I think the love she found with my and Alex's father was different."

"How so?"

"She had known her first husband most of her life. He was chosen for her by her father, who was Vanax. It was a good match and would have endured had her husband lived. But it was not the sort of fierce, all encompassing love that transforms the soul."

Royce stirred his tea. "I thought you didn't care for Byron?"

"What has he to do with anything?"

"Oh, I don't know, that business about love and the soul just sounded like something he'd say."

When he saw her expression, Royce relented a little. "Not that he'd put it as clearly, he seems quite incapable of that and, of course, he'd be talking only about himself."

A shade stiffly, Kassandra said, "It is possible to dislike bad poetry and still respect the power of true love."

"Perhaps it's just a difference between men and women, one of many."

"Byron is a man."

"Ah, well, as to that." Royce shrugged. "Best not to tread there, I think. Have some more apple tart."

"Ignorance is not . . ."

"Oh, lord, I know! May we speak of the far more amenable subject of our mutual niece?"

"Oh, yes, let's. Isn't she the most adorable baby you have ever seen?"

"As I have seen very few babies," Royce teased, "I suppose I would have to agree."

"Fie on you! You know perfectly well she is exquisite."

"Yes," Royce admitted, but he was looking at Kassandra as he spoke. Indeed, she had the sudden, heady sense that he saw perhaps too much. The moment was so intimate, the connection between them so strong. She braced herself.

"Why are you called Kassandra?"

She set down her fork and carefully dabbed any crumbs from her mouth. "You do not like that name?"

"It's a lovely name, but you will agree, it has certain allusions — tragic Troy, the princess who could see the future but went unheeded. Surely, your parents knew of that when they chose it for you."

"Yes, they knew."

"Why, then?"

"We are, as you pointed out, linked by family."

He remained silent, letting her decide whether or not to tell him in her own time and her own way. Slowly, she said, "Joanna can find things."

"She has that gift and thank God for it. Last year, she found me."

"Women in your family are born with unusual gifts. Not in every generation, but from time to time. This is so, is it not?"

"It is, but what has that to do with —"

"About the year 1100, a member of your family came to Akora."

"Yes, he sent artifacts back. They are still in the library at Hawkforte."

"But he remained on Akora. Because we keep our history very carefully, we know what happened to him. His descendants live still among my own family."

"So we are distantly related."

"*Very* distantly," she emphasized. "Going back about seven hundred years. The ancestor we share, being a man, had no gift of his own but he seems to have brought the tendency for them to Akora. At any rate, his female descendants have, from time to time, displayed unusual abilities."

Royce was silent for what seemed like a very long while. Outside in the vines near the windows, birds began returning to their nests for the night. Dusk was settling over the city.

"Kassandra," he said gently, a wealth of understanding in that single word.

She felt a sudden relief simply that he *knew* and that, with this man, she would not have to hide so vital a part of herself. "It was not my original name but the one given to me when my gift became apparent."

"You truly can see the future?"

"No, I can see possible futures. Different paths lie before us. We choose our own fates."

She watched him mulling that over and saw the moment when the question formed in his mind. "Have you," he asked, "seen us?"

"Not exactly," Kassandra replied. She met his gaze unwaveringly. "I realize that's not a good answer and I'm truly not trying to be evasive. It's just that sometimes what I see is very unclear."

"That must be frustrating," Royce said.

"It can be."

"But perhaps in this case, it's for the best." He stood and offered her his hand. She took it and also rose. His palm against hers was warm and roughened by calluses. She had a sudden, piercing memory of him grasping a sword.

"I think I prefer for matters to unfold on their own," he said.

"People generally do." She was pleased that her voice was steady when she felt anything but.

They walked together to the drawing room door. "It has been an eventful day," Royce noted with what she thought was admirable understatement. "You should get some rest."

"And you." Joanna had told her that he slept inside now *sometimes*. Would he tonight?

"Royce —"

He had released her hand but turned to look at her. "Yes?"

"I was there when you were brought to Ilius after your rescue. I have some idea of what you endured." Indeed, the memory of the pale, gaunt figure he had been would haunt her forever.

His face hardened and for a moment she feared he would suspect her of pitying him. That, she could not bear. "I did not mean —" she began.

"It's all right," he said. "What happened is in the past. I'm grateful to have survived it but I do not intend to let it haunt me the rest of my days."

He took her hand again, raised it to his lips, and smiled. "Or affect any of those futures you may see."

"Certainly not," she murmured and tried to ignore the fact that her toes were curling again.

Chapter
SIX

Outside, in the last fading light of day, Royce paused to breathe deeply in the hope that it would clear his head. He had become an uncle on this day, for which he was deeply grateful, yet it was the princess from a hidden land who commanded his thoughts.

She was . . . unusual, not to say unique. Beautiful, to be sure, but he was no stranger to beautiful women. She had wit and humor, grace and honesty, all attributes he valued more highly than mere appearance. Yet there was no getting around the fact that the way she looked, and more particularly the way she felt in his arms, had an effect on him at once predictable and profound.

She was his sister-in-law and for all that they were not *apodos* — he grinned at their brief misunderstanding over the word — neither was she the sort of woman with whom he could envision anything other than an entirely proper and serious relationship. The very sort he had no room for in his life at the moment.

But then there was the fact that she made

him laugh. And that she was so damn easy to talk with. And that he saw the love in her eyes when she spoke of the niece they shared, and knew this was a woman whose spirit was warm and generous.

By God, she could kiss. Was it true that she had never done it before? Yes, he knew it was, for Kassandra would not stoop to lie. She had far too much pride and sense of her own worth. He was the first to kiss her. It made him feel quite absurdly pleased and rather dangerously possessive.

His driver appeared just then, hastily retying his stock as he came round from the back of the house where he undoubtedly had been well fed. The outriders came with him, lighting the torches that would illuminate the way home while keeping any ne'er-do-wells at bay. Boys from the stables hurried up with the horses, likewise well fed and rested.

Royce waited patiently, occupied with his own thoughts. He was an uncle. Someday he would show Hawkforte to Amelia and tell her about the part of her heritage that flowed from there. They would walk the stone battlements that had stood for more than nine centuries, not as old as Akora to be sure, but respectable all the same. It was odd to think that if he had no children of his own, Amelia would inherit Hawkforte. Odder still that just then he felt a powerful yearning for children, whereas before he had never given them much thought.

Kassandra could see the future. No, the possible futures. She called it a gift but he suspected it was far more of a burden. She had seen nothing to do with them . . . exactly. But she had seen something, of that he was quite sure, that she was not telling him.

He frowned as he got into the carriage.

Ridiculous, really, that he couldn't just walk, but London was increasingly unsafe these days. Only this morning, before being called to Joanna and Alex's residence, he had been at Carlton House, hearing the fevered rumors that the Luddites were offering a hundred guineas for the head of the Prince Regent. Sweet lord, that would have the man even deeper in his cups than he was already.

Alex had been right to want Joanna to go to their own manor at Boswick or to Hawkforte. Still, with the men they had brought up to London, their residences were well-enough protected. Unfortunately, the same couldn't be said for the rest of the city.

If only the Prince Regent would rouse himself from the stupor of drugs and self-pity he seemed to slip more deeply into each day . . . If he would stop seeing his own subjects as potential enemies and any challenge to the status quo as the preface to revolution . . . If he would turn what was actually a decent-enough mind toward improving his kingdom . . .

If horses had wings, Royce would be home already. As it was, the carriage clattered through the all-but-empty streets a few minutes longer before depositing him at his front door. He nodded to the men keeping guard there and to the footman who admitted him, then went directly upstairs, stripped off his clothes and tumbled into bed, where he dreamt of a raven-haired beauty with laughing eyes and a delightful little girl . . . no, wait, that seemed to be a boy . . . playing on the battlements of Hawkforte.

Kassandra, too, slept but only fitfully. She woke several times to what she thought was the sound of Amelia crying but that was hushed so quickly she could not be sure. At first light, she was up again but felt compelled to wait for some sign that the new parents were stirring. That she got when a somewhat rumpled and unshaven Alex wandered into the morning room.

"Everything all right?" she asked at once.

He ran a hand over blurry eyes and nodded. "Fine, couldn't be better. I must have slept — oh, I don't know — twenty or thirty minutes over the course of the night."

Kassandra couldn't help it, she laughed. But she also poured him a cup of tea and gestured for him to sit. "I'll warrant you didn't sleep night before last either with Joanna beginning her labor. You know, you don't have to stay awake and on watch constantly. Amelia will be well looked after even if her exhausted father steals some sleep."

He grinned despite his fatigue, drank half the tea in a gulp, and nodded. "I know, I know. It's just that she's so damned fascinating. She has the littlest fingers and toes, and the biggest yell. She looks right at me and I can just see she's figuring out what she wants next."

"Probably so. How is Joanna?"

"Magnificent. She seems to glow from inside. Of course, she was sensible and slept when she could."

"As you must. Go," she instructed, assuming a sisterly right. "There are only a dozen or so guest rooms in this house. Find one of them and sleep."

He considered that as a parched man would eye a bubbling fountain. "I just might."

"You will," Kassandra said firmly. "I will keep Joanna and she-who-must-be-obeyed company."

Alex managed a weak chuckle but he did go. Kassandra waited no longer. She commandeered the tray Sarah had assembled and carried it up herself. Joanna was awake and chatting with Elena. Brianna was busy giving Amelia a bath, an experience the baby seemed to enjoy thoroughly.

"Tea," Joanna said with delight. She patted the bed beside her. "Sit. Did you see Alex? Did you convince him to get some sleep?"

"Yes and yes. Poor man, he looked done in."

All the women chuckled at that, understanding as they did that even a man trained to the rigors of battle could find a newborn baby overwhelming.

"And Royce?" Joanna asked.

Kassandra hesitated just a moment. The memory of that kiss was still far too fresh. She feared to stumble over it. As smoothly as she could, she said, "He went home last night for some rest of his own."

Joanna cast her one sharp look and smiled. "Good. I'm sure he'll be back as soon as he can."

"Bearing gifts, no doubt. I suspect shortly there will be nothing left in London for other newborn babes. And speaking of which . . ." She reached into the deep pocket of her skirt and withdrew from it an object perhaps six inches in diameter, wrapped in silk. "I have a gift for Amelia."

"Her first," Joanna said with delight as Kassandra placed it in her hands. Quickly unwrapped, the gift was revealed to be a golden ball engraved with ancient carvings. Joanna stared at it in bewilderment. "A golden ball . . . but I saw that . . ."

Kassandra nodded. "In the dream you had. I was startled when you said as much. I picked out this gift for Amelia months ago. Watch . . ." She took the ball back for a moment and threw it lightly between her hands. Each time the ball sped through the air, it sang with haunting musical notes.

"Amazing," Joanna said as Kassandra returned the ball to her. "How does it make that sound?"

"Some of the engravings on the ball cut all the way through the surface, creating a pattern of very narrow slits. When the ball is thrown, air flows through the slits and causes the ball to sing. Only about a dozen of these were ever made and each has a different song."

Studying the ball, Joanna said, "It is very good of you to give this to Amelia, but are you sure? So rare a gift for a young child —"

"I want her to have it. It was mine when I was little."

"But you should keep it for your own daughter."

A shadow moved through Kassandra. She pushed it aside hastily. "If I ever have one, she and Amelia can play with it together." Quickly, she added, "Alex says you glow and he is right."

"Oh, did he say that? How sweet. He is the dearest man and already a wonderful father, as I knew he would be. Tell me, what was he like as a boy? Phaedra has told me some stories, but not nearly enough."

"Can there be enough?" Kassandra teased, but only briefly, for she was glad enough to oblige. Indeed, she was happy to speak of anything other than her own future. Of that she did not wish to think at all.

So a pleasant week passed. As Kassandra had anticipated, the house soon overflowed with gifts. Many were indeed from Royce, who, relishing his role as uncle, showed a rather alarming fondness for objects of large dimensions. These included a hobbyhorse the size of a small pony, a playhouse with two floors that fit into the nursery only by virtue of that room's high ceiling, and most remarkable of all, an "automaton" — a mechanical figure of a life-sized boy who could be prompted to beat the drum hung round his neck with admirable vigor. As Amelia spent most of her time sleeping and the rest eating, it was difficult to tell which of these gifts she liked best, but she did gaze with apparent interest at the automaton each time it was set to work.

Other gifts were of more modest proportions though no less lavish in their quality. Dolls seemed to be the favorite, some possessed of entire wardrobes any lady of the *ton* would envy. Jewelry was also popular. Amelia quickly became the oblivious recipient of a quite nice set of diamond earbobs sent by the Prince Regent himself, several pearl necklaces, and half-a-dozen bracelets. Nor was her mother forgotten. The house soon overflowed with bouquets accompanying notes of congratulations and well-wishing. Joanna dutifully set aside a portion of each day to respond to the notes, and dispersed most of the flowers throughout the servants' quarters, where they were duly appreciated.

Amelia's arrival provided the family with a ready excuse to decline both visitors and invitations, the former being considered injurious to the baby's health and the latter being simply unwanted. With Royce joining them each day, they were content and more to be only in their own company. Kassandra knew the peaceful interlude would end soon enough, for the world always found a way to intrude, but she had no warning of the exact circumstances in which that would occur. Perhaps her joy at her niece's birth held the dark visions at bay.

They came, not as visions but as reality, on the second Monday of the month, May 11, a day that dawned to sultry warmth that seemed to herald an early summer. Late in the afternoon, when Royce suggested Kassandra accompany him for a stroll, she readily agreed. There had been no repetition of the intimacy between them on the day of Amelia's birth. He was unfailingly polite and congenial but seemed content to keep a proper distance. While she regretted that, Kassandra told herself it was for the best. All the same, a walk would do her good. She had not been away from the house since Amelia's arrival and felt the need for a change of scene.

They strolled through St. James's Park in the direction of the river and shortly found themselves in the pleasant environs of Whitehall.

"You might find this interesting," Royce said as he gestured at the buildings before them. "Over there is Westminster Palace. Construction on it began almost eight hundred years ago. Young by Akoran standards, I know, but about as old as you'll find here."

"It's quite impressive," Kassandra said honestly. "Is that where Parliament meets?"

"In the part called Westminster Hall. Would you like to see it?"

Kassandra allowed as to how she would and they walked in that direction. They were entering the darkly paneled lobby that served the House of Commons when an odd sound rang out, rather like a crack, Kassandra thought. She was wondering what it could be when Royce suddenly grabbed hold of her and without warning, pushed her against a nearby wall, putting his own body between her and the lobby.

"What on earth . . . ?" she exclaimed. Even as she tried to look over his shoulder, he yanked open a nearby door and shoved her into what appeared to be a small cloakroom.

"Stay here," he ordered and disappeared. Outside, in the lobby, she could hear footsteps pounding and men shouting to each other. Very quickly, she understood why.

"Mr. Perceval is shot! Mr. Perceval is shot!"

Perceval? Spencer Perceval, the Prime Minister? *Shot?* Disbelief filled her.

Cautiously, she eased open the cloakroom door and peered outside. The lobby thronged with men, but through the crowd she could see a still form lying on the floor, bleeding copiously from a wound to the chest. As she

134

watched, two gentlemen approached and picked up the body, carrying it into a nearby office. Scarcely had they done so than loud cries went up.

"Shut the doors! Let no one out!"

The doors through which she and Royce had entered minutes before were slammed shut and secured.

For a moment, silence descended, broken when a grim-faced man emerged from the office into which Perceval had been taken. He looked deeply shocked. Kassandra could not hear what he said but she had no need to do so. Instantly, his meaning became apparent.

"Where is the murderer?" a voice cried out.

"Find the murderer!"

So Perceval was dead. The Prime Minister known for his profound intolerance of reform. The man she suspected had contemplated an invasion of Akora to further his own aims. Dead.

At whose hand? Not an Akoran's, of that at least she could be sure. There were very few Akorans in England besides herself, and all those were in service to Alex, who had chosen each and every one. Besides, to kill an enemy in such a way was dishonorable. A duel would have been different, but to shoot down a man while he had no chance to defend himself . . .

Who had done it?

The answer was not long in coming. As cries for the murderer to be revealed continued, a slender, dark-haired man with regular features, in ordinary dress, looking little different from the dozens of other men thronging the lobby, announced suddenly, "I am the unfortunate man."

As he still held a pistol grasped in his right hand, Kassandra saw no reason to disbelieve him. Neither, apparently, did anyone else, for he was seized immediately and roughly searched. Almost at once, another pistol was found in his trouser pocket. Both weapons were taken away.

Seeing him disarmed, agitated members of Parliament pressed closer, demanding to know why he had done as he had. So vociferous were they in their interrogation that the man had little opportunity to answer. He tried several times, breaking off when their voices overrode his own, but eventually he did manage to speak.

"Want of redress," Kassandra heard him say, "and denial of justice."

And that, it seemed, was that. Perceval was dead, his assassin hurried away upstairs to face a hastily summoned magistrate, and nothing left to show what had occurred, save for the blood still staining the lobby floor.

She was staring at it when Royce took her arm. "We must get you home."

"I don't want to sound a dreadful hypocrite," she said as he guided her down a long corridor and out a back door of the palace, "but poor

Perceval. No one deserves to die like that."

"People very rarely get what they deserve. Hurry now."

They were outside, facing the river. "Why the haste?" she asked.

"There's a mob gathering."

"To protest Perceval's death?"

He handed her into a carriage waiting for them, apparently by his arrangement. Taking the seat across from her, Royce said, "Good lord, no, to celebrate it. Perceval was roundly hated by the common people."

"They will actually rejoice at his death?" She could not imagine such a thing no matter how loathed the man might have been.

"Strenuously," Royce said, "and, I expect, riotously. I picked a bad afternoon to suggest we go for a walk."

Alex certainly thought so, for he was at the gate of the Mayfair residence, mounted and accompanied by outriders, about to go in search of her when their carriage drew up.

"You've heard?" Royce asked him as he handed her out.

Alex nodded grimly. "I suspect all London has heard. Where will you be?"

"I'm going back to Westminster. I want to get a better sense of what this is about."

"Any idea who did it?"

"A disgruntled subject apparently, one of a very great many. You have adequate guards?"

"Since we had the foresight to bring men up from Boswick and Hawkforte, I do. You will be careful?"

"I'll watch my back," Royce said as he returned to the carriage.

Kassandra had no opportunity to say anything to him before he was gone.

She was staring after him when Alex dismounted. At his urging, they walked up the path to the house. Behind them, she heard the iron gates clanging shut and the sound of chains being wrapped around them.

"You are unharmed?" her brother asked.

She swallowed against the lump of worry in her throat and nodded. "Completely, but quite bewildered. Has this sort of thing ever happened before?"

"The killing of a Prime Minister? No, but the English did chop off a king's head less than two hundred years ago."

She shook her head in wonder. "They can seem so civilized."

"It is deceptive. Come inside now."

She did as he said, listening as he gave orders to deploy men around the walls and at the upper windows of the house where they would have a view of anyone approaching. Desperately, she wanted to believe such preparations were unnecessary but her better sense told her otherwise.

Finding Sarah, she sent the maid to Joanna on her behalf. "Please tell her I am fine and will join her as soon as I've freshened."

"I will, Your Highness, and glad I am to see you well."

In her room, Kassandra bathed quickly and donned a new dress. She supposed she was being superstitious, but she did not wish to be near Joanna or Amelia while wearing anything that had been so close to violent death.

She found her sister-in-law in a chair next to the window, Amelia in her arms. At once, Joanna held out a hand.

"Thank heavens you are all right. What a dreadful business."

"It is," Kassandra agreed, taking a seat across from her. Quickly, she added, "But I am certain we are quite safe here."

"Oh, I'm sure we are, too, although others may not be so fortunate. Royce came back with you, didn't he?"

"Of course, he wouldn't let me return alone."

Joanna gave her a level look. "But he didn't stay, did he?"

"He went back to Westminster," Kassandra admitted. "He wanted more information about what is happening." Because she could not stop herself, she added, "I hope he will not stay away long."

"He will be all right," Joanna said gently.

Kassandra nodded but her emotions felt entirely too raw to comment further. Instead, she distracted herself with Amelia, who was awake and looking around attentively. The women admired the child and chatted until the distant shouts from the city beyond the high walls increased until they could not be ignored.

The day was fading and from the window, Kassandra made out the flicker of bonfires burning in the streets. When the breeze changed direction, she smelled smoke. The shouts grew louder and more raucous, with a drunken edge. It would be dark soon in a city teetering on the brink of lawlessness, and still there was no sign of Royce.

Alex came up several times to reassure them that there was no trouble near the house. And perhaps also to reassure himself that they were not unduly alarmed.

"I am quite tired of sitting here," Joanna announced when he came again. "I would like to go downstairs."

"I don't think —" he began.

"For pity's sake, Alex, I will walk down if need be."

"You will do no such thing."

"I am fine, really and truly fine. Elena says so, I say so, everyone else knows so, even you. But if I have to stay within the four walls of this room tonight, I shall go stark, raving mad."

"Don't you think you're exaggerating just a little?" He tried to sound stern but the curling at the corners of his mouth undid the effort.

"Stark, raving."

"You will not even think of going into the garden?"

"Wouldn't enter my mind." Satisfied she had won, Joanna held out Amelia to Kassandra and suffered herself to be lifted into her husband's arms.

Having carried her downstairs, Alex deposited her in the family parlor with admonitions to stay put. He went back outside to check on the men. Kassandra glanced at the mantel clock, seeing that it was getting on toward nine o'clock. Perceval had been dead almost four hours and there was still no sign of Royce.

"You need to eat something," Joanna declared and rang the bell. All the footmen were with Alex but Sarah appeared promptly. She looked a little pale.

"Everything all right?" Joanna asked.

"Oh, yes, my lady." Sarah glanced toward the high windows. "It's just that noise . . . awful, isn't it?"

"You know that Lord Boswick will not allow harm to come to anyone here?"

"Certainly . . ."

"Truly, he won't," Joanna said gently. "But I think there are times when people are more comfortable staying close together. We'll come down. We can have tea and sandwiches, get out a deck of cards, gossip like mad, and never mind anything else."

"Come down . . . my lady? . . ."

"Ask Mulridge if you aren't sure. She'll tell you we did this sort of thing all the time at Hawkforte. Truth is, I miss it."

"Oh, well, then, I wouldn't want to go against Mulridge, my lady." Indeed, Sarah shuddered a bit at the thought. But she recovered quickly and insisted on helping Joanna down the steps to the kitchens, where she was received with surprised delight.

Seated at the wide table in the center of the spacious room, Kassandra quickly saw the wisdom of what Joanna had done. They were surrounded by women; not only all the female house servants from Cook on down but Elena and Brianna, who shortly joined them as did Mulridge herself. Whatever self-consciousness might have existed was melted away by the presence of Amelia, for none could resist cooing over her. Tea flowed in copious amounts, sandwiches and cakes appeared, and with Joanna's gentle prodding, a spirit of feminine camaraderie quickly took root.

"They'll be sorry tomorrow, of course," Cook said of the people who had gone out into the streets to celebrate Perceval's death. "They'll have to live with the consequences, won't they?"

She was a broad, plain-faced woman who had grown up at Boswick and had the same solid sense Kassandra associated with Akoran women. "I would like to know who did it," Kassandra said as she nibbled on a tea cake. In the company of the women, her stomach was not so knotted and she found she had an appetite.

"Fancy, you were practically there," Sarah said. "I would have fainted dead away."

"You'd have done no such thing, Sarah Merrick," Joanna exclaimed. "You come from better stock than that. Why I'll wager if you'd seen the villain before he acted, Mr. Perceval would still be among the living."

"Oh, my lady, I don't know about that!" But Sarah was clearly taken with the notion and did not mind a round of teasing about her hypothetical heroism.

"Still," Cook said at length, "what comes next won't be pretty. Fat George has just been waiting for an excuse to bear down all the harder on the common people." Abruptly, she caught herself and flushed. "Sorry, my lady, I mean no disrespect."

Joanna shrugged. "He is fat and his name is George. If he doesn't want people putting the two together, he ought to make more of an effort to rule properly."

"Is he truly your ruler only by birth?" Elena asked. She had learned a great deal of English in the months she had been in the country and had no difficulty making herself understood.

"We have an hereditary monarchy," Cook intoned. "Isn't it the same on Akora?"

"Not precisely," Elena said. "Let us just say we would not accept the sort of ruler who could be called Fat George."

"What would you do about him, then?" Cook asked.

"That is a good question," Brianna interjected. She was seated at the table near

Kassandra but her attention kept drifting to Amelia, who made her smile. "The Americans have elections and throw out rulers they don't like."

"Oh, the Americans!" Cook exclaimed. "They're nothing but trouble. Why my dear Uncle John went over to fight them when they had their rebellion."

"What happened to him?" Mulridge asked.

"I don't know rightly, he never came back."

"He wasn't killed, was he?" Joanna asked.

"Why no, he just never came back. Settled in a place called Con-nec-ti-cut or something of the sort. Quite astonishing, really. He'd been a perfectly sensible man till he got over there."

They were musing over the fate of Uncle John when footsteps sounded on the stairs to the kitchen. "Here you are," Alex said. "Been looking all over for you. You might have left a note."

"Where did you think I'd gone?" Joanna asked with a smile. She held out the plate of cakes to him. "Have some, they're awfully good."

The presence of his lordship had a quelling effect on the chatter of the women, but Alex did not notice. Having assured himself that his wife was in good hands, he grinned at his daughter, took two of the cakes and departed.

When he was gone, Cook rose. "Here we are sitting about while I'm sure those men outside would like a nice tea." She got to work briskly, and didn't object when Kassandra insisted on helping. Joanna, of course, was not allowed to do anything, which made her grouchy until Kassandra suggested she could cut the sandwiches. When all was ready, Sarah and Brianna carted everything upstairs. They returned almost at once.

"My lady," Sarah exclaimed, "Lord Hawkforte has returned."

Kassandra leaped to her feet. She paused only long enough to note Joanna's knowing smile before dashing up the stairs.

Chapter
SEVEN

Blasted man, he was in the garden talking with Alex, although to be fair it looked as though he had only just gotten there. He seemed all right but then he was the sort to hide any injury. She was quite sure he had a bruise on his forehead.

"What happened to you?" she demanded before she had come to a full stop in front of him.

"Oh, hello, Kassandra," Royce said with a smile. "What's got you racing about?"

"What's got me . . . ?" Of all the utterly stupid questions. Did it not enter his tiny male brain that she might just possibly be concerned about him? "Why nothing," she snapped, "absolutely nothing. *Good night,* Lord Hawkforte."

She had turned on her heel and was marching away when Royce caught hold of her arm. Laughing, he pulled her back to him.

"Easy, spitfire. God, you're fun to tease! Are you holding up all right?"

"Holding up? Of course I am. How did you get that bruise?"

"Bruise? Oh, this. Got hit with a brick, I think. Nothing to it."

"I suppose not, given the obvious thickness of your skull."

Grinning, Royce said, "I tell you, Alex, she's everything I ever heard about Akoran women. 'Warriors rule and women serve.' I can certainly see how well that works."

"Never said it worked," Alex grumbled. "More of a goal, really. Call it an ideal."

Kassandra glared at them both. "I'm so pleased to see you're enjoying yourselves while London burns."

"London isn't burning," Royce said more seriously. "Oh, there're fires lit and plenty of people dancing around them. They've broken into the taverns and made free with the drink. For the moment, that seems to have satisfied them."

"Did you learn anything else?" Alex asked.

"The killer's name is John Bellingham. He has some sort of grievance against the government, nothing special to it. At any rate, he tried to get Perceval's help and, of course, got nowhere. Seems to have decided life wasn't worth living but wanted to kill the Prime Minister first. Funny thing is, he's dreadfully worried about Perceval, hopes he didn't hurt him."

"But you said he wanted to kill the Prime Minister," Kassandra reminded him.

"So he did. The problem is, he doesn't seem to realize that Perceval the man and Perceval the Prime Minister were one and the same. Kill the hated symbol and you've also killed the human being."

"He's mad," Alex said flatly.

" 'Fraid so," Royce agreed. "Not that it will help him any. He'll swing before a fortnight's out."

"You will kill a man who is clearly not right in his mind?" Kassandra asked.

"Not me personally," Royce said dryly. "But a mad *king* doesn't get treated very well in this country. You can't expect much for a mad murderer."

Alex nodded somberly. "I'd appreciate it if you'd stay here tonight. The men are doing a good job but another pair of eyes wouldn't go amiss, just in case things do take a turn for the worse."

"Of course I'll stay. Better here than Carlton House, and if I go home, I'm sure to be summoned there." He shook his head in disgust. "Prinny will want everyone arrayed round his bed, moaning over the rabble and envisioning us all being guillotined."

"That man really has to get a grip on himself," Alex said.

"As long as you're staying," Kassandra said with forced patience, "you might let Elena take a look at that bruise."

"Don't see the point," Royce replied. At her exasperated look, he grinned again. "But I wouldn't say no to a cup of tea."

She snatched one off a nearby tray and shoved it at him. "Here, have your blasted tea."

"Play nicely, children," Alex murmured and went off to check on his men.

Morning came but brought no relaxation of vigilance, nor did the days that immediately followed. Inevitably, Royce was called away to Carlton House and Alex with him. They returned wearied and frustrated.

"Perceval's been buried privately," Royce said as they all sat together in the drawing room. "The authorities feared there would be riots if they tried to give him a state funeral. Bellingham hangs tomorrow."

"Perhaps things will quiet after that," Joanna suggested.

Her husband shrugged. "Perhaps."

"I have been thinking," she went on, "what with the trouble and all, Amelia and I could go down to Boswick or Hawkforte, either one. Kassandra can come with us. It's lovely at either manor this time of year and it would make a nice change from London, especially . . . well, under the circumstances."

Kassandra looked swiftly to her brother. She knew full well that this was a major concession on Joanna's part, who had steadfastly refused to leave London because Alex could not accompany her. That she was offering to do so now meant she understood fully how unsettled and dangerous matters were likely to remain.

And yet, Alex did not seem eager to take up

that offer. Indeed, he made no direct response to it at all.

Instead, he gestured to the pile of envelopes on a silver tray on the table in front of them. "I see you've had another note from that Byron fellow."

"Actually, Kassandra has," Joanna said. She was frowning slightly, no doubt at the change of subject.

"Does he write to you often?" Royce asked.

Kassandra shook her head. "Two or three times, I think. I haven't taken much notice."

"What on earth does he want?"

"Why nothing, so far as I can see. They're just chatty sort of letters."

"I don't really understand why he would be writing to you at all."

"He's fascinated by Akora. He said so when we met at Melbourne House." She picked up the most recent missive and glanced at it. "Mostly, he just seems to be lonely. There isn't much social life at the moment, what with the troubles and all."

"Have you answered?"

"No, actually, I haven't but I can't see that's your affair."

Royce flushed slightly. "I just don't think it's a very good idea for you to become involved with him."

"I'm not involved with him."

"Well, good, then."

They sat, glaring at each other, until Joanna

cleared her throat. "I'm so glad that's settled. Tell me, do you think the two of you might manage to be a quarter hour in each other's company without finding something to squabble about?"

"We do not —" Kassandra began only to break off when she realized Joanna was right, sparks did tend to fly when she and Royce were together. Partly she supposed that was because of the tensions surrounding them, but she knew full well that it also came from unresolved desires on both their parts.

"I am sorry," she said. "I would not for the world wish to abuse your hospitality by being an ill-tempered guest."

"Nor would I," Royce added quickly.

"Good," Joanna said. "That's quite enough penitence. Now perhaps one or both of you gentlemen" — under her gaze, Royce and Alex stiffened slightly — "would like to tell me why my very generous offer to remove to the country has not been greeted with cheers of male relief."

It fell to Alex to do so. He hesitated only briefly before saying, "Everything is fine at Hawkforte and Boswick."

Joanna's eyes widened slightly. "That's good to hear, particularly as I had not considered otherwise."

"However," Alex went on, "major disruptions are spreading beyond London. The roads are not safe."

"I see . . . of course, we could simply *sail* to Hawkforte and avoid the roads altogether. We've done that often enough."

"We could —"

Silence fell as Joanna gazed at her husband. Finally, she said, "You have something else in mind."

"I am not prepared to discuss it right now."

Kassandra only just managed to conceal her surprise. Instinctively, she looked at Royce. *He knew.* It was there in the cool gold shadows of his eyes, which met hers directly. *He knew and he approved.*

"I think I will go up now," Joanna said. Uncharacteristically, she appeared on the verge of tears.

"Sweetheart," Alex said, rising.

She held out a hand, forestalling him. "No, it's all right. I just think I should go up. It's been a rather tiring day." When he moved to help her, she shook her head firmly. "No, stay here. I'd actually like to be on my own for a bit."

She left, carrying Amelia. Alex stood, watching them go. He cursed softly under his breath.

Royce rose and poured Alex a brandy, handing it to him. "She'll be all right. She's a strong woman."

Alex took the drink but scarcely sipped it before setting it aside. With a visible effort, he wrenched his attention back to the matter at hand.

"Royce knows of your gift," he said to Kassandra. It was not a question but she nodded all the same. "Then I think he should know the rest."

When she did not object, Alex said, "Last year, Kassandra foresaw a British invasion of Akora. That was how we knew of the threat and were able to act against it."

Royce cast her a quick look that held no surprise. "I assumed as much when she told me what she can do."

"Good," Alex said. "Then you will understand that after Deilos's defeat, we were all relieved that the visions of an invasion stopped."

"Yes, of course . . ."

"Unfortunately, they have returned."

This time, Royce was startled. "You said nothing of this."

"I only learned of it myself a short time ago." To his sister, Alex said, "We believed that if there was indeed a British plan to invade Akora, Spencer Perceval would be behind it. It was consistent with his overall policies and as Prime Minister, he was in the best position to act, although he did deny any such intention to no less than the Prince Regent himself."

"I understand all that . . ." she said.

"Has Perceval's death made any difference?" Alex asked. "Does the threat of invasion still exist?"

Kassandra stared at him in surprise. She had not thought of that. Always, in her mind, she had associated the threat of invasion with Deilos, who ought to be dead but might not be. She had thought very little about Perceval's role, if at all. But if his part had been significant . . . and he was now dead . . . there was a chance, however faint, that everything might have changed.

"I don't know. I have not sought vision since leaving Akora."

"Never mind, then."

He would not ask her, she realized. Knowing as he did that the search for the pathways of the future could be painful and exhausting, Alex would never even suggest that she make the attempt. Nor would she ever wait for him to ask.

"If you will excuse me," she said, rising.

Both men also stood. Her brother looked at her with concern. "Kassandra, you don't intend —"

"You worry too much," she said, and touched his arm gently.

Outside in the hall she paused for a moment, listening to the sounds of the house. At this hour, it was likely that Elena was in the garden and Brianna in the library. The servants would be below. Mulridge . . . there was never any telling where she might be but as she seemed to keep largely to herself except for tending Joanna and Amelia, that didn't really matter.

Joanna herself had gone to her room with Amelia, which meant the nursery would be empty. Amelia did not sleep there yet, her parents preferring to keep her close until she had weathered the first few months of life. But she was carried up to visit the nursery from time to time. It was a warm, sun-dappled place, full of playful murals, toys awaiting their young mistress, and days not yet born filled with the promise of happiness.

Slowly, Kassandra mounted the stairs. Never had she tried to seek vision in such surroundings, but now she felt drawn to do so. As she entered the room, she paused, looking around. The floors were slightly worn in places where generations of Boswick children had played, including her own and Alex's father. The tall windows were open, admitting the fragrances of the garden. She breathed in deeply as a sense of peace stole over her.

Royce's automaton boy stood in a corner, eyeing her solemnly. The playhouse where Amelia would someday clamor with her little friends was set against one long wall. In what would be its front yard, the hobbyhorse waited patiently.

Waited for the future to arrive and become the present. One future out of all the many possibilities. One from all the branching, twisting pathways she saw fading away into eternity.

She took another breath and let her eyes close slowly. Her hands rested on the carved footboard of the bed Amelia would occupy one day. Here, in this room, in that unknown future, the baby asleep downstairs in her mother's arms would be a little girl . . .

A little, laughing girl with honey-hued hair and sparkling eyes . . .

"Ring around the rosie, pocket full of poesie . . ."

The high, lilting voice of a child . . . very young . . .

"All fall down . . ."

"William, give me that!"

"The mechanical boy . . . he needs repair . . ."

"What a marvelous room. The nursery, you say?"

Too far, she had gone too far. Her breath came in pants. Tension built mercilessly behind her eyes. Back . . . back . . .

And away, away from the nursery, the house, the city . . . Akora . . . *home* . . .

She saw it, then, as though she had not left: the cerulean sea, the curving rim of the islands, the lemon groves in flower . . . and Ilius, glorious Ilius, gleaming in the sun . . .

And the red . . .

Her mind shied away, denying, was drawn back.

The red serpent, moving along the roads, up from the shores, ever higher, climbing inexorably, banners flying, men in red coats marching, drums beating, cannons roaring . . . The black smoke swirling like an evil, living thing, parting to reveal the bodies lying broken and unmoving . . .

Her throat tightened, she could not breathe.

On and on the dead were heaped. She must not look . . . must not see their faces . . . for she would know them. Atreus, Alex, her beloved brothers, dead. Her cousins and uncles, all the men of her family, and so very many more . . . dead . . . Boys, women, girls . . . fighting to the last for the land they loved. Dead.

"Nooooo!"

The scene veered suddenly, hurtling her at breakneck speed along another path, into another possibility. She saw the shining city of Ilius at peace, glimpsed her family alive and well, saw herself . . . climbing a hill to a place she knew . . . saw a man emerge as though from the bowels of the earth. Deilos! Alive, smiling at her maliciously. Deilos . . . coming at her, murder in his eyes, but she was ready, she was prepared, she knew what she had to do. For Akora, for all she loved, for the future that must be whatever the cost. She felt the hilt of the blade cool in her hand, felt the power within her as she drove it into the man who would destroy all she held dear. Felt, too, the pain as he struck at her in turn, his last act, looked down and saw her life's blood flow, the price paid that Akora would be safe.

The terrible scene released her. She fell a great distance, sobbing, fell and fell and fell . . .

And was caught . . . in strong arms, against a hard chest, cradled close and enveloped in the present where . . .

"God damn it! How could he let you do this?"

Royce.

Relief filled her. She was safe, protected, she did not have to fear or struggle or do anything except hold on to him with all her might as he lowered them both to the floor. With infinite tenderness, he stroked her hair, crooning soft words of comfort, willing her to come back to him.

Her breath steadied even as her mind cleared. Slowly, she looked up at him. "I am all right, really."

Her voice sounded very far away even to her own ears. It did not seem to reassure him.

"Alex should not have let you —"

"It was my choice, not his. I had to know."

"Perceval . . ."

Her throat clogged on the words but she managed to utter them. "His death changes nothing, at least not for Akora."

Royce said nothing but he tightened his arms around her. She sat up slowly. Gazing round the nursery, she said, "I wonder why I never realized before that a place so devoted to the young and all they represent would be a good place to seek vision of the future they will inhabit."

He drew her closer yet, resting his chin on the top of her head. "You were crying."

She nodded, her hands wrapped around his forearms, still desperately needing his strength.

"What I saw cannot be allowed to come to pass. At all costs, it must be prevented."

She raised her head, meeting his eyes. "No price is too high."

"It's only a possible future," he reminded her. Gratefully, she left him in ignorance.

"Yes, only possible. Please, help me up."

He did so quickly but still did not let go of her. "You want to tell Alex." His voice was hard.

"Don't be angry at him, this was not his fault."

"Is it always like this? So painful and frightening? . . ."

"No, not always. Sometimes it is actually gentle and even pleasant." Desperate to lighten the mood, she smiled softly. "For instance, I saw Amelia months ago, when first I learned of her. She is going to keep her parents very busy!"

He relaxed slightly. "I thought as much. We have a long history at Hawkforte of women who know their own minds."

"She will be another." She straightened, savoring his closeness, wishing it could endure forever. "You love Hawkforte."

"I am a part of it," he said simply. "I'm not sure exactly what that means but somehow it seems as though I was there before I ever actually was and that it will always be with me."

"I think there are only a very few places on earth like that."

"Is Akora one of them . . . for you?"

"I suppose, in some ways." She could not tell him more, not speak of the strange yearning she felt for another place, another home somewhere between dream and memory.

Royce was looking at her, concern shadowing his eyes. "Kassandra . . . do you know why Alex wouldn't agree to Joanna going to Boswick or Hawkforte?"

She nodded, glad that on almost all matters she could speak honestly with this man. "He means to send her to Akora. It is a hard choice but I can understand it. The threat to Akora is still in the future. The danger in England is real right now."

"If there was no threat any longer to Akora, he would be able to go with them."

She nodded. "Yes, but under the circumstances, that is not possible. There will have to be a new government now, won't there? Alex will need to be here to do all he can to safeguard Akora's interests." Softly, she added, "It will be very hard for them. They have not been separated since they wed, and there is also Amelia. This is all very unfortunate."

Cautiously, Royce asked, "You realize it is not only Joanna who must go?"

She sighed deeply. "Somehow I thought that waiting so long to get here meant I would have more time once I did arrive."

He squeezed her waist gently. "You will come back."

No, she thought, she would not. Not if her vision was correct, and it had rarely been wrong. Her mind reeled from it. Instinctively, she sought refuge in a shell of normalcy. "I have a few days yet, at least. Perhaps time for another trip to Gunter's, assuming the streets are peaceful enough?"

"If I have to bring the shop to you, I promise you shall not go off without all the toffees you can carry."

"Actually, I prefer the lemon drops."

"So be it," he said.

Together, they went down the stairs.

"Atreus's instructions are very clear," Alex said.

It was several days later. Bellingham was dead and buried, and London had sunk into a sullen stupor roused only by anxiety over who would form the new government. The Whigs hoped for a second chance, while the Tories jockeyed to hold on to power. Fat George kept to his bed.

"Kassandra is to return to Akora on the ship that brought this message. There is to be no delay and no discussion."

"Should I resent the implication that I would argue over the Vanax's clear directive?" Kassandra asked softly. She was too tired to muster more than so mild an objection. Sleep eluded her, which was just as well. Her dreams were filled with images of blood.

"Only if you wish to pretend you would not have done so if circumstances hadn't so worsened in the meantime," Alex replied. His tone was affectionate for the sister who, unexpectedly, was giving him no trouble.

"I am resigned," Kassandra said. In fact she was not, but she preferred to keep the anguish of her heart hidden. It was as well that she part from Royce now. Her feelings for him were a danger, threatening as they did to tempt her from the path of duty.

"I certainly am not," Joanna said. She was standing near the window from which she had been gazing out at the garden, lost in her own thoughts, but now she turned her attention to her husband. "And I will not pretend otherwise. Hawkfortes have been safe at Hawkforte for nine hundred years. I see no reason why I cannot go there."

"Need I remind you," Alex asked stiffly, "that you are Atreides now, as is our daughter?"

"No," Joanna said, "I need no reminding." A deep sigh escaped her. "But I have said how I feel, you know it well, and now we have little time left. I would not waste it in acrimony."

At once, Alex went to her and took her in his arms. She leaned her head against his broad chest. Royce and Kassandra exchanged a glance. As one, they rose and slipped from the room, leaving the couple to their privacy.

Outside in the garden, Royce said, "Marriage has mellowed my sister. There was a time when she would not have given in so readily."

"She loves him and in that loving, she can never win by besting him. Even if she were somehow able to persuade Alex to her view, she would still lose because she would know he was unhappy and worried. That is no victory."

"You make love sound like a trap," he said wryly.

Kassandra's response was entirely serious. "Oh, it is. A honeyed trap, to be sure, but a trap all the same. Where love enters, freedom departs."

He stopped, standing in the shadow of a graceful old willow tree, and looked at her. "You surprise me. I thought women were all for love."

Candidly, she said, "I think women, like men, enjoy the notion of being loved. After all, it confers a certain power. But to be *in love,* that is a different matter."

"Have you never been in love, then?"

Had she? Was she? Or was she just precariously close?

"I love my family."

He smiled faintly. The sun, filtering through the delicate branches, revealed the thick fringe of his lashes, the straight blade of his nose, the surprising, sensual fullness of his mouth.

That mouth . . . that kiss . . .

"I should go back inside," she said.

"And I should — and must — go on to Carlton House."

Her sympathy was immediate. "The Prince Regent again?"

"Again and always." He looked rueful. "Somehow, he thinks me the man to reconcile Whig and Tory."

"That's absurd. The only person who can do that, if it can be done at all, is the Prince Regent himself."

"It is difficult to lead from the bottom of a bottle, whether of brandy or laudanum."

Royce took his leave then, gracious as always. Kassandra remained in the garden a little while longer until she could be reasonably certain the deep current of her yearning for what could not be was not clear for anyone to see. Only then did she return to the house, there to begin preparations to return to Akora.

With her she took a leaf of the willow tree, plucked from where he had stood, in the sunlight of that day already swiftly fading into the past.

She felt a little foolish in the doing but that did not stop her; she took the leaf anyway and later, in her room, folded it carefully within the pages of Miss Jane Austen's *Sense and Sensibility*, a world in which love truly did exist and all managed to work out precisely as it should.

Chapter EIGHT

Every journey, Kassandra thought, seemed to have the same rhythm to it. Whether the product of long months or mere days of planning, anticipating and preparing, the actual moment of departure always arrived in a great rush.

From the carriage window, she stared out at the docks of Southwark where she had first set foot in England scant weeks before and from which she would shortly leave. The streets were crowded with people, most ill-garbed, many with the gaunt stamp of hunger or disease on faces prematurely aged. But among them, like bright-plumed peacocks strutting their privilege, strolled the wealthy. The whip-wielding constables of London had brought what passed for peace back to the streets but it was no more than a thin and bitter crust laid over a cauldron of simmering resentment.

Alex was right to be sending them away, but knowing that, as he surely did, made his task no easier. He sat on the bench across from Kassandra, Amelia tucked within the crook of his arm, his free hand holding Joanna's. The couple had said nothing since leaving the Mayfair house, their silence eloquent of their shared unhappiness.

Another carriage followed, this one bringing Elena and Brianna who were also returning to Akora. They had needed a separate carriage to accommodate the crates of precious books they were taking back with them, as well as all the chests holding the seeds and cuttings of medicinal plants that Elena had accumulated during her visit.

Outriders accompanied the carriages, keeping the curious well away. As they neared their destination, the crowd thinned and finally vanished of its own accord. Before them was a stone quay bracketed on either side by warehouses. No sign declared the ownership of the property but it was well known all the same and was the reason why the residents of Southwark gave it wide berth.

At the end of the quay, a ship rode at anchor. It was only one of a hundred or so ships in port at the moment, vessels of every size and description, gathered from over a good portion of the world. But it was also unique.

As Kassandra stepped from the carriage, she looked up at the tall mast splitting the sky and from it, to the curving prow of the mighty vessel, rising higher and higher until it ended finally in the horned head of a great, red-eyed bull.

The ancient symbol of Akora. The reminder to all who cared to look upon it of the fierce will and might of the Fortress Kingdom.

And yet for all that, to her, simply a ship of the sort she had seen every day of her life in the harbor at Ilius.

The captain, alerted to their arrival, hurried onto the dock where he greeted Alex respectfully. The two stepped a little apart to speak. Other men appeared and began loading the baggage on board. The wind was freshening and very soon now the tide would turn.

Kassandra remained where she was until finally there was no reason for her not to board. About to step up the gangway, she hesitated and looked back down the length of the quay past the warehouses.

Where was Royce? She had thought he would come, if not to say good-bye to her, surely to bid farewell to his sister and niece. She had seen him last two days before at supper. Since then, she knew only that he had been extremely occupied. Yet he would not let them go with no word at all . . . would he?

It seemed he would, for there was no sign of him. The last of the trunks and crates had been taken aboard, and Alex and Joanna had gone to her cabin to make their farewells in private. Soon, very soon, they would be gone.

Fine, then, it was for the best. She turned, head high, and climbed the last few steps to the deck, almost reaching there when the sudden clatter of a carriage made her look back. Instantly, her heart leaped. Before the carriage wheels rolled to a stop, Royce dropped down lightly onto the quay.

"Good morning," he said with a smile.

"And to you," she replied, hoping for all the world that she sounded merely cordial. "Joanna is on board, if you'd like to say good-bye."

"She's with Alex, I presume. I think they should have as much time together as possible." He nodded to the footmen who jumped from the carriage and began . . . unloading several trunks . . . ?

"Did we forget something?" Kassandra asked.

"I certainly hope not. It's too late to go back for it now."

"But what . . . ?"

Just then, Alex appeared on deck. He looked strained yet in command of himself. Seeing Royce, he managed a faint smile. "There you are. Thought for a moment you weren't going to be able to get away after all."

"Prinny stalled as long as he could," Royce said. "But not even he could refuse the request of a brother monarch."

"Request?" Kassandra stared at them both. "What request?"

"Oh, didn't I mention it?" Alex asked with feigned innocence. "In the same letter with his instructions that you return home, Atreus said he would like an opportunity to meet Lord Hawkforte. Said he thought that would — how did he put it? — 'facilitate the establishment of mutually beneficial relations between the Kingdoms of Akora and Great Britain.' Yes, I think that was it."

Was it remotely possible that she had heard him correctly? "Atreus wants to meet Royce?"

Alex nodded. "He was rather clear about that."

"And you chose not to say a word?"

Her brother looked apologetic, but not excessively so. "Truth is I wanted it to be a surprise for Joanna. Thought it might cheer her up, make things a bit easier for her. You understand."

Oh, she did, and instantly felt quite ashamed of herself. Just because she was caught between shock and joy, delight and dismay, she could not forget the feelings or needs of others.

"I see," she murmured, not daring to look at the golden-haired man who stood on the quay, gazing up at her, his expression watchful and, she feared, all too knowing.

"You don't have any reason to object to Royce going along, do you?" Alex asked.

"No, no, of course not, don't be absurd, why ever would I? And, of course, Joanna will be comforted. It was really quite good of you to think of it, Alex."

"Yes, well, hopefully this whole business will be over soon and we'll all be back together, but in the meantime —"

Kassandra did not hear the rest of what he

said. The shock of Royce's arrival had pierced the careful wall she had placed around her emotions. Even as it crumbled, she looked at her brother, really looked at him, so familiar and so dear. The anguished thought rose up in her that she might never see him again.

If her vision was correct . . .

And it had rarely been wrong.

"I'm sure this will be a great solace to Joanna."

"I'll just go find her," Royce said as he stepped onto the deck. There was a question in his eyes, a shadow of concern when he looked at Kassandra. Try though she did, she could not fully conceal her distress.

Considerately, Royce left her alone with the brother he no doubt thought she would miss during the few weeks — hopefully not more than a few months — of their separation.

"Kassie," Alex said gently, using the name only he had ever called her by, "you're not really so upset, are you? Everything will work out, you'll see."

She mustered a weak smile. "Oh, I'm sure it will."

Barely had she spoken than he sighed and opened his arms. She went into them, hugging him fiercely, willing herself to remember this moment, every sound and scent, every touch and thought, to cherish each, to keep the memory where it would always be fresh and true.

If only . . . if only . . . time could stop, heart-beat suspend, and the moment last forever.

If only.

Water splashed on the pilings beneath the quay. The tide was turning.

Kassandra remained on deck as the Thames Estuary faded into the distance and the vessel approached the Strait of Dover. There, close to the Flanders coast, they were joined by four Akoran warships that took position on either side to escort them into the Channel and beyond.

The appearance of the other vessels surprised her, but upon reflection, she realized it should not have. With the threat of an invasion of Akora renewed, Atreus would be inclined to take additional precautions. He also would not let pass an opportunity to make a show of force in waters frequented by both the British and French navies.

She lingered until the freshening wind reminded her that garments suitable for a London day in late spring were not really adequate at sea. Shivering slightly, she went below and shortly found her way to her cabin.

It was one of a group of cabins situated toward the bow of the ship. Ordinarily, they would be occupied by the vessel's officers, but on this occasion, they had been turned over to the female passengers. Royce, she supposed, would be invited to share the crew's quarters.

She suspected he would enjoy being among the Akoran warriors, being a warrior himself at heart.

Her cabin was small but comfortably furnished with a wide bunk, a writing table, and a large wardrobe. Graceful murals of Akoran life enlivened the walls, solace for the men who, tough as they undeniably were, missed their homes when they were away from them. Adjacent to the sleeping area was a bath, complete with a shower of the sort Joanna confessed to having been so fascinated by during her first voyage on an Akoran vessel. Kassandra smiled at the thought that while Akora might acquire certain advances from beyond its shores, it was far ahead of the rest of the world when it came to plumbing.

As she had directed, the trunk with the clothing made for her in England was in the hold. The one brought to her cabin held garments in the Akoran fashion. With a sense of mingled regret and relief, she removed the dress she had donned that morning and folded it away.

Half an hour later, she knocked on the door of Joanna's cabin. Joanna herself opened it. She, too, had changed into Akoran garb. Her eyes were slightly red-rimmed but other than that, she looked much her old self. Amelia was asleep in the cradle brought aboard for her.

"Come in," Joanna said, standing aside to admit her. "Royce has gone to get settled."

"I'm so glad you will have his company."

"As am I. It was quite a surprise." She hesitated a moment before asking, "You did not know?"

"I hadn't a hint. Alex truly did want to surprise you but I think both he and Royce were concerned the Prince Regent might not agree to let him go."

"That would be so like Prinny," Joanna said. She went over to the cradle, checking to be sure Amelia still slept, then took a seat near the porthole. "I have many regrets about leaving England but I confess parting from society is not among them."

"You know Alex did what was best."

"I suppose . . . no, that is not fair, I do know he was right. But, sweet heaven, it hurts!"

Kassandra went to her quickly, kneeling down in front of her, and took Joanna's hands in hers. "It won't be for long, I promise. Amelia will have her father back and you will have your husband."

Hope flared in Joanna's eyes. "You have seen —"

"No, not precisely." She could not lie about her visions, not ever, no matter how much she might wish to. "I cannot tell you that but I am certain all the same." Very certain because she had seen what would be needed to avert an invasion of Akora. To prevent the terrible red serpent creeping over the roads, bringing with it the swirling smoke and everywhere the bodies of the dead. Seen and accepted.

"How I hope you are right," Joanna said with a sigh. "I know it is very weak of me but I cannot bear the thought of being apart from him."

Kassandra smiled gently and got to her feet. She glanced at her niece, sleeping peacefully, and felt a moment's fierce gladness that there would be a future, despite all.

"Not weak," she said, "never that. You and my mother are the two strongest women I know."

"That is kind of you." Joanna's face brightened. "Phaedra will be so happy."

"She would meet us halfway if she knew you were coming with Amelia," Kassandra predicted. "And that doesn't require a vision to know!"

"I'm looking forward to surprising her and Andrew as well."

"My father will be thrilled. I must say, I'm glad they're back from America. They had a wonderful time there, but we were all anxious for them to come home."

"I seem to recall Alex suggesting there was some particular reason for their return. Was there?"

Well aware that Joanna was trying to distract herself, Kassandra nodded. "Father thinks there is going to be another war between the United States and Great Britain. He's quite convinced of it."

"Surely one war was enough."

"Perhaps not. At any rate, I think Mother wanted to come home as well. She says now that her children are marrying, she needs to settle down."

"She has her eye on you, I take it?" Joanna teased.

"No, actually on Atreus. He is the oldest, after all. Mother told him when Alex married that he really must choose a bride."

"Which he has still managed not to do."

"It's hard for him," Kassandra said. "With matters unsettled on Akora, if he marries into one of the noble families, he risks alienating all the others. He could simply take a bride from among the people, but she would have to be the sort who can deal with the demands of the position. Besides, at heart I think Atreus is something of a romantic."

"He wants to fall in love," Joanna said.

"He would deny it, of course."

They were entertaining themselves with thoughts of Atreus's future bride when Royce appeared. He stopped just beyond the door and stared at them. "Good lord."

"I believe you know my brother," Joanna said wryly, "the *diplomat?*"

"I'm sorry . . . I didn't mean . . ." Though he tried his utmost, he could not keep his gaze from devouring Kassandra. She looked so . . . utterly, exquisitely feminine. Kassandra as he had known her in England and yet more.

The gown or whatever it was called that she wore, more of a tunic really, was made of some filmy white material that left her arms bare and clung to her small waist before falling to her ankles. Her hair was unadorned and tumbled in thick ebony waves that seemed to hold within them the glint of moonlight on deep water. She smelled good, too, he realized, some combination of jasmine and something else he couldn't recognize, very different from the cloying perfumes of society chicks.

"Royce . . . ?" Joanna spoke with gentle amusement.

"What? Oh, yes, sorry . . . you just both look rather different. Lovely, of course, just different."

"It is the Akoran style," Joanna said, "and much more comfortable than our English clothes."

"I imagine so." Particularly since there didn't seem to be all that much of it. Barely had he entertained the thought when he realized it was not true. Filmy as the garments might appear at first glance, they were actually much more modest than the diaphanous creations some society ladies sported.

"I hope you've been made comfortable," Kassandra said. She was doing her best not to look at him but the effort was futile. He had removed the frock coat in which he'd come aboard and wore only snugly fitted breeches, a loose shirt, and boots. The thick mane of his golden hair was windblown. Against his summer tan, his eyes appeared greener than usual and fringed by sun-kissed lashes. He looked hard, rugged, and utterly male.

"The captain seems a good sort," Royce said, "and the men have been very welcoming. I must say, Joanna, I can understand now why you've been complaining about the plumbing in England. When I get back, I think I'll look into putting one of those stand-up contraptions in at Hawkforte."

"It's called a 'shower'," Joanna said, "and just wait until you see the bath tubs."

"Something to look forward to," he said with a grin, and went over to the cradle to check on Amelia.

The following day saw them turning south out of the Channel and into the open sea. From there, they would drop down past Spain and Portugal to the Strait of Gibraltar but instead of turning east into the Mediterranean, as most shipping did, they would strike out westward to the fabled land beyond the Pillars of Hercules, Akora.

After luncheon, enjoyed on deck, Royce got out a map and began studying it. He had spent the morning among the men, helping to set the sails and taking his turn at the crow's nest high on the center mast. The day was bright, the wind steady and the sky clear but for a scattering of fluffy clouds that only served to emphasize the deep blue helmet of the heavens. The rhythmic clank of the rigging and the occasional creak of the hull reminded him that he had spent far too much time of late in London and, for that matter, on land. A sailor to his soul, he was enjoying himself thoroughly.

"It's amazing to think we had no real idea of what Akora looks like until last year," he said, "and even now, there're only a few of us who know."

"Why is that?" Brianna asked. She and Elena were sharing lunch with them, accompanied by Amelia, who was awake and content in her mother's arms.

"Look here," Royce said, spreading the map out before her. "Imagine you're on a British ship, say, in the waters around Akora. You can't get too close because the Akoran navy won't let you. The best you can do is try to chart the coastline using a spyglass. Right here, on the north coast, you notice what looks like an inlet and you see something similar when you get round to the south side. But that's about all you can see. As far you know, Akora is one large island with no harbors, nowhere even to anchor safely, nothing except a couple of inlets which don't look like much. She must keep her fleet at sea, you suppose, supplying it from smaller boats, but you can't really imagine how and that only adds to the mystery. In fact, since you can't see *anything* along the coast except impenetrable cliffs, it's easy to understand how the legends of a Fortress Kingdom got started."

"But Akora isn't one big island," Brianna said. "At least it hasn't been for thousands of years, ever since the volcano exploded."

"That's the surprise," Royce said. "It certainly was for me." He pointed toward the "inlet" on the southern coast. "On my first voyage here, I arrived from this direction, coming directly out of a gale that had caught me off the Gulf of Cadiz. My boat was coming apart when I saw what I thought was just an inlet and realized it was the only chance I was going to get. I thought if I was lucky, I'd be able to follow it until it ran out and I ran aground. Instead, I found myself hurled up what was really a strait and into the Inland Sea, which I'd had no idea even existed."

"The drowned heart of Akora," Elena said quietly. She broke a crusty roll and dipped it in the remnants of the fragrant fish stew called *marinos* that had to be among the very best dishes Royce had ever tasted. "When the volcano exploded, it tore the original island in two. The sea rushed into the center."

"It's amazing anyone survived," he said.

"They would not have," Kassandra agreed quietly, "if not for some of the sacred caves underground that sheltered them from the fires that followed the flow of lava. Even so, if the invaders had not come shortly thereafter, everyone left would have starved to death."

Royce rolled up the map, putting it away

carefully. He thought she looked a little pale and wondered why. Surely, she should be happier to be returning home?

"It must have been difficult to accept invaders as rescuers," he said.

"They were not accepted," she said flatly, "at least not for several generations. It took that long to work out an accord between the old ways and the new."

"Change can be difficult to accept under the best of circumstances," Royce observed.

Joanna broke off cooing at Amelia and said, "Change is coming to Akora once again, hopefully this time far more peacefully."

Kassandra nodded. "Change must come. Akora cannot fall behind the rest of the world. That would leave us far too vulnerable."

"The Vanax, in his wisdom, will guide us through whatever lies ahead," Elena said confidently. "After all, he is the Chosen."

"By ancient ritual," Brianna said. "Ancient *and* mysterious, conducted in the sacred caves of which the Princess spoke just now. Very few have any idea of what is involved. We know only that when it is over, the Vanax has been chosen."

"It might be interesting," Royce said only half-facetiously, "to send all the various crowned heads of Europe down into those caves. I'd wager damn few of them would even manage to get back out, much less end up as 'chosen.'"

His own frankness surprised him, suggesting as it did the depths of his frustration with England's monarchy. He must be more relaxed and at ease even than he had realized. Perhaps that was what had also prompted him to speak, however briefly, of his previous visit to Akora.

In the almost two years that had passed since the first time he set eyes on the Fortress Kingdom, he had said virtually nothing about his experiences there to anyone. Joanna and Alex knew the bare outline of what had transpired, for they had rescued him from the hell in which he had found himself, but not even they knew very much. He preferred it that way even though he realized that his reticence had come at a price. The nightmares were less frequent now but they still happened, and only recently had he begun to sleep within four walls again.

He had recovered physically from nine months spent slowly starving in a dank cell, waiting to be used as bait to spark the invasion the traitor Deilos imagined would bring him to power. Freedom had never been so sweet to him as it was now. But somewhere deep inside, he knew, lurked the desire for revenge. If Deilos still lived . . .

He glanced at Kassandra and was surprised to find her gaze already on him. She saw too much, he thought, and not only in her visions. Yet he could not find it in himself to mind. There was some strange comfort in the sense that he was not alone with painful thoughts.

Another day passed and another. The closer they came to Akora, the stronger memory grew. Royce gave up sleeping in the crew quarters and made his bed on deck. In this, he was not alone, for the farther south they sailed, the warmer it became. He threw himself into the hard, physical routine of the voyage, doing his share and more of the work. In slack times, he joined the men in their sports — knife throwing was popular, as was wrestling. Distantly, he was aware that he was earning the Akoran warriors' respect, but what mattered most was that he did not think too much.

Inevitably, he was conscious of Kassandra. She was always there — on deck, with Joanna, cooing to Amelia, or simply staring off across the sea lost in her own thoughts. They shared meals together but little else. In the close confines of the vessel, there was no opportunity for private moments and that, he thought, was fortunate.

He dreamed of her, lying on the deck at night, lulled to sleep by the motion of the ship. He saw her as he had the first time, twirling round and round, laughing with sheer happiness. And as she had been on the nursery floor, tormented yet valiant.

He slipped from the dreams to stare at the swelling moon and wonder why the shadows never fully left her eyes.

Ten days after leaving Southwark, he woke to the smell of lemons.

It was not yet dawn. Merely the thinnest ribbon of fire shone against the eastern horizon. Most of the other men were not yet stirring, only the night watch was awake. Royce sat up slowly and looked around.

Lemons.

That made no sense at all.

He got to his feet, stretched, rubbed a hand over his jaw, and decided so long as he was up, he ought to shave. And still he smelled lemons.

A door opened near the bow. As he watched, a slender figure emerged and went to stand by the railing. Though her back was to him, he knew her at once.

He closed the distance between them with a soft tread she could not possibly hear. All the same, she turned to him.

"Good morning," he said.

Kassandra nodded. She drew the cloak she wore more closely around her and glanced up at the still-shining stars. "You are awake early."

"So are you. Tell me, why do I think I smell lemons?"

Her full mouth — that so soft, so sweet mouth — curved in a smile. "You smell Akora."

"Akora . . ." In the heady fragrance that threatened to swamp his senses? Or was it the woman herself who made him feel that way?

"The lemon groves are in bloom," she said. "The wind passing over the hills picks up their scent and carries it far out to sea. Take a breath, slowly . . ."

As he did, she said, "There is wild thyme and oleander, as well. Those who have traveled away from Akora — Alex, my parents, myself — know that no other place on earth smells like home."

He could well believe it, for the scent entranced him, but even more powerful was the awareness that their destination was near. "How much longer?" he asked.

She lifted her head, taking the measure of the invisible just as he and every other sailor would. "With this wind, we will sup tonight in Ilius."

The stars were returning, following in the train of the setting sun, when they entered the harbor at the foot of the royal city. Royce was on deck, where he had been since waking. Since the first sight of land in late afternoon, he had scarcely been able to take his eyes from Akora.

Confusion warred with elation. He knew his memories of that first arrival were fragmentary at best. He had battled the gale for hours before being blown into the Inland Sea, and had barely reached shore alive on the island that was to become his prison. A blow to the head had rendered him only semi-conscious so that he scarcely remembered being captured by Deilos's men. But even so . . . he thought he knew what Akora looked like: a harsh and rocky place, cruel and unforgiving.

What was this, then? This seeming paradise

of verdant hills dotted with white temples and prosperous farms, of golden beaches and azure waters?

They had come through the southern strait, just as he had done, but instead of being blown wildly toward the cluster of three small islands in the center of the Inland Sea — the only remnants of the drowned part of Akora — they had hugged the shore of the large eastern island called Kallimos, the name meaning *beautiful,* and in this case well deserved. Far to the west across the Inland Sea, visible only with a spyglass, was the equally large western island of Leios named for its fertile plains. But it was Ilius that held his attention. He knew he had been taken to the city after being rescued by Joanna and Alex. He had spent several days in the royal palace, being cared for by Elena, but of that he remembered almost nothing at all. Nor did he recall very much about his departure for England. It was only during the voyage home that he had returned to himself.

Perhaps that was why everything looked so new and different, that and the fact that he came as a free man, not a half-dead prisoner. Whatever the cause, there was no denying that the land was breathtakingly beautiful.

"No wonder people have wanted to keep this place to themselves," he said.

Beside him, Kassandra nodded. Softly, she said, "You saw Akora at its worst. Now I hope you will see our best."

It seemed he already was, for scarcely had they entered the harbor than he realized he was looking at a city unlike any he had ever seen before. Ilius rose before him, climbing up the hill that rose out of the sea, tier on tier of houses that all seemed draped in flowers, roads winding among them to reach the top where stood the royal palace, gleaming crimson in the rays of the setting sun.

"It is immense," he said while still trying to absorb the dimensions of what he saw. The entire top of the hill appeared to have been sheared off, replaced by a complex of columned buildings.

"We have been building it for more than three thousand years," Kassandra said wryly. "And we have an aversion to tearing anything down. There are rooms in the palace that date from the original construction."

"Three-thousand-year-old rooms? Are they still in use?"

"Of course, everything is kept in excellent repair."

"It's hard to imagine. In Europe, we think anything a few centuries old is venerable. Here I suppose you'd still call that 'new.' "

"Yes, we would, although that is a word we don't have much occasion to use."

Still staring at the palace, Royce shook his head in amazement. "It's as though ancient Rome and Athens, even the temple cities of Egypt, were still alive and flourishing, as though nothing had ever deteriorated or been destroyed."

"Every child learns of the great struggle for survival that had to be waged after the explosion. It is deeply engrained in us that what we have is precious and must be protected."

He looked again toward the city, trying to comprehend what he was seeing. No other people on earth had managed to bring so much of their past intact into the present. Yet the Akorans had also accomplished the even more difficult balancing act of preserving their culture while still allowing it to grow and change. The achievement spoke to their tenacity and to a subtlety of mind both rare and admirable.

It was all he had ever imagined during the uncounted hours in the library at Hawkforte, studying the artifacts his ancestor had sent back from the Fortress Kingdom centuries before. A young boy's curiosity and wonder had become the determination of a man and brought him to this moment.

A moment he realized just then would not have been so precious were it not for the woman sharing it with him.

"You said," he reminded her, "that you knew what happened to my ancestor who came here. That there are records?" When she nodded, he asked, "Will you show them to me?"

"Of course, if you like. I will be happy to show you that and more." She broke off just then and looked to the quay they were fast approaching. Her eyes suddenly brightened, free for once of the shadows that lurked in them.

He was wondering at the cause of that when the answer became evident. A man and a woman stood on the dock. The man was tall, broad-shouldered and very fit despite being well into his middle years. The woman was of a similar age but still slender and lovely. She had ebony hair much like Kassandra's and, indeed, looked like an older version of her. At sight of the vessel, they both smiled warmly and waved.

"My parents," Kassandra said with delight.

Royce stood back a little as the vessel nestled gently against the quay and dropped anchor. Scarcely had it done so than Kassandra alighted and was swept up in her parents' embrace. They stood together for some minutes, chatting happily, before Kassandra turned back to Royce. With a smile, she gestured to him. He came forward and was introduced.

"The Lady Phaedra and Lord Andrew Boswick," she said with what he thought was pardonable pride. "Please to welcome Lord Royce Hawkforte."

"Good to meet you," Andrew said, offering his hand.

Royce took it with pleasure. "I must say, sir, for a dead man, you look remarkably healthy."

Andrew laughed, as did his wife and daughter. "The fiction of my death has proven very useful," the older man said. "After I washed up on these shores more than a

188

quarter-century ago, I quickly realized I wished to make my life here." He looked warmly at his wife who smiled in return. "But I was never at ease with the notion of forgoing my responsibilities in England. Fortunately, my son, Alex, was both willing and able to take them up. As the Marquess of Boswick, he has been ideally placed to help Akora emerge into the modern world."

"I gather you have been busy in America for the same purpose?"

"We just returned from there," Phaedra said. "I wouldn't have minded staying longer but Andrew has the idea there is going to be another war."

"The Americans are seething," her husband said. "The British practice of boarding American ships at will, seizing their seamen and impressing them into the Royal Navy has rubbed the pride of the young nation raw. Hotheads are calling for war and I think they are going to get it."

"Are the Americans in a position to wage another war against Britain?" Royce asked.

"Not at all. Their military is small, poorly equipped, and in disarray. However, that is precisely the same situation they confronted when they launched their Revolution, and we all know the outcome of that."

"Enough," Phaedra declared as she took her husband's arm. "I have heard quite enough talk of war. Now that my daughter is home, I wish only to —"

"Mother . . ." Kassandra smiled broadly.

"What, dear?"

"I think you should know I did not come alone."

"Why, of course you didn't, dear. You brought Lord Hawkforte with you."

"True but —"

Phaedra wasn't listening any longer. Her gaze had focused once again on the deck of the ship, and the woman who had just emerged.

The woman and what she carried in her arms.

"Joanna? . . ." Andrew murmured on a note of wonder.

Their daughter-in-law smiled warmly as she said, "There is someone I would like you to meet."

Chapter
NINE

The earth revolved suddenly, changing places with the sky, which hovered at an odd angle for just a moment before hurtling out of sight even as the ground returned with a vengeance.

Grunt.

It hurt but not all that much. Certainly not enough to prevent him from getting right back up. Royce leaped to his feet agilely, faced his opponent, and grinned.

"You'll have to do better than that."

Atreus smiled in turn. "I intend to."

Both men wore only loincloths, their powerful bodies oiled and glistening in the sun. They stood in a sand arena surrounded by stone benches, empty now except for the dozen or so men shouting encouragement.

"Sure you want to take part in the Games?" Atreus asked, getting a chokehold around Royce's throat.

Royce grabbed hold of his arm, planted his feet firmly apart, and neatly flipped the Vanax of Akora onto his back. "Absolutely," he said.

Atreus lifted himself out of the dirt and

laughed. "Well done, Englishman. You learn fast."

"I'd damn well better around here," Royce muttered, but his smile never faded.

He had been on Akora two days and in that time had probably acquired a larger collection of bumps, scrapes and bruises than he'd ever had before in his life. Yet he felt good, damn good actually. Atreus was all right. He was tough-minded, that was clear from the moment they met a day after Royce's own arrival. The Vanax had returned from a week's journey reviewing the coastal installations. He was still covered with the dust of the road when he summoned Royce to his private office deep within the labyrinth of the palace. Since then, the two had hardly been apart. Royce knew Atreus was taking his measure but he didn't mind, for he was doing precisely the same in reverse. So far, he liked what he saw.

"The finest athletes from all over Akora will come for the Games," Atreus said a short time later when they broke off and headed for the showers. "It's a chance to renew acquaintances, catch up on news, and win everlasting fame."

"Sounds good," Royce said. He was already fantasizing about the blissfully hot water that soon would be pounding down on his battered body — hot water, how in hell did they do that? — when he said, "Who came up with the idea? Did you borrow it from the Greeks or did they borrow it from you?"

"That depends on who you mean by the Greeks," Atreus said as they entered the preparation rooms. He accepted a towel from a servant and handed another to Royce.

"We're not certain where the original inhabitants of Akora came from. Tales survive of a great voyage but that's all. However, those who came after the explosion were from Greece. Not the Greece of Athens or Sparta but much earlier, the Greece of those who did battle on the plains before Troy."

"The Myceneans," Royce said, still astounded by the thought.

Atreus nodded. "They held Games to honor the bravest warriors when they died. That was the beginning of the tradition. The first Games on Akora were held in the Year Ten after the cataclysm. They have been held every year since without exception."

"Something tells me that if I wanted to, I could find a list of every man who had ever participated in the Games over the past three thousand years."

"Of course," Atreus said. "It's all in the libraries. Kassandra mentioned she was going to take you there."

"If you have no objection."

"No, none at all," Atreus assured him as he dropped the single garment he wore, stepped under a spout and flipped the lever to start the flow of water. The spout was set high in a tiled wall but Atreus was a tall man, as tall as Royce himself, and his head came within inches of it.

"I have one other question," Royce said, "about the Games."

"What's that?"

"The Greeks of Athens participated in their Games in the nude. I notice the men of Akora wear loincloths."

"The Athenians barred women from attending the Games," Atreus said over the rush of the water. "While we're more relaxed about nudity here on Akora than I understand you Europeans are, we don't go quite that far."

"You never considered excluding the women?"

"We may have at one time or another. It just never worked out."

"Why is that?" Royce asked as he began lathering soap over his chest, avoiding the more tender spots. "We've all heard that 'warriors rule and women serve' but frankly, it doesn't seem to have much impact."

"There's a catch to it," Atreus said.

Royce grinned at this affirmation of what he had suspected. "I had a feeling there might be. Women can be very persuasive."

"It's not just that. There is a sacred prohibition on Akora against any man ever harming a woman. It's a legacy of the time when the priestesses of the old way and the warriors of the new finally reached an accord. A man who harms a woman is shamed for life, as he well deserves to be."

"Joanna told me something about that last

year." She had cited it as evidence that the men who held him captive, and who had later tried unsuccessfully to rape her, could not possibly be in service to the Vanax because no Akoran leader could risk bringing infamy to his name by allowing such villains into his service.

"There are all sorts of ways to do harm," Atreus said. "For instance, if we held Games and said the women couldn't come, they would be disappointed and unhappy, therefore harmed, therefore we cannot do any such thing."

Royce shook his head, admiring of the ideal, indeed wishing it could take root in England, but amused all the same by what he realized must be the consequences. "It must not be particularly easy to be an Akoran man."

Atreus laughed at the very notion. "Let's just say we have every incentive to develop superb negotiating skills."

Royce was still chuckling over that as he dried off and donned the clothes he had left on a shelf. Atreus did the same and together they emerged back into the arena. Several more groups of men were practicing, some wrestling, others at the long jump, still more throwing javelins and discus. They acknowledged their Vanax as he passed and exchanged words of mutual encouragement.

Outside in the street, Royce noticed that just as when they had arrived, the people nodded and greeted Atreus with real pleasure but with no hint of ceremony. He was their leader, the Chosen, yet he was also one of them. Royce tried to imagine Prinny maintaining authority in such a relaxed manner but found that impossible.

They had walked perhaps a quarter mile in the direction of the palace when Royce noticed a crowd gathering up ahead. From the corner of his eye, he saw Atreus stiffen. As they neared, and others became aware of them, the crowd gave way sufficiently for Royce to see that a word had been written on a wall in large yellow letters.

HELIOS

Only that, nothing more, yet it seemed to have people excited and even, Royce thought, apprehensive. Several glanced nervously at Atreus, who merely looked at the wall and said nothing. Within minutes, young men arrived and began wielding brushes covered with whitewash. Before very long, the word had vanished.

Atreus walked on and Royce with him.

They came around a corner only to confront the same again.

HELIOS

A sigh escaped Atreus. This time he did not pause but continued on. They were near the

196

palace when Royce said, "Would you mind telling me what that is about?" Not for a moment did he believe it was commonplace for Akorans to go about writing on their walls. The entire city was far too beautifully maintained for any such thing to be the custom.

"Helios means sunshine," Atreus said.

"I knew it had something to do with the sun but why write it on a wall?"

"It is a symbol; you might even say a code. Helios is at once the name and the demand of the rebels who believe change is not coming quickly enough to Akora. Among other things, they want government to be much more open and directly accountable to the people, in the sunshine as it were, rather than in the shadows as they claim we are now."

"I see . . . but why write it on walls?"

"They believe, or so they say, that there is little tolerance on Akora for dissent. They are taking the opportunity of the Games to make their feelings known."

"What will you do?" Royce asked.

Atreus shrugged. "Nothing. My priority at the moment is to discover why Kassandra is having visions of a British invasion of Akora again and what, if anything, Deilos may have to do with that."

"You think it is possible that Deilos isn't dead?"

"There are others besides him who may believe I am trying to bring too much change, including conservative members of my own council, but I do not seriously believe them capable of initiating action against me. That leaves Deilos."

Quietly, Royce said, "I would very much like him to be alive."

Atreus stopped walking and looked at him. "Why?"

"So that I can kill him."

"For vengeance?" the Vanax asked.

"Partly," Royce admitted. "But mainly because he needs killing. Left alive, if indeed he is, he will only go on hurting the innocent."

Atreus resumed walking. Shortly, he said, "Kassandra was right, you have the heart of a warrior."

They seemed to be doing well together, Kassandra thought, as she watched her brother and Royce approach. They looked at ease in each other's company, but then she had expected that they would be. The Lord of Hawkforte and the Vanax of Atreus were very alike in many respects: both proud, honorable men; both leaders; both capable of great strength and equal gentleness.

The one was her brother and she loved him dearly.

The other . . .

She would be very foolish to think about him.

And it was so very difficult not to.

"There you are," Atreus said, giving her an affectionate smile. They had spoken briefly about her going off to England without telling him of her returned visions. Atreus had expressed his surprise, not to say his disappointment, but he had listened to her explanation that she had believed it vital for her to visit England and accepted it even though she had no notion what, if anything, the trip had accomplished. As always, his actions were shaped by his deeply rooted commitment to justice and fairness. Beyond that, he simply trusted her. The knowledge was humbling.

"Waiting for us?" he asked.

Waiting for them . . . for him . . . for Royce . . . "Why no," Kassandra said, suddenly unbearably self-conscious. "I was just on my way to the libraries and happened to see you coming. I trust you've had a pleasant day?"

"Certainly an energetic one," Royce replied. His eyes did not leave her. "The libraries? Would you mind if I came along?"

Flustered and trying hard not to show it, she shrugged. "Why no . . . I suppose not . . ."

Atreus cast her a quick glance, frowned slightly and settled the matter. "That sounds like a good idea. Royce, I'll see you at dinner."

The two men bid each other farewell. When Atreus had gone, Royce said, "The Vanax has been explaining to me about the Games."

Kassandra noted the bruise directly below his

right eye. "I would say he has been doing more than just explaining."

"He showed me a thing or two," Royce admitted. "I returned the favor. I'm looking forward to competing."

"Are you? Competing, I mean? Are you sure that's wise? The competition is very fierce and men have been known to be injured."

Softly, he asked, "Do you think I would be afraid of that?"

"No, of course not. I didn't mean to suggest . . ." Damnable male pride always there waiting to be tripped over. "Never mind, I'm sure you will do very well. What events have you chosen?"

"The stade-race," he said, naming the short foot race that was considered the hallmark event of the Games, "the javelin-throw and wrestling." His excitement was palpable for all that it was contained and suddenly she understood why. He was a man of pride and strength, to be sure, and he would relish pitting himself against similar men. But he had been fascinated by Akora since tenderest boyhood. To actually be there, and to take part in such a thoroughly Akoran event, was likely the fulfillment of a dream.

"May Fortune favor you," she said softly and led the way toward the wing of the palace that housed the libraries.

The vast double doors stood open, revealing a long, gracefully proportioned room a hundred feet wide and several times that in length. The ceiling soared fifty feet over their heads, vividly painted with murals of Akoran life. Light flowed from broad windows ranged above a balcony that ran all the way round the room. The walls were lined with shelves for books and cupboards for scrolls. Long, polished tables were equipped with comfortable chairs, inkwells and lamps. Dozens of scholars were at work, served by busy librarians coming and going with material for them.

"I have never seen anything like this," Royce said quietly. There was a note of reverence in his voice. He clearly understood that he was in a temple of knowledge.

"What you see here," Kassandra said, "is only a small amount of the entire collection. Much more is stored underground."

"Is it possible to see that?"

She nodded. "That is where we are going. The documents you want, regarding your ancestor, would be on one of the lower levels."

She led him to a door set between tall bookshelves, opening it to reveal a stone staircase curving downward. Clerestory windows high in the stairwell admitted light, yet the rapidly cooling air made it clear they were beneath the surface.

Shortly, they entered a large chamber filled row upon row with shelves that seemed without end. A librarian, informed of their request, handed them a lamp and provided careful directions. They walked past the shelves for perhaps five minutes before finally finding the location they were looking for.

"This is absolutely astounding," Royce said as he set the lamp in a nearby bracket. He was shaking his head in amazement. "Forgive me for putting it this way, but don't you people ever throw anything out?"

Kassandra laughed very softly. She withdrew a small leather-bound volume from one of the shelves and carried it to an alcove where she set it on a table. Carefully, she opened the book and began turning the pages. "In the spring of the Year 2594 after the cataclysm, a great storm struck without warning . . . a *xenos* was found clinging to the mast of a destroyed ship . . . he was taken to the home of Horatio the fishmonger and from there to the palace . . ."

"Year 2594," Royce repeated. "What would that be in the Christian calendar?"

"1100 A.D., I think. This may be him . . . listen . . ."

"The *xenos* recovered from his injuries . . . he described great battles on the continent of Europa for control of various holy places . . . he named his home as . . ." She looked up eagerly. "It translates to Fortress of the Hawk."

"Hawkforte," Royce said, his excitement matching her own. "Does it say anything else? Does it tell what happened to him?"

Kassandra riffled through several pages and nodded. "It tells a great deal." She handed him the book. "Perhaps you would like to read it for yourself? It is permitted to borrow books from the library so long as you promise to take good care of them."

He turned the volume over in his hands, looking at it. "Yes, of course I will. We have some very old books in the library at Hawkforte. I know they have to be handled gently."

"Oh, this one isn't very old, not more than eight centuries. If you want to see really old books . . . scrolls, actually . . . we have to go much farther."

"No, that's all right. I've enough to keep me occupied with this." He gestured to the book he held. "But perhaps another time."

"Perhaps," she replied, reluctant to think beyond the present moment. It was so quiet in the depths of the library. The shadows cast by the lamp alternately concealed and revealed his features. She was suddenly, vividly aware of being alone with him.

"We should go," Kassandra said softly.

He reached out, his hand brushing her arm. "Why?"

"Because . . . you should rest before the Games tomorrow."

"I'm perfectly well rested. Why are you so nervous?"

"I am not."

"Just a moment ago, a tiny flutter sprang to life in your throat . . . right there." The tip of his finger touched a few inches below her chin where her life's blood flowed. Touched and lingered.

"Don't," she said, and meant to draw back but somehow didn't.

At once he withdrew his hand, not far, just enough. "All right, but you haven't answered my question. You were not so nervous in London when I kissed you."

"We should not have done that."

"But you allowed it, you said so yourself."

"I was feeling . . . reckless."

"Reckless?"

"Certainly, don't you ever feel that way?"

"Oh, yes," he said, very softly. "I know exactly what reckless feels like. In fact, I'm feeling that way right now."

He bent his head, slowly, deliberately. There could be no question but that she knew what he intended — and had ample time to stop him.

But her arms felt like lead hanging at her sides and she could not seem to bring herself to move . . . or breathe . . . or do anything except wait until . . .

The touch of his mouth on hers shattered the slim hold she had managed to maintain on her self-control. She moaned deep in her throat and arched into him, taking the heat he offered . . . taking, taking . . . and giving. The taste and touch of him filled her. The hard wall of his chest and thighs pressed against her, the strength of his arms holding her close, the fierce sense of his strength rising up to meet her own need, were all more than she could resist.

But resist she must. Flickering like stubborn fire at the edges of her mind was the knowledge that she was not free to follow her heart. She had to — *had to* — remember that duty came before all else.

Her breasts ached and deep within her she felt a pool of heat, pulsing to its own rhythms, preparing her for him. It would be so easy . . .

Gasping, Kassandra wrenched away. The effort sent pain driving through her. She bit back tears, stared for an instant into his bewildered eyes, and reached for the only protection she had — truth.

"I am," she said and heard her own voice shaking. "I am," she began again, more firmly, "not free to do this."

She saw then pain that mirrored her own and almost reached out to him. Only sternest discipline stopped her.

They stood in the circle of light cast by the lamp, surrounded by the centuries of history of the land she would give her life to protect. Would give . . . most likely very soon. The visions had been clear. Somehow, in some way, her death would protect Akora. So be it. Never, not for an instant, had she considered shirking her duty. But sweet heaven, the temptation to do so was there, deep within the golden shards of his eyes.

Because there was only one lamp, and because she would not leave him in darkness, Kassandra walked away alone. Far in the distance, where the librarian had his table, she saw a tiny pinprick of light. Ignoring the tears burning down her cheeks, she moved toward it.

Royce was largely silent through dinner. He ate a little of the various dishes, drank a very little of the excellent wine, and listened to the talk of the others gathered around the table — Atreus, Joanna, various other family members and friends — but he spoke almost not at all. Kassandra had not joined them. She had sent word through a servant that she was indisposed. Elena had offered to go to her but she demurred, saying that was not necessary.

What in hell was wrong? What possible impediment could there exist to the simple acknowledgment of their feelings for each other?

Granted, there was nothing simple about the way he felt. She had him tied in knots, beguiled, bewildered and just plain baffled.

If this was love — and he had a sinking feeling that it was — heaven help him.

Later, as he walked Joanna back to her apartments, he asked, "Is Kassandra betrothed?"

She stopped in mid-step and stared at him. "What? Of course not. If she were, I would have told you or Alex would have or Atreus certainly would have mentioned it. We wouldn't have left you in ignorance."

"And why's that?"

His sister had the grace to look abashed. "It isn't precisely a secret that the two of you are drawn to each other."

"And here I thought we had everyone fooled," Royce said dryly.

"I'm afraid not," Joanna said with a smile. "Why did you ask if Kassandra is betrothed?"

Because the thought that she was stopped from responding to her feelings for him because of a commitment to another man was less painful than the possibility that she found those feelings unacceptable for a princess of Akora. Only very slightly less painful, but in snatching at straws, he was not going to be overly picky.

But of that, he would say nothing.

"No reason in particular. It's late. If I'm going to make a decent showing tomorrow, I'd better get some rest."

Well aware that his sister was far from satisfied by that reply, he took his leave before she could ask any more questions he was not inclined to answer.

She had avoided dinner but she could not avoid the Games, nor did Kassandra truly wish to do so. After tossing and turning all night, alternately blaming herself for having any feelings at all for Royce and longing to act on them, she was desperate for diversion.

Besides, Royce would be there.

A weary groan escaped her. She stumbled out of bed, made her way into the bathing room, and stood under the shower until the shadows of the night slunk away, however reluctantly.

Through the high windows of the chamber, she could hear the sounds of the crowd gathering for the Games. Life surrounded her in all its dearly familiar glory. The temptation to seize while yet she could, proved too much. She dressed hastily and went out, running down the steps to the palace courtyard as she always had as a child, sometimes hurtling so fast that she stumbled and skinned her knees. She did not now but she did arrive just a little breathless and in disarray, which she supposed made it fortunate that people were far too distracted to notice her.

The vast courtyard in front of the palace was filled with yellow banners. Some hung from the walls, others floated over the ground, all were printed with a single word:

HELIOS

The rebels. She knew of them, of course, had heard Atreus speak of them. They had made other efforts over the past year or so to bring their views to the attention of the people. But this was the first time they had come within the grounds of the palace itself.

HELIOS

Openness, accountability. On the surface, it was hard to argue with. But she knew how often Atreus had to juggle conflicting interests and concerns so that everyone felt satisfied. He worked behind the scenes, a master diplomat and negotiator, patiently and skillfully crafting the outcome that served all best. If discretion was gone, subtlety forbidden, what then?

Chaos, she thought and sighed deeply. The demand of the rebels for faster, deeper change made no more sense than did that of Deilos for no change at all. Atreus was caught between the two. She did not envy him even as she knew he was uniquely suited to meet the challenges of his position. He was, after all, the Chosen.

He was also, by what she saw of him just then, annoyed. He stood in the courtyard, hands on his lean hips, surveying the profusion of banners. Going to his side, she strove for lightness.

"You cannot fault their industry," she said.

He turned and mustered a smile for her. "True, but I could wish it directed more productively."

"Any idea who did this?"

"No, they were quick and clever." Thoughtfully, he added, "They would need to know the routine of the palace, when the guards are changed and so on."

"You think they have adherents within the palace itself?" The notion was startling, not to say disturbing.

He shrugged. "I wouldn't discount the possibility, but enough of that. Are you recovered?"

"Recovered?"

"From whatever indisposition kept you from joining us for dinner last night."

"Oh, that, yes, of course."

"I am relieved to hear it." His gaze narrowed. "As, I am sure, Royce will be."

Her gaze darted to his and as swiftly withdrew. This brother saw too much by far. "Yes . . . well," she said, "you had better get on, hadn't you? The opening ceremonies must be about to begin."

Atreus raised a hand, summoning the chariot that appeared before him. The matched pair of grays pawed the ground eagerly. "Come," he said and offered his hand.

She went because to refuse would raise too many questions she did not want to face. Atreus drove the chariot at a speed that would have been deemed foolish in a man less skilled. Normally, he would not have done so through the city streets but they were empty that morning, everyone having already assembled for the Games. Very quickly, they reached the arena. He drew rein just within the shadows of the long, vaulted tunnel leading to the sun-bright field where the competitions would take place.

Kassandra alighted but not before touching her brother's arm gently. "May Fortune favor you," she said.

"I will need it," he replied with a grin. "I'm listed for the chariot race."

"*What?* . . ." She spoke to dust, for already he had urged his horses on and was entering the arena. The roar that went up at the sight of him was deafening. It pummeled her even as she struggled with her shock. The chariot race was the most dangerous event, by far. It was a rare year when men entered in it were not injured and sometimes even killed. Atreus loved horses and loved to race them. As a boy, long before he became Vanax, he had delighted in tearing over the plains beyond Ilius, besting all who dared to take him on. But since being Chosen, he had forsworn such activity, accepting that the life now in service to his people was not his to risk as he might have wished. Privately, Kassandra had been at once relieved but concerned that he was giving up too much of himself for the role he must fulfill. Now, it seemed, he had decided to make the role fit him instead of the other way around. She supposed it was a sign of his maturity even as inwardly she quailed at the danger to him.

Saying a quiet prayer for him, she climbed the stone steps to the first tier above the arena floor. Joanna was already seated, as were many others of the Court. Phaedra and Andrew were a few tiers away in the midst of a group of their friends. They nodded at sight of her but kept their attention on the parade of athletes led by Atreus, who emerged for the start of the Games.

As trumpets blared and priestesses released white doves into the air, Kassandra sought Royce among the hundreds of supremely fit, eager men awaiting the beginning of the competitions. Quickly enough, she found him. He was dressed as were all the other men, in a loincloth and nothing else. The golden mane of his hair was pulled back at the nape of his neck, a sensible precaution for one who intended to wrestle. The broad sweep of his shoulders and chest made her eyes widen, never mind when she looked farther down to his heavily muscled thighs and . . .

It was quite warm for early June. There didn't seem to be a breath of air in the arena. She sat down but could not keep from fidgeting.

Boys came by with skins of water and she accepted one but it didn't seem to help. The first event began. It was the long distance race, twenty circuits around the clay track along the outer perimeter of the field. The competitors were closely matched and stayed bunched together, as they likely would until very near the end. People took the time to settle down, still chatting among themselves as they brought out snacks, soothed overly excited children, and generally prepared to enjoy the day.

Eventually, three runners broke from the pack and vied with each other for victory. The crowd stirred, many getting to their feet for a better view and to cheer on a favorite. In the final seconds, one man burst through the ribbon at the finish line to wild acclaim.

The crown of oleander leaves had been placed on the winner's brow and the clay track swept clean before the next event began. Kassandra was scarcely aware of it, for she knew the stade-race came after. Joanna spoke to her and she must have replied but she had no idea what was said.

The wait for Royce to appear seemed to drag out forever but finally he was there with the other men, stretching to limber up, then setting his right foot in the marble sills embedded in the clay ground to give a steady start.

A moment later, the heralds' trumpets sounded and the runners were off.

Chapter
TEN

Instantly, Kassandra jumped up, straining to see Royce. The pounding feet of the racers raised a cloud of dust along the track but she was able to make him out all the same. Her heart leaped when she saw that he was staying very close to the front. Truly, he was a magnificent man with the hard, lithe body of a warrior and the heart to match. Watching the rhythmic surge of his muscles as he sprinted down the track, she could scarcely breathe. He personified an ideal of male beauty and grace that made her doubt creation could possibly hold anything more thrilling.

A roar went up from the crowd as the racers tore across the finish line. Royce was right there among them but was he . . . had he . . . ? No, she saw, he had not come in first. That honor went to a dazed young man who, realizing what he had done, smiled hugely even as tears of joy coursed down his cheeks. Well he might be so overcome because he would be honored throughout Akora for his victory.

But so it seemed would Royce who, she saw now, had come in second. The achievement of the *xenos* visitor thrilled the crowd. The thousands of spectators were on their feet, shouting their approval even as some streamed onto the field to lift both racers onto their shoulders. She caught a quick glimpse of Royce looking startled but happy as he was carried by, and even managed to wave to him.

"He did so well!" she exclaimed to Joanna who was also waving. "Did you see that? Isn't it amazing? He had only a few days to train."

"He did wonderfully well," Joanna agreed. "Royce always loved to run along the beach at Hawkforte. Aside from sailing, it was his favorite recreation. But I don't know that he's ever been in an actual race before."

"He's listed for the javelin-throw and wrestling," Kassandra said, still unable to contain her delight.

"Yes, I know," Joanna said with a gentle smile. "I'm sure he will acquit himself nobly. Certainly the crowd has taken him to their heart."

The crowd was not alone in having done so, Kassandra thought, but not even worry over her wayward emotions could dim her happiness. Nor could she help but think that there was no harm in that. So long as she remained firm in her resolve — and she would — surely it was no sin to snatch a little pleasure from life?

Eased in her conscience, she gave herself up to the excitement of the next event, although since Royce was not in it, her attention was not so riveted. It returned in full force when he emerged for the javelin contest. She thrilled to the sight of him on horseback, wearing only the white linen kilt pleated and belted around his waist that was the common garb of Akoran warriors. His bare chest and arms gleamed in the sun as he urged his mount forward, grasped the first javelin of gleaming teak, drew back slightly on his right side and ahead on his left, rose in the saddle using the powerful muscles of his thighs, and let fling the weapon with power and grace. It struck very close to dead center of the target. As the crowd roared, Royce turned his horse swiftly, grasped the second javelin, and hurled it as accurately.

"How could he possibly know how to do that?" Kassandra said in astonishment as Royce grinned and acknowledged the spectators' approval.

"He's read Xenophon," Joanna said dryly. "Memorized him, actually, by the look of it." When Kassandra continued to look at her in bewilderment, she said, "Xenophon wrote a magnificent treatise on the art of mounted warfare. He gave very precise directions for all sorts of activities."

"So it appears . . . Royce may not win but he will acquit himself honorably."

Indeed, he did, finishing third only because twin brothers from the island of Leios, already legendary for their prowess with the javelin, came in first and second. The trio went off, once again hoisted on shoulders, flushed with success.

Next was the oldest and in certain ways the

most demanding of the events, another race, but this one requiring the competitors to run in full armor while carrying weapons. The racers needed not merely great strength but also immense stamina. Kassandra remembered that it was Alex's favorite event. He had won it three times in the previous five years, and would certainly be entered if he had been on Akora.

A soft sigh escaped Joanna. Kassandra put an arm around her shoulders and hugged her gently. "I would not be at all surprised if you sit here next year — Amelia will be walking by then and will make you frantic — and watch Alex run himself into the ground wearing a hundred pounds of metal while racing under the noonday sun."

Joanna laughed and even managed a smile. "Do you promise?"

"Oh, yes," Kassandra said, and meant it with all her heart. She would do everything — and anything — necessary to make sure that could occur.

"In that case," Joanna said, "lemonade for all." She raised a hand, summoning the vendor.

Shortly thereafter, the wrestling commenced. And very shortly after that, Kassandra began looking away only to be drawn back again and again to the painful spectacle. Royce did well, all things considered, but he was thrown into the ground again and again. He managed a few very good throws of his own, but wrestling was an art learned almost from infancy. He took his defeat in good humor, which Kassandra could not share, as she was too busy wincing with every fall he took.

"It's over," Joanna said finally. "He's fine, really. A little bruised but otherwise all right."

"He should have had more sense."

"They should all have more sense but they don't. They're men and we love them for it."

Amelia chortled just then, drawing the startled gazes of her mother and aunt. She laughed just exactly as though she had understood them and agreed entirely.

More events followed even as the vendors offered sticks of grilled meat and vegetables, small loaves of fresh-baked breads, more drinks, pennants with the pictures drawn on them of the most renowned competitors, and the ever-popular wooden whistles the crowd loved to blare at the high points of the Games.

Royce joined them in time to grasp a stick of meat for himself. He devoured it with relish. "I've had the best time! The spirit here is incredible. It's competitive, to be sure, but everyone supports each other. I was getting advice from men I was about to go against right up to the very moment the competitions began."

"That's wonderful," Joanna said and handed him a mug of lemonade. "You look absolutely awful."

"I showered," he replied, a bit defensively.

"She means the bruises," Kassandra said. She thought "awful" was going too far, for the truth was, he looked magnificent. He was a bit battered, however, as was to be expected. All the competitors were the same.

"These are nothing," he insisted, gesturing to the livid black-and-blue splotches with which he was adorned, and with the enthusiasm of a boy, added, "I won two silver bracelets. Here." He handed one to each of them and beamed as they put them on.

"Thank you," Joanna said sweetly and leaned over to kiss his cheek.

Kassandra stared at the bracelet, turning it round and round her wrist. In her quarters, there were chests fitted with silk-lined drawers that held precious jewels given to her because she was a princess. She wore them on occasion and enjoyed them. But never had she received anything so lovely as that simple silver bracelet won by sweat and skill in the Games.

"It's very nice," she said, and felt his gaze even as she refused to meet it.

The chariot race was about to begin. Word had spread that Atreus was entered and people were tense with excitement. As soon as the drivers appeared on the track, guiding their powerful teams into position, the crowd was on its feet. Kassandra and Joanna exchanged anxious glances but Royce looked enthralled.

"Magnificent horses," he said. "What are the chariots made of?"

"Wicker," Joanna said quietly. "They're intended to be very light and maneuverable at high speeds. Unfortunately, they provide no protection at all for the drivers."

"Surely Atreus won't take unnecessary chances," Royce said.

"He won't intend to," Kassandra agreed. "But he is as competitive as anyone else, and in the heat of the race . . ."

"He will remember that he is Vanax," Royce said, "and behave responsibly."

Joanna nodded. "I'm sure it will be so. Look, the heralds are in position."

A moment later, the stadium resounded to the blast of trumpets and the chariot race began. The pounding hooves of the horses could barely be heard over the steady roar of the crowd. Approaching the first turn, the drivers maneuvered to be in the lead. Wheel axles flashed dangerously close and several teams of horses threatened to shy into each other.

When the turn was completed, Atreus had the lead but he was closely pursued by the other drivers, one of whom only just managed to squeeze past him as they raced down the straightaway toward the next turn. Kassandra leaned forward anxiously, her stomach clenching at the dangerous maneuver. Still, she was not surprised to see it. No one would feel required to give her brother quarter because he was Vanax, which was as well because he would have taken any such behavior as a mortal insult.

At the second turn, one of the chariots near

the front entered the curve just a little clumsily. Halfway through it, the driver lost control. His chariot lifted entirely off the ground, the wheels spinning in midair. Kassandra had a glimpse of the man's startled face before he and the chariot flipped entirely over. The tracings were torn loose and the horses ran free, posing an instant threat to the other competitors, who only just managed to avoid colliding with each other and the wreckage.

The instant the remaining chariots were passed, a crew ran forward to retrieve the stunned but mercifully still-living charioteer who limped off as men, mounted and waiting for just such an event, rode down and drove the errant horses into chutes to either side of the arena and from there into paddocks. The danger was just barely past as the remaining chariots continued into the second loop.

Atreus had the lead again, and was driving with skill and daring. Like everyone else, Kassandra was on her feet. There were five loops in all. If he could hold his lead . . .

The horses thundered down the track, their powerful bodies straining right along with those of the men fighting to control them. They were almost at the first turn again. Kassandra saw Atreus pull back very slightly on the reins, the tactic of a seasoned driver, even as he shouted encouragement to his team.

The turn was upon them, the horses taking it well. Atreus's lead was opening up. He was two . . . no, three yards in front of the next closest driver when . . .

A clap of thunder tore through the stadium, shaking the stone tiers of seats, the ground, and seemingly the very air itself. So shattering was the sound that Kassandra could see people's mouths moving in shouts, screams or simple bewilderment, but she could hear nothing. She wanted desperately to move but couldn't seem to do that either. Her limbs felt frozen.

Royce was under no such impediment. Even as the wave of sound still reverberated through the arena, he grabbed hold of both women, careful of Amelia cradled in her stunned mother's arms, and forced them down into the shelter of the stone benches.

"Stay here," he ordered. "Don't try to move until we're sure there aren't more."

Kassandra heard him as though from a great distance, but his words still made no sense. *More what?*

Not that it mattered, for just then she became aware of the hideous scene before her. Horses were screaming . . . or was it men? An entire section of the arena's outer wall had come down onto the track. Drivers and their teams were trapped under it. Men were racing from all sides of the arena, some already struggling to pull away the heavy blocks of stone and rescue those caught beneath them.

"*Atreus!*" Frantically, Joanna grabbed Kassandra's arm. "Do you see Atreus?"

"No . . . he was right there . . ." Right near the portion of the track where the wall had collapsed. The same realization seemed to come to the crowd as a whole, for as one the shout went up.

"The Vanax!"

The Chosen. The man the people of Akora counted on to preserve the past while guiding them into the future. The living link between all that had been and would be.

A broken link?

Everything in Kassandra cried out against it. This was not right. This was not what she had seen. This should not be.

What, in the name of heaven, was happening?

"Stay here!" she said to Joanna. "Keep Amelia safe."

"Wait! What about you?"

"I'll be all right," Kassandra called as she ran down the nearby stone steps. "I have to find Atreus!" And Royce. He was there somewhere, in among the men. She had to be with him, had to do anything and everything she could.

Yet even as she began pushing her way through the frantic crowd, searching for Royce, the thought still burned through her mind. Amid all her visions, why had she caught no glimmer of the danger to Atreus?

And not only to him, for already she could see half-a-dozen injured men being laid out carefully on the track. Four were conscious, in pain but alive. The other two were not moving.

Healers were hurrying to those who could still benefit from their help. She saw Elena, calm in the midst of chaos, and Brianna following behind her, looking very pale.

More wounded were being brought out of the rubble along with, she feared, several more dead. Some of the horses had also perished and they, too, would be mourned, for the Akorans were a horse-loving people. But it was on the living that efforts had to be concentrated.

Realizing she lacked the strength to move the stones, Kassandra stayed out of the way of the men, who quickly formed a human chain to dismantle the collapsed wall. Large blocks were moved swiftly hand to hand. The warrior training almost every Akoran male received benefited them now as they worked together smoothly.

Through the still-swirling dust, she caught sight of Royce, sweat-streaked and covered with grime as he hoisted one of the larger blocks. Andrew was with him, helping to maneuver a stone to one side. Royce dropped down onto his knees and reached farther under the debris.

Moments later, men gathered around him, blocking her view. She pressed closer, desperate to see. Elena brushed past her, but Brianna stopped and put her hand on Kassandra's arm. Everything seemed to be happening in slow motion, as though time itself had been blown off course by the explosion.

"Princess," the young woman said in a voice

so faint and shaken she could scarcely be heard, "what could have happened?"

"I don't know," Kassandra said. Brianna looked so ill that Kassandra wanted to stay with her, but just then a cry went up from the men. Turning, she saw a limp body being drawn from the rubble.

A wave of cold drove through Kassandra, almost bringing her to her knees. For a terrible, black instant she knew nothing at all. When she was next aware, she was clinging to Brianna, who had only just managed to remain upright herself.

"Atreus," Kassandra whispered, for she was capable of nothing more. All her shock and pain, all the ache of love turned to terror resonated in his name.

Half-a-dozen men, themselves caked with dust and splattered with blood, lifted the still form. Grim-faced, they formed a guard of honor. The crowd grew silent as they moved past, carrying their precious burden. Only the wailing of a few frightened children punctured the eerie quiet.

The Vanax of Akora was taken to a tent being set up swiftly near the center of the track. Kassandra followed. She could not feel her legs and was unsure how she managed to move but move she did. Desperate need drove her forward. She was recognized and people cleared a path for her. Several murmured in sympathy but most were too shocked to say anything.

Atreus had been laid on a table when she reached the tent. His hair and skin were covered with stone dust but the livid red wounds along his chest and limbs were still all too evident. Blood was caked on his forehead. He lay unmoving. Men stood in small groups nearby, not talking, scarcely breathing. Elena was with Atreus, her hands moving over him swiftly.

"He lives," she said after what seemed an eternity. Before relief could grab hold, she added, "But his injuries are grave."

A deep murmur ran through those assembled in the tent and from them out into the crowd filling the arena. Kassandra stood, still feeling bathed in ice, and imagined the news spreading farther, through the streets of the city, over the hills and across the Inland Sea, reaching all of Akora but not stopping there, going beyond, out into the world.

To England?

The Vanax was wounded and with him, Akora itself. An enemy seeking opportunity could scarcely find a better moment.

Was this then the source of her renewed visions of invasion? Perhaps, but still her failure to see the danger to Atreus tormented her. Try though she did, she could not understand how that had happened.

Nor could she do anything to help her brother no matter how desperately she wished otherwise. Elena and several of the other healers were at work. They would do everything within their power but the outcome would depend on Atreus's own strength and the vagaries of Fate.

Arms wrapped around herself to ward off the bone-deep chill that had taken hold of her, Kassandra stumbled back outside. Her mind, dazed and reeling, returned again and again to the same thought: If only she had seen, if she had tried harder, sought vision more often, been wiser . . . If only . . . She should have been able to do something, anything, to prevent this horror, yet it had come all the same. She had failed, horribly and abysmally and for no known reason. Tears clogged her throat and seared her eyes but she would not let them fall. The strength of generations rose within her. She could not, would not fail again.

She stood for a few minutes, numbly watching as the rescue efforts wound down. All the injured were in the care of the healers. The dead were being carried away. Men were moving over the rubble, Royce among them. They were studying the stones and the debris lying amid them. As she watched, they collected several items and set them carefully aside.

What were they doing?

She walked a little closer, watching. Some of the men beside Royce were known to her. She recognized them as being among the corps of engineers charged with maintaining the buildings, roads and bridges of Akora, and with other, highly specialized tasks. Unless she was very much mistaken, the particular men going through the debris were skilled in the most advanced tools of war.

Royce saw her just then, and frowned. He broke off talking with several of the engineers and came to her side. "You should not be here," he said.

She stared at him for a long moment, gazing at his beloved face. The pain of Atreus was bad enough; how would she feel if Royce, too, had been among the casualties?

A thought for another time, for the coldness within her born of shock and fear was hardening fast into something altogether different. Something unyielding and resolute. It was the princess more than the woman who answered him. "I have seen Atreus and the others. I want to know why this happened."

When still he hesitated, she lifted her head and looked at him directly. Her own voice sounded strange to her, yet she knew it revealed who she was at the core of her being. "It is well to remember that I, too, am Atreides. Be assured, I will not forget it."

She saw the flicker of surprise in his eyes and heard the caution in his voice as he said, "The wall collapsed as the result of an explosion. We have found fragments of wood, some from barrels, some probably from a wagon parked on the other side of the wall. We have also found traces of gunpowder."

For all her resolve, Kassandra could not help but be shaken. She stared at him in disbelief. "What are you saying?"

His voice gentled, tinged by worry for her. "This was a deliberate attack."

"Hawk Lord . . ."

Royce turned toward the man calling to him. He accepted the piece of yellow cloth the man held out and examined it carefully.

"Does this look familiar?" Royce asked, handing the fragment to Kassandra.

"I'm not sure . . ."

His face was grim as he took the evidence back and continued staring at it. "I am," he said. "I saw what was in the palace courtyard this morning. It's the same fabric used for those Helios banners."

"You think the rebels — ?"

"We will know more when we have assembled the evidence."

Slowly, Kassandra nodded. Though shock heaped upon shock, she had no doubt of what she must do. "*All* the evidence," she urged. "Every scrap of it. You say there were barrels, I want to know how many. Gunpowder, how much? Who drove the wagon? Did any witnesses see it being parked? For that matter, who saw anything that could possibly be of any significance?"

She raised her voice slightly so that the men standing nearby would hear. "The rebels, if they can be so identified, will be detained. But all will be done in accordance with our laws."

Atreus was . . . indisposed. He would recover, she could not think otherwise. Alex was away on a far shore. It fell to her. She was Atreides. All her life, in some sense she had not understood, she had been preparing for this. It was there within her, her strength and her reassurance. She could do this. She would do it.

"The law, above all, will be upheld," she said. "No one will act beyond or outside the law. That must be clearly understood. Whatever pain we feel, whatever anger, the law is above that. Let no man or woman question this."

They were all listening to her, Royce and every other man gathered there. They *saw* her and, in that moment, she saw what they saw. Atreides. The first of her family had stepped forward more than three thousand years ago onto a landscape of fire and death. In all the time since, through all the challenges, the line had never broken.

It would not break now.

Come what may, the line would hold.

"Send heralds," she said, and heard her own voice, steady and sure. "Tomorrow will be a day of prayer. Let the people refrain from work. Let them go into the temples. Let them pray for the well-being of the Vanax and all those injured, but let them also take comfort in the knowledge that Akora is and will always be."

They cheered, with surprise at first, a little hesitantly, but then in the deep-throated voices of men whose relief is heartfelt. The world had trembled, the walls had fallen, but the House of Atreides remained strong and upright. All was as it had always been.

She walked through the crowd, feeling their need and their strength, touching the hands stretched out to her, listening to the voices calling her name.

Atreides . . . Atreides . . .

Not Vanax, for she was not that. She was not the Chosen. But she was . . . what? Whatever, whoever, she was not alone. Royce was there close to her side. He said nothing, only looked at her with those green-gold eyes that saw so much. Near him, she felt the tightness in her ease.

He went with her to the room in the palace where Atreus was brought. He stood by her side as she stood beside her brother and prayed as she had never prayed before in her life.

He was there when her brother's counselors came, good men for the most part, although there were one or two she doubted. Came to offer their sympathy and assess her.

Not the Vanax. Not the Chosen.

But Atreides.

And later, much later, he was there when exhaustion overcame her finally. It was he who lifted her onto the bed in her chamber, who pulled back the covers, who held her when the tears struck and who stayed, through the long night into the dawn.

Chapter
ELEVEN

Kassandra looked at the silver bracelet on her wrist. The sunlight streaming through the high windows had warmed the metal. Or perhaps it only felt that way because she was so cold. She had slept, fitfully to be sure but still slept, bathed, dressed, eaten, gone through the motions of responding to people when they spoke to her, and yet she felt as though some essential part of herself was encased in ice.

Yet she had also wept. Emotion was there, real, acute, even agonizing. Her tears were hot even if the rest of her remained frozen.

It was the day after the bombing of the Games. She had to think of it that way, had to remind herself over and over of what she still had such difficulty grasping — the attack had truly happened and it had been deliberate. Someone, or more likely some group of people, had struck at the very heart of Akora, killing and maiming without mercy.

Word had been sent to Alex, but it would be ten days or more before he could receive the news, and as much again before he could reach Akora.

Services would be held that afternoon to honor the dead. She would be present, of course. Those who lived away from Ilius would be escorted home by honor guards. Soon the smoke of the funeral pyres would stain the sky.

And life would go on . . . somehow.

She roused herself to listen to what the magistrate was saying. He was young for his trusted position, scarcely forty years old, but she remembered that Atreus thought very highly of him, enough so to name him chief legal officer for the district that included Ilius.

"All evidence is being secured in a central location here in the palace," Marcellus continued. "Fortunately, the fire that resulted from the explosion was put out very quickly. While most of what has been recovered is in fragments, we do have one very large section of a metal wheel rim of the sort commonly used on wagons."

"The metal is badly bent," Royce said, "and partially melted but it is still recognizable."

He had been with Marcellus and the engineers all day, returning to the palace only when the final pieces of evidence had been recovered from the site of the explosion. Although he had no official standing, he had stepped in without hesitation. The other men accepted him, perhaps because they had taken his measure in the Games, perhaps because he was, at the core, a natural leader.

"As the Hawk Lord says," Marcellus agreed, "there is no doubt that what we have are the remains of a wagon, a fairly large one at that. In addition, there are smaller fragments of metal that appear to be the bindings of barrels."

"Did any witnesses notice this wagon?" Kassandra asked.

Marcellus consulted the tablet he carried. "As I am sure you will understand, the people are very eager to cooperate with the investigation. As of about an hour ago, men of my office have received statements from one hundred and twelve witnesses. Almost all these people entered the arena from the side where the explosion occurred. They recall seeing a large wagon parked next to the wall. Whatever it carried was covered with canvas. They didn't think much of it except several noticed it was parked right up against the wall but still blocking part of the street. They had to walk around it."

"Whatever drew the wagon," Royce said, "whether horses or mules, appear to have been unhitched and led away some time before the blast, probably to ensure that the wagon would be difficult for anyone to try to move. An old woman who lives in the street next to the arena and who was not attending the Games because her daughter-in-law was in labor recalls seeing a man near the wagon minutes before the explosion. He was bending over, possibly lighting the fuse, so she didn't get a good look at him. Her daughter-in-law called to her just then, she turned around to answer her, and was blown across the room by the explosion. Rather amazingly, she wasn't injured."

"Is her daughter-in-law all right?" Kassandra asked.

"She gave birth to a healthy son very shortly thereafter."

Out of death came life, she thought, and smiled wearily. "That, at least, is good news. Was anyone else suspicious seen near the wagon?"

"All sorts of people," Marcellus said. "Either three men or four or possibly more . . . they were young or they may have been old . . . they all had dark hair but several did not . . . they were shouting slogans or they said nothing . . . they were holding yellow banners or they weren't . . . One witness thinks he saw a fellow who looked like the person he thinks he saw painting one of those Helios slogans on a wall in his street several days ago, but he isn't absolutely sure."

"However," Royce interjected, "there is no doubt that yellow banners of the sort left in the palace courtyard were in the wagon. We have found more pieces of them, some even with letters still visible. They spell out Helios."

"The advocates of Helios have engaged in small acts of vandalism to communicate their views," Kassandra said, "but they have never behaved violently. It is difficult to believe they would have turned from painting slogans on walls to killing innocent people."

Royce and the magistrate exchanged a quick glance. Quietly, Royce said, "There is another witness, an older man very certain of what he saw. He happened to glance up and says he saw a man climb onto the upper wall of the arena, straddling it so that he had a view of the track but could gesture to someone in the street. As Atreus took the lead and came toward the turn, the man says this fellow on the wall waved to someone below."

"You think it was a signal," Kassandra said. Her stomach clenched. Bad enough had become worse yet.

Royce nodded. "They must have used a short fuse, but even so, there would have been time to get away. There is a narrow alley between buildings right near where the explosion occurred. Someone who darted in there would have been protected from the worst of the blast."

"And would have been able to get away without being seen," Marcellus added.

"This man on the wall," Kassandra said, "what did he look like?"

"Dark-haired, very fit, typical Akoran male except for one thing. The witness says he had a yellow banner draped around his neck."

Kassandra stood. She walked a little distance away to stare out the windows. It felt very odd to be in Atreus's office without him also being present, but she had chosen it both for the privacy it offered and to maintain as much normalcy as possible. The room was furnished simply with a single large table set on the flagstone floor. Several small bronze statues and two larger pieces in marble — all Atreus's own work — were nearby. From boyhood, he had shown great promise as an artist. Had he not been Chosen, it was likely he would have lived happily as a sculptor.

She ran her hand over the smooth bronze head of a rearing horse and thought of the brother who lay a short distance away, still unconscious, still fighting for his life. Their mother was with him as was their father, the man who had taken the fatherless boy to his heart and raised him as his own son. All over the city and beyond, the temples were full. The markets were empty, businesses shuttered, and nothing stirred in the harbor below. The life of Akora hung suspended along with the life of its leader.

Looking at Royce, she asked, "You believe this was an attempt to assassinate the Vanax?"

Very gently, he said, "The evidence suggests that."

"So it would seem . . ."

"However, I think it would be a mistake to jump to any conclusions about who is responsible. The wagon filled with Helios banners and gunpowder, the man on the wall with a banner draped around his neck . . . we seem drawn to a conclusion we can hardly miss and perhaps that's the point. Someone may be trying to lay the blame for this on the rebels."

"With respect, Hawk Lord," Marcellus said, "there is no evidence of anyone else being involved."

"There is Deilos," Kassandra said. Because of his high position, Marcellus knew what had transpired the previous year, but most Akorans did not. They were only aware that the scion of a respected house had disappeared, rumor had it in a storm, and what remained of his family — an aged mother and two sisters — had been taken under the protection of the Vanax.

"Deilos is dead," Marcellus said, and looked from one to the other of them for confirmation neither could truly give.

At length, Kassandra said, "Round up anyone you can reasonably connect with the painting on the walls and the banners in the palace courtyards. Charge them with anything you can — vandalism, littering, creating a public nuisance, whatever."

The magistrate frowned. "What of the bombing?"

"If you can find direct evidence to connect them to it, do so. At the very least, they will be off the streets. If this crime is of their making, they will have no opportunity to try again. And if they have been used by someone else, that person, whoever he may be, will not be able to continue hiding behind them."

Slowly, Marcellus said, "When the people learn we are arresting members of Helios, they will draw the obvious conclusion and turn against them with rage."

"All the better then that the rebels be taken into custody," Kassandra said, "if only for their own protection."

Marcellus drew himself up, inclined his head and said, "As you say, Atreides, so will it be done."

When the door had closed behind him, Royce said, "You realize that while your instructions are logical, they may also be unfair."

"I realize I may be ordering the arrest and detention of innocent people, if that is what you mean. Can you suggest a better course?"

"No," he admitted.

"I may be making a terrible mistake."

"No," he said again, "you are doing very well."

Her heart lightened, so profound was the effect of his support. "Do you really think so? You have been responsible for the well-being of your people at Hawkforte. You know what that is like to lead. Do you truly believe I am doing well?"

He came closer. She was caught in his gaze, unable to look away because she could not muster the will to do so. He was so important to her, this man . . . this hope . . . this future, all tied together in some way she could not understand but could only fumble toward.

"Do you remember what you said," he asked, "when I kissed you? When we kissed?"

"No," she said honestly. "I remember very little except what you made me feel."

He smiled, pleased, but said, "I called you a girl. You said you are a woman. You are right and the difference really does matter."

He was closer still. She felt the warmth of him seeping into her, chasing out the cold. "You can do this, truly. You are a woman of sensitivity and courage, and you are Atreides."

"I am so afraid."

"Of what?"

"Of making a terrible mistake, of betraying my people, of failing in my responsibility."

"Good. No, don't look so dismayed. There are times when fear is our friend. It sharpens the senses and hones the reflexes."

"If Atreus dies . . ."

"Alex will come home. You would not face that by yourself. But Atreus will not die."

"How do you know that?"

"I don't, but it stands to reason, doesn't it? He did not die when the bomb exploded almost on top of him. He did not die when the wall came down. He did not die in the night when everyone knows spirits weaken. He is young, strong, he has expert healers to help him and the prayers of his people. Why then do you fear he will die?"

"I fear . . ." Her hands twisted. She took a breath, willing calm. "I did not see this."

He was silent a moment, looking at her. She felt his surprise and his understanding. "I wondered about that," he said. "What did you see?"

"What do you mean?"

"Just what I said. You saw something, I'm certain of it. Nothing else explains the way you have been."

"Oh, really?" Desperately, she sought time, delay, anything to help her deal with this man and his knowledge of her. "And just how have I been?"

"You and I, we are drawn together."

"A kiss, no more."

"Kassandra . . ."

Her name on his lips was caress and reprimand all at once. "You know there is far more than that and yet you pull away."

Startled, she took shelter in the only protection she had — duty. "I have responsibilities."

And feelings, heaven help her, feelings for him so powerful she feared they would deter her from the path she must walk if Akora was to survive. Feelings . . . growing with every breath she took.

"You are not betrothed."

He had asked about her? She was surprised yet tentatively pleased. All the same, she could not reveal that lest those tempting, treacherous feelings overwhelm her. "Have you ever thought what you imagine is between us may be more of your own making than of mine?"

"No," he said honestly and looked amused.

"What I saw . . . is of no importance. All paths to the future are uncertain. Nothing matters now except that Atreus live."

She half-expected him to offer the usual words of comfort and reassurance but this was Royce, the Hawk Lord, and she should have known better.

"Atreus matters, but not above all else. Whether he lives or dies, Akora must be preserved."

"You are English and yet you say that?"

His eyes flashed. She saw in them all the pride and strength of the lineage and the man. "English is not another word for enemy, no matter what you have seen and what you believe. I remind you, *Atreides,* you yourself are half-English."

He was right. She was part of the red serpent she had seen, come in fire and death. But she loved the father who had made her so.

"Come," Royce said, and held out his hand. "Your parents would be glad of your company."

She went with him, holding fast to his warmth, and stood again by her brother's bed, surrounded by hushed murmurs and fathomless fears. She knelt to pray and rose with renewed resolve.

Atreus would live or die.

Akora would be preserved.

"Summon the Council," she said, and knew what she must do.

Incense swirled on the air. Kassandra watched it rise in tendrils into the late afternoon sky. It was very still in the vast courtyard in front of the palace. Despite the presence of so many thousands of people in the only place on Akora large enough to hold them all, there was hardly a whisper of sound.

The prayers were almost over. Soon the bodies would be taken away and the crowd would disperse. The city was calm. Arrests of the rebels were proceeding swiftly. Marcellus assured her that all those who could be identified would be in custody by nightfall, before people could be tempted to take matters into their own hands. That, at least, they would be spared.

She looked to one side where her mother stood. Phaedra was exhausted but composed. Until now, she had not left her son since he was brought to the palace. Joanna was with her. She met Kassandra's gaze, her own dark with worry. Unspoken between them was the wish that Alex could be there. He was not but Royce was, standing a little distance behind Kassandra. She could not see him but she knew he was there all the same, knew and drew comfort from him.

The priest and priestess were almost finished. On the final words of the prayers for hope, for redemption, for life everlasting, gongs were struck. The sound reverberated gently but persistently, echoing off the surrounding walls of the palace.

It was over. Kassandra waited until the

guards of honor had lifted each of the dead and walked in single file through the silent crowd and out into the streets. Some would be carried to the hill beyond Ilius where the dead were given to the heavens. The rest were bound for the ships awaiting them in the harbor and their own journey soon on the celestial road all must ultimately walk.

When the last of the bodies had gone, she turned and led the way back into the palace. Within the cool, shadowed walls, a little of the tension left her. Her shoulders slumped slightly but she was careful to conceal her weariness. Too many eyes still watched.

The counselors were there, five men in all. There had been six members of the council but after Deilos's betrayal and disappearance the previous year, Atreus had not been inclined to replace him. Of the five, three were solid men Kassandra knew she could rely on to do what was right. They were dismayed by what had happened but willing to give her their full support. The other two were a different matter.

Mellinos caught her eye just then and inclined his head gravely. He was almost sixty, rather vain about his appearance, and considered himself a guardian of Akoran virtues and traditions. While he did not overtly oppose Atreus's determination to bring about change, he had not failed to raise objections and concerns at every turn.

And then there was Troizus, the ever cautious and circumspect. He was younger than Mellinos but looked older by virtue of his sagging jowls and perpetually creased brow. There had been talk the previous year of a marriage between Deilos and one of Troizus's daughters but it had come to nothing, for which Troizus was no doubt grateful. He and Mellinos had avoided being caught in Deilos's fall, but that did not mean their views had changed.

Could she trust either or both of these men? When she had met with the Council earlier and announced formally her intent to take up the duties of her brother pending his recovery, no one had demurred. But her action was unprecedented in Akoran history. That, alone, would upset Mellinos. As for Troizus, she simply did not know what he was likely to do. Either man, or both, might seek to betray her.

Which suited her perfectly.

The attempted assassination of Atreus had failed, not only because he still lived but because she had placed herself squarely between the traitors and the chaos they had intended to bring to Akora. By doing so publicly and formally, she had made herself a target.

A target they would have to come out into the open to reach.

She had failed to see the danger to Atreus and through him, to Akora. But she would not fail in this. Whoever the traitors were, she would draw them out and she would destroy them.

On that, she was entirely resolved.

But to succeed, she had to make quite sure no well-meaning person close to her guessed her intent. That included Joanna and her parents, who understandably enough would be appalled, but most particularly it meant Royce.

Of them all, he presented the greatest challenge. His strength added to her own could prove vital, but he saw so much, so clearly.

Even now, as he stood nearby talking with Joanna, Kassandra was aware of him watching her. She nodded but did not approach them. For the next hour, she made herself available to a steady stream of visitors, exchanging a few words with each, listening to their concerns, and thanking them for their expressions of support. The effort wearied her yet further but she knew it was both needed and worthwhile.

Finally, she was able to slip away. She went first to Atreus's quarters where she spoke with Elena.

"The Vanax's great strength of body and spirit serves him well now," the healer said. "However, until he regains consciousness, we cannot know the full extent of the damage he has suffered."

"But you think there is at least a chance that he will recover," Kassandra prompted, clinging to hope.

"Recover, yes, if he survives the next few days. But whether that means he can regain all his former capabilities, I simply do not know."

The thought of Atreus living yet unable to

function fully was too painful to contemplate. After a few words with her parents, who remained at the bedside, Kassandra left.

Royce was waiting for her in the corridor. Seeing him, a little of the grief and dread weighing her down lifted, but only until she remembered that she must conceal her plan to draw out the traitors.

"How is he?" Royce asked as they walked toward her quarters.

"The same. I gather the next few days are critical."

"You are tired."

She nodded. Listening to Elena, she had felt as though the last of her strength was being drained from her. The mere effort of putting one foot in front of the other required concentration. "It's been a very long day. I thought I would lie down briefly."

"A sensible idea, although it would be better if you stopped for today. Surely you have done enough."

She cast him a quick look, wondering if there was any chance he understood what she had truly done, but his expression held only gentle concern.

"Thank you," she murmured, and touched his hand for just a moment before seeking the shelter of solitude.

Royce remained in the corridor, looking at the closed door to Kassandra's quarters. The anger he had felt growing within him all day would no longer be denied. Yesterday, she had turned to him in trust and need. Today, she would barely look him in the eye. Every instinct he possessed told him something was very wrong.

He could see she was exhausted and possibly not thinking entirely clearly. He did not want to read too much into her actions but that meeting with the counselors, what had been the purpose of it? She had done nothing except formally announce the steps she had already taken. Why feel called upon to do any such thing when it was only likely to provoke the more conservative among them?

Since the bombing, he had seen Kassandra emerge as a woman of strength and determination even beyond his expectations. It was difficult for him to believe that she did anything without deliberate purpose.

But he could be wrong. She had been thrown into a horrible situation and she was exhausted. He might be looking for meaning where there was none.

He might also be chasing thoughts in circles leading nowhere. He, too, was tired, although he had no intention of resting. Instead, he went in search of Marcellus, finding the magistrate just where Royce expected him to be, in the room where the evidence was being assembled.

"An ordinary, nondescript wagon," Marcellus said as he got to his feet from where he had been kneeling beside the pile of debris that was slowly being reassembled. "Unfortunately, there seems to be nothing to distinguish it."

"Is there a possibility it was stolen?" Royce asked as he studied the pile of charred wood and metal.

"It could have been but there have been no reports of any such theft."

"What about the barrels?"

The magistrate shrugged. "There's really nothing to be said about them other than they were barrels. Except for a few strips of metal, they were completely destroyed. However . . ." He gestured to the space over the floor where the pieces of the wagon had been laid out. "We can estimate the size of the wagon and from that, the maximum number of barrels it could have been carrying — about twenty."

"Twenty barrels of gunpowder," Royce said slowly. "That's a considerable amount."

Marcellus nodded. "It is consistent with the damage done."

"The question then is who would have access to so much gunpowder?"

"I am making inquiries."

"In the meantime, are the rebels saying anything?"

"You mean the alleged perpetrators of minor counts of vandalism and public disorder?" Marcellus corrected with a grimace. "Nothing useful. They claim complete ignorance of the explosion and express outrage at being suspected of it."

"Of course, they would —"

"Exactly."

"If they were innocent," Royce concluded.

"Well, yes, I suppose they would but they would do the same if they were guilty."

"As you said, nothing useful. The gunpowder sounds like our best hope."

"That will take some time. It isn't all that difficult to produce."

"Not by someone with access to saltpeter, sulfur and charcoal," Royce said. "There was a time when we made gunpowder for ourselves at Hawkforte. The only ingredient difficult to secure was the sulfur."

"That would not be a problem on Akora."

"Why not?"

"Sulfur crystals abound on the three small islands of the Inland Sea. We think they resulted from the volcanic explosion there."

At the mention of the islands, Royce stiffened. He knew them all too well, although he had only ever set foot on one. Phobos, Tarbos and Deimatos — the names all meaning *fear* because of the terror that accompanied their birth in fire and death — were the sole remnants of the drowned heart of Akora. It was Deimatos that had a very personal meaning for him, for it was in a tiny cell on that island that he had endured the captivity from which he had been rescued barely half-alive.

Returning to Akora, he had thought to put the last vestiges of the suffering he had experienced on his first visit to rest once and for all. He had failed to consider that the nightmare might not be over. That it might, in fact, still be going on.

But now he was not trapped alone in it. So was Kassandra . . . and Atreus . . . and ultimately all Akorans, for it was they who would suffer most if the fabric of their world was ripped apart, this time not by nature but by man.

He could not allow that to happen. Akora was a reality worth protecting, but it was also a dream of what people could accomplish with brave hearts and bold minds. Never would he stand by and let it perish.

"Will you tell the Atreides?" Marcellus asked.

Royce nodded. "She was retiring for the night but if she is not already asleep, I will tell her now."

He was thinking of exactly what he would say to convince her to let him help as he walked quickly back down the corridor to Kassandra's quarters.

Chapter
TWELVE

"Princess Kassandra is not here, Lord," the servant said. She was a slender, middle-aged woman with dark, silver-streaked hair twined in braids around her head. More to the point, she looked entirely serious.

"Sida . . . it is Sida, isn't it?"

Pleased, the woman nodded. "It is, Hawk Lord."

"I thought the Princess intended to retire for the night."

"That may be but she went out a few minutes ago. Indeed, if you hurry, you may be able to catch her." She pointed down the corridor that linked the private quarters of the royal family to a recess little more than a height and width of a man. "Through there, my lord."

He went quickly and found himself on a curving staircase set into an inner wall of the palace. The steps led down to a landing where there was a small wooden door. Royce opened it and found himself looking at a path leading toward the city. He saw no sign of Kassandra nor could he imagine why she would have gone that way. The stairs continued to lead downward. He shut the door and followed them, but not before taking one of the lanterns hanging nearby.

Remembering the vast catacombs of the library, he thought he might emerge into something similar but the steps led much deeper into the ground. The temperature fell rapidly and he smelled . . . not the sea but the tang of mineral springs similar to those he had visited in Bath several years before.

At length, the steps ended and he found himself in a large chamber. Holding the lantern high, he saw that the surrounding walls were carved with niches in which were set several hundred statues, most of them life-sized depictions of men and women. So detailed were the carvings that he had the sense he was looking into the faces of individuals who had truly lived.

Beyond the statue room was a vast arch. When he stepped through it, the flagstone floor ended and he realized he was walking on cool, damp earth inside an immense cave. Lamps were set in brackets all around the cave. Several of them had been lit, enough to reveal a chamber so large as to rival any cathedral in Europe. Far above, slender cones he knew to be stalactites hung in glittering hues of white, pink and green. Similar stalagmites rose from the floor of the cave. They formed aisles that led to a deep rock edge at the far end of the chamber.

Where Kassandra stood. She was dressed in shimmering white, her hair tumbling in thick, ebony waves down her back. As always at the sight of her, his body tightened. He strove to ignore that and was helped just a little by his intense curiosity about the place in which he found himself.

Her attention was focused on the stone ledge. He moved forward, his tread silent against the earth, well aware that he was intruding on her privacy and reluctant to disturb her, yet drawn to her side all the same. Something gleamed in the light cast by the lamps . . . something red.

He breathed in sharply, struggling to come to terms with what he saw. A . . . ruby? No, that couldn't be and yet it appeared so. An immense ruby jutting up out of the stone ledge, gleaming as though with the fires of the earth.

Kassandra's hands rested on it lightly. Her eyes were closed. Her features appeared composed but as he watched, a tremor rippled through her and she sagged suddenly.

He was there in an instant, catching her to him. Gently, he lowered her to the ground in front of the ledge and knelt beside her. Concern for her well-being drove out all other thought.

"Kassandra . . . what's wrong?"

She did not respond at once but lay in his arms unmoving. Her skin felt very cold, colder even than the temperature in the cave. Her eyes opened and she stared at him unseeingly.

"Kassandra." His voice was low and urgent. He bent over her, shielding her with his body from any danger, striving to somehow make her warm again.

"Royce . . . ?"

"Thank God! What happened to you?"

"I was . . . seeking vision." Her gaze cleared a little more. "What are you doing here?"

"Seeking you. I thought you meant to rest."

"I did and could not."

A long shudder went through her, exhaustion mingling with dread. He felt it and drew her closer. "What is this place?"

"A temple," she said slowly. Her voice was low and slightly husky. She coughed and began again, sounding stronger. "Ancient when Akora was young. When the volcano exploded, some people sought shelter here. They were among the few to survive."

"I can see why. We must be deep underground."

"Yes, very deep." She sat up, gazing at him. "Are you sure you should be here?"

"Why, is it forbidden?"

"No, not exactly, although very few ever come here. I was thinking of what Joanna told me . . . of your difficulty sleeping inside." Quickly, before he could reply, she said, "It is remarkable that you have recovered so well but there are bound to be lingering effects."

He grimaced but answered her honestly. "It is true I had that difficulty but I was determined to overcome it and have done so. Besides, none of that matters. You said you came seeking vision?"

She nodded toward the ruby. "I don't know why exactly, but the crystal helps me."

"That's not really a ruby, is it?" If it were, it would have to be the largest ever found by far.

"It is, for all that its size may mislead you. There have been others like it found in these caves, although none quite so large." She waved a hand in the direction of what appeared to be tunnels leading away from the caves. "There are diamonds as well in far greater quantity than the rubies. We have used them to acquire what we wish from the outside world."

Royce shook his head in amazement. With hindsight, he realized he should have questioned the source of Akora's wealth but it was used in so restrained a manner that the thought had not occurred to him. He did not doubt that was deliberate.

"No wonder Akora has sought to keep its secrets from the world. Men would seek to come here for the gems alone."

"So we realized long ago."

He stood, drawing her with him but still holding her close. "Did you find the vision you sought?"

Her eyes went blank for a moment, worrying him, but she recovered quickly. "I came here really to try to understand why I didn't see what happened to Atreus. I still don't know the answer to that but I know the situation is becoming more complex."

"Why is that?"

Her eyes were wide and filled with shadows. "There are so many paths branching away from each other, like the limbs of a great tree. It is difficult to see which one we walk, much less where it will lead."

His arms tightened around her. He hated the thought of her alone in this cave, struggling with the gift that was also a curse. Hated even more the thought of her venturing out in some way beyond the reality in which they both were, trying to walk paths into futures that might never exist. How easy was it for a person to become lost in such places? To never find her way back again?

"Couldn't you have waited until you were not so tired?" he demanded more gruffly than he intended.

"Perhaps, but I have learned I must try when the moment seems right. At any rate, you said you had something to tell me?"

He realized she was trying to deflect him but let that happen all the same. There was no point burdening her with his fears and concerns. She would have no answer for them save the requirements of duty, and that he simply did not want to hear again.

Briefly, he explained what Marcellus had told him. Kassandra listened and nodded. "The gunpowder produced for the use of the army is well regulated. It is stored only in royal armories. But from what you have said, it would not have been very difficult for someone to produce an illegal supply."

"The reality is that anyone could have gone out to one or more of those three islands and collected sulfur crystals. All the same, I can't help thinking of Deilos."

"His family controlled the island of Deimatos almost from the time it was nothing but a burnt cinder sticking out of the Inland Sea. I suppose that is why he felt safe imprisoning you there. But after his disappearance, it and all his lands passed to the Vanax."

"Even so, Deilos would know it well."

"Yes," she agreed, "he would." She thought a moment and said, "I will ask Marcellus to send men there to investigate. Hopefully, if Deilos has been active on the island, they will find evidence of him."

"The interior of the island is riddled with caves. A man could hide there for years and not be found."

"That is true; even so it is worth the effort."

They stepped a little away from each other. There was nothing more to keep them in the cave yet Royce was loath to leave. Above, the world would intrude as it always did. Here they were alone, if only for some little time.

"This looks like a remarkable place," he said.

So quickly that he could not help but wonder if her thoughts had been similar, she said, "It is that. Would you like to see more of it?"

He allowed as to how he would and smiled when she took his hand.

They went deeper into the cave, past the stone ledge and the ruby that gleamed there, beyond the circle of light cast by the lamps Kassandra had lit. Guided by the lantern Royce carried, they followed a natural tunnel carved out of the stone until they came to a place where the lantern was not needed.

"There are tiny creatures here that produce light," Kassandra said. "Alex showed them to me under a microscope."

"Where are we?" Royce asked as he looked around. He saw water nearby and what looked oddly like a . . . beach. And yet they were deep underground. He also noticed that the temperature seemed considerably warmer.

"I'm not sure," Kassandra admitted, "but this seems to have been a part of Akora before the explosion. Even though the area where we are survived, it went through great upheavals. Areas that were on the surface ended up buried. This seems to have been one of them."

"Is that a . . . temple . . . ?" He was looking at a small building glowing greenish-white in the eerie light. A row of columns held up the pointed roof.

"Yes, it is. We think it may have been used to offer prayers for those who were venturing out to sea. There seems to have been an inlet here that led to the sea but it was covered over and all that remains is a mineral spring that comes from deep within the earth."

"That's what I smelled . . . and the source of the warmth?"

She nodded and knelt beside the water. "It is actually drinkable although it tastes salty. We think this stream helped sustain the survivors so that they could remain underground until the worst of the lava flows and explosions ended."

"This is an incredible place," Royce said as he looked around. "I feel as though I've stepped back in time."

"That's what I've always felt whenever I came here. Somehow, I don't think this was just one more temple long ago. I think it was extremely important to the people who lived here, which is why they sought sanctuary near it."

"Are there any statues inside, anything that might have represented their gods or goddesses?"

She hesitated just a moment, or perhaps it was his imagination. Taking his hand again, she said, "Not exactly, but let me show you what is there."

They went together into the ancient temple. The air was very still and smelled of age. He knew no other way to describe it. He wondered what he would see, and thought he was prepared for almost anything, yet he was surprised all the same.

"What is that?" he asked.

"A face," Kassandra said. "We don't know if it is a man's or a woman's, it could be either. It was carved into the stone so long ago that the features have softened a great deal but you can still make it out."

So he could, just as he could see the flow of water running over the carving and the moss growing in every crevice of the stone. The face seemed to be fading in and out of the earth itself.

"This water is greatly valued," Kassandra said. "Even today, we bring ewers of it to the temples for blessings."

She looked at him again, a bit anxiously, he thought, but as before the impression was swiftly gone. Bending, she cupped her palm, caught sparkling drops of water and drank.

The liquid slipped down her throat, cool, clear and incredibly pure. She drank a little more and felt the tension easing from her body, little by little, almost imperceptibly at first, but gathering in strength with each passing moment.

"Why don't you try it?" she suggested and stood aside so that he could do so.

As Royce bent to catch the water in his hand, Kassandra almost reached out to stop him but drew back at the last moment. He was a strong man, it would still be his choice. The water was merely . . . encouragement.

From time immemorial, Akoran husbands

and wives had enjoyed a goblet of the water taken from the buried temple on their wedding night. Years later, old couples basking in the sun would remember it fondly and share secret looks of tender passion.

Of course, it was also possible that the water did nothing and all was mere legend. She wanted to believe that, for it eased her conscience, but the heat seeping through her made her uncertain.

She stared at Royce as he drank, watching the ripple of the water ease down his throat. He was such a beautiful man, so perfectly formed in body and mind. The memory of him on the field at the Games, on horseback wearing only a kilt, his powerful muscles flexing as he threw the javelin, haunted her dreams.

Ever since then, she had been living in a nightmare. Atreus . . . the danger to Akora . . . her own death the price to save both family and home . . . all seemed to close around her until she could scarcely breathe.

Until the moment when she emerged from her desperate, futile quest for vision to see in Royce's beloved face the future for which she yearned with all her heart.

A future that in all likelihood was impossible.

That being the case, was it so terribly wrong to steal a little happiness in the fleeting present?

She cupped her hand, caught the gleaming flow of water and drank again. Royce did the

262

same. She was right, he had never tasted water more satisfying.

When he had drunk, he took a deep breath and felt his lungs fill with the mingled scent of lemons and jasmine, the perfume he already knew, for it clung to her skin.

That satiny smooth skin. Would it feel cool to his touch as it had earlier or would she be warm now here in the cradle of the earth?

He had to know.

His fingers brushed over the curve of her cheek, lingered . . . Her lashes drifted down, so long and soft, up again, and he found himself gazing into fathomless eyes.

"Royce —"

"Hush," he said and gathered her to him.

She was slim and strong in his arms, her body molding to his. Her lips parted, accepting the hard thrust of his tongue as he tasted her deeply. He wanted to go slowly, knew he should, and found the effort entirely beyond him.

He had waited so long . . . not mere weeks but lifetimes it seemed . . . time without beginning or end, stretching out endlessly yet coming finally to this moment.

Surely, he was not alone in believing they had been coming to this moment since that fog-draped morning in London when he first set eyes on her?

Her hands were on his shirt, pulling it loose.

Shock roared through him. He had not expected this. She was gently reared, a virgin, he had thought to go very slowly — heaven help him — always mindful of her innocence. But her passion seemed to match his own and she was fire in his arms, in his hands, in his dreams.

"Sweet heaven," she said, gasping softly. "I want you so much!"

Somewhere on the planet there was a man who could withstand such words from a beautiful woman in his arms.

Of course, that poor fellow was a eunuch, which absolutely did not bear thinking about.

Royce groaned in relief, offered thanks to any and all deities who might feel they were due, and lowered her gently to the ground. Far in the back of his mind, he knew what he was doing was momentous. Kassandra was as far from a casual encounter as it was possible for a woman to be. He knew that and accepted it. Indeed, the depth of his feeling for her transformed pleasure into something vastly more.

He brushed aside the silken fabric covering her shoulders, letting it slip down her arms to reveal the curve of her breasts and stared at the smooth paleness of her skin against his sunburnished hand, a hand that he noticed shook slightly. As well it might given the intensity of the hunger roaring through him.

"You are the most beautiful man," Kassandra said, and ran her hands under his shirt and over the flat, hard planes of his chest.

He gasped and moved to stop her. "I really would like this to last."

She stared into his eyes. "It already has lasted weeks . . . in London, on the ship, here. Just how much more endurance do you think either of us should have?"

"That's true, but you . . . are a virgin . . . we have to go slow . . ."

She laughed, her breath hot against his throat. Pleasure burned through him as her tongue touched the lobe of his ear. "How many virgins have you lain with, Hawk Lord, that you are expert in such matters?"

"None . . . Stop doing that . . . No, don't stop . . . I can't take much more . . ."

"You don't have to," she said and pushed away from him, rising to stand on the golden beach buried in the heart of the earth. Holding his eyes, she undid the slim belt around her waist and let it fall.

He truly did need to breathe and any minute now, he'd remember how. But just then there was nothing he could do except gaze at Kassandra as she slipped her gown down the rest of the way over her high, rounded breasts and past her narrow waist where it caught on the gentle swell of her hips.

Far in the back of his mind, it occurred to him that he was being seduced — by a virgin. The sheer absurdity of the situation filled him with tenderness that only increased when he saw Kassandra falter slightly and cast her eyes down in a sudden flash of shyness.

In that moment, the fierce battle he had been waging for self-control was won. Suddenly, nothing mattered except the brave, honest, tantalizing woman standing before him.

He reached out a hand and drew her back down onto the soft ground beside him.

"You," he said honestly, "are the most amazing thing that has ever happened to me."

"How can that be?" she murmured against his chest. "You have had other women, adventures, an entire life in the wide world."

"That's true, I have, which must mean that you are amazing indeed."

She laughed, shy again but delightfully so. He took the opportunity to turn her so that she was lying beneath him. Her hair caught under her, making her wince. He drew it out gently, savoring the dark, silken strands as they ran through his fingers, and drew tendrils over her breasts, laying them gently, brushing them away, watching all the while as her nipples hardened.

And yet he scarcely touched her.

Amazing indeed, exquisitely responsive and above all, honest. With all her beauty, intelligence and mystery, if he had to think of one word to describe Kassandra it would be *honest*. He could not imagine her ever betraying anything she held dear just as he could never do so. Honor and all it bred was the common ground between them.

Not that intense passion didn't matter, too.

He caught her face between his hands and kissed her repeatedly, his mouth trailing along the delicate curve of her cheek and jaw, lingering over her throat where the pulse of her life beat, returning again and again to her lips, tracing their contours with his tongue before thrusting hard and deep. He was rewarded by a soft moan as she arched in his arms. Their tongues played as their bodies strained toward each other. He slid his thigh between hers, still managing to go gently, and felt the wet heat of her.

She was shaking and couldn't stop. She could not get close enough to him, touch him enough to satisfy the fire raging in her. Wave after wave of pleasure coursed through her and it, too, was not enough.

She was not ignorant. Older women spoke plainly and sensibly of the force of passion. She understood what a man and woman could find together . . . or at least, she had thought she did.

This . . . *this* was something so vastly beyond her imagining.

He touched her again, as though he understood perfectly what she needed, and she gasped, her hands gripping his shoulders.

"Royce . . ."

"My way," he said though his voice was little more than a grunt, "damn it, we do this my way."

And that apparently meant that she was going to be sweetly tortured, subjected to the most ardent caresses until her peak of arousal became so intense that she truly could not bear anything more. And until the very determined, astoundingly controlled man who drove her to that point was satisfied that the moment had come.

He was very large, she realized far back in the fragment of her mind that was still functioning. He must have considered that, must have taken such care because she was a virgin and . . .

A cry, not of pain but of pure and utter pleasure broke from her. It rose past the little temple buried in the earth, into the vaults of the cave and seemingly to heaven itself.

Much later, arms wrapped around each other's waists, they came through the cave and up the winding stone steps. Watching Royce replace the lantern on its hook, Kassandra had a vague sense that more time had passed than she had realized. No light shown through the crack of the door that led to the outside. In the hours they had spent below, day had ended and night had begun.

Atreus.

They went together to his quarters. Phaedra and Andrew were still there, as was Elena. The healer looked tired but relieved.

"The Vanax opened his eyes briefly about an hour ago, my lady. He did not speak, but still it is a hopeful sign."

"He is going to live," Brianna said, emerging from the shadows. She looked pale but determined. "I am convinced of it."

"And the others?" Kassandra asked, buoyed by heady hope.

"They are improving," Elena said.

Kassandra breathed, drawing in the sweet scent of Akora in the night. "When this is over," she declared, "we will have a day of thanksgiving. No, several days. We will feast and sing. We will gather flowers in the fields and fill Ilius with them. We will wear garlands and drink wine."

Quietly, Royce said, "When this is over. When those responsible have been brought to justice."

"Oh, yes," she said and turned from the bed of her brother to look at the man who had taken her into realms unknown. "When justice has been done. When peace and security are restored. When Akora is safe."

"Let it be as you say," Phaedra murmured and embraced her daughter.

Holding her mother in her arms, Kassandra had a sudden, piercing memory of herself as a child, being comforted by Phaedra. Phaedra who was so constant and reliable a mother, so good and true a friend. Who always knew what to say and do.

Who now needed comfort.

"It will be," Kassandra said, and in that moment felt immeasurably older than she had scant hours before, as though the years had overtaken her and made a breach with the childhood she had not known until then still clung to her. She let it go with a little sadness, but knowing the time had come to move beyond.

Andrew stepped forward, her father but also a husband, dearly loved and loving. He took Phaedra from her. Over her shoulder, he said to his beloved daughter, "I believe you need to rest."

"She does." Royce stepped forward. "Elena, send word if anything changes."

The healer nodded. "As you say, Hawk Lord." Her smile was gentle, her eyes wise.

"I am fine," Kassandra insisted as he led her back out into the corridor. There was no fight in her, she realized with a start. She was willing to be guided by him, at least at this moment.

"When did you eat last?" he asked. Before she could answer, they entered her apartments. He took the hammer beside a small gong and struck it to the beaten metal.

"Eat? I don't know —"

"My point. Ah, Sida . . ."

The servant materialized as if from air. "Hawk Lord," she said, bowing. "Princess." Her mouth twitched slightly in a smile.

"Food, Sida," Royce said. "Whatever won't take very long."

"You," Kassandra said when they were alone again, "are becoming rather bossy."

"I have always been," he said and grinned,

twisting her heart. "You just didn't notice. Where's the bath?"

"The what?" Why was he thinking of that?

"The bath. You have the most incredible plumbing on Akora. It was amazing on the ship, but what I've seen here beats all."

"I'm so glad you think so . . ."

"Bath . . . there it is." He went through, into the spacious room and looked around approvingly. "Very nice. What are the pipes made of?"

She followed. "Copper . . . I suppose. They were clay very long ago but they've been copper for centuries."

"That's what I love about Akora," he said as he turned the knobs on the immense tiled tub, causing water to gush from the spigots shaped like swans. "Plenty of history. In England, if we go back more than a few hundred years, we're all fragmented, too much lost. But not here. Here you've got everything safely tucked away."

"We try . . ."

"You certainly do. Take off your clothes."

"What?"

"You heard me, take off your clothes. Is this some kind of bathing oil?"

She looked at the crystal bottle he held up and nodded slowly. "Yes, it's honeysuckle . . . I think."

He grimaced. "I can stand that, I guess, at least on you." He began undoing the breeches he had only lately redonned.

"I don't think . . ."

"Oh, good, it's quite an overrated activity for a woman."

At her outraged gasp, he laughed. "I've said it before and I'll say it again, you are fun to tease. Now get in the tub."

She was going to say no but he was already naked and that distracted her sufficiently that when next she noted anything at all, she was in the same state and lounging in hot, scented water.

"You're a terrible man," she said languidly.

Terribly beautiful there in the glow of the lamps holding the night at bay. Terribly enticing as she gazed at him, swept by the memory of what had passed between them, still resonating to the echoes of the pleasure he had revealed to her.

"I am that," he agreed and smiled.

He rubbed the soap between his hands, then rubbed his hands over her. She gave up any pretense of thinking and gave herself up to his ministrations. He seemed pleased by her docility, so much that she was moved to right the balance between them. By the time she was done, he was gasping.

"How do you know so much?" he asked.

"Innocence, not ignorance," she said, and rose dripping from the tub. Her knees held, which surprised her. She reached for a towel, gave it to him and took another for herself. Aware of him watching her, she began to dry herself . . . very slowly.

"No fair," he muttered and rose to follow her.

Sida brought them food: warm rounds of fresh-baked bread sweetened with honey, paper-thin slices of ham, golden cheese, deep ruby wine, and little pears possessed of succulent sweetness that they licked from each other's lips.

They ate on the bed before the wide window thrown open to the night. Crickets chirped and far off in the trees an owl hooted. Through wisps of cloud, they watched the moon watching them.

Satisfying one appetite led to satisfying another, which took a very long time indeed. When the moon had set, Kassandra stirred. Against his heated skin, she murmured, "I feel so guilty."

She had thought him asleep but at once his arms tightened around her. "For God's sake, why?"

"Atreus . . . the others . . . all the trouble that has come to Akora and yet I am happier than I have ever been in my life."

He sighed a little and touched his lips to her brow. "And you think that's wrong?"

"No," she said, tentatively at first but again with more conviction. "No, I don't. It simply *is*, now in this moment, and that will have to be enough."

He said something more but she was sinking

into velvety darkness and did not hear him. Nor was she aware when he pulled the covers over them both and lay, holding her close, awake and thoughtful through what remained of the night.

Chapter
THIRTEEN

Marcellus stood in front of the wide table that served Atreus as a desk. The surface was cleared of all papers, empty of everything except the pen and the inkwell the Vanax customarily used. Kassandra had made no changes, neither adding nor subtracting, nor did she sit at the table. She could not imagine doing so while her brother lived.

The magistrate carried his usual tablet but, Kassandra noticed, he consulted it less frequently than he had a day before. Now he seemed merely to hold it as a talisman of sorts. He looked as though he had slept, some at least, and he was freshly groomed. Most importantly, he appeared calm and matter-of-fact.

"I will tell the men to concentrate their efforts on Deimatos, as you have said, Atreides, but not to overlook any clues that may be found on Phobos and Tarbos."

Kassandra nodded. "Good. Now tell me of those who have been arrested. How are they faring?"

"Well enough, I suppose. They are all rather

young, none more than mid-twenties, and naturally their families are concerned. But we have seen to their comfort. Several have acknowledged, I would say even bragged of, painting their slogan on the walls and releasing the banners in the palace courtyard. But they insist they did nothing more."

"What of the man seen on the arena wall with the yellow banner around his neck? Do any acknowledge him?"

"No, in fact they insist he does not exist."

"Perhaps he does not," Kassandra said slowly. "After all, there is only one witness who claims to have seen him."

"Three," Royce said quietly. He stood off to one side, near the windows. Kassandra was not so pale as she had been the previous day but he knew she had slept very little because he had slept not at all, content instead to keep watch over her. Too soon she had awakened and far too quickly after that, the day had begun in earnest. Since then, the pace had not slowed for a moment.

She was, after all, the Atreides.

"Two more witnesses have been found," he explained. "One is a woman who was seated on the other side of the arena from the older man who came forward earlier. She, too, noticed the man with the banner around his neck. The other is a young boy, about eleven years old, who saw the same man. Their descriptions vary somewhat and no one got a really good look at his features, but they all agree he was there and he was wearing a yellow banner around his neck."

"It may mean nothing," Kassandra said thoughtfully.

Royce nodded. "Or everything."

They stared at each other for a long moment.

Marcellus cleared his throat. "You will understand, Atreides, that we are under some pressure to bring the miscreants to trial."

"Yes, of course," she said, forcing her attention back where it must be. "How unfortunate that the Chief Magistrate, being the Vanax himself, is indisposed. I am sure that when he has recovered, my brother will deal with the matter expeditiously."

"That could be some time, Atreides."

Her voice hardened. "It will be what it will be. In the meantime, all those detained are to be treated with utmost consideration and courtesy."

"But they are not to be permitted their freedom?" Marcellus asked mildly.

"No, they are not. I think we can all agree that matters remain unsettled and emotions are running high. Therefore, it is best that the supporters of Helios stay where they can be kept safe and secure."

Marcellus might have remarked that those being detained were not likely to agree but he was not a man given to stating the obvious. Instead, he said, "Work continues to clear debris from the arena. Rebuilding of the wall should be underway by tomorrow."

"I am pleased to hear it."

"On an unrelated matter, if I may, the olive groves are coming into bloom."

"Good, the usual ceremonies will be observed."

Marcellus hesitated. His eyes darted to Royce, who caught the look in them and asked, "What does that involve?"

She did not answer at once but stared out over the city. He had the sense that she was very far away and found himself resenting that. Still, he remained silent, waiting until finally she returned to him.

"There are rituals. They aren't elaborate, it's really just a matter of going out into the fields, saying a few appropriate prayers, that sort of thing."

Marcellus spoke up. "Ordinarily, that would be done by the Vanax. The people are pleased to see him at such a time. It is a reminder of the continuity and order with which Akora has been blessed."

"Atreus has always enjoyed such events," Kassandra said softly. "He likes to get out among the people, to talk with them and most importantly, to listen."

"Therefore," Royce said, "you will do as he normally would?"

"Yes, I think that is best. Thank you, Marcellus. I appreciate your diligence."

When the magistrate had gone, Royce said, "Your concern about keeping the members of Helios safe and secure might also extend to yourself, don't you think?"

She plucked an imaginary fleck of dust from the skirt of her white tunic and thought suddenly that as she was no longer a virgin, she could wear other colors. Except to do so without marriage would surprise and alarm her people, not to say also her family. Perhaps that was just as well, for she had neither time nor energy for the subject of new clothes.

"Myself?"

He came round the desk to stand near her. He had showered that morning and no longer smelled of honeysuckle. She must not think of that.

"To all intents and purposes, you have assumed your brother's authority. Do you not think that whoever sought to kill him may now look upon you as a target?"

Something moved behind her eyes that he could not grasp but knew he did not like. "I am not the Vanax."

He tried a different tack. "What would have happened if you had not stepped forward as you did?"

"I don't know what you mean."

Anger stirred in him. She was being purposefully obtuse, he was certain of it. What he did not know was why. "Of course you do. If you had not picked up the reins of power, what would be happening right now on Akora?"

"The same that is happening. We are mourning the dead, praying for the injured, and getting on with life."

"You don't think there would have been any confusion . . . panic . . . uncertainty . . . ?"

"I suppose there has been some of that."

"No, not what is but what would have been. Has any Vanax ever been assassinated?"

She looked genuinely shocked by the mere question. "Of course not, that is unthinkable."

"The unthinkable almost occurred two days ago. How, then, can you say everything would be as it is if you had not stepped forward, not been recognized as the Atreides?"

"I am Atreides, it is my family name."

"*The* Atreides, that is something different, something there has never been before. I hear what they call you. You hear it, too. More to the point, I hear their relief and their trust. They are looking to you to hold things together until Atreus recovers enough to resume his duties."

"As I have every intention of doing." He thought her smile forced. "Would you like to accompany me to the olive groves?"

He summoned patience, reminding himself of his feelings for this woman and for Akora. "Yes, I would. Who else will be coming along?"

"The counselors, I suppose, some clergy, a few others."

"Any sort of guard?"

"Of the sort the Prince Regent always travels

with?" She wrinkled her nose. "We don't stand on such ceremony."

Anger stirred, the hard-edged sort that demands action. Something was wrong. Either she was not the woman he thought her — intelligent, aware, perceptive — or there was something else . . . He turned the idea that he was entirely mistaken about her over in his mind and found it collapsed on the most cursory examination. He *knew* Kassandra. What he did not know was what she was keeping hidden from him or why.

"I was thinking more of a guard to see to your protection. There is nothing ceremonial about that."

She shrugged lightly. "It is not our custom."

He forced a smile of his own. "Neither is someone trying to kill the Vanax."

Her eyes were very wide and dark but anyone looking at her would see a woman who appeared completely composed. Anyone, that is, but Royce. Moment to moment, heartbeat to heartbeat, he was more certain than ever that Kassandra had something in her mind he definitely did not like.

"I believe it best serves my people to behave as normally as possible," she said.

"And you will do whatever serves them best, won't you?"

There, just for an instant, her eyes flickered and her mouth — that so-soft, so-enticing mouth — trembled.

"I can hardly do less. Perhaps it would be better if you remained here and helped Marcellus."

"No, I don't think so. The last time I was on Akora, I really didn't get a chance to see much. I'd rather not pass up the opportunity now."

"Well, then you must come," she said, and this time her smile was genuine.

With the efficiency he was coming to regard as normal on Akora, arrangements were made by afternoon. Two of the counselors would come with them, Mellinos and another man named Polydorus whose estates were within the area they were to visit first. Most of the other members of the Council were already on their lands, bringing both the news of what had happened and the reassurance of their presence. Only Troizus remained in the capital where, he informed them, he believed it was his duty to be.

Before departing, they went again to see Atreus. At Andrew's insistence and with the help of a potion provided by Elena, Phaedra was sleeping. But Joanna was there, sitting beside the bed, holding her brother-in-law's hand.

"He was conscious for a few minutes earlier," she said. "I believe he recognized his mother and Andrew as well."

"Did he say anything?" Kassandra asked softly. She thought Atreus looked a little less pale than when she had seen him earlier in the day, and prayed that did not signal the onset of fever.

Joanna shook her head. "No, but Phaedra spoke to him and he blinked." She glanced up, seeing the expression in Kassandra's eyes. "I know, it is so little, but we have to hope."

"What does Elena say?" For the first time since Atreus had been brought into the tent at the arena where the injured were being cared for, the healer was not at his side. She, too, was getting desperately needed rest. But Brianna was there and she answered.

"His heartbeat is strong, Princess, and there is no sign of infection. The greatest source of concern remains the blow to his head."

"If he does not regain consciousness soon . . ." Kassandra did not finish her thought. There was no need. They all knew that the longer Atreus remained unconscious, the less chance there was that he would ever recover.

Quietly, Brianna said, "My aunt has gone to rest because she is considering the possibility that surgery may be needed."

"Surgery . . . ?" Kassandra repeated. "On the Vanax?" And not merely any form of surgery but the most difficult and delicate, that performed on the brain itself.

"I have not been told of this," she said and felt the tremor in her own voice.

Joanna smiled but her eyes were strained. "It hasn't really been discussed and it may turn out to be completely unnecessary."

"How long . . . ?" Kassandra began. She

283

broke off, aware of how shocked and dread-filled she sounded.

"Elena has not said how much longer she thinks it is wise to wait," Brianna replied. "I think it must be different in every case." She turned and looked at Atreus. "He is very strong."

"He will need to be," Kassandra said and went forward to the bed where she bent and took her brother's hands in hers. Urgently, she whispered, "Atreus . . . hear me . . . we love you, we need you. Return to us from wherever you have gone. Find the road back and take it. It is not your time. *It is not.*"

Royce touched her shoulder. The contact drew her back out of the dark pain that threatened to swallow her. "They are waiting for you," he said.

She went from the room, from the palace, out into the day so bright it hurt her eyes. She mounted the beautiful white horse brought for her and rode with Royce beside her through the streets. She waved to the people and accepted their greetings — some shy, some heartfelt, a few cautious and uncertain. And all the while she thought of Atreus.

So, it seemed, did Royce, for as they left the city behind and turned east toward the fertile hills and valleys beyond Ilius, he asked, "What sort of surgery is Elena considering?"

Rather to her surprise, she did not mind speaking of it with him. On the contrary, to be able to do so somehow made it less frightening. "It is called trepanning, the removal of a small piece of bone from the skull to relieve pressure on the brain."

"I have heard of that but . . ."

She glanced over at him and saw that he looked very grim. "English doctors are familiar with this?"

"Some may be, although I don't think any of them actually perform such a procedure. It's difficult to imagine anyone doing so."

"Elena is very skilled at it."

"You mean she's actually done it before?"

"Yes, a few times."

"That's extraordinary," he said. "But then, so is everything about Akora."

She turned away for a moment to wave to a cluster of children. They grinned with delight, jumping up and down in their eagerness. "After all your years of imagining us, I hope the reality is not proving disappointing," she said as they continued on.

"On the contrary," he replied, and his eyes were suddenly warm as they moved over her.

She laughed a little, self-consciously. Mellinos was riding behind them and she saw, out of the corner of her eye, that he stiffened and looked at her disapprovingly. Kassandra repressed a sigh. She supposed the tradition-bound counselor believed he should be beside her rather than that honor being given to a *xenos* nobleman. But Royce was a member of her family through marriage, and not even Mellinos could criticize her for being escorted by a male relative.

The closest of the olive groves lay only a few miles beyond Ilius. The road came up over a rise so that before they saw the trees, they saw a sea of white blossoms unfolding before them.

As they rode down into the grove, the trees rose around them. They were widely spaced so as to assure sufficient sunlight, but even so the sight was startling.

"This is one of the oldest groves on Akora," Kassandra said softly. She glanced around, looking at the trees she had known all her life. Over there she saw the concourse between ranks of trees where she and Alex had played tag on summer days while the young Atreus accompanied their grandfather, who was then Vanax, during the prayers. And there, under that very old, immense tree, she and her mother had sat only a few years before, talking of the years to come, the dreams they both had. How often she had come here, how easily she had presumed what had been for so long would always be.

"I should think so," Royce said. He was looking around carefully, absorbing the sight of trees in some cases fully forty feet high in thick bloom. Their trunks were vast, gnarled and twisted. Leathery, lance-shaped leaves glowed green on the side facing the sun, silver underneath. "I have seen olive groves in Greece and the Levant, but they do not look like this."

Kassandra, who had been to neither place, asked, "How do they look?"

"More haphazard, some trees in bloom, others not, none bearing so thickly as the least of these."

The farmers were coming out to meet them. Kassandra drew rein and began to dismount. Before she could do so, Royce threw a leg over his horse, slipped easily to the ground and held out his arms to her. She went into them readily but stepped apart at once, too aware of how great the temptation was to do otherwise.

They were greeted with eager smiles and a palpable sense of relief. She was suddenly very glad that she had come.

Polydorus presented several of the local people. Kassandra spoke with them, exchanging the usual courtesies, only to break off suddenly when she saw Royce bend down, take a handful of dirt and rub it between his fingers thoughtfully.

When he noticed that she and the others were watching, he said, "It's good earth. Sweet, moist." He rose, dusting off his hands, and glanced around. "What kind of irrigation do you use?"

That was all that was needed. At once, the local people were vying with each other to explain where the ditches were and the sluices, how they were managed and maintained, when the first of them had been laid down — in dim memory — how rarely the supply of water failed and what was done when it did. Royce listened intently, nodding from time to time, injecting a word or two, but mostly just attending to what was said. Finally, he remarked, "We irrigate at Hawkforte using a system begun by my ancestor who gave his name to the place, but regularly updated. I have never understood why others have been so slow to take up the practice, but it does require great care."

Polydorus nodded, a pleasant man, round-faced, bright-eyed, at home on the land. "Even a year or two of neglect can destroy an irrigation system. The ditches collapse, the sluices deteriorate. It takes constant vigilance."

"It does," Royce agreed. "Of course, then there's the matter of fertilizer."

Kassandra pressed her lips together to restrain a smile. Her English gentleman, he who moved so easily amid the highest reaches of the Court, was a farmer at heart. Every step he took, everywhere his eye turned, his easy rapport with the country folk, all spoke to it.

"I had no idea the *xenos* cared about such matters," Mellinos murmured. He stepped carefully, unwilling to dirty his robes.

"The *xenos*," Kassandra replied, "is lord of a vast estate in England. His family has cared for that land for almost a thousand years. Obviously, it is very close to his heart."

"Then he will want to return there," the counselor observed and smiled at her sudden look of consternation.

They gathered at a makeshift altar for the prayers. A table had been carried out into the orchards, draped in white linen and set with a bowl of flowers. Incense was lit and the prayers said. Kassandra had little to do save for being present, but toward the end, she stepped forward as tradition required, took the silver ewer of water from the priestess, and poured it carefully into the ground. As she did so, she recited the ancient admonition spoken by her ancestors back into the far distant past.

"Give to us as you will, take from us as you will, Mother of us all. Let your blessings shine upon us who are your children."

Scarcely had she finished than the local people gathered round to express their gratitude and bring out refreshments. More tables were set up, a group of musicians struck up a soft tune on drum, lute and harp, and wine flowed. The mood was subdued, no doubt because of fears about Atreus, but even Mellinos unbent as bread was broken and dipped in the golden-green oil of the previous year's olive pressing.

Tasting a bit of goat cheese pressed on him by a smiling old woman, Royce looked for Kassandra. He saw her in the center of a circle of women, some young, some old, most in between. She was talking with them and smiling.

She hid behind smiles, he thought. Not always, for there were times when her smiles were completely genuine, but too often, and especially of late, she hid.

Or more correctly, she was hiding something.

He tried to push away the thought but it proved difficult to dislodge. He wanted, needed, to believe in the honesty between them but doubt was creeping into his mind. Perhaps that was his failing, not hers. He was too accustomed to the intrigues of the English Court, the false promises and betrayals, the constant maneuvering for power at all cost.

Akora was different, not simpler, it would be a mistake to think that, for it was a very old and complex society. Perhaps it was that people seemed to share more — ideals, beliefs, values, even wealth were all held much more in common. But not power, he reminded himself, at least not enough to satisfy the followers of Helios.

He looked around the venerable orchard, beyond the people to the roads and hills. They were out in the open, an easy target for an enemy who had dared to come into the very heart of Ilius. And yet, he had to admit that anyone coming toward them would be seen immediately. Kassandra had refused guards but there were many sturdy young men among the local people who looked as though they had undergone the usual warrior training. Royce did not doubt they would fight fiercely to protect her.

Perhaps she had not been mistaken to come here. Perhaps she was hiding nothing at all.

Perhaps he was just so in love with her that his normally good sense had flown away like so much thistledown.

Love. He took a swallow of the wine handed to him and reassured himself that he could deal with the situation. He had always known that love existed, that it was real and a force to be reckoned with. His parents were proof of that, but more lately he had seen the same phenomenon with Joanna and Alex. Truth be told, he had wished from time to time that he might experience it himself, not that he really expected to, for it seemed damnably rare. Yet here it was, clear and unavoidable.

He loved her. Well, of course he did. She was a very easy woman to love — beautiful, passionate, courageous. No, that wasn't true. He wanted truth from her? He had to give it himself.

There was nothing easy about her. What he had dreamed of in the innocent days of youth was commonplace to her and, he realized, the same was true in reverse. In a very real sense, they were dreams to each other. Could dreams become reality?

But she was more, so much more. She was a princess, daughter of an ancient line, bred to lead and to rule. Wasn't that evident in the way she had stepped forward to take her brother's place, insomuch as anyone could?

The Atreides.

A new idea for Akora and for him.

If Atreus died, Alex would come home but would he become Vanax? Not necessarily. Alex was honorable to the bone. He might well recognize that his sister had a special relationship with Akora that he himself could not equal.

Kassandra was as much a child of duty as was Royce himself. She would never put her own wishes above the good of Akora.

Please God and all the heavens, let Atreus live and not only for the sake of the man himself or his kingdom. He grimaced, startled by that purely selfish wish even as he realized it was wildly unlike him.

Did love make one selfish? Perhaps, but he would offer no apology for it. He wanted Kassandra safe and free to live her own life . . . with him.

The wine was cool and tart on his tongue. He drank again and watched her, a woman of extraordinary grace, holding out her hands to the women on either side, who joined with her and began to dance, slowly at first, then more quickly, dancing beneath the sun filtering through spreading branches of the ancient olive trees. Some of the women were very old and the pace was kept gentle for them. They danced with purpose and with dignity, but also with joy. It was there in their lined faces, in the movements of their bodies that seemed to recall other times, other pleasures. The younger women smiled, but he sensed they were all more restrained than they would have been ordinarily because of the Vanax and the shadow that hung over them. Yet still they danced, as they must have for untold generations there in the olive orchard. Dancing despite pain and grief, dancing because the day was golden and tomorrow would come.

The men joined them. They formed an outer circle around the women, hands held high. They moved with strength and power, with pride and certainty. And they called to Royce to dance with them.

He went, he supposed because of the wine, and found to his surprise that he knew the steps. As though he had danced like this somewhere, sometime, in distant memory. But not here, not on this land. At Hawkforte, where his heart lay.

The drums beat faster, the lute soared higher, the notes of the harp rose plaintively to the heavens. A few stray white blossoms shaken loose by the breeze drifted over them.

Kassandra turned her head, away from the circle of women, and met his gaze.

They rode home into the setting sun that turned the whitewashed walls of Ilius to crimson-gold. Sida met them shortly after they dismounted with news that Atreus slept peacefully and Elena was satisfied to wait at least a little while longer.

Kassandra felt relief seep through her so profound she had to imagine steel in her spine to keep herself upright. She was still very far from done.

"Mellinos," she said, pretending not to notice how the counselor winced when he dismounted, "you will join us at dinner, will you not?"

"Dinner, Princess? I had rather thought . . . given the activity of the day . . ."

"Dinner," Kassandra repeated firmly. "Ah, Troizus, I thought you would be about. Come as well. We will eat oysters and talk of old times."

"Old times," the sag-faced counselor murmured. He shifted his eyes from her to Royce and back again. "You are too young to have had any old times, Atreides."

She laughed and swept them all into the palace. Over her shoulder, she said, "Dinner, but do not worry, we will not linger late."

They did not, although they did eat oysters as the Atreides had declared, on half-shells set on beds of salt-encrusted ice. With them came small, sweet shrimp in a sauce Royce could not identify but found delectable, a salad of tangy radishes and fragrant greens, and many other things, all accompanied by wine he thought tasted of sunshine.

They talked — he was not sure of what — history and legend, intertwining. At one point, he heard himself saying, "Arthur was real, I am sure of it. His time is dark, much is lost, but the memory of the man himself is too great to be mere myth."

"A hero arises," Mellinos murmured and helped himself to more wine. "It is ever so in the most dangerous of days." He blinked owlishly, because of the wine and the long day, and looked at Kassandra as though her presence surprised him. "A hero . . . or . . ."

"A heroine," Troizus said. He raised his goblet in salute. "Isn't that what you were going to say, old friend? A heroine is as good as a hero, don't you think?"

"I don't know," Mellinos admitted. "It is different."

Troizus nodded, raised cup to lip again but, Royce noticed, did not swallow. "This is a time for difference," the counselor said. "We stand on the edge of a new world."

"Heaven preserve us," Mellinos muttered and rose with some difficulty. He sketched an inebriated bow. "Princess, I must bid you good night before I disgrace myself."

She smiled, a real smile that lit her eyes, and held out a hand to him. "Never could you do that, Counselor. Your honor is your armor."

He blinked and returned her smile with his own. "The first of the Atreides said that. Your family —" He hesitated, still holding her hand, and said, "You have never failed us."

"We are only men and women," she said, "as capable of error as all the rest. Yet here, in this place, we seem called to something higher."

"The Fates have favored all of us here on Akora," Mellinos said, "and the Atreides above all. Pray they do not withdraw their favor now."

He went, with dignity, leaving behind him a pool of silence into which Troizus said, "He has always been a tad superstitious, for all that he is my good friend."

Kassandra raised an eyebrow. "Really? I see no rabbits' feet dangling from him."

"Oh, nothing so obvious, but he believes in destiny as though it were a real force to be reckoned with."

"And you do not?" Royce asked.

"I believe in chance, not design. A wise man seizes the opportunities that come his way." He set down his cup and the liquid in it flashed in the light of the torches. Still full, Royce noted, and wondered at a man who would not drink sunshine. "I will bid you good night as well, Atreides," Troizus said. "The moon rides high and I am for my bed."

When he was gone, Kassandra tipped back her own goblet and drank. Her hand shook just a little as she set the empty cup down.

"I would like to see Atreus before I retire," she said and held out a hand. Her smile was weary but of such beguiling sweetness that he felt stabbed by it.

They went together into the silent room where Elena sat beside the bed, keeping watch. Near her, on a pallet on the floor, Brianna slept but fitfully.

"He is far away," the healer said, "but the cord that links him to us remains strong."

Kassandra stared at her brother, pale against the damask sheets. "How long?" she asked.

"I don't know," Elena answered honestly. "A few days, a week perhaps, not more than that. He must return or we must act."

A while longer they lingered, watching the silent rise and fall of Atreus's breathing. Finally, a sigh escaped Kassandra. She bent and surprised Elena by kissing her very lightly on the cheek. "We all rely on you," she said, "and you have never failed anyone. Remember that and be easier in your heart."

The healer blinked and clasped her hand.

A short while later, Royce escorted Kassandra to her quarters. At the door, he stopped. It was late and all around them the palace was very quiet. Nothing stirred in sight or hearing. He thought of how soon the sun would rise and bring with it all the demands of the day, pressing down upon her. "You need to rest."

"I need . . ." She did not finish but only held out her hand to him as she walked backward into the room, gilded in moonlight.

Chapter
FOURTEEN

Three days . . . of olive groves, incense, prayers and wine. Of vigils beside Atreus's bed and murmured consultations with Elena. Of time stretching out and slowing down in the way it often did just before leaping forward explosively.

And in between, the nights. Stolen time, Kassandra thought, and refused to harbor guilt. Each instant was precious to her.

In the brilliance of the days, as she moved through duties that swiftly became routine, she found herself suddenly remembering a moment, a touch, a whispered word cherished in the night.

Royce was, she decided, the sort of lover women dream of. In the velvet hours, in his arms, she found a different world, one without pain or fear, without loneliness or dread, a world in which nothing existed except love and the joy it bestowed.

She who had always delighted in the dawn now woke to it with regret.

Atreus did not improve nor did he weaken.

He simply continued, unknowing and un-moving. Soon, very soon, a decision would have to be made. She dreaded the thought even as she knew it could not be avoided.

Often, her mind sprang out across the sea to thoughts of her other brother. Word was speeding to Alex by fast ship but, even so, it would still be days before he knew, and longer still before he could return. Assuming, of course, that developments in England allowed him to do so.

Rumors circulated along the quays, up the roads leading from the harbor, past the great Lion's Gate before the palace and into its hal-lowed chambers. Rumors born on the wind of great events happening beyond Akora.

It was said the Emperor Napoleon, he who sought to bestride the world like the ancient Colossus, had turned his sights toward the vast plains of Russia. Kassandra found that difficult to believe, for that land, though very distant from Akora, was well known to her people. Surely, only a fool or a madman would believe it ripe for conquest. Was Napoleon one or the other, or merely made complacent by what must seem the habit of victory? They would know soon enough.

Other stories were also told, rumors of war between England and America where former colonists nurtured the upstart notion that having won their liberty in fire and blood, it should be respected. Instead, they found their vessels boarded, their seamen impressed, their fishing rights violated, and themselves mocked as weak and helpless. Andrew, who had lived among them, believed they were neither.

"Disorganized," he said when the talk at dinner turned in that direction, "and much in love with the sound of their own voices, for every man must have his say. But they have tasted freedom and they will not surrender it easily."

"I pray it does not come to that," Phaedra remarked. She was eating a little more than she had been, but still looked worn and pale. "So much pain and all for what? Life is far too short to be wasted in such a way."

As her husband gazed at her with gentle concern and Kassandra fumbled for some words of comfort, it was Royce who said, "But the contributions of a life spent upholding what one truly believes in can have consequences far into the future, don't you think? Like the ripples of a stone thrown into a pond."

He was a caring man, Kassandra thought as she recalled that moment when her mother's eyes lightened just a little, and one who saw perhaps too much. But he had been speaking of Atreus, not of herself. She had no reason to believe he sensed the dark forces driving her.

Three days. On the morning of the fourth, she left the room in which her bed still held the heat of night's passion and went directly to the courtyard. Royce and assorted members of the

Court awaited her. Mellinos had begged off and Troizus was occupied in Ilius, as usual, but there were some two dozen in the party. She worried it might be too many for her purposes but had not sought to discourage anyone lest she raise questions she did not wish to answer.

They proceeded down the winding road to the harbor, greeted along the way by citizens of Ilius. Kassandra thought the mood in the city was still subdued as all awaited word of the Vanax, but in many ways life was returning to normal. But then it had to. Children had to be fed, crops brought in, businesses run. Perhaps there was comfort in that.

The harbor glistened a dark and regal blue beneath the morning sun. Beside the stone pier, a bull-headed vessel awaited them. The party boarded and very shortly the anchor was raised. A freshening wind filled their sails, carrying them out onto the Inland Sea.

Coming out of the port of Ilius, they passed many other vessels. Seeing the pennant of the Atreides family flying from the center mast, the sailors raised their oars in salute. Kassandra stood on the bow, waving in acknowledgment until her arm ached and her smile felt frozen.

Finally, when they were far enough beyond the harbor that there were no longer any vessels near them, she relaxed, if only a little. A small sigh escaped her.

"Beautiful day," Royce said. She turned to find him nearby, lounging against the railing.

He wore the kilt of an Akoran warrior, which, she had to say, suited him extremely well. It also allowed him to blend in, at least a little, with the rest of those accompanying her.

"It is that," she agreed.

"Leios," he said, naming the island that was their destination. "Place of Plains. That's what it means, isn't it?"

She nodded. "Leios is about the same size as the island of Kallimos we have just left. But it is very different. Instead of the hills found on Kallimos, most of Leios is a flat plain."

"It's part of the original Akora, before the explosion?"

"Yes, along with Kallimos. But both still suffered very severely from the eruption. So far as we can tell, the major magma flows were in the direction of Leios, which was covered by lava. Very little in the way of artifacts has ever been found there."

"But the land is fertile?"

"Very. We grow wheat, rye and barley there, but mainly Leios is famous for its horses."

His gaze brightened. "We raise horses at Hawkforte."

"So Joanna has told me." Softly, she asked, "You miss it, don't you?"

"Hawkforte? Yes, I suppose I do but don't read too much into that. I miss Hawkforte when I'm in London, which is no great distance away. In fact, the only time I don't miss home is when I'm actually there." The wind ruffled his hair. He smoothed it down absently. "You must feel the same way about Akora."

She was distracted, staring at the thick strands of gold she remembered stroking in the night, recalling how silken they felt compared to the roughness of his unshaven cheeks in the same hours, against her breasts and thighs.

"What? Oh, yes, I suppose, but truth be told, I always dreamed of leaving Akora."

"As you have done."

"I mean for longer, farther . . . not that it matters." How foolish of her to think of that. She was bound to the land, linked by blood and fate. For her, there would be no wider world.

"That's something I've always admired about women."

"What is?"

"The strength they have to leave all that is familiar and make a place for themselves in a new land. If we ever really thought about it, we'd realize that women have done that far more than have men. After all, it's usually women who are given in marriage, sent off to live with the clan over the next hill or considerably farther away." He looked out across the water, squinting in the brightness. "What is it Ruth said? Your people will be my people? It took courage to say that."

"Ruth of the Bible? I have read that story. It is very moving."

"The Bible is full of strong women."

He flexed broad shoulders and watched the

dolphins who had appeared beside the vessel, darting in its wake, leaping with playful abandon. Among them glided small fish, only a foot or two long, with winglike fins, who rose from the water to speed over the surface as though in flight.

"Fish who fly?" he asked with a smile.

"Only one of Akora's wonders. Look there, to starboard, you see how the color of the water changes from deep blue to a much lighter green?"

When he nodded, Kassandra said, "If you dive there, you will find a shallow reef and in among it, the ruins of what appears to have been a good-sized house. Somehow, it escaped complete destruction even as the waters closed over it. People have retrieved small objects within what is left of the rooms: a few statues, shards of pottery, even some fragments of tile mosaics."

"No trace of the inhabitants?"

"No, but perhaps they escaped."

They both knew that was unlikely. The fate that had overtaken most of Akora had been inexorable.

"Do you think they had any warning at all?" Royce asked.

"Those who survived left records indicating that the explosion was preceded by ground tremors and the venting of steam that went on for some time. They had seen the same and worse from the mountain before, so many were not alarmed."

"They thought themselves safe?"

"I imagine they did, but then people always want to believe that, don't they? They want to go about their everyday lives, tend to their ordinary concerns, and not look very far beyond."

"Even in the shadow of a volcano?"

"Even then." She pointed off into the distance. "I'm not sure, but I think there may be a squid out there."

Royce looked where she directed, studying the dark shape that rippled beneath the water. "Big," he murmured.

"Fifteen, perhaps twenty feet long. See how the dolphins are veering away and the flying fish with them? They don't really fear the squid; he doesn't prey on them, but they give him wide berth all the same."

"I'd do the same."

"Squid is a delicacy," Kassandra said. "But we do not trouble the largest among them."

"Too dangerous?"

"Too tough — the meat, that is. They aren't worth the effort."

He laughed at that and looked at her with such warmth that she thought it prudent to glance away, which she did manage to do if only very briefly. His gaze drew her back and she found herself looking once again into green-gold eyes that saw far too well.

"I should have realized you Akorans would not turn from any challenge," he said.

"Even so, we pick our battles."

"Yes, I rather think you do."

Silence drew out between them. She did not want to contemplate what he meant. They were bound for Leios, Place of Plains, on a day of shimmering loveliness.

What would be, would be.

"No olives this time?" Royce asked.

She shook her head but did not look at him again, keeping her eyes on the water cleaved by the fast-moving hull. "Not on Leios. In fact, it would be a good idea not to mention olives. The people there eat olives, of course, and use the oil, but they believe the growing of grains far surpasses the tending of orchards."

"So there is rivalry between Kallimos and Leios?"

"Of a sort, I suppose, but nothing of any seriousness. It is too bad Brianna couldn't come with us."

"Her family is from Leios?"

"Yes, and I'm sure they miss her, but she will not leave Elena." Not at so harsh and difficult a time when the healer might well be facing the greatest challenge of her life.

"Kassandra, I truly believe Atreus will recover."

He meant the words as comfort and she accepted them as such. When he moved closer and put an arm lightly around her waist, she made no effort to draw apart. Let those who saw think what they would. For this little space of time, she was content to be not the Atreides but simply a woman.

Your people will be my people. How she longed to make so heartfelt a declaration. How bitter was the knowledge that she could not.

At mid-afternoon, a dark smudge appeared off toward the north. Kassandra said nothing of it and hoped Royce would not notice. For a time, she thought he had not, but he said, "Is that Deimatos?"

She pretended to look then, as though for the first time, and knew he was not fooled. "It is."

He was silent for several minutes as she agonized, wondering what horrible recollections of his captivity on that island were tormenting him. Finally, he said, "I thought it was larger."

"Experience can be deceptive."

"So I see. Marcellus's men are still there?"

"I believe they left today. They sent word ahead that they have found no trace of sulfur mining on the island."

"If the sulfur is in crystals left by the volcano, it wouldn't really be necessary to mine for it, would it?"

"I suppose not. Such crystals could be found lying on the ground or, more commonly, in caves. But there is no sign of anyone living or working on the island."

He stared off at the distant rise of the island. "You know that some of the men loyal to Deilos were never captured."

"I know that is a possibility but since we were never sure exactly how many men he had, we cannot know if any are still at large. Even so, without Deilos himself to lead them, it is not likely they could accomplish anything."

"You are assuming that Deilos is dead."

"No," she said softly. The dark memory of her vision in the nursery rose within her, like the long rolls of thunder that warn of an approaching storm. "I'm not assuming anything." Except that she would do her duty.

"That is just as well. It would take weeks, if not months, to properly search all the caves beneath Deimatos. And even then, we might find nothing. If he lives, he could be on Tarbos or Phobos. They, too, are uninhabited and riddled with caves."

"If he lives," she said, "he may not even be on Akora." But she knew otherwise, or at least she thought she did. The sun went behind a cloud just then, making her shiver.

Leios came upon them by mid-afternoon. To Royce's eyes, the flat, undulating island seemed to rush up out of the horizon. He stared at the verdant fields waving green and gold in the gentle breeze, and felt the brush of home.

To the west, a promontory etched with golden beaches reached out into the sea. Beyond, the land curled inward, offering the gentle protection of a bay where a harbor nestled. It was far smaller than Ilius, comprising only half-a-dozen piers and what looked like a warehouse or two. Royce could see buildings beyond, but as the land was flat, it was impossible to judge how far the town might extend.

The crowd gathered on the piers was more easily judged. He guessed there were several thousand people with more still streaming in. They waved as they saw the vessel. As it drew nearer still, a cheer went up.

Kassandra went ashore a short time later to be welcomed by the elders of Leios, accompanied by the twin brothers who had come in first and second in the javelin competition at the Games. One had suffered minor injuries in the explosion but was recovering quickly. The other was unharmed. They greeted Royce with easy camaraderie and bowed respectfully to the Atreides.

"Our prayers for the Vanax are constant," one of the elders said. "Night and day, without surcease, we entreat Creation to preserve him for us."

"I thank you," Kassandra said softly. She looked at the men and women around her, old and young, people of pride and dignity but counting on her to say something, anything that would relieve some measure of their concern.

She sympathized but she could not lie to them.

"My royal brother needs your prayers," she said, "as do I. We have all been thrust into a situation where history and tradition cannot guide us. We can count only on each other and our own best judgment."

They nodded at the wisdom of this and the honesty. She was, Royce thought, as they had already known she would be. Or at least, as they hoped. She did not disappoint them, but then it was not in her nature to ever do so.

In the fields, where he looked with a farmer's eye at the ripening strands of wheat, she said the prayers and made the offerings as she had already so many times before. But her attention was no less nor was her sincerity. In some way, each time was the first for her.

Afterward, they enjoyed a simple country dinner amid rolling pastures not far from the harbor. Tents were set up where they would spend the night, there being little accommodation nearby. He already knew the population of Leios was close to that of Kallimos but it was far more spread out. Even so, it seemed many had journeyed considerable distance to welcome the daughter of the family that had served them for so long.

Her tent was set a little apart from the others but otherwise was much the same as the rest. He supposed this would be the case even if it was occupied by the Vanax himself. Very little attention seemed given to rank on Akora. Certainly, there was none of the elaborate ceremony and ritual that characterized Prinny's Court. For that, Royce was grateful, for he had little patience with such vanities.

All the same, he could think of one sensible

precaution commonplace in England but lacking here. Prinny went nowhere without guards. Kassandra, by contrast, had none. For days, he had told himself it did not matter because she was surrounded by loyal Akorans who would never let her come to any harm. But night was coming on swiftly. Her tent was far enough away that she could call for help without necessarily being heard.

Of course, she might also cry out for pleasanter reasons.

Decided, he moved through the thickening dusk, drew aside the tent flap, and stepped inside.

Kassandra was just finishing her bath. It was an indulgence to cart about the canvas-and-wood tub that had to be filled laboriously with buckets when she could have managed with just a basin. She admitted as much, but savored the bath all the same. After the long day, and the days before it, she needed the calming peace of hot water and blessed quiet.

She would have lingered longer but the water cooled rapidly. Rising, she reached for the towel she had left on a stool beside the tub.

Only to have it handed to her.

She gasped and whirled around to find Royce surveying her with obvious appreciation. "You were very far away," he said.

"I was not!" Grasping the towel, she wrapped it around herself even as she felt ridiculous for doing so. It was hardly as though the man had not seen her naked before. Seen, touched, tasted, savored . . . Never mind about that now.

"You walk too quietly," she accused.

"A hideous failing," he replied, looking pleased with himself. He glanced around the tent. "Cozy."

"Comfortable, as I am sure yours is."

He raised a brow and with it, beckoned a blush. She was not a hypocrite. He had shared her bed for four nights and were they in the palace, he would be sharing it again. It was just that they were out in public, as it were, with none of the privacy to be found in her own quarters.

But she had not moved away from him on the ship and, truth be told, she did not want to do so now.

"You are caught," he said. At her puzzled look, he added, "On the horns of propriety. It's an awkward place to be."

"I'm not trying to conceal anything."

"I realize that, but you are trying not to make a display of what has happened between us, not force people to deal with it at a time when they are deeply concerned and anxious."

"Yes," she said on a breath of relief. He truly did understand. "That's it exactly."

"Kassandra . . ." He reached out a hand but let it fall without touching her. "Whatever lies ahead of us, my concern right now is for your safety. You are alone here in this tent and it is set a little apart from the others. If you like, I'll sleep outside but I'm not leaving you by yourself tonight."

She had not thought of that, had not considered that he would be worried about her in such a situation. Belatedly, she realized that her own vision had blinded her. She knew this was not the time or place, but he knew nothing of the sort.

And he wanted to protect her. He really did.

Tears stung her eyes but she would not let them fall. The towel was a different matter. She went to him without it.

He moved, his lips trailing down the silken line of her back to the exquisitely sensitive spot at the very base of her spine. There he lingered, blowing lightly on her skin, touching her with just the very tip of his tongue.

She cried out softly and writhed against the mattress, trying to turn, but that he would not permit. He held her firmly, his hands clasping her hips, pressing her down. With his legs, he straddled her. She could only turn her head, her eyes smoky with passion's fire.

"Enough," she murmured, half-plea, half-demand.

"I think not." His own voice sounded harsh in his ears but he could not help that. His control was strained to the limit. Hunger for her was a roar within him, eclipsing almost all else save for his utter and absolute determination.

She would remember this night when the dark thoughts he suspected came too often were upon her. She would remember it when she felt torn between her desires as a woman and her duties as an Atreides. Moment to moment, heartbeat to heartbeat, she would remember him, them, and everything they shared. He would damn well make sure of it.

Still holding her, he pressed lightly along the curve of her buttocks, letting his fingers curl into the apex of her thighs. She jerked beneath him and he thought, though he couldn't be sure, that the pillows muffled a curse.

"So soft," he murmured, "so smooth and sleek, so perfectly formed. You really are exquisite." As he spoke, he slid a finger into her cleft, stroking just lightly enough to be intensely arousing without offering any hope of release.

"Damn you!" This time he heard her quite well and would have chuckled had he any breath. Still restraining her, gently but implacably, he stroked her again, more insistently, and was rewarded with a moan.

The sound of his own heartbeat thundered in his ears, but still he held back. Again and again, he touched her lightly, then altered the rhythm and pressed hard for just an instant. Her cries came one after another but they only spurred him on. Not until a red mist moved before his eyes did he lift her, push her legs farther apart, and with a single, driving thrust, bury himself in her.

Her climax was instant and deep. It drew from him his own, bone-jarring in its intensity but still not enough. When she would have moved then, he pushed the fragrant ebony hair away from her neck and sank his teeth lightly into her nape.

"No," he ordered and reached round, cupping her breasts, his thumbs rubbing over her distended nipples.

"Royce . . . I can't . . ."

"You can, you will, we both will." Already, he was hard again and becoming more so by the moment. He pulled her up farther, bowing her beneath him, and thrust again and again until the world shattered.

When he finally slumped away from her, they lay for some little time entwined in each other and the bed covers. Were the circumstances different, he easily could have drifted into sleep, but a strange sort of desperation seemed to grip him. Nor was Kassandra immune to it. She rose above him, a pale vision of loveliness, and tipped back her head so that her hair fell over her buttocks, onto his thighs.

"Were you making a point?" she asked, gazing down at him.

He ran a hand lazily from the damp, dark curls between her legs up over her smooth belly, savoring the creamy warmth of her skin and the quiver that ran through her even as she tried to remain impassive. "Was I? I think the question really is am I?"

At her startled look, he lifted her, moved slightly, and slid her down his hard, thick length.

"*Royce* . . ."

That note of amazement in her voice was really quite pleasing, he thought, just as it became impossible to think at all.

Chapter
FIFTEEN

When Kassandra awoke, she was alone in the tent. She lay for a few moments, staring up at the ceiling as she tried to order her thoughts.

Had it been a dream or had she . . . had Royce . . . had they? . . . Well, yes, they had if the dual sensations of utter satisfaction and lingering tenderness were any indication.

Cautiously, she rose from the bed and dropped a simple white sheath over her head. Ignoring the sudden tingling of her nipples as the fabric touched them, she stuck her head outside the tent in the hope of finding hot water.

It was there, in a covered bucket set in the sun. With a sigh of relief, she took the water back into the tent, filled a basin, and washed. When she was properly dressed and had brushed her hair until it gleamed, she could think of no further reason to linger. Assuming an expression she hoped revealed nothing of the turmoil of her thoughts, she went out to face the day.

The elders of Leios and many others had remained with the royal party overnight. They were clustered by an open tent from which breakfast was being served. Kassandra exchanged greetings, accepted a cup of milk laced with honey, and tried hard not to look around for Royce. Just as she was wondering where he could have gone off to, he appeared in the company of the twin javelin throwers. Seeing her, he stopped, and for a moment simply looked. Whatever he saw must have pleased him, for his smile was slow, devastating and utterly male.

But his address, when he spoke to her, was entirely proper. "Good morning, Your Highness. I trust you slept well."

Two could play this game, she decided. He looked just smug enough for her to want to take him down a notch or two. "Alas, I did not. There was something rather annoying and persistent in my tent . . . an insect of some sort, I think."

Royce had just taken a swallow of lemonade. He coughed and cleared his throat. "An insect? Really? Are you sure it wasn't something larger?" He leaned a little closer so that only she could hear him. "Considerably larger, Princess, and very . . . attentive, shall we say?"

Fighting a fierce blush, she pretended great interest in the sweet breads and fruits set out on wooden platters. "I really can't recall," she murmured, and endured Royce's chuckle with as good grace as she could muster.

They left a short time later, journeying inland on horseback along the winding roads cut between fields of grain. The day was as golden as the harvest promised to be. Kassandra's self-consciousness fell away as she took simple pleasure in Royce's company.

Several times over the course of the morning and afternoon, they stopped to bless the crops and meet with local folk. Always their reception was the same — warm, appreciative, with expressions of concern for Atreus and sympathy for his family.

That night their tents were pitched near a lake surrounded by fragrant pines. Once again, Kassandra did not sleep alone.

The next day, they reached the fabled horse plains of Leios.

"The ground here is thick with lime," Kassandra said as they rode along, the hooves of their mounts raising little puffs of dust. "Grass that grows in such regions seems to endow the horses who feed upon it with unusually strong bones."

Royce nodded. He looked out over the fields, watching the magnificent animals that galloped across them or grazed quietly. Somewhere deep within him, the ever-present chord of home reverberated. "It is the same at Hawkforte and in other places, Ireland for instance. Always, where there is lime, there are strong horses."

"Leios provides horses to all of Akora. It is said that while the bull god is worshipped elsewhere, here the horse god reigns supreme."

"Are the two really different?"

She shook her head, appreciating his perceptiveness. "People need something familiar to help them understand what they are part of, yet which is also so much more than themselves."

A short time later, they drew rein in the center courtyard of a good-sized estate. A man hurried out to meet them. Royce recognized him as Goran, one of the counselors who had returned to his own lands to be with his people as they grappled with the enormity of what had happened.

"Princess," Goran said as he came forward, "your presence honors us. I trust your journey has not been difficult?"

"Not at all," Kassandra replied as she dismounted and smiled at the slim, balding counselor. "And you, Goran, do you fare well?"

He shrugged and spread his hands almost apologetically. "I confess to relief at being beside my own hearth but I feel torn as well, thinking I should be in Ilius instead."

"You will know when it is time to return there," Kassandra said with confidence. Atreus had always described Goran as "solid" and she had been given no reason to disagree.

"The Vanax," he said gently, "we hear there is no change."

"Not for the better but neither for the worse. He is in the best of hands."

"Oh, I have no doubt of that, none at all. Elena saved my dear wife during a most difficult childbirth. I don't know what we would have done without her." For a moment, Goran looked lost in the recollection of that brush with tragedy but recovered himself quickly. "Well, then, come along, if you will. I have a trio of new colts to show off."

One had been born only a few hours before and remained nestled beside his mother in a straw-lined stall. But the other two were old enough, at a few days of age, to be out in a paddock. There they took tentative little runs on spindly but strong legs, darting about in small bursts but never straying far from their dams, who eyed them with patient tolerance.

"See that one there," Royce said, pointing to the colt with a white blaze on his forehead. "He reminds me of a colt born last year at Hawkforte, a stallion who looks to have real promise."

"Will you race him?" Goran asked.

"Probably, but only for a year or two, then he'll go to stud."

The counselor chuckled. "Not a bad life."

"I should say not," Royce said and laughed in turn.

Kassandra was content to allow them their male moment and said nothing.

"Are there any wild horses in England?" Goran asked later as they were walking back toward the main house where they were to stay the night.

"Very few," Royce said, "although some are

said to remain in Scotland and parts of Ireland. Why do you ask?"

"There are wild horses here on Leios. We chose long ago to leave them so, but we watch them and when we see one of particular strength and courage, we let him come to our mares."

"A wise idea."

"I had a notion you would approve," Goran said and smiled.

That night, Kassandra slept alone, or at least she tried to. Goran's home was comfortable but not overly large. There was none of the privacy of the palace and less even than in the tents. She reassured herself, when she retired after dinner, that Royce understood her choice of discretion. Even so, as the hours dragged on and sleep proved elusive, she wondered if she would find any rest at all.

At length, she gave up the effort. She was sleeping nude as always, and donned a shift before leaving the room. It fell only to her mid-thighs but was adequate for modesty's sake. With so much idle time, she had woven her hair into a single thick braid that lay over her shoulder.

The moon was high and surrounded by a halo that shone violet toward the outer edges but changed across the entire spectrum to red on the inside. The nimbus extended in a perfect circle far out across the heavens. So brilliant was its radiance when added to that of the moon itself that, had Kassandra wished, she could easily have read by the light. As it was, the glow cast long, black shadows of trees and buildings across the pale ground. Her own shadow preceded her as she walked out into the small garden Goran's wife lovingly maintained in the atrium at the center of the house.

There she sat on a stone bench and listened to the gurgle of the fountain. The air was perfumed with the scents of jasmine coupled with herbs and sweet grasses. Weariness crept over her but it was not the sort that jangled nerves. Rather, she thought that if she remained in so peaceful a place a little longer, she might be able to return to her room and actually sleep.

She was contemplating doing that when an odd sound nearby caught her attention. She turned, looking over her shoulder, trying to discern the source of the noise. Just as she did so, there was a sudden *woosh* in the air to her right and in the same instant, she felt herself hurtled to the ground.

For the space of several heartbeats, she knew only that something very large and hard was holding her down. A man . . . Instinctively, she began to struggle but stopped almost at once as Royce rasped near her ear, "Be still."

He lay over her, his body entirely covering and protecting her own even as he lifted his head and looked in all directions. She caught a glimpse of him in the brilliant glow of the moon and shuddered inwardly. She *knew* this man, had lain with him, yet at that moment, she understood that he would be a truly terrifying enemy, capable of killing without hesitation or mercy.

"Royce," she said again and touched his arm gently. "I am all right."

He looked down then, into her face. She thought he had not heard her but gradually his expression cleared. He rose, holding her, and still keeping her within the protection of his body, carried her swiftly away from the fountain into the shadows around the edge of the atrium. Pressing her back into the darkness, he said, "Stay here until we know what has happened."

She thought he meant to go and investigate but he had another intent entirely. Without hesitation, he took a step away from her, planted his feet squarely apart, and standing in the silver light of the moon that illumined his features so that they resembled chiseled stone, he called out, *"To the Atreides!"*

Men came from all sides, pouring into the garden. Some were yanking on tunics, others already had their swords drawn. They came swiftly and with purpose, none stumbling or uncertain. Goran was among them, along with his sons, one of whom could not have been more than fourteen. There were older men as well, some really quite old but still ready and willing to answer the call, indeed likely they would be insulted by any suggestion they should do otherwise.

How had he known? she wondered in a tiny space of time before the men surrounded them. Was it because he was a warrior himself and understood that loyal, honorable men will always rally to save a true leader?

Royce said a few quick words and the men fanned out. Torches were brought, turning the atrium as bright as day. Women appeared, a few calling from windows, but most keeping out of the way once they knew the Atreides was unharmed.

Quickly, the red tile that had come very close to striking Kassandra was found. Several of the younger men climbed onto the roof and within minutes, the source of the tile was found.

"Here, Hawk Lord!" one of the men called. "A tile is missing and several others are loose."

Leaving Kassandra with Goran, who was visibly agitated, Royce climbed up to take a look. He returned grim-faced.

"Your roof is in good repair," he said to the counselor.

"It is," their host agreed. "I have never allowed it to be otherwise, but that portion of the roof was newly tiled only this past spring. I am certain it had no defect."

"Even so," Kassandra said soothingly, "it was only a tile and no harm was done. I certainly appreciate everyone's concern but . . . ."

They were not listening to her. At Royce's

order, the men were moving out in groups beyond the atrium, although some stayed behind to guard her, also at his instruction.

"What are they doing?" she asked Goran. "Where are they going?"

He looked at her in surprise, as though she should have known. "To search for the intruder, of course, or intruders." When she still looked puzzled, he said, "The Hawk Lord understands what I told him, that the tile could not have come loose by itself. But someone standing on the roof, or perhaps crouching there, could have accidentally loosened it."

"An intruder . . ." She was about to say there was no evidence of any when she realized how very foolish that would be.

Deilos. She could not know for certain that it was him or even anyone he had sent, but she did know someone had been watching her. A shiver moved down her spine. Instinctively, she wrapped her arms around herself.

No, not someone. Two someones. Royce had reached her far too quickly to allow for coincidence. Even if he also had been unable to sleep and had come out into the garden, she would have seen him . . . but for the fact that he had not wanted her to do so.

He was watching her. For good purpose, she knew, but still the thought was distressing. When the time came, as she was certain it would, she had to be free to act without interference.

She had to be free to die, because in her vision nothing less than that stopped the red serpent from swallowing Akora.

Her stomach clenched as she fought a wave of nausea. By all that was divine, she would not think of that now! Royce was out there, hunting an enemy who might well be the very same man who had already come close to killing him once before.

"Go after him," she urged Goran.

"After the intruder, Atreides?"

"No, after Royce, after the Hawk Lord. He . . . he does not know these lands and I'm sure he would welcome your wise counsel."

Goran was not fooled for an instant. He looked at her gently. "I believe he prefers for me to stay with you, Atreides. That is only right as you are a guest in my house. Your safety is both my honor and my duty. Now if I might escort you back to your quarters?"

It was the sensible thing to do, of course, but the thought of being within four walls for who-knew-how-long before Royce returned was more than she could bear.

"I would rather remain here," she said. When Goran hesitated, she added, "You cannot believe any intruder is still near enough to be a danger to me. But even if he were, I have no doubt you and your household guard would defend me nobly."

The gleam in the counselor's eye made it quite clear he knew she was managing him. He also realized he could not refuse her.

"As you wish, Atreides, but it may be some time before they return."

"I am content to wait," she replied and meant it . . . then.

It was more than twelve hours later, in mid-afternoon, when Royce finally returned. Kassandra did not remain in the garden all that while, although she was there until long after the sun rose. Finally, drooping with fatigue, she allowed herself to be led away by Goran's wife, who tucked her into bed as she would one of her own daughters and stayed with her as she drifted into sleep.

Even then, she slept but fitfully and woke after only a few hours, while there was still more opportunity for her to wait. This she did with varying degrees of patience, worry, and finally, when fear for him banished all her efforts to reassure herself that he would come to no harm, anger.

It was right then that Royce returned.

He found her more or less where he had left her — in the garden. She was dressed in a gown of white silk and her hair was braided with flowers. He had no way of knowing that Goran's wife, the sweet-natured Alla, had done that in an effort to raise Kassandra's spirits. Nor did he comprehend the emotions that had cascaded through her as she awaited him. He saw only that she was beautiful, safe, and *his*.

On that last part, he was absolutely determined. Through the long, frustrating hours of a hunt that proved infuriatingly futile, he had decided there was not going to be any doubt about that. It was all well and good that Kassandra had responsibilities to her people and her land, and that she had the strength to live up to them. He admired that unstintingly and did not hesitate to support her in every possible way.

But it changed nothing. She was his. He had waited his whole life for her and he would allow nothing — absolutely nothing — to come between them. Let Deilos beware, though much good it would do him. The traitor was a dead man, did he but know it, his life measured in mere minutes from the instant he fell into Royce's hands, as he surely would. Long had he contemplated Deilos's reward for keeping him imprisoned and nearly bringing about his own death. Gladly would he have killed him for that alone. But this was different. He would kill Deilos not for himself but in the sure and certain knowledge that by doing so, he removed a danger to Kassandra.

Kassandra who stared at him with an odd gleam in her eyes. She saw before her a man streaked with dirt and sweat, who came to her as from battle. Yet, blessed Fortune, he bore no wounds. No blood touched his skin.

No blood.

The anger in her ebbed away.

"You did not find him," she said. She knew, though she shied from the knowledge, that had he found the enemy, he would have come to her stained with blood.

"I will," he said simply and took hold of her. He did not do it with any particular gentleness and he did not seem to care that he dirtied her gown. He held her hard as though he needed to draw the very breath of her life into himself. Heaven help her, she could not resist. Her body molded to his as naturally as though she had always done so.

"You will come to no harm," he said, and she felt then the tremor that went through him.

Tears clogged her throat. How desperately she wanted him to be right. How clearly she knew he would not be.

She would not think of that now . . .

"Come into the house," she said softly. "You need to bathe and rest."

"I need you," he said, but let her take his hand and lead him inside.

Discretion was forgotten as Kassandra put away all thought of it and turned her attention to Royce. Servants came with food and unguents she requested for the scrapes and bruises she found when she helped him to undress before stepping into the deep tub in the bathing chamber beside her room. He grimaced a little as he did so but remained in good humor so long as she was near. When she returned from speaking with the servants, he glared at her suspiciously.

"What have you there?"

"An ointment. It will not sting."

She had spoken carelessly and regretted it immediately when his glare turned to outraged astonishment.

"You jest," Royce said. "I have no need of any ointment, much less assurance it will not *sting*." He curled his lip when he spoke, then ducked his head under the water and came up throwing droplets in all directions, mainly on her. "Some soap wouldn't go amiss."

"Here." She held out her hand, but not so close that he could take the small round of soap she held. Instead, she said, "You have a broad back indeed but I think I can manage to scrub it."

"I need no nursemaid," he growled but sat up all the same, giving her access.

She knelt beside the tub, wet a sponge, rubbed the soap over it and went to work on his back. It was very broad and about as yielding as a granite wall. Cupping her hands, she poured water over his head and washed his hair. He groaned softly as she dug her fingers into his scalp, prompting her to continue doing so until his head wobbled a bit loosely on his neck.

"Enough," he growled. "I prefer to keep my wits about me."

"Really? You seem willing enough to forgo them from time to time."

He shrugged shoulders honed to steel. "Sheer folly, that and the fact that you make me forget I have any wits to keep."

"It isn't folly," Kassandra said softly. She rinsed his hair and moved around the other side of the tub to kneel in front of him. Water darkened her gown, making it all but transparent in places.

Royce frowned. "Sweet heaven, woman, don't you think you're enough of a temptation as it is?"

"I have no idea what you mean," Kassandra said primly and gave her attention to his chest. When she was done with that, there was the rest of him. His very long legs with the iron-hard muscles bulging in his thighs and calves received particular attention, but so did the soles of his feet and each individual toe.

He groaned again and let his head drop back, but he was smiling when he did it. Quietly, he said, "The whole damn time I was out there, I was thinking about you. Maybe that got in the way of my concentration, I don't know. But we were able to track him a good two miles before we lost the trail."

"Track who?" Kassandra asked, as though she did not know.

"Deilos," he replied emphatically. "I'm sure it's him."

Despite the warmth of the bathing chamber, coldness darted through her. Royce could not know what she had seen and what it meant. He could not. She had been too careful to keep her vision of Deilos and herself hidden. But for all his love of the land and his understanding of it, the Hawk Lord had the spirit of a warrior and the instincts to match. He had knowledge of his own beyond her ken, despite her efforts to understand it.

"How, if you never found him? How can you be sure?"

"I just am." The light in his eyes dared her to contradict him.

When she did not, he was mildly placated but that faded quickly as she made to finish the job. "That's enough," he said quickly. "I'll do the rest."

"Looks as though it will take you awhile," Kassandra remarked. Deliberately, she sought escape in sweet distraction. "I had no idea you'd enjoy having your feet rubbed so much."

"A man can't have any little secrets, can he?" He sounded gruff but he didn't look that way. And he came to join her in the bedroom with admirable swiftness.

Later, lying on sheets damp because Royce had not taken much time to dry himself, Kassandra said, "We must return to Ilius."

"Good idea," he replied. He sounded sleepy, as well he might after two nights with no rest, the hunt for Deilos and the extremely pleasant hour they had just spent. But he was not so drawn into dreams that he did not add, as though to himself, "Lure Deilos there, make it tougher for him to get near you, then finish him off."

As plans went, it was impeccable in its ruthless simplicity. She did not doubt it could succeed admirably well, save that she must not allow it to do so.

She would not think of that now . . .

"Sleep," she murmured, and nestling against him did the same.

Two days later, they sailed back into the harbor of Ilius. As the city neared, Kassandra's hands gripped the deck railing so tightly that her knuckles shone white. She had no news fresher than two days, that being the latest word to have reached Leios before their departure. If Atreus had . . .

She closed her eyes for a moment, opened them again to strain for anything she could see.

If her brother had died, fires would be burning throughout the city. People would be offering up favored possessions, however small, to accompany the Chosen on heaven's path. In the temples, the altar fires would burn night and day as the priests and priestesses did the same. And in the palace . . .

In the palace, no fire would burn, no food be cooked, no water drawn, no lamp lit. There would be only the terrible, wrenching mourning for a life cut short and a people cut adrift.

And then the search, the hope, the prayers as

the rituals were carried out to find the new Chosen. Once that had taken two long years. Often, it took months. Akora did not have years, nor even months. Not with the red serpent waiting.

If her brother was dead . . .

She lifted her eyes to the sky and saw there . . .

White clouds, fluffy like the flax that grew in high summer's fields. Golden sun bathing the city in its radiance. And here and there, scattered throughout the city, the thin white tendrils of very normal, very blessed cooking fires.

Nothing more.

Relief rose in her so profound she could not breathe.

"He lives," she gasped and saw by Royce's smile that he, too, knew.

"He lives," she said again and laughed a little through her joyful tears.

Barely had the ship docked than they hastened together to the palace. Andrew met them as soon as they entered the family quarters.

"We would have come to the quay," he said after he had embraced his daughter and shaken hands with Royce, "but Phaedra cannot bear to leave him."

"How is he?" Kassandra asked, and as she did, she clasped Royce's hand.

"Atreus lives," Andrew said quietly. "He opens his eyes from time to time, and Phaedra believes he recognizes us, but I am not convinced. All the same, twice I thought he moved a finger as I spoke to him."

"So little," Kassandra murmured. Yet the world, for still her brother lived.

"Elena is there now," her father said. He looked at her gently. "We must decide very soon."

Decide on surgery that could restore the Vanax or kill him. That might save Akora or send it plunging into chaos. Decide while Deilos waited, plotting, just out of sight.

"Soon," Kassandra confirmed, and saw as though she held it in her hand, the last grains of sand begin to flow through the hourglass of her life.

Chapter
SIXTEEN

"The surgery involves removing a small piece of the skull," Elena said quietly, "in the area where the Vanax suffered the worst injury. I estimate the piece removed will be about one inch in diameter, however it is impossible to know for certain until the procedure is underway. There is a possibility it could be necessary to remove more."

The family was seated around a long table in the room Atreus used for council meetings. Kassandra was there, as were Phaedra, Andrew and Joanna. They had asked Royce to join them. Brianna accompanied Elena.

"The removal of the bone is done to relieve pressure on the brain?" Andrew asked.

Elena nodded. "That is its purpose. But I must be clear with you. As you know, the Vanax suffered a concussion, concussion-jarring of the brain; not necessary to crack skull which means his skull may be cracked. At this time, I cannot say how deep the crack may be or how much more difficult it may make the procedure."

"In other words, you could begin and find

you have a serious problem?"

"Yes, that is possible. It could, for example, make it necessary to remove more of the skull."

"He could not survive that," Phaedra said, very low. "No one could."

"There are cases in our medical logs of people who had very sizeable portions of their skulls removed and lived. However, I cannot tell you that they recovered fully."

"What happens after the bone is removed?" Kassandra asked.

"We do our utmost to guard against infection," Elena replied, "and wait in the hope that the easing of pressure on the brain will allow it to heal itself. If that occurs, the Vanax will regain consciousness. There will be a significant period of convalescence but the bone of his skull will grow back and eventually most or even all of the opening made in the skull will heal over."

"What if the injury is so deep within the brain that relieving pressure on the surface does not help?" Kassandra asked.

"Then he will not recover, Atreides. In that case, the surgery will probably hasten his death."

Andrew reached over and took Phaedra's hand. Quietly, he asked, "Is there truly no other alternative?"

Elena shook her head. "Someday we may be able to see into the brain and better understand what happens within it, but right now it remains a great mystery. We can wait, as we have been doing, but the Vanax is weakening. Not even a man as strong as he can continue in an unconscious state indefinitely."

"You are recommending the surgery?" Kassandra asked. She wanted to be very clear about that.

But Elena was not prepared to give so definitive an answer. "I am informing you that if the surgery is to be done, it will have to be very soon. If we wait much longer, the chance to perform the procedure with any real hope of a good outcome will be gone because the Vanax will have weakened too much to endure it."

"And if we go on as we have?" Kassandra prompted.

"There is still a chance the Vanax can recover on his own. I have searched the medical records and found reports of patients who were unconscious in some cases for as long as several weeks and still awakened. Some of these went on to recover more or less fully."

Her gaze went around the table. "After a few weeks, there is no chance of recovery because it is impossible for us to keep the patient properly nourished. Even now, while we are managing to give the Vanax water and a thin broth, we cannot give him food. In the end, the lack of nourishment will kill him as surely as anything else."

"If there was a way to give him food —" Royce said.

"Various methods have been tried in the past," Elena said. "They have all led either to respiratory problems that bring on death or to infections that have the same result." Softly, she said, "I am sorry. I know the choices are not good. If you wish to simply wait, I will understand. Indeed, I cannot tell you that is not the best decision."

Those around the table fell silent. Their faces revealed the struggle each waged with grief and hope. Finally, Andrew said, "I think we must ask ourselves what Atreus would want us to do."

"He has never turned away from a challenge," Phaedra said with a weak smile. "Even as a little boy, he was always running on ahead, always so eager to see and do." Tears spilled from her eyes. Her husband went to her and took her in his arms.

Quietly, Andrew said, "I believe I know what choice Atreus would make if he could, but this is more than the decision of a family. Kassandra, the people look to you. For their sake, what do you think should be done?"

It was what she had hoped would not be said, but she understood the fairness of it. In stepping in as she had, she had taken on all sorts of responsibilities, including that of helping to decide what would happen to her brother.

Even so, she said, "We cannot decide this for the sake of the people. As much as they love their Vanax and depend on him for guidance, we must make this choice for Atreus's sake alone."

She looked to Royce. "If you were he, what would you want?"

He did not hesitate. "A chance to live, however slim it may be. I know this is a very difficult decision, but unless you have some reason to believe Atreus is going to recover on his own, the surgery may be the only chance he really has."

They all looked at her, in their eyes the silent question: What, if anything, had her gift revealed to her?

Never would she tell them. That much, at least, they could be spared. Instead, she said, "I truly believe Atreus will recover, but we must do everything possible to help him." She spoke on the cusp of hope and nothing more. All her efforts to seek vision of Atreus and his fate had failed. There was nothing left save prayer. Let her choice be right, all her choices. Let them be right for Atreus, for Akora, for Royce, for her family and, at least in some sense, for herself.

She stood, feeling the tension in every bone and muscle. Soon, very soon now, it would end. "Elena," she said, "please prepare to perform the surgery."

The smell of burning sulfur filled the room Elena had chosen. It drifted out the windows and through the corridors. Traces of it found their way into the furthest reaches of the palace. Smelling it, people stopped what they were doing and stood silent. Many bowed their heads in prayer.

The evil spirits were being driven out of the place where the surgery would take place. Tradition dictated it be done, and none were inclined to question that. But just before she went to ready herself, Elena said, "I cannot explain why, but when surgery is done in a room purified in this manner, patients tend to develop fewer fevers or infections afterward."

While the sulfur burned, Elena bathed, then withdrew alone for a period of meditation. Meanwhile, the family remained with Atreus. Unspoken among them was the knowledge that this could be the last time they would see him alive.

When all was in readiness, Atreus was taken carefully from the bed where he had lain for more than a week and carried into the room where the surgery would be done. It was just after noon. Light streamed through the high windows covered with gauze as Elena had ordered. She did not wish to be distracted by an insect that might enter by chance.

Below in the courtyard, people were gathering. Although no official announcement of what was about to occur had been made, word had spread. Priests and priestesses moved among the crowd, offering comfort. Beyond, the city of Ilius slowed almost to a stop. So quiet did it become that the chirp of birds in the trees was the most audible sound.

The family accompanied Atreus down the corridor from his quarters to the room but did not enter it. Elena had requested that only the bare minimum of people do so. She believed this best preserved whatever effect the burning sulfur had created.

Just as he was carried inside, Kassandra was swept by an almost irresistible desire to do something, anything that would prevent what was about to happen. She pressed her lips together tightly but even so, a soft moan escaped her.

Royce put a strong arm around her waist. "I think it would be better if you waited elsewhere."

She nodded, not trusting herself to speak. It would be some time yet before the actual surgery began. Elena had explained that first she would examine Atreus to be certain his condition had not deteriorated to a dangerous level. Then the Vanax would be carefully washed and prepared. Only after that was all done would she proceed.

"Where would you like to go?" he asked.

She shook her head. "I don't know . . . not far . . ." Not in case she had to be summoned quickly.

"Surely, in so immense a palace, there is somewhere special to you?"

She thought for a moment before the answer came to her. "Come," she said, "I want to show you something."

They went through the maze of corridors that wound through the palace until they came to a part Royce judged to be very old. Although in impeccable repair, the floor sloped from both sides into the center where centuries of feet had trod.

Before long, they reached broad double doors that opened to reveal a large, high-ceilinged chamber. At the far end stood a chunk of marble a little over five feet high. Someone had carved it just enough so that it was possible to see the compelling features of a woman beginning to emerge from the stone.

"This is Atreus's studio," Kassandra said. She gestured at several other statues, some completed, some barely begun, and at the worktables holding smaller creations, some in clay, others in bronze.

"I don't believe he would mind our being here," she went on, "and this is the place where I feel closest to him."

"I can see why," Royce said, and looked around slowly. He realized at once that he was being given an extraordinary insight into the soul of the man most people thought of only as the Vanax of Akora. Atreus was that, but he was also a truly gifted artist.

"How much time is he able to spend here?" Royce asked.

"Not nearly as much as he would like but he steals a few hours now and then, occasionally even a whole day."

She nodded toward the small cot set up in one corner. "Sometimes, he sleeps here when he works until exhaustion overcomes him."

Studying a small clay study of a runner that looked so real Royce would not have been surprised to see it sprint across the table, he asked, "Do you think he regrets not being able to do just this?"

"He has never said so but there must be times when he wonders what his life would have been like were he not the Chosen."

"It isn't something he wanted?"

"No, I don't think so. Because he was the eldest son of the family and our grandfather was Vanax, people did wonder if it would be Atreus. But when the time came, I think he would have been delighted to discover it was someone else."

"Could that have happened? Could anyone have come forward and said he believed himself to be the Chosen?"

"Certainly, so long as he was willing to undergo the trial of selection."

"Which, as I recall, you don't want to discuss."

She smiled apologetically. "I don't mean to be mysterious. The truth is I don't know much about it myself. Only the Chosen really knows what it involves."

"But when this trial is over, it's obvious that a person is or is not the Chosen?"

"Well . . . yes . . . among other things, only

the Chosen can survive it."

Royce nodded slowly. "I thought it might be something like that, otherwise why wouldn't Deilos have challenged Atreus for the position of Vanax when he had the chance?"

"How I wish he had, for then he would have been dead long before now."

"That certainly would have saved us a great deal of trouble," Royce agreed.

Barely had he spoken than he discovered he was even more correct than he would have thought.

It began simply enough — a sound from the distance, not really alarming, just voices growing louder. But very shortly thereafter came the deep reverberation of gongs, similar to those Royce had heard at the funeral services for those killed at the Games, but more ominous and urgent.

Kassandra paled. "Quickly! Something has happened."

She ran from the room, Royce close behind her.

Before they got very far, they smelled the fire. The odor at once was but was not like that of the sulfur burned earlier at Elena's behest. There was something similar about it, yet it was thicker, deeper, more deadly.

Reaching the end of the corridor, they hurried down a flight of steps and emerged out into the main courtyard of the palace in time to see crews of men attempting to douse flames that were spreading rapidly. It appeared as though the ground itself was on fire. Where the flames reached the outer walls of the palace, the very stone seemed to ignite.

Already a line of men were passing buckets of water; but when thrown on the fire, the water appeared to do nothing. The flames seemed to be impervious to it.

In the tumult of the effort to fight the fire, Royce caught sight of Marcellus. He stepped in front of the magistrate, who was rushing forward to take his place on the water line.

"What happened?" Royce yelled above the roar of the flames. "How did this start?"

"I don't know," Marcellus said, coughing as he breathed in lungfuls of the cloying smoke. "We can discover that after we've put it out."

"The water isn't working. What kind of fire can't be put out by water?" When the magistrate looked at him blankly, Royce grabbed his shoulder and shook him hard. "Think, man! And while you're at it, look! This is no ordinary fire."

Swiftly then, Marcellus steadied. He stared at the fire as his eyes turned hard and grim. "You're right, the water has no effect." He raised his voice, shouting to the men nearest him. "Get blankets, quickly! This fire must be beaten out!"

Seeing for themselves the sense of what he said, the men obeyed. Some ran for the stables, empty as any horses that had been there when the fire began had already been led to the greater safety of the paddocks beyond the palace. Others raced inside to grab every blanket, tablecloth and other large piece of fabric they could find. Within minutes they were back and beating at the fire with all their strength.

Slowly, so slowly, the flames began to lessen and finally to flicker out. Even so, there were patches that were still flaring up a good half-hour after the first alarm had been given.

However, by then attention had turned in other directions. One man lay dead, not from the fire but from an arrow shot precisely through his neck.

"I'm sure he's the one I saw throwing the pots, Atreides," a young boy told Kassandra when he was brought to her to relate what he had witnessed. "He had them in a rope sling and he threw three of them, one right after the other. Everywhere they landed, the fire sprang up instantly."

He looked to Royce and the other men standing nearby. "I know it doesn't make any sense but that is what I saw. No one set the fire. It simply appeared where the pots smashed."

"Did you see the man shot?" Royce asked.

The boy shook his head. "No, Hawk Lord, by then all I saw was the fire."

"Remove the body," Kassandra directed, "and let us give thanks no one else was harmed." She looked at the blackened ground and the walls of the palace blistered by the heat of the fire. "This could have been much worse."

"So it seems," Royce said slowly. He looked at her, then toed the ground, watching it crumble, before glancing from where the dead man lay toward the walls of the palace. "The arrow came from there."

Kassandra followed the direction of his gaze.

"Given the dead man's position," Royce said, "and the direction the arrow in his neck is pointing, it was shot from up on that wall."

"Perhaps an alert guard saw what he was doing," Kassandra suggested.

Royce looked unconvinced but he had no chance to comment, for just then an angry murmur went up from the men removing the body. The dead arsonist's tunic had slipped slightly, revealing a swatch of yellow beneath it.

Marcellus stepped forward quickly and withdrew what proved to be a yellow banner. A single word was printed on it:

HELIOS

"Again the rebels!" the magistrate exclaimed in disgust. "Truly, is there no end to their perfidy? How many more do they seek to kill and maim?"

"Rather convenient of him to identify himself so clearly," Royce remarked.

"With respect, Hawk Lord," Marcellus said, "I realize you think we are being led to a false conclusion, but you will admit the evidence against the rebels is clear, while there is no evidence whatsoever of anyone else's involvement."

Royce shrugged and looked again to the wall. "I don't know that and I won't until the guard is found who killed this man. Let him come forward and claim his just reward for the great service he rendered."

Marcellus looked puzzled. "Of course, he will do so. I'm sure we could find him now if we asked."

"Do you really think so? I don't. In fact, I don't think any such guard exists." Royce gestured to the dead man. "I think this fellow was likely killed by whoever sent him into the crowded palace courtyard where he was sure to be seen and captured. Unlike the explosion at the arena, there was no way for this man to commit his deed and still escape. Had he been taken alive, he might have told us who was behind this. But he can't because he is conveniently dead."

"Even so," Marcellus said, "the banner —"

"May signify anything or nothing." Royce turned to Kassandra. In an abrupt change of subject, he said, "Atreides, I am sure you are very concerned about the Vanax. Perhaps we could step inside and inquire as to the progress of the surgery."

Before Kassandra could reply that they were not likely to know anything until Elena had finished her work, and that, at any rate, she thought it her duty to remain where she was, Royce took her arm and led her away. So swift were his strides that she had to run a little to keep up with him.

"Where are you going?" she demanded. "Elena will send out word when —"

Royce rounded a corner of the palace and stopped abruptly. No one else was about. Everyone had already been in the courtyard or been drawn there to fight the fire. They were alone. He turned her to face him. "What was it?"

"What was what? What are you talking about?"

"Whatever was in those pots. Whatever caused fire that water couldn't put out. What was it?"

He was still gripping her arm, not painfully but with no intent to release her. She looked away. "Royce . . . ."

"Tell me. I must know what Deilos has."

Because he would go against him, no matter what the risk to himself. Kassandra's throat tightened painfully. "Why do you think I know?"

"Because you did not ask."

So simple an answer, so stark a mistake. Were he anyone else, she would still have denied. As it was, she winced at her own foolishness. "You have to understand . . . almost no one knows."

"Knows what?"

"Akora must be able to defend itself."

"I have never said otherwise. What has that to do with this?"

"Two years ago, when the visions began of Akora being invaded, my brothers realized that despite all our efforts, we really were vulnerable."

"I know this. Alex secured cannons from foundries in England that the government never had any intention of selling to him. He was on his way back here with them when Joanna stowed away so that she could come in search of me."

"Yes, we got the cannons but we didn't look for help only from outside. We also looked deep within our own knowledge. You know what the library here is like . . ."

"Vast, almost unimaginable, a treasure trove of thousands of years of thought and discovery."

She nodded. "And what have people been doing for thousands of years? Inventing ever more ingenious ways to make war, some of them kept so secret as to be forgotten long ago."

He thought a moment . . . another. She saw the moment when he knew, for his eyes flashed with mingled horror and disbelief. "My God, you've rediscovered Greek Fire."

"The Byzantine Greeks invented it," Kassandra said wearily. She suddenly felt overwhelmingly tired. "They used it to destroy any who came against them. It allowed them to preserve their empire for centuries."

Royce nodded slowly. "And they kept it so secret that the knowledge of it was lost . . . everywhere except here. You rediscovered how to make it."

"We never intended to use it, except if we absolutely had to."

"Someone has used it, Atreides. Someone just used it to make a very effective point. Do you have any idea what would have happened if there had been more men, throwing more pots? How many do you think would have died out there in the courtyard? How many would be screaming in agony even now?"

"Stop it!" Kassandra demanded. "Do you imagine you are telling me anything I don't already know? The enemy is striking at the very heart of Akora. Not just at the Vanax but at the spirit that makes us what we are. This is an enemy who seeks to make us afraid, to make us look at one another with suspicion, to wonder moment to moment if disaster is about to strike again. No people can long endure that and live in peace with one another."

They looked at each other. Slowly, Royce said, "Unless a hero arises. Isn't that what Mellinos said? Someone will come forward who promises to save them, to restore everything to the way it was. The people may not like him, they may even fear him, but sooner or later, they will listen to him."

Kassandra took a deep breath, willing herself

to calm. "I think you may have just described Deilos's plan."

"Could he have found out about the Greek Fire?"

"It is possible," she admitted reluctantly. "He was on the Council. He might have seen or heard something he should not and used his authority to learn more."

"Does the formula involve sulfur?"

She hesitated only a moment. "Yes, sulfur is used. So is the black oil that seeps from the ground in some places and . . . other things."

He did not ask her what they were. She had the clear sense that he truly did not want such knowledge.

"Deimatos must be searched again," he said, "and the other small islands as well."

Kassandra nodded. "We must act quickly. Time is very short."

Royce still held her, but gently. He drew her closer, his breath warm against her cheek. "Kassandra . . . you know if Atreus . . . that is, if he doesn't make it . . . there will have to be another trial of selection, won't there?"

"Yes, there will . . ."

"Is there any way Deilos could pretend to undergo it and survive? Could he convince people he was the Chosen when he really wasn't?"

She answered emphatically, without a shadow of doubt. "No, absolutely not."

He set her back a little so that he could look

at her. "How can you be so sure?"

"I saw Atreus when it was over. There were . . . signs. They are unmistakable."

"And these signs, they are known to any man or woman on Akora?"

"No . . . they are known only to a few . . . to those initiated into the deepest mysteries."

"Deilos, is he one of the initiated?"

"No, certainly not." The very idea was absurd. "Only a very few are, and he would never qualify."

"Right now, how many people are there on Akora who would know whether a man claiming to be the Chosen truly was or not?"

"I don't know exactly . . . not many." Horror filled her as the full implication of what he was saying sank in. So few people to stand between a ruthless madman and the power for which he lusted. "Twenty perhaps . . . not more than thirty."

Regretfully, he said, "You are more vulnerable even than you thought."

Desperately, she shook her head, trying to drive out the terrible possibility he conjured with cold logic and reason. "Never in the long history of Akora has anyone attempted to become Vanax through treachery."

"Then you have been very fortunate because it is not all that difficult to do away with twenty or thirty people. They wouldn't even necessarily have to be killed. They could be locked up somewhere." His eyes darkened.

"Deilos is good at that."

"This is unthinkable. If such a thing were to happen, Akora truly would be destroyed."

"Then we must see to it that it does not happen," Royce said grimly. "One way or another, Deilos must die."

A faint laugh broke from her, startling them both. "There is such irony to this," she explained when Royce looked at her in surprise. "Deilos sought to kill Atreus, in all likelihood. But were Atreus able, he would tell you Deilos should not die. He would say he should be taken alive, if at all possible without endangering others. That he should have a fair and open trial with the charges against him made public and every opportunity provided for him to defend himself."

"That's all very laudatory," Royce said. "But you must realize if there was the same kind of openness about the process by which the Vanax is selected, if more than just twenty or thirty people knew how to confirm that choice, it would be impossible for anyone to attempt to usurp that office?"

"Are you saying you think the proponents of Helios are right?" she challenged.

"Not if any of this violence truly is of their making. But if they are simply being used, as I suspect, then yes, I do think they have a point."

He waited for the shock and even the anger he thought she was sure to express, but instead Kassandra merely sighed. "Perhaps that is true.

I honestly don't know. It may be that Akora has to change in more ways than I have considered. But that is a question for another time." She looked to the sky and the distance the sun had moved since noon. Softly, she said, "Elena must have begun by now."

"Then let us go in. At the least, we can share the wait with Joanna and your parents."

But when they entered the palace, there was no sign of the rest of the family. They were not gathered in the corridor near the room where the surgery was to be performed, nor could they be found anywhere else nearby when Kassandra and Royce went to look.

"Perhaps they were drawn away by the fire," she said finally. "It's possible they are even looking for us."

"Perhaps they are —" Royce began, only to break off when he saw his sister hurrying toward them.

"There you are," she exclaimed. "I sent servants to find you but in all the confusion in the courtyard —"

Kassandra's hands clenched together tightly. "Atreus . . . is he . . . ?"

"He is unchanged," Joanna said. At Kassandra's bewildered look, she gestured to a bench set beneath one of the windows that lined the corridor. "Come and sit down."

"No, just tell me. What has happened?"

Brother and sister exchanged a look. Gently, Joanna said, "When the fire broke out, Elena

357

had not yet begun the surgery. She delayed in order to see if there were any injured who needed her help." She looked again to her brother, who moved closer to Kassandra. "As she went to inquire, she tripped and fell down a flight of stairs."

"No . . . She could not have. We need her —"

"Kassandra, Elena broke her arm. She will be all right but she cannot possibly perform the surgery."

She really should have sat down, Kassandra thought belatedly. Of all the possibilities she had imagined and feared, this was not among them.

"Is there anyone else?" Royce asked.

Was there? Was there another healer who could be trusted with the life of the Vanax in so delicate and dangerous a procedure?

"There is an older man," Joanna said. "He is the healer who trained Elena, but he is close to eighty now and has not done any surgery at all in a decade, much less anything so difficult."

"Anyone else?" Royce persisted. "Surely she has students of her own?"

"She does, but none of them has ever done this procedure on a living patient. They have only practiced on animal skulls."

It was Kassandra who reached the inevitable conclusion. "Then it cannot be done. Whatever we may have wished, the surgery is not possible."

Joanna nodded. "It may be this is for the

best. The surgery could have killed Atreus."

"And doing nothing may have the same effect," Kassandra said. Confusion whirled through her. She had seen nothing in her visions of the attack on Atreus, hence nothing of its outcome. She was as unknowing as any ordinary mortal in this matter.

And yet, for all that, there was still hope.

And even, remarkably enough, the faintest touch of humor.

"You know," she said as they moved down the corridor toward her brother's quarters, where he once again rested, "there is at least a possibility that Deilos may have saved Atreus's life."

"Should that be the case," Royce said matter-of-factly, "I will enjoy telling him that before he dies."

Chapter
SEVENTEEN

"He was here," Royce said emphatically. "Right here in this city and, I would wager, probably within the palace itself."

"You don't know that," Marcellus said. Barely had he spoken than he grimaced. "I seem to always be saying that to you, Hawk Lord, in one way or another. Please do not misunderstand me. I mean no disrespect nor do I dismiss the notion that you may be right. But I am a magistrate. My understanding of truth revolves around the presence of evidence."

"Then consider the man himself," Royce suggested. "Do you believe Deilos would entrust so essential a mission as the murder of a subordinate to someone else? If he did, he'd just have to kill *that* man himself to assure his silence . . . or another . . . or another. There would be no end to it. Sooner or later, he would have to act."

"What you say is reasonable," Marcellus acknowledged, "provided the man in the courtyard was murdered."

"No palace guard has come forward to say he shot that arrow."

"There was a great deal of confusion —"

"Not that much," Kassandra interjected. They were in Atreus's office once again. There, at least, she felt she could be assured of some degree of privacy. The palace overflowed with people, or so it felt. All the counselors were present, including those like Polydorus and Goran who had gone home for a time. They told her only that they thought it was right they be there, but she knew what was in their minds. Elena's injury and the consequent impossibility of the surgery were no secret. Everyone understood that one way or another, time was running out. Atreus would recover very soon on his own or he would die. In either case, there was a natural instinct to be together and close to the center of events.

"I think," she continued, "we must acknowledge that the Hawk Lord is correct; the man who set the fires likely was murdered to assure his silence. There is a person behind all this and I believe it is Deilos. He must be stopped."

"I have no quarrel with that," Marcellus replied, "but we have scoured Ilius from one end to the other. If the enemy is indeed hidden here, I would like to know where."

"He may not be here any longer," Royce said reluctantly. "He may have withdrawn to a safer place to wait." He did not have to say what would be awaited. They all knew he meant Atreus's death.

"We have also searched Deimatos and the other small islands," Marcellus said.

"They are riddled with caves," Royce pointed out. "To search them thoroughly could take months."

"That is true," the magistrate acknowledged.

"If Deilos and his supporters take shelter on one of those islands," Kassandra said, "it will be Deimatos. His family owned it and he has known it from tenderest childhood. Additionally, the sulfur and other ingredients he would have needed are available there."

"We waste time sitting here," Royce said. "We should be searching Deimatos again."

"We?" Kassandra raised a brow. "You mean you, do you not?"

"I would not mind the opportunity."

She stared at him across the width of the office. "You want to kill Deilos."

Royce shrugged. "I have made no secret of it."

Kassandra moved away from the window where she stood, walked to Atreus's desk and touched it lightly. Her brother possessed the wisdom of the Chosen. She did not nor, in truth, would she wish it. They had different roles to play. But somehow she must find her own wisdom now.

"Deilos and any who follow him are not foreign enemies," she said quietly. "They are not something remote and distant from our soil. They are *of* Akora, as much as we would like to deny it. We must defeat them in a way that honors our laws and our traditions. Only then can we truly say the enemy is no longer among us."

Marcellus was nodding before she finished. "What are you suggesting, Atreides?"

"I'm not really sure," she admitted. "But I believe we must have patience as well as courage. We must not do as Deilos expects but rather as is right for Akora."

"He will expect us to come after him," Royce said. "The attack on the palace may have been an attempt to lure us into doing exactly that." He stood and walked near to where she stood, studying her all the while. She could not see what was in his eyes but his smile chilled her.

"He will have prepared the ground," Royce continued as though he saw it all in his mind's eye. "He will think himself ready for us."

"He may be right to think that, for he has a terrible weapon," Kassandra said. Her chest tightened painfully. "To go into the caves on Deimatos could be suicide. The lives of hundreds of Akoran warriors — and your own life — could be lost."

"But not to hunt him," Royce rejoined, "to simply lie in wait, will afford him more opportunity to strike."

"There is that risk," she acknowledged, "but I still think this is what we must do." She spread her hands, willing him to understand, praying he would do so and that in the process, he would understand her as well. Understand and perhaps ultimately forgive. "Akora has always been a place of life, not death. We wrested life from a shattered world. We rebuilt it stone by stone and seed by seed. Our devotion to life — to every *individual* life — has always been our greatest strength. Deilos tempts us to forget that, but we must not. We must be truer to ourselves now than we have ever been."

"Blood lust runs high," Royce said matter-of-factly. His gaze lingered on Kassandra. "There is a certain challenge to resisting it."

She breathed then, slowly and softly so that he would not notice her relief. "I entrust this to you," she told him softly. "It will take great skill and persistence to flush out those who seek to harm us without unnecessary loss of life, but I am sure you can do it."

"It will also take men," he said dryly. "Not many but the best."

"You shall have them," she assured him, "and anything else you need."

And with that, in her heart, she let him go.

Except that he did not go, not just then. There were arrangements to be made, men to be assembled, supplies to be organized. Her plan was well and fine, but there were simple practicalities to be observed.

So he said, so he explained as he prepared to sail on the morning tide.

Which left the night.

She had not considered that. In making the decision to send him to Deimatos, she had not thought that there would be time for any long farewell. She had imagined herself busy, hurrying between her brother's bedside and all the demands that fell to her, as she had been for so many days.

And yet in those days, in those nights, there had been so much more.

She was thinking of that as she went to visit Elena. The healer was resting as comfortably as possible while yet she grappled with the shock of what had happened to her.

"I never fall," she told Kassandra. "Absolutely never. Even when I was a very small child just learning to walk, I did not fall."

"But we all fall from time to time," Kassandra said, trying to comfort her. The older woman was not in pain, for Brianna had slipped a soothing powder into a drink when Elena refused to take it outright. But she was badly agitated.

Elena seemed not to hear her. "I have walked down those same stairs a hundred times, even more. I have run down them more often than I know. Why would I fall just then? *Why?*"

"You were concerned. There was the possibility others were gravely injured."

"Nonsense. I would not react in such a way. I went calmly and purposefully. There was no reason for me to fall."

"And yet you did."

"And yet I did," Elena agreed. "On such foolish accidents, far too much can hinge. If the Vanax dies . . ."

"It will not be your fault. Now rest, for you know full well that is the only way you will recover."

Kassandra left Elena's quarters a short while later and returned to her own. She entered reluctantly and looked around, caught between hope and dread that Royce would be there.

He was not. She faced an empty room, an empty bed and empty hours. Oh, she would go down with him to the harbor in the morning. She would stand beside him and make it clear he went with her authority, on her behalf. She would bid him and all the men who sailed to Deimatos Fortune's favor. She would even mean it.

Royce would have to face his demons on Deimatos, where he had been held in such brutal captivity, but it was to his benefit that he do so. He might well discover men still serving Deilos hiding there and she had no doubt he would capture them. But of Deilos she was quite convinced he would find nothing.

Deilos was in Ilius.

The note brought to her scant hours before told her so.

She took a bath. Doing that always made her feel better. Or at least it always had. Were she to marry Royce and live with him at Hawk-

366

forte, she would have to learn to do without such luxuries. Or perhaps not, for he had expressed interest in Akoran plumbing and might look to import it.

What *was* she thinking? What absurd disorder of her mind prompted such a notion? Surely, she did herself no good allowing her fancies to wander in so painful a direction.

Rising abruptly, she toweled herself dry with such fury that her skin glowed pink. Leaving the wet cloth on a stool, she walked naked back into the bedroom.

That was odd, she didn't remember lighting any lamps, yet one glowed softly near the bed.

Illuminating the perfectly formed, perfectly nude body of a man stretched out at his leisure, his powerful arms folded behind his hand and a tantalizing smile playing over his hard mouth.

"Royce . . ." She spoke and knew it only when she heard her own voice.

He looked her up, down, up again. Heat followed his gaze. "Marcellus offered to see to the arrangements."

"How very thoughtful of him."

"Come here." He did not move, did not hold out a hand, did not so much as beckon her. He simply directed.

She could, of course, refuse. She could remark on his high-handedness. She could pretend some sort of prickly annoyance with him.

But then, it was her bed.

"I was planning to go to sleep," she said, and

lay down on her side facing him. Gracefully, she bent one leg and rested her head on her arm, all the while watching him.

"You look like an odalisque."

"I hardly live in a harem."

"No, that's true, you don't." He turned to face her, a lock of golden hair falling over his forehead. It was really quite unfair that any man could be so devastatingly handsome. "I cannot imagine you any man's slave."

"I am relieved to hear it." Delicately, she added, "The other night, in the tent, I rather got the impression you were of a different mind."

He had the grace to blush, just a tiny bit. "Because I wanted the upper hand?"

"You wanted . . . everything."

He did not deny it. "I have not found it precisely easy to be the lover of the Atreides."

Ah, was that it, then? He had sought a rightening of the balance between them because he was uncomfortable with the power she had assumed?

"There have been ruling queens in England," she said. "The great Elizabeth, for instance. How would you have managed with her, I wonder?"

He laughed at the notion, looking suddenly boyish now that his admission was made and not rejected by her. "But she was known as the Virgin Queen, so it would not have been an issue."

"Do you think she was, really?"

"I hope not," he said honestly. "Her father chopped off her mother's head, her half sister was a religious fanatic who came within a hair's breadth of killing her, and she lived much of her life under threat of assassination by traitors seeking to usurp her throne. At the very least, she should have found some personal happiness."

"That can be elusive." And far too fleeting. She glanced toward the wide windows. Too soon it would be morning.

"I think," she said very softly, "that it's my turn."

He was, to his credit, an extremely strong and self-disciplined man. Nothing else could explain how he bore the sweet torment she inflicted. He had wanted to right the balance between them? She needed to do the same. Even more importantly, she was desperate to imprint the memory of him within herself so deeply that it would survive anything, even death.

Akora was a place of life. But death had come all the same, violent and premature death, and it was not done yet. Death hovered too close, driving her. She lingered over him, savoring the scent and touch of him, every sound he made, every stroke of his skin, every mindless, explosive release they found together.

Such a beautiful man. And yet, oddly, as she lay beside him in a brief interlude of respite, she had the sudden, fleeting image of a raven-haired boy playing on high stone walls close by a sea that was not Akora's. How very strange.

"You have no brother," she said.

He murmured what might have been agreement. No brother, a sister to be sure, but whence then came the raven-haired boy? An illusion, perhaps, no more for all that there hung about him the same undulating glow that lit the edges of her visions.

But this could not be one of them, for it did not hurt. On the contrary, she felt suffused with calm as though nothing in all existence could possibly trouble her.

The boy . . . laughed and spun a stone into space, whirling and whirling, landing somewhere she could not see to send ripples in all directions . . .

A stone cast into a pond. Royce had said something about that to her mother. Something about a life upholding beliefs . . .

She should not sleep, time was too short. Already, her weary eyes opened to glimpse a rim of gray against the horizon.

No, not yet! Not so soon. Tears stung her.

"Kassandra? . . ."

He sounded sleepy and rumpled, a man pulling himself from exhaustion's well because he cared enough to do so.

"Ssshhhh," she murmured and lightly stroked his hair. "It is nothing."

He murmured something, her name again perhaps, and gathered her close. Tucked into the curve of his body, she lay awake, wide-eyed, and willed the raven-haired boy to return, but he did not.

"May fortune favor you," Kassandra said. The ranks of men drawn upon the quay nodded as one. They were all young, handpicked and supremely fit. Men of the legions who guarded the palace. Men who would welcome the opportunity to avenge the Vanax but who would gird themselves to the higher demands of justice.

Royce stood before them. He wore the kilt of an Akoran warrior. His hair was held back from his brow by a thin strip of leather. The sun had tanned his skin to a burnished gold. From his taut waist hung a sword belt. His left hand rested on the hilt of the blade.

"Perhaps you should have brought your cane," she said softly.

He remembered in a moment and laughed. "I regret that I did not. In fact, I should have brought a hundred of them. Can't you see all these fine men fitted out with sword canes?"

The image was so preposterous — Akoran warriors marching into battle wielding canes — that she laughed suddenly. Those nearest looked at her in surprise. Instantly, she sobered. She should not have done that. The moment was too fraught.

"I truly do hope you will be careful," she said, and resisted the impulse to reach out to him.

"I am ever cautious," he said, and she saw something move behind his eyes that momentarily stung her. But it was gone so swiftly she was left to blame her imagination.

The tide turned, as it ever would. She stood, her spine rigid, and tried to think of some last words to say to him but none came. He leaned forward suddenly, kissed her lightly on the cheek, and said, "Try not to worry too much."

A thousand replies welled up in her but none found voice. She stood, silent and alone, and watched him sail away.

In the palace, she went to find Amelia. She had seen almost nothing of her niece since the explosion at the Games and was startled by the change in her. She was bigger to be sure, and her hair was a little thicker, but mainly she was much more alert. The child's blue eyes, already blurring into her mother's hazel, seemed oddly old for so young a face.

"How is she sleeping?" Kassandra asked Joanna, for this ever seemed to be the question to ask new mothers.

"Tolerably well. She still wakes around midnight, nurses and goes back to sleep until about six o'clock. That really isn't bad."

"She is a beautiful baby."

"Indeed, she is. You are missing Royce already."

"I didn't . . . he only just left, why would I miss him?"

"Oh, for heaven's sake, Kassandra, I miss Alex when he walks out of a room. Do you really expect yourself to be different?"

"You love Alex."

"Of course I do, and you love Royce."

She gave off admiring her niece and pretended not to understand. "I have never said so."

"I rarely mention the fact that the sun comes up every morning. My failure to do so has absolutely no effect on the event itself."

No, it did not. Nature in all its mystery went right on despite the concerns of piddling mortals.

She loved Royce.

Well, of course she did. How could she not? She had known she loved him for a long time now, probably since that morning in London spinning round and round. Her mind had never settled since and her heart certainly had not.

It made no difference.

Love, like, lust — no gradation in the path of feeling could change her course.

But she did love him and just then, she gathered the knowledge to herself and hugged it closely. There was an odd sort of comfort in it.

Deilos's note. It had come in a pot of calla lilies brought by a young boy hired for the purpose. He had waited until she was walking across the courtyard, then approached her.

"Gentleman said to give you this, my lady."

He looked at her shyly, as though grappling with the thought that she was real enough for him to be speaking to her.

She took the pot, sniffed the lilies, thinking even then that she had never liked that particular variety.

"Who gave you this?"

"Don't know, my lady. Gentleman never said his name."

She paused then, looking at him over the blossoms that were already beginning to brown around the edges of petals white as fish bellies.

"What did he look like?"

The boy thought. "Old, not so old as my father though, so young, I guess. Thin in the face but set up well enough."

Deilos . . . or a thousand other men. But how many would send her lilies?

She thanked the boy, sent him on his way. In her quarters, she looked harder at the pot.

And in the doing, found the note with its so unnecessary threat: Come or he would unleash the Greek Fire. Thousands would die.

No, they would not. But death would come to Ilius on this bright summer day. So it had been given to her to see.

She lifted her niece and held the soft, warm body of the baby snug in her arms. Amelia's heavy head drowsed on her shoulder. She made little bubbles of saliva as she breathed in and out.

"You should have a child of your own," Joanna said.

A raven-haired boy, playing on stone walls hard by the sea.

"You loved growing up at Hawkforte, didn't you?"

"I did," Joanna agreed. "Even after my parents died, it was a special place."

"Yet you left it."

"I had no choice. So long as Royce was missing, nothing else mattered."

"There must have been a moment though, some instant when you doubted." Immediately, she regretted saying that. It was too personal, she had no right.

But Joanna seemed to feel differently. She nodded without hesitation. "I still have dreams about it." A soft laugh escaped her. "I am standing on the dock at Southwark, the same one we left from to come here. All I can see before me is an Akoran warship with its vast bull prow gleaming in the darkness. Off in the distance, the boys I hired to distract the guards are doing their best. The moment has come, I have to act. But I hesitate. I cannot move my legs. I am overcome by doubt and confusion."

"And . . . ?" Kassandra prompted, desperate to know the rest.

"And nothing. I awaken, until recently, beside Alex. What really matters is that I know it is a dream. I *did* act. I gathered up all my courage and I ran, not away from the ship but straight toward it. When there was nowhere left to run, I jumped." She looked down at her hands. "There have been times, waking from that dream, when I still feel the rope I used to pull myself up toward the porthole, hard and rough against my skin. It is as though it is all happening again."

"Echoes," Kassandra murmured. "Creation seems filled with them, echoes of what was, what could have been, even what is to come."

"You feel them?"

"Sometimes," Kassandra admitted. She lowered her gaze, savoring the soft brush of Amelia's hair against her cheek. "She is a dear child."

Who woke just then, fussed a little but did not cry. Instead, Amelia looked at her aunt, not with the unfocused gaze of a baby but quite intently. She opened her mouth, closed it, opened again like a little bird. Her brow wrinkled and she glared.

"I think she's trying to tell you something," Joanna said lightly. She took her daughter, rested her upright against her shoulder and gently patted the baby's back.

"I must go," Kassandra said. Her legs felt stiff but she stood on them all the same.

"Royce will be all right," Joanna reassured her.

"I pray so," Kassandra said, and went from the room into the fading light of day.

In the corridor near Atreus's room, she hesitated. The urge was in her to visit with her brother once more. But he remained unconscious. He would have no awareness of her presence and time was fast fleeting. Besides, Phaedra and Andrew would be with him. There was too real a chance that her parents would feel something amiss in her.

Better just to go.

She hurried because if she hesitated a scant moment, she feared she would falter. Quickly, quickly through the rooms and corridors she had known all her life. In the courtyard, she forced herself to slow lest she draw curious glances. But the moment she was beyond the Lion's Gate, she was almost running.

As Joanna had run and when there was no more room to run, leaped.

But Joanna had leaped into life, whereas she . . .

No, don't think, only hurry. Time was short already. She heard her breath as she climbed the road that led up beyond the city, higher and higher, until she came at last to a small plateau in which nestled a half-circle of stone tiers gathered round a stage.

Phaedra had brought her to the theater the first time, while yet she was very small. She remembered the excitement, the anticipation, remembered walking up holding her mother's hand.

How she loved this place.

And how ironic that Deilos would choose it.

Alone, he had said in the note, and alone she was. He could not know it did not matter. Her visions were clear — if she died, the red serpent did not come to Akora. And here, in this place she knew so well, this was where she had seen her death.

All the world's a stage, the great English bard had said. How well he knew.

The theater at this hour was empty. She entered through the passage that led between several tiers of seats and came up the aisle toward the stage. She did not set foot on it but stopped just short and turned round.

There was no sign of anyone. So far as she could see, she was the only person in the theater.

Was the note a trick?

Her mind had just begun to entertain that notion when she heard a noise . . . odd, unknown . . . but growing louder.

She looked again and saw, there in the center of the stage, something rising.

The floor of the stage was folding away and a platform was emerging from the earth.

Deus ex machina, she thought. The god in the machine. It was a staple of plays, the sudden intervention of a divine being raised to the stage from a hiding place below. Sophisticated audiences tended to titter at it, as it was considered a cliché.

She felt no urge to laugh. Indeed, only terror filled her as she stared at the man who strode out onto the stage and smiled at her.

"Princess Kassandra," Deilos said. "How very good of you to come."

Chapter
EIGHTEEN

"I believe you left me little choice," Kassandra said.

His mouth stretched farther, showing his teeth. It was not a smile but rather, she thought, more like the grinning rictus of death. A shiver ran through her. Above all, she must not think of death now. The time for thought was long past. Only action mattered. "But that was my intent," he said. "You are too . . . elusive."

"Elusive?" She willed calm, took a step toward him. "But I am here."

"So you are." He bounced forward, waving his arms, then clenched them around himself before abruptly letting go. Finally, he settled on a pose of one foot thrust forward and one hand on a hip. She wondered if he thought that looked noble.

"I wanted to marry you," he said.

Her stomach clenched. She had known, of course. Atreus had mentioned it to her two years or so before, just in passing and with her answer a foregone conclusion.

Marry Deilos. The very notion was absurd.

"As I am sure the Vanax told you at the time, I had no interest in marrying."

He waved a hand dismissively. "Oh, yes, Atreus said something to that effect. Naturally, I knew better. He simply did not think me good enough for the exalted Atreides family."

"He told you the truth. I did not wish to marry. I wanted to be free."

Deilos frowned, puzzled. "Free? What do you mean?"

"Just what I said. I wanted a greater measure of freedom than I thought could be found within marriage. Above all, I wanted to be able to travel."

"Why?"

He seemed genuinely bewildered, as though she had announced her fervent desire to eat dung.

"You have ventured beyond Akora," she reminded him. "Surely, you know the excitement of the wider world."

"There is no excitement," he said flatly. "I went only from necessity and nothing more. Akora is all the world that matters."

"Then why do you seek to destroy it?" She spoke not wisely but because she truly did want to know. What could possibly spur a man to act as Deilos had done?

"Destroy it?" He looked outraged. "I do no such thing. How dare you say that? I want only to preserve Akora."

"By attempting to kill the Vanax and entice Akora's enemies to descend upon her?"

He made no effort at denial but merely said, "You mean the British?" Again, his hand fluttered, the hand of this man who dismissed so much save the violent fantasies of his own mind. Those were all too real to him. "The British are nothing. We would take them easily, and in the process, the people would rally, become one again with the old ways, the right ways. The British are merely a tool."

"I daresay they see themselves differently."

Loftily, he declared, "That is of no matter. They would serve my purpose, but perhaps now that will not be needed. Atreus will die. You and I will marry. The people will be relieved. They will rally to me."

"You have it all planned," she said, though the bile rising in her throat made speech almost impossible.

"It will be as it is meant to be." He came closer, looking at her. She had to force herself not to move away. Slowly, delicately, she slipped her hand into the hidden slit of her tunic, the one she herself had cut knowing it would be needed. "There are rumors about you."

"Rumors?"

"That you bear a gift, some say a curse. Other women in your family have been like that." He frowned. "I should not wish any of our daughters to be marked in such a way, but then I prefer you bear sons."

"A man does not always receive what he prefers."

"But I will because I serve Akora. Even so, answer me. Are the rumors about you true?"

Her hand closed, hard and firm. She took a breath, willing strength. "As I do not know their content, I cannot say."

"You see the future. That is why you bear the name you do."

"Perhaps my mother liked the name."

"Did she? Odd, considering what happened to the original Kassandra. She was killed, wasn't she? Sacrificed on Achilles' grave."

"So legend says."

"You see the future."

"You may believe anything you like."

He came at her suddenly, one hand raised, his face twisted. "Do not provoke me. I know what you are. An unnatural being, an unnatural woman, claiming power for yourself or trying to. I have no patience with any of that. You will be my wife. You will serve me and Akora. It will be your privilege to do both."

Nearer, but not yet near enough. She wanted to scream but spoke softly instead. "To do so will cause me hurt and that, as you know, is forbidden."

"Ah, yes, the bargain of the priestesses and the warriors. Your family engineered it, I have no doubt. But I repudiate it. Women will serve, as they were always meant to do."

"And you will rule?" Disgust filled her. How had Akora nurtured so venomous a serpent? He rejected everything that had been developed and protected over so many centuries.

"My family should always have ruled," Deilos said. "It was you Atreides, concocting that absurd fiction of a trial of selection, then ensuring only your own candidates could survive it. You stole what should have been ours."

"There have been Vanaxes who were not Atreides."

"Perhaps they did not bear that name but they were Atreides all the same, born of Atreides mothers or wed to Atreides wives. It was always you, but no more. Oh, I will wed you, for the people will be satisfied by no less. But you will have no say in anything I do."

"Will I? Tell me, how did you survive last year?"

He looked blankly at her for a moment, then reddened. "When your dear brother did his utmost to kill me? But he could not. Don't you see, I am destined to live . . . to rule. I cannot be defeated."

"Then you have nothing to worry about, do you? You went into the Channel in the midst of a sudden gale. How is it you did not drown?"

"I was born aloft by the sea god."

"The sea god . . . ?" He believed it, she realized. He absolutely believed he had been saved by divine intervention. She had never considered that he might think that way, but now she saw the odd, twisted sense of it. He was not the Chosen, could never be, but he could believe himself favored all the same above other men. He was mad enough for that.

"You doubt, don't you?" Deilos demanded. "But that's because you are an unbeliever at heart. You follow a false faith. The gods of sea and storm are real. They make themselves known to me."

"Truly, the gods move in mysterious ways. What of the ancient spirit of Akora? Do you think that favors you, too?"

"There is no ancient spirit. It is a fiction of you Atreides."

She had expected him to say that but even so, she shivered inwardly. He was beyond hope.

"Enough," he said abruptly. "We will return to the palace together. You will announce our marriage, which will take place at once."

She knew what she had to do then. To say no, to defy him, to make very clear she would never become part of his insanity. He would be goaded into killing her and he would succeed. But he would have to come very close to do that and when he did . . . she would be ready.

She breathed in the sweet morning air and took one last look round the theater. Her thoughts were of her mother and father, her brothers and most especially of Royce. How she longed for him!

And yet, she would not shirk her duty. Never that.

"No," she said and waited for the step into eternity.

"No?" Deilos repeated as though she spoke a strange, unknown language.

"I will not marry you. I will never do anything you wish. I will defy you with every breath. Never while I live will you succeed."

There, it was done, and if there was any mercy in the Universe, it would be over soon.

He came closer and she shuddered, for in his eyes she saw the light of true evil that had taken possession of his soul. Because he had allowed it to do so, she reminded herself. Because he had yielded to the seductiveness of power and vanity that doomed him. He raised his hands, his fists flexing. "You cannot stop me!"

Closer . . . closer . . . the struggle to stand still and not try to flee was almost more than she could bear.

Her hand tightened, began to draw forth. She had been trained, as she had hinted to Royce. Every Akoran woman received such training, not because there was anything to fear from Akoran men but in simple recognition that the world could be more uncertain and dangerous than anyone wished.

She had done very well with her training. Her instructors had said it was her Atreides blood, but she had seen her father at sword practice and suspected his heritage also played a role.

A little closer . . .

She would kill Deilos. Deilos, dying, would

kill her. They would be linked in death but not in eternity, please all that was Holy.

Akora would be safe. This she had seen.

Her blade flashed, drawn swift and sure. Deilos saw it coming and reacted at once, just as she had seen him do in her visions. He was warrior-trained, honed for battle and maddened by the lust for power. The knife he yanked from the scabbard at his waist lunged toward her with deadly speed.

A heartbeat . . . her heart beating . . . once more . . . only once and then . . .

A roar of wind blasted past her, knocking her off her feet. A surge of power unlike any she had ever known seized her, like mighty wings soaring high . . .

She was wrapped in a strange stillness, hurtling in a direction she had neither seen nor suspected.

Her heart beat again and she felt time beat with it, a moment of time she had never expected to know.

Part of a world in which she had never imagined she would be.

And yet she was, indisputably, alive not only to the world but also to the strength and fury of the man holding her.

To Royce. The Hawk Lord, true in every way to his name, for he was, just then, a predator of such deadly intent she could scarcely bear to look at him. Scarcely endure the light of pure rage in his eyes.

"Damn you," he said and leaped, sword drawn, to face Deilos.

Who was gone.

Royce existed in a cold, silent well where time crawled and feeling did not exist. That was fortunate, for he was distantly aware of fury unlike any he had ever known, just beyond the edges of his mind. Rage best held well at bay. He stood, deliberately separating himself from the woman who gazed up at him, her eyes wide, dark, impenetrable.

He could not think of her or of the pain twisting in him. Not now, not yet.

He stared into the darkness where part of the stage had dropped away. Where Deilos had gone. Blade in hand, steel glowing in the failing light, the Hawk Lord leaped.

And fell an unknown distance, landing agilely. For a moment, he stood utterly still, not breathing, only listening and hearing nothing until . . . To his left, the way he judged to be west, a shower of pebbles rolled down an incline. He followed the sound, plunging into a tunnel faintly lit by ventilation shafts cut to the surface.

For a moment, only a moment, the walls seemed to contract in on him. Illusion, he reminded himself, and the gift of the very man he hunted. Bared, his teeth gleamed whitely in the dimness. He ran, easily and effortlessly, his tread silent against the damp earth.

A half mile on, the tunnel veered south. Royce smelled the sea. He redoubled his efforts and was quickly rewarded. Up ahead, not all that far, he could hear running steps. Whatever else he was, Deilos was in good shape. He moved quickly, too quickly for a man scrambling to escape any way he could. There was no hesitation, no indirection. He knew where he was going.

Just then, the tunnel curved again. Running, Royce miscalculated and struck the wall, dislodging loose rocks that fell with a clatter. Up ahead, Deilos stopped. In the sudden silence, his voice was high and shrill. "I know you're there!" he screamed. "Bastard Englishman! *Xenos!* For your interference, you will die!"

Cursing under his breath, Royce flattened himself against the tunnel. He did not care to dwell on the irony of the man whose life he had inadvertently saved wanting to take his own.

"You can't escape, Deilos. The Atreides is willing for you to stand trial. You'd be well advised to take that offer while you can."

"The Atreides?" Scorn mingled with the rage fueling Deilos, all but choking him. "That abomination! I should have killed her. By all the gods, I will! Her and all the rest of them. I will cleanse this land —"

His tirade continued but Royce was no longer listening. The threat to Kassandra eclipsed all else. Heedless of his own safety, he moved forward quickly. And saw the glint of water. An underground stream running into the Inland Sea. Deilos's planned escape route, complete with a small boat awaiting him.

Mad the traitor might be, but he got full marks for strategy.

Now or never, Royce thought, and hurled himself away from the wall, straight at Deilos.

Who anticipated his coming and was ready. He raised his arm, clutching in his hand what looked like a small clay pot. He grinned wildly as he threw it straight at Royce. "Die, Englishman! Die for her and for Akora! Writhe in flames no one can extinguish!"

Greek Fire exploded on the floor and along the walls of the tunnel. It would have splashed onto Royce himself had he not only just managed to leap back. Scant inches separated him from the fire that ignited instantly. The heat of it seared him, but even so, he did not retreat farther. If the flames climbed no higher, he could jump them. At least, he thought he could. It was worth the try . . .

But the flames did mount, so high they brushed the ceiling of the tunnel and so hot Royce had no choice finally but to pull back. Through the dancing fire, he only just made out Deilos, laughing as he entered the boat and launched it into the swift-moving river.

Kassandra had watched Royce vanish into the bowels of the earth. She had managed to stand and was distantly pleased that her legs held her. She could see well enough but the world seemed out of kilter. Beneath the ordinary sounds of birdsong and the distant rhythms of the city remained the odd rush of wind. Or was it her own blood still, incredibly moving to the rhythm of her heart?

Time passed, framed by disbelief and dread. Enough time for fear to shatter numbness and make her mind a canvas of terrifying images. What was happening to him? Where had he gone? Was he safe?

Her throat constricted painfully but she was scarcely aware of it. She could only stare into the abyss and pray he would be restored to her. Her faith was boundless but even so, when there was movement in the darkness, a stirring that swiftly resolved itself into a beloved form, she scarcely dared believe that her prayers had been heard.

The dying sunlight gleamed all around him, in the gold of his hair, over his bare, burnished skin, gilding him like an ancient god. He walked toward her swiftly, sheathing his sword as he came. His eyes never left her.

His hand closed on her arm. He did not hold her cruelly or painfully, but she felt the strength in him all the same and had to force herself to stand very still lest she tremble.

She was . . . afraid? Yes, deeply afraid of a man she would never have believed it possible that she could fear. Of a man she trusted absolutely with her heart, her body and her spirit. A man she would have said could move mountains because of his utter and unshakeable nobility.

A man who just then terrified her because she saw in him what she most feared in all the world. Not death, she had faced that and astonishingly still lived. But something far worse, the death of something so rare and precious she would have done anything to protect it.

Of love.

"Royce . . . I did what I had to . . . nothing more, nothing else. Please try to understand. I am Atreides, I have responsibilities, I had to —"

"Enough!" He spoke not loudly but low and hard, like steel scraped against stone. "I saw what you did. How you lured him to you. You've never carried a knife, not in the time I've known you. What did you imagine, that you could kill him?" He laughed harshly, without a shred of humor.

"Yes, I would have killed him! Deilos would have died. I saw it."

"You what?" He stared at her, understanding dawning even as it was resisted. "You saw it? You had some *vision* of this?" His hand tightened, becoming painful. "What did you see? Tell me!"

"I saw Deilos die. I saw Akora safe. Here in this place where we have spun our legends and shared our history. Isn't that enough?"

"If it is all, it is enough, otherwise no. What else did you see?"

She could lie. She could tell him that was all. But she was Atreides, honor was her shield. And, God help her, she loved him.

"I thought I would die as well."

"You saw . . . your own death?" His face twisted at the words, as though he sought to expel them from his very soul but could not for they clung to them both.

She nodded. "That day in the nursery, I saw it. Akora could survive if I killed Deilos, but doing that would mean I also had to die." At the look of horror on his face, she cried out. "Oh, please, understand me! I did not want to! I wanted to live just as anyone would. But there seemed to be no choice."

With steel in his voice, he said, "I remember very clearly you telling me that you could see *possible* futures. We choose our own fates, you said. Isn't that true?"

"I did say that." In the magical hours following Amelia's birth when she had succumbed to treacherous temptation and let herself draw close to him. "But I could see no future for Akora except that which required my death."

"And it didn't occur to you that you ought to tell someone this? That you just possibly ought to mention it instead of taking the whole bloody burden of the whole bloody mess on your own shoulders?"

"Who should I have told? Atreus, who would have kept me locked up to protect me? Alex, who would have done the same? Or perhaps I should have told you, Royce? But I already know what you would have done because you have done it. You prevented me from doing what I was supposed to do and now Deilos, instead of being dead, is still alive and at large."

"You *blame* me for saving your life?"

"No! Oh, God, no, I don't mean that at all! But you have hurtled us into a future I have never seen and I don't know what to do!"

He shook his head, as though dazed, but she was not fooled. He was still enraged, she could see that clearly, but she could also see beyond to the deep hurt welling up within him. That, more than anything, tore at her. She fought back tears even as she fought the terrible urge to cling to him, beg his forgiveness, do and say anything she had to in order to ease the pain ripping at them both.

"Did you think?" he asked, very low so that she could barely hear him. "Did you think for one moment how I would feel?"

How he would feel? Her mind was blank, her being frozen. She could not speak or move or do anything at all to defend herself.

For in truth there was no defense.

She had not thought.

She had assumed.

"I . . . we . . . wanted each other."

"Wanted? What in hell does that mean? I . . . damn it . . ." He broke away, breaking free of her, walking to the far edge of the stage. It was only a few yards really but it might have been eternity.

"I . . . cared about you," he said, the truth wrenched from him. "Did you think how I would feel after you were dead? Did it occur to you that I and any others who . . . care for you would suffer?"

She stood discovered and condemned. The knowledge chilled her more than fear or approaching death or anything she had yet experienced. So intent had she been on what she believed to be her destiny, indeed her mission, that she had allowed herself to consider nothing else.

"I wanted to live," she said, very low.

"But you did nothing to make that happen. You marched straight into death."

"Yes, but while I lived . . . I wanted to live." Had it been an act of consummate selfishness, this need to grasp life while yet she could? Was she a terrible, callous person for having failed to consider how he would feel?

The answer was stark and cruel. She could not shirk it no matter how desperately she tried. However right her motives, she had hurt this man who had deserved instead her most faithful care.

"Royce . . . I am sorry."

He shook his head again, shrugged and turned away, renouncing her as he renounced her contrition.

"It does not matter," he said, and she was

394

terrified that he was right.

"It does! I should have thought, should have realized. It is just that I have been so overwhelmed ever since I thought my life had to end soon."

"Akora matters," he said as though she had not spoken.

To her it did, but so did he. Oh, God, he mattered so very much. He was her life, her happiness, her hope for the future and the black-haired boy . . . A future she had not truly seen, merely conjured, wishing for what seemed even beyond imagining.

"Where are you going?" she entreated, for he was walking away, striding as a man will to a distasteful but necessary duty.

"To finish this," he said, and did not look back at her.

She went after him. Pride could not stop her nor could duty, for she was now in a world she did not know. She felt newborn in some strange sense and the feeling was both heady and liberating. She was *alive*. No doubt there had been more astounding miracles, but not for her.

Royce went directly to the docks where the men she had thought were on their way to Deimatos awaited him. They observed his coming stoically. Her own presence raised eyebrows, literally, but they were far too well schooled to display any reaction beyond that.

"Spread out," Royce directed. "Take whatever ships you need and block both straits, north and south, from the Inland Sea. Let no one come or go from Akora until you are told otherwise."

At once, Kassandra saw the wisdom of his orders. Deilos would be cut off from retreat. He would be forced to seek refuge within Akora. The men sprang to obey the one they called the Hawk Lord. That, too, did not escape her. They respected her as Atreides and looked to her to protect the stability they had always known. But when it came to fighting a deadly enemy, they turned instinctively to one they would follow gladly into battle.

So had it always been among men. So, she supposed, would it always be. Creation conspired that men and women should share their strengths.

When the warriors had dispersed, she looked to Royce. "What are you going to do?"

She might have spoken to the air, for he did not answer her. She saw no hint in him that her question had even been heard. He was closing her out, sealing himself from what was and what would be. The realization churned in her, making her feel, for just a moment, as though she could not go on.

But she would, of course. She had done as she had done. She was as she was. Perhaps he could never forgive that. Her spirit rebelled at the thought. She reached out, beyond restraint, and grasped his arm. His skin was warm, not rough precisely but without the smoothness of her own. As always when she touched him, she felt a start, even a sort of tingling, as though they were different sorts of forces that inevitably clashed before coming into alignment.

"You are going to Deimatos."

His eyes were hooded, like the hawk's. "Is that a question, *Atreides,* or an order?"

"Order? I am not such a fool! You are not a man to be ordered. You are going because you believe Deilos will go there."

"As a badger to his hole."

"I would go with you."

His brows rose. There was bitter humor in him. "Would you?"

Pride stirred again. She ignored it ruthlessly. "Yes, I would. I want to go with you."

"Because you are Atreides."

"No, it has nothing to do with that. I want to go because I love you."

He flinched. She saw that and was pleased. Far too much was at stake to indulge in fairness. Let him be stabbed by truth. Let it sink deep within him to draw out the poison of hurt and anger.

"Deimatos is the place of your demons," she said. "I would rather not have you face it alone."

"You were willing enough to have that happen when getting me out of the way served your own ends."

It was her turn to feel the dart of truth. She

took the wound and did not care. Instead, she flung her hair back, her head high, and glared at him. "Think as you like, condemn me as you will, but I would still go with you."

She feared he would refuse, but instead he looked at her with eyes that seemed chiseled from stone. "I do not trust you out of my sight," he said, and deliberately removed her hand from him.

And so they went. Not alone, for that would have been foolish, but not with any great number of attendants that would have alerted Deilos had he been watching. Kassandra suspected he was not. She had felt, indeed almost smelled, the fear in him when the Hawk Lord came and all his grand, deluded plans shattered like so much ill-cast glass. He would go to ground, gather round him his faithful following and his deadly weapons, and await what was to come.

Royce was not waiting. On board the small vessel carrying them and a few handpicked men, he spread out a map. The warriors gathered around him to study it. Kassandra was closed out again, blocked by broad backs and wide shoulders, by the intent murmur of men preparing for battle.

She climbed up on a hatch and peered over them. The map looked simply drawn but still contained a good amount of detail. She almost thought she recognized it but she could not be sure.

If Royce saw her looking, he gave no sign. When he was done, he folded the map away. The men dispersed in small, mainly silent groups. They sat, stretched out on the deck, looking out over the water with hard eyes.

"Where did you get the map?" she asked. In such a gathering of men, her woman's voice sounded odd even to her own ears. Royce looked at her and did not answer. She stared back, determined.

"From Joanna," he said finally. Deliberately, he added, "Alex trusted her with it."

That hurt, of course, but it did not stop her. At least he was talking to her. If she could keep him doing that, he would not be so able to close her out.

"Where did Alex get it?"

Again, he hesitated. "Either he drew it or Atreus did."

"Wait . . . . I remember something about the two of them and Deimatos. I think they got in trouble with father for going there."

"They damn near got themselves killed but they seem to have had a lot of fun in the process."

Well, yes, of course they would have, and Royce would understand that entirely. Indeed, had the opportunity arisen, he would have shared in their "fun."

"Of what use is this map?" she asked.

Still grudging, he said, "It's of the caves."

"Marcellus should have had that when he

sent men over to search."

"He did have it but there was no time to investigate every passage and chamber."

"You intend to do so?" Her stomach churned. She who had never been seasick in her life but was very much afraid that she might be about to start.

"Your brothers spent months, from what I understand, exploring the caves. They may have reached the deepest reaches of them. If they didn't, it wasn't for want of trying."

"No wonder father was so angry. They could have been lost or hurt."

Royce shrugged. "Some of the passages are actually rivers running underground for long distances."

"Joanna said something about there being a lot of water in the caves."

"There certainly seems to be."

"But you must know, water cannot protect you against Greek Fire."

"That's true," he said, and returned his attention to the map.

Chapter
NINETEEN

The craggy shores of Deimatos rose out of the sea shortly after midday. At the sight of them, apprehension surged in Kassandra. She fought it down, willing herself to calm, for truly she could not do less. A few of the men talked quietly among themselves, several napped. None looked at all apprehensive about the battle in which they might shortly be engaged. That was the warrior way, she supposed. They were trained to it from earliest manhood and it served them well. With her own emotions at the breaking point, she could not help but envy them.

The island being too worrisome a sight to long contemplate, she turned her gaze to Royce. He stood near the bow, looking out over the water at the approaching shore. Like the other men, he appeared imperturbable. His features were hard, his eyes narrowed against the glare of sunlight off the water. As she watched, his hand moved lightly, almost caressingly on the hilt of his sword.

Nine months he had been held in a cell

carved out of stone and all but buried in the ground. Nine months with little food or water, scant light and less hope. Nine months that had almost killed him and that would most likely have driven a lesser man to madness.

For months afterward, he had struggled to recover physically and mentally. Only recently had he been able to sleep inside again on any regular basis.

Now he was returning to the place of his suffering and, quite possibly, to the man who had inflicted it.

He had set himself apart from her, and not just by the length of the deck. Far more, perhaps insurmountable, lay between them. The thought made her heart hurt but it could not stop her. She went to him quietly and stood beside him as the ship rocked beneath their feet and the shore came ever closer.

He shouldn't have brought her. He should have sent her back to the palace to stay with her mother and Joanna, where she would have been perfectly safe so far as there was any safety while the foul business of Deilos remained unsettled. If nothing else, that might have left him freer to concentrate on what needed doing.

Instead, he was hard-pressed to think of anything except the faint scent of her skin wafting to him on the sea breeze, the soft murmur of her gown, and the all but irresistible impulse to draw her to him. She felt so damn good in his arms, as though she truly belonged there, and, truth be told, he had never felt as right anywhere as he did when she held him to her heart. But that was all before, burned away in the realization of what she had done — and what she had been prepared to do.

She would have died.

Cold washed over him. He had to remember that . . . *had to.* His parents' deaths had been bad enough, but he had found the blessed resiliency of childhood and rebuilt his life. This was different. She would have left him to a void of anguish and loss from which he doubted very much he would ever have been able to recover. At the very least, believing what she had about her fate, she damn well should have kept her distance from him.

Her hand brushed his. He stiffened and made to pull away but his effort fell short or perhaps his intent was weak, for her fingers caught his and held on tightly.

Several moments passed. The shore sped nearer. The men began to stir.

Kassandra turned her face away but not before he saw the silver glint of her tears. "Don't die," she murmured. "Please don't."

The wind blew harder.

Deimatos appeared to be deserted. Not so much as a stray rabbit crossed their path as they climbed the short distance from the anchorage inland toward the largest entrance to the caves. On the way, they passed a narrow trail, really no more than a bare stretch of dirt. Already the grass was beginning to return, with the result that the trail might have gone unnoticed had not the trees and rocks surrounding it been all too familiar to Royce. They were almost the last sight he had seen before being thrown into hell.

Down that path was the prison in which he had nearly perished. He could still smell the dank stone and fetid moss, still remember the relentless cold that seeped into his bones even on days when the brilliant sun visible through the tiny slit of a window had mocked him with especial cruelty. To that barred window he had clung when he had the strength to pull himself up to it, staring out across the water at the white tower just visible on a nearby island. From that cell he had been taken to be led, he thought, to his death.

But the man who had walked that narrow path was not the man who glanced at it in passing and did not so much as flinch. Life truly did hold the promise of rebirth, he realized, but only at a cost. The pain of the past no longer had the power to hurt him but the pain of the future twisted in his gut with vicious sharpness.

She would have died.

He could not forget that, could not set it aside even for an instant. His shock and horror, his pain and anger had only grown stronger and more settled as the hours wore on and he had time to contemplate what she had done.

Akora has always been a place of life. So she had said, but for Akora she would have died. Without saying anything to anyone, without asking for help, without even giving him a chance to save her.

She had sent him away. To free herself for the embrace of death.

"Damn her."

"What did you say?" Kassandra asked. She walked beside him, really ran a little, for he devoured the ground with his pace. The veil over her hair had come loose and tumbled about her shoulders. She was slightly breathless and her eyes were very wide.

"Nothing," he replied and kept going, determined not to look at her or think about her or . . . He slowed slightly, one hand on his sword, the other clenched. "I said nothing."

"Oh, I thought . . . never mind."

"When we get where we are going, you will do exactly as you are told. Do you understand?"

"Yes, of course, but where are we going?"

"There," he said, and pointed to the top of the hill ahead of them.

"I know this place," Kassandra said a short time later when they had climbed the hill and could see much of Deimatos spread out beneath them. She had to speak up to be heard over the rush of the waterfall nearby. "Joanna told me of it."

"She and Alex escaped from the caves through there," Royce said and pointed.

From the wall of stone rising far above the ground flowed a rush of water that tumbled, glistening in the fading sun, down and down and down until it came to rest finally in a pool frothed by the force of the torrent crashing into it. The sight was beautiful but the thought of riding that current of water was terrifying.

"It is amazing that they lived," Kassandra said softly.

He agreed with her but would not say so. He wanted to say nothing at all, to close himself off entirely from her, but the effort seemed beyond him.

"It was their only way out," he said, "after Deilos's men sealed them up in one of the caves."

A shudder ran through her. He saw it and knew she understood what her brother and sister-in-law must have experienced when they realized they had no hope of escape but to dare the underground river with all its treacherous dangers.

"You think Deilos is down there somewhere," she said.

He nodded. "He has had time enough to reach here and to hide himself."

"There are miles of caves."

"Probably. There are also twenty-three entrances . . . or exits."

Her eyes flew to him. "Twenty-three? You know so exactly?"

"Alex and Atreus knew. They mapped each and every one." He gestured to the men who had followed them up from the ship carrying wooden litters stacked with barrels taken from the hold.

"We will split up," Royce said, "into teams of four." He divided the men quickly, showing each on the map where they should go. When he was done he pointed to the sky. "When the width of a man's fist doubled stands between sun and sea, then will we act. Be ready."

"Act how?" Kassandra asked when they were alone, save for the trio of men who had remained with them. "What are you going to do?"

"Trap a rat," Royce replied and smiled.

He was punishing her, of course. She realized that well enough. He was angry and hurt by what she had done. Being a warrior, the anger would rule, at least for the moment.

But he had brought her along and for that she could not help but be grateful.

Now he was fooling with what looked like barrels of gunpowder.

Not fooling. She had to believe he actually knew what he was doing. But the memory of the arena, the roar of sound and the screams that followed, made her stomach churn.

"Those are for . . . ?" she asked.

His back was to her. His very broad, very

powerful back she had racked her nails down a time or two. He did not turn but he did reply.

"Choices," he said and continued with his work.

It grew cooler as the sun slanted westward. She squinted at the horizon and tried to imagine how much longer it would be before a man's fist doubled would cover the distance. Not long, she thought, not long at all.

The barrels of gunpowder were linked by fuses and set at the very edge of the hill just above the waterfall. If they were exploded, it was likely the opening through which the water flowed would be blocked.

Royce stood, hands on his hips, and looked out beyond the hill. The wind riffled his hair and the warrior's kilt that was his only garb. To her eyes, he looked wild and untamed. And deeply loved.

In this world where she had never thought to walk, she could admit the true feelings of her heart. Joanna had known, but then she was a woman who had accepted the irresistible nature of love and could recognize it at work in another.

I love you, Kassandra thought, but gave no voice to the words. It was enough to say them within herself and marvel at their resonance. How powerful they were, how compelling, how like the very man to whom she would have directed them had circumstances been different.

I love you. The wind made her eyes tear,

nothing more. She blinked hard but refused to turn away. The sight of him was too precious.

Their shadows lengthened across the ground. Royce raised his arm, rippling with muscle, and sighted down it to his clenched fist. Almost . . . not quite . . . a few more minutes . . .

"You are not going into the caves," she said, finally letting herself believe.

"Not if I can help it," he replied and stiffened slightly, listening.

The first roar of sound came from the west, well out of their sight but heard clearly all the same. A second and third followed rapidly. Then there was only a single, vast explosion that seemed to go on endlessly. So intense was it that Kassandra felt the ground tremble beneath her feet. Instinctively, she reached out to Royce.

He caught her to him, sheltering her against his body. She felt a moment's fierce joy at the realization that he had not hesitated to protect her but the sensation was fast fleeting. Barely had the last tremors subsided than he put her from him.

He glanced toward the barrels of gunpowder. She saw the struggle in him and wondered, scarcely breathing, what decision he would make. One more fuse lit, one more explosion and Deilos would be trapped, buried alive within Akora itself. No doubt there were some who would find that fitting.

Was Royce among them?

He bent down near the fuse, looked from it to the hill's edge as though gauging the distance and the effect.

"It would work," she said because she knew it to be true. "You would leave him no way out."

"And leave no assurance that he was dead."

"The map —"

He straightened, wiping off his hands. "Could be incomplete."

"You know that is not likely."

He looked at her then, really looked as he had avoided doing almost entirely. She felt his gaze to her marrow and could not turn from it even as the knowledge of how much she had hurt him made her wish to do so.

"In point of fact," he said, "I know very little, certainly less than I thought I did."

"Royce —"

He gestured curtly, cutting her off. "Enough." He moved closer to watch the rush of water emerging from deep within the earth.

The sun set, further chilling the air and revealing the glory of the stars but slightly dimmed by the waxing moon. Kassandra sat farther back from the hillside away from the spray of water and drew her knees up to her chest. She was distantly aware of being cold but could not manage to care.

Many of the men returned, leaving behind only a few to guard the sealed entrances. The rest took up positions near the waterfall.

Royce paced, crossing and recrossing the

same length of ground silvered by the horned moon. She watched him bathed in light, gilded by droplets of water, precious to her eyes.

Time passed, future becoming present becoming past. She breathed in the scents of the night and marveled again that she lived. She would see the sun rise on a world she had never expected to know and in that world she would have to make some life for herself.

A thought for later. Now there was only the moon, the man and the moment.

She stood, surprised to find her legs stiff and aching, and went to him. He saw her coming and stopped, watching her with guarded eyes.

"Deilos can wait," she said. "Even with the caves sealed off, if he has supplies, he could last for months."

"He could but he won't. Patience does not march with vanity."

"You think him vain?"

"I think him deranged. Don't you?"

"Oh, yes, corrupted by the lust for power and convinced of his own invincibility. But he must know you are waiting here."

"He will not come alone."

A terrible sense of foreboding seized her, not a vision but the simple fear of a woman for the safety of the man she loved. "Seal the cave." When he looked at her in surprise, she said urgently, "Really, what chance is there that he could escape? He will die . . . eventually and without the need for any more risk of life."

He was tempted, she could see that. Tempted to close off the last exit from the labyrinth of caves and leave the men in them — those who had held him captive — to suffer a long and terrible death. He had prepared for that, readied himself to do it, and still he did not. The fuse remained unlit.

"If I do that," he said to himself as much as to her, "this matter will remain unresolved. People will want to believe Deilos dead and Akora safe but they won't know for sure. Already, there is too much uncertainty to add yet more."

He did not have to say anything else; she understood all too well what he meant. Atreus might die and Akora face the challenge of finding new leadership. At the very least, the people had to know that the man who had brought such grief to them had himself been brought to justice.

"We wait," Royce said. He gestured to two men below, summoning them to him. When they arrived at the top of the hill, he gave his orders quickly and succinctly. "Remain here with the Atreides. Guard her well."

The men glanced at her, nodded. Kassandra wanted to protest but knew the futility of that. If battle came, the top of the hill was the safest place to be. Of course, Royce would not be there. He would be below, in the thick of it.

And she would be able to do nothing but watch.

Her gaze fell on the gunpowder. Flint and tinder were nearby. It would be so easy . . .

The moon rose higher and in the doing, seemed to shrink. But its light remained bright enough to bathe the world in a sea of silver.

She could not see Royce any longer. He was hidden somewhere in the woods beyond the waterfall along with the rest of the men, save for the two set to guard her. She felt a moment's sympathy for them, knowing how they would chafe at missing the action.

They waited. She wondered what was happening in the caves. How many men were in there with Deilos? Were they convinced by now that the only remaining way out was the underground river and the waterfall where it emerged from the earth? Would they dare that treacherous route knowing they might drown in the process?

Deilos would, she was certain of that. He would trust himself to his gods of sea and storm.

And he would bring the Greek Fire with him, for the river could not harm it.

She walked a little closer to the barrels, feeling the guards watching her but knowing they would do nothing unless she tried to leave the hilltop for a more vulnerable position. If she merely bent down with her back to them, blocking the action of her hands, she could strike flint to tinder and . . .

Betray Royce? Fail to be what he needed and

deserved. He had earned her trust, had in truth every right to demand it.

He was the warrior, not she. Her courage was steady and her instincts good, but it was he who walked with the god of battles.

She stepped back, still staring at the barrels but no longer tempted to touch them. Rather, she put her faith where she knew it belonged, in the man who had earned it, and sent with it a heartfelt prayer that he would succeed.

Scarcely had she done so than a scream pierced the air, muted by the rush of water but audible all the same. Kassandra ran to the edge of the hill just as a dark shape hurtled from the caves, riding the flume of water. Almost at once, another followed and another.

Not screams, she realized belatedly, but the bloodchilling shouts of warriors as they rushed the enemy. Desperate men riding the stream of water down into the pool below, then scrambling out quickly to hurtle the pots they carried toward the trees . . .

That must surely explode in flame, banishing the night and threatening to turn the surrounding glen into an inferno. In which Royce and his men were trapped.

"No!"

Her scream was frantic. Terror beyond any she had ever known threatened to consume her. She turned desperately, with no true idea of what she would do, certain only that she had to do something. But before she could take a step,

414

the two men charged with protecting her were there.

"Atreides," one said gently, clearly mindful of her horror, "look."

She followed the direction he indicated but at first saw nothing, only more of the human missiles shooting out of the caves, surviving the plunge and letting loose with their deadly cargo.

Or trying to. The fire was striking metal, the metal of a shield wall raised by Royce and his men who stood behind it in tight formation, unshrinking as fiery blow after blow came at them, such extraordinary discipline testament to both training and courage. Again and again, the pots exploded and the shield wall held. Fire did ignite, burning against the metal. She could only imagine that the men must be protecting their hands and arms, most likely with the heavy leather gloves used in the training of horses and for other tasks. Fire also struck the berms of earth she saw had been dug in the deep shadows cast by the trees, forming a barrier between the waterfall and the forest beyond. But earth did not burn well any more than did metal ultimately. The Greek Fire seared both, to be sure, but inevitably the terrible flames meant to bring agonizing death began to flicker out.

As for Deilos's followers . . . many of those who tried to emerge from the pond got very little farther before, inexplicably it seemed, they began to fall, first one, then another and another. Only after she witnessed half-a-dozen of them go down did Kassandra realize there were archers stationed in the surrounding trees. Again and again, invisible in the shadows, arrows flew. Again and again, the men of Deilos met the swift and merciless hand of justice.

Hope stirred within her and with it tremendous pride in the man she loved. All along she had believed Royce possessed the heart of a warrior. Now she realized he also had the mind and spirit of a true commander, one well able to lead his men to victory.

Except that it would not be true victory until Deilos was dealt with. Was he one of the men down there, dead or wounded in the pond, or immediately around it? She strained to see but without success. The hill was too high, the smoke from the fires still obscured the glen and clouds moved across the moon.

Just before they did, she saw Royce move forward, big and relentless in the smoke, striding through it with his sword unsheathed. He called to his men to close in, cutting off any chance for their foes to escape, and began going among the fallen, checking each and every one, living and dead.

Kassandra had seen enough. Nothing, not even her well-intentioned guards, could keep her on the hilltop. She darted past them, ignored their startled shouts, and ran down the steep path to the pond. Royce saw her coming and straightened. He waited until she was very close before he said, "You do not belong here."

She ignored his anger as best she could and held her ground. "It seems safe enough. You have done a magnificent job."

Her praise clearly surprised him. He was grappling with it when one of his men shouted. Just then a dark shape hurtled down the waterfall into the pond. At the same moment, the moon emerged from behind the clouds and shone her light directly on the water.

And the man who sprang from it.

Kassandra had a moment, only a moment, to wonder if Deilos might not be entirely wrong that some power favored him. But not the ancient gods of sea and storm, of that she was quite sure. Those old fellows were only one more face of Creation, the life force that suffused the Universe. But there was another force, very different, to which men had long since given the name of Evil. Whatever its origin or its purpose, she could not say. She only knew that she had felt its malevolent presence from time to time when she walked the pathways of the future.

Perhaps it favored Deilos, perhaps it even moved within him, for he came from the pond seemingly with strength beyond that of ordinary men and faced with sneering glee the warriors who confronted him.

"Alive!" he exclaimed. "How can you still be alive? What mystery is this? What taunting twist of fate?" He looked round at his own men lying dead or wounded and showed no hint of care for them. "Fools, stupid fools. How simple a task I set you. Kill. How hard is that, especially with the weapon you were given?"

His gaze shifted to Kassandra and she felt the full blast of his rage. "You, foul woman, violator of the natural order. I should have killed you when I could."

She might have answered but just then Royce moved, putting himself between her and the man whose every word was provocation. The Hawk Lord's blade flashed in moonlight. He moved it but slightly, gesturing.

"Come."

"To what?" Deilos demanded. "Captivity? The mockery of a trial you offered? I think not!"

Barely were the words uttered than Deilos leaped, his own sword drawn, flinging himself straight at Royce. He meant to die, Kassandra realized even as horror rose within her, but he also meant to kill. In Deilos's twisted mind, it would be better to die by the sword than live defeated. Perhaps he even imagined some paradise awaited him or perhaps it was not Deilos at all who gazed from eyes reddened by smoke and fire.

"Royce!"

His name screamed in her mind but the warning remained unuttered. She was the daughter and sister of warriors. Never would she so foolishly distract one challenged to mortal combat.

"Get back," Royce called to his men, his voice hard as the steel of his blade. The night turned cold as the Hawk Lord said softly, "He is mine."

How they had danced in the gallery of the London house, Royce and Alex together, moving with strength and grace, swords flashing on that sun-filled summer day. How the unique power of good men, their courage and their will, had shone in them.

This was different.

Here death hovered, not death that was the gateway to the life beyond, but death, the servant of despair and destruction. It leaped and gamboled with Deilos's mad strength, it slashed and speared and turned to strike again.

But Royce — beloved Royce — was its match.

He had been born for this, Kassandra thought distantly, there amid the bold towers and verdant fields of Hawkforte, honed in blood and sinew, his warrior's heart unflinching.

The clash of steel rang out over the roar of the water, filling the glade. Deilos was a master swordsman but raw hate drove him and it was a clumsy spur. It made him just a shade impulsive, just a fraction off, just an instant too late or too soon, with every blow striking only Royce's steel.

They circled the small field of battle, never taking their eyes from one another. Royce's stamina was vast, Deilos's almost but not quite its equal. Breathing harder, sweat pouring from him, he roared his frustration.

"Damn you, *die!*"

"Not here," Royce replied calmly. "Not now. A year ago, perhaps, but moment to moment makes us anew." He moved closer, turning slightly, gauging the moment as he confronted the man who would kill him if he could but, far more to the point, would have killed Kassandra.

Would still, did he ever get the chance.

The sword felt right in his hands, though he had wielded it for only a few days and then only in practice. It felt made for him, perfectly balanced and attuned to his every move.

The night air drifted around him, whispering in moonlight. Far in the back of his mind, distant voices seemed to murmur, the deep and resonant voices of men he knew in a way he could never explain. Men of his own proud line, reaching back in time through centuries. Men who had fought always to protect the good and preserve the right.

Men who were with him now. His own father, his presence so vivid and real that Royce would not have been surprised to see him standing beside him. But beyond, generation after generation, stood men Royce knew had been with him in some way all his life and who always would be because he was one of them now and eternally.

And yet he stood alone, as each of them had stood alone at some time, facing an enemy who called from within him the darkest and most savage of his own emotions. Hate, fury, a ravenous hunger for vengeance that would never be satisfied until Deilos's blood poured from him to nourish the ground his fire had blackened.

Akora is a place of life.

The words rose suddenly from deep within Royce, in the hidden chamber of the soul reserved for ultimate truths. Memory surged, of himself as a young boy in the library at Hawkforte, first falling under the spell of the Fortress Kingdom. Of wet afternoons and windswept nights idled away studying the artifacts his ancestor had sent back. Holding them in his hands, turning them this way and that, feeling the power within them even when he could not give it a name.

But he could name it now; he knew what it was. He had found it everywhere on Akora, in the faces of ordinary men and women as well as in the strange, moss-wreathed face peering from the stone of the sacred cave.

Above all, he had found it in Kassandra.

Kassandra who, believing herself under sentence of death, had never abandoned her fierce commitment to life.

Deilos's chest rose and fell like a bellows for

hell's fire. By moonlight, he looked a sickly gray.

"You can't kill me! You can't! The gods favor me! I am meant to rule Akora!"

"Akora is a place of life," Royce said quietly even as he moved, flowing with wind and moon, his sword moving too quickly to be seen.

Deilos stared at him uncomprehendingly. The words meant nothing to the man who had imagined himself the rightful ruler of the land whose very essence he did not grasp to the slightest degree.

A moment and another passed before Deilos screamed. Truth he could not grasp, but he could take frantic hold of the stump of his wrist from which sword and hand had fallen as one.

Royce bent, took moss from the water's edge, untouched by the fire, and wiped his blade. He slid the sword back into its scabbard without glancing at the traitor whose screams went on and on without end.

"Bring him," the Hawk Lord said to his men and turned toward the sea.

Chapter
TWENTY

Marcellus met them on the quay accompanied by a company of soldiers. The magistrate wore an air of quiet satisfaction as he watched Deilos and his men being loaded into the wagons that would take them to prison.

When the last was gone, he bowed to Royce. "A task well done, Hawk Lord."

"Your task now, Marcellus. I can't say I envy you."

"Which is why you are a warrior and I am a judge, lord. Each to our own paths." He turned to Kassandra. "Your lady mother requests that you come directly to the palace, Atreides."

"Do you know why?"

"I regret, I do not."

Apprehension washed through Kassandra. Coming into the port of Ilius, she had scanned the sky as before for any sign of the smoke that would indicate Atreus was dead. Seeing none, she was relieved, but now she feared the worst. Instinctively, she turned to Royce.

"Come with me?"

Even as she asked, she realized he was

watching her. His manner remained distant but he did not refuse.

"If you wish." A chariot awaited them. They stood together yet apart as it sped up the hill toward the Lion's Gate.

Entering the vast courtyard, Kassandra thought everything looked as it had before. There was no sign of any important development but that meant little. Her parents might have chosen to keep such knowledge secret as they awaited the outcome of events on Deimatos.

The moment she stepped into the private area of the palace, away from prying eyes, she dropped all pretext of calm and broke into a run. She had almost reached the doors to Atreus's quarters when they opened and a young woman emerged.

Brianna . . . her fiery hair a tangled mess, her tunic looking as though she had slept in it. Brianna . . . whose head was bent and whose shoulders appeared slumped.

Kassandra stopped suddenly, unable to take another step or ask the question that screamed within her mind. Only the hard warmth of Royce's hand closing around hers anchored her to hope.

She clung to the comfort he offered even as Brianna belatedly became aware of their presence. She lifted her head, clearly fighting exhaustion, and . . .

Smiled. A huge, brilliant smile to strip away

weariness and banish fear. A smile of such radiant glory it seemed as though a sliver of the sun shone forth from within her.

"The Vanax has awakened," she said, and laughed even as tears of heartfelt relief coursed down her cheeks.

Heedless of her own tears, Kassandra hurried into the room. Her parents were sitting beside the bed. Joanna stood nearby. Elena was next to her, the healer's right arm supported by a sling. They were all attentive to Atreus but Phaedra turned her head as her daughter and Royce entered, and her smile rivaled Brianna's.

"He is asleep again," she whispered, "but he woke about an hour ago. He knew us. Oh, Kassandra, he *knew* us!"

Mother and daughter embraced, both weeping, as Andrew stood and held out a hand to Royce. "Praise God you have both returned," he said gruffly.

"Not alone," Royce replied. "Marcellus is in his glory."

Andrew's eyes sharpened. "Deilos . . . ?"

"And two dozen of his men, all that remain I believe. We flushed them from the caves."

"He means that quite literally," Kassandra interjected. She could not stop smiling any more than she could hold back the tears of relief that continued to flow. For the first time in far too long, she found herself laughing. "I've noticed the English fascination with our plumbing. Perhaps that is what inspired so ingenious a solution."

"Not the waterfall?" Joanna gasped and laughed as well.

Her brother nodded modestly. "Of course the waterfall. You and Alex managed it much better than did Deilos or any of the others. Those that survived are all injured . . . one way or another."

"How unfortunate," Andrew remarked, his tone making it clear he thought otherwise.

"I suppose I should see to it that my assistants have all they need," Elena said. She bowed before moving toward the door.

Phaedra caught her hand in passing. "Atreus . . . ?"

Gently, the healer said, "He sleeps peacefully, which will speed his recovery. He recognized you, he spoke a few words, he understood what was said to him and he can move all his limbs. Truly, we are blessed." She looked down ruefully at her injured arm. "I can even accept this, knowing it prevented surgery that was not needed and might have done great harm."

"Still," Andrew said, "he would not be recovering but for your excellent care."

"So true," Phaedra agreed, and rose to embrace the healer. "We will never forget what you have done."

Clearly pleased but also embarrassed, Elena took her leave. A short time later, Joanna followed her. She looked long at her brother before departing. Her eyes were filled with loving concern. "You have been to Deimatos."

He nodded, imperturbable in the moonlight flooding Atreus's chamber, challenging the lamps that glowed warmly. "Twice. The second time was better."

Joanna sighed. She touched his arm gently. "I am very glad."

Kassandra watched the easy interplay between them. They needed so few words: a glance or two, a quick touch. The communication between brother and sister was direct and clear, shaped by a lifetime of love nothing could ever change.

The envy she felt appalled her. She turned away and found herself looking at Atreus. He seemed very pale, lying there against the smooth linen sheets. His hair had ever been dark as night but now it appeared even more so, as though all color drowned in it. The hard lines and planes of his face seemed accentuated. He looked . . . not older . . . but almost eternal, like a sculpture he himself might make. His chest rose and fell smoothly, without effort.

The Vanax would live.

And more than that, he would recover completely. He would be Atreus again, the strong, indomitable brother she knew and loved. He would resume his life and his duties, which essentially were one and the same.

She would be free.

The thought seemed unworthy yet she could not banish it. She would always be Atreides, but she would no longer be *the Atreides*. People would remember what she had done, they would speak well of her. But they would be immensely relieved to get back to normal.

As was she herself.

No longer *the Atreides*. But still Kassandra?

At her birth, her parents had named her Adara. It meant *beautiful* and she had always supposed it was the sort of name given by doting parents. But when her "gift" became obvious while yet she was very young, her name had been changed. It was meant to serve as a reminder of what happened when the warnings of a true seer of the future were ignored.

She could not remember being Adara. She had always and ever been Kassandra.

Was she still? If she sought vision now, would it be revealed to her?

At the mere thought, rejection welled up in her. She had no wish to do any such thing. If she never saw a glimmer of any possible future again, she would be thrilled beyond words.

But she had a duty . . . did she not? She must stand sentinel against the dangers confronting her people.

Atreus slept so peacefully. How she longed to do the same. But more than that, she longed to live . . . normally. As Joanna did and her mother and so many other women she had known. Taking the future as it came, surprises and all.

Royce had surprised her. She had not foreseen what would happen between them. Had not guessed when she was drawn to England for some purpose she had thought concealed from her . . . but was it really? Or was it right before her eyes, the man who had saved her and Akora both? The man who had looked at her with such rage and pain when he realized the terrible choice she had made.

Her whole body tensed. She rose suddenly and walked to the nearest window, hoping the night breeze would cool her.

"Kassandra." Her mother spoke, always vigilant as a mother will be. "Is something wrong?"

She turned swiftly, too aware of Royce's nearness. "No! Of course not. Atreus is well. Nothing else matters."

"We all rejoice at the good turn Atreus has taken," her father said. He, who had lifted her high while still she was a child, who had made her laugh and wiped her tears away. He who knew her so well. "But a great deal more matters."

"Akora will be safe."

"Thanks to you and Royce, and ultimately to all of us."

The Englishman, who had come as a castaway to the Fortress Kingdom and stayed to love a princess, said, "In that safety lies the well-being of each and every individual, including you. So heed your mother's question. Is something wrong?"

No, yes, everything. Oh, God, what could she

say to them? They loved her, trusted her, respected her. She counted their good opinion above the stars themselves and could not bear the thought of ever disappointing them.

"I am . . . tired."

"Then you must rest," her mother said.

Phaedra left the bedside of her son and went to her daughter. She took her in her arms as she had while yet she was so small. Too soon ago, time too fleeting. They both knew that, there in that moment.

"Rest," Phaedra said. "Atreus lives, Alex comes, Deilos faces justice. You have done so very well. Now let gentle sleep knit up your care."

"I love you," Kassandra said and felt the fierce truth of that love flowing through them both.

Her mother drew back a little and looked at her, really looked as one soul to another. All she felt was in her eyes as she said, "I rejoice in your life. You fill me with gladness."

Apparently, it was a day for tears. They burned her cheeks as she hugged her mother and saw, over Phaedra's shoulder, Royce walk quietly from the room.

She did not go after him. Pride did not stop her nor did duty. But fear, raw and stark, put the brake on impulse.

She knew, because she stooped to ask, that he was within the palace. He had gone to speak with Marcellus and the other men. Sida brought her that information without expression, brought as well a tray of calming tea and sweet biscuits.

"Eat," the servant said. "Your mother will not forgive me if you take ill."

"When have I ever done so? Name once when I have ailed?"

"You had the measles when you were eight."

"I have forgotten that."

"Some of us have not. We feared for your life." The servant pursed her lips. "Not for the last time."

"All I have ever tried to do was what I thought was necessary." Did none of them truly understand that? Did they all condemn her?

Was she doomed to that most loathsome of emotions, self-pity?

She shuddered at the thought and drank the tea. It helped, a little.

Sida undid the brooches that held the tunic at her shoulders and eased the garment from her. She dropped a sleeping gown over Kassandra's head and turned back the covers of the bed. "There comes a time when it is right and fit to lay down burdens."

"A new world . . ."

"Perhaps, I know not of such things. But it is the world in which we find ourselves, praise the Creator, and we must manage as best we can."

The linen was very cool against her back. Sida drew a cover over her, walked to the windows, and closed the shutters. The room fell into shadows.

"Sleep," Sida said softly and went away, leaving Kassandra to her dreams.

They came in fits and starts, fragments of memory and imagination. She was on Deimatos again and terrified, then back in the house in London, spinning round and round in the sun. Royce was there and the dark-haired boy — oh, how she loved them both! She heard her brother's voice, Atreus as he had sounded in the long ago days before he went into the caves and emerged the Chosen.

"Look, Kassandra, look at the size of this fish!"

They were on the banks of a river, along with Alex, and they were all very young. The fish, on the other hand, was very large and gleamed bright silver in the sunlight. They ate it grilled, with lemons and pepper, and it was succulent on her tongue.

"Grandfather is dead."

Alex's grandfather and her own, the one in England where Alex had to stay. He had written to her explaining why. Akora needed him there. The world was changing. The Fortress Kingdom could not risk falling behind.

She missed him terribly and dreamed of seeing England for herself. As she had done . . . with Royce.

A moan pierced her dreams. She heard it and awoke uneasily. Night had fallen. She sat up in the bed, her body stiff from having lain unmoving in the grip of exhaustion.

The bed, where Royce had come to her, felt barren. She left it suddenly and kept going, straight from the room, dragging a cloak with her. Flinging it on, she went along the corridor that ran beside the family quarters and down the stairs to the courtyard.

The square that thronged with people at all hours of the day looked vast and dark, filled with shadows. As a child, she had imagined it to be the largest place in the world. Even now, she thought it might be.

On the walls beyond, the nightwatch kept vigil. She turned away, lest they see her. Where could she go? The caves beneath the palace were replete with taunting memories. There she had sought vision and there, too, she had found Royce. She could not bear to confront them now.

The public rooms of the palace would also be empty but they held no attraction for her.

She could go to the libraries but they, too, were a place of memory.

There was always the roof.

The vast roof of the palace covering several acres and holding within it one particular place of magic and mystery that had always drawn her.

A staircase around a nearby corner led upward. She climbed slowly, wondering when she had last been there. Several years ago, to be sure, before the world closed in around her.

She had been . . . eighteen, perhaps? And enchanted with the stars.

There were other places on Akora where those who knew of such things charted the skies, places hidden away beyond the touch of light where even the smallest outside fire was forbidden. But the first of such places, the oldest and still the most respected, was on the roof of the palace itself. Legend had it that even before the original parts of the palace were built, the earliest inhabitants of Akora had observed the skies from the top of the same hill.

Kassandra believed that, for she had seen the ancient records kept in the library, detailing the movements of the constellations, how they shifted in shape and position over the ages, and how even the star pointing to true north changed.

Parchment after parchment bore the painstaking observations of astronomers long dead, men and women whose writing made them seem eternally alive. Individual hands could be recognized, and the dates noted when people seemed especially tired or perhaps cold. There were even personal observations:

"How glorious the heavens! How insignificant are we who attempt to understand them, yet how enobling the task."

"How I would rather be with Polydorus tonight!"

"What tug is this I feel, like the tide drawing me not to the sea but to the stars? Why do I feel my home is there?"

"My feet are numb!"

"A comet! I have seen a comet! There is purpose to my being here."

"Only a fool forgets his dinner under such circumstances. Count me among that sorry brotherhood."

"The new lenses are ready. What will they reveal?"

"We are so very small."

But for all that, so stubbornly alive.

In the distance, she could see the portion of the roof that was a garden, created long ago and still faithfully nurtured. Between it and her was a vast expanse of tile and stone, almost all of it empty save there, toward the north where the dome housing the observatory was just visible.

She walked toward it slowly, taking due care to stay on those parts of the roof laid out as paths.

The moon had set, leaving behind a sky blazing with stars. By their light, she could make out the city below. So late was the hour, so deep the night that nothing stirred along the flower-draped roads twining among snug houses and prosperous shops. Likely even the cats were asleep by now.

It would be dawn soon. The watchers who

charted the sky were retiring to their own rest. Several passed her as she neared the observatory. They nodded respectfully but did not tarry, weary as they no doubt were.

By contrast, she felt all too awake and alert. The cloak she had thrown on seemed to hang like a dead weight from her shoulders even as it tangled around her ankles. She kicked it aside impatiently and kept walking. Her skin prickled, not with cold, for the night was only pleasantly cool, but with agitation she could not repress.

At length, she came to the observatory. The dome was just under ten feet in height and constructed of steel plates smoothly welded together. A large gash arching across the top of the dome divided it in half. Just inside the opening and peering from it was the telescope.

It was a source of pride that the telescope was of Akoran design and manufacture. True enough, much had been learned from the achievements of the great Galileo Galilei and the equally impressive Isaac Newton, but much had already been known. Although the present instrument had seen first light, as the astronomers said, scarcely a decade before, already there was eager talk of how to improve it.

The surface of the dome felt cool beneath her hand. She touched it lightly as she looked up at the stars. They filled the sky, blazing in such quantity that they almost seemed to blend together. The vast sea of stars men called the

Milky Way draped across the sky from the northwest. Within it and dimmed by its glory was the constellation of Cassiopeia, the doomed queen condemned for her treachery. Not far from her, farther to the west, the great hero Perseus chased across the sky. It was a night for warriors; Orion trod the sky toward the southwest.

She had a special fondness for Orion. His was the first constellation she was able to recognize with any reliability, aside from the Dippers, of course, but they were so easy anyone could find them. Orion had always fascinated her. She imagined herself hunting with him across the skies and dreamed of the extraordinary vistas such a being of the stars would see.

She must be dreaming now for another warrior appeared toward the southwest, not against the velvet darkness of the sky but much closer. A warrior she could see very clearly from the proud set of his head and the sweeping breadth of his shoulders to the steady hand resting on the hilt of his sword.

A warrior who walked toward her as the night wind ruffled the thick mane of his hair turned silver in starlight.

"*Royce* . . ."

He was with the men . . . or asleep. He could not possibly be there.

"We seem fated to meet in all sorts of unexpected places, Atreides." He spoke with a faint edge of mockery, as though her surprise

437

amused him. But she sensed weariness in him as well and had to fight the urge to go to him.

She gathered courage to her as she would a cloak. "We do indeed, Lord Hawkforte. One might truly think there is such a thing as Fate."

"Except there isn't. There are only different possibilities for us to choose among."

"So it has always seemed to me."

"And you would know, wouldn't you, Atreides? It's fair to say you're expert on the subject."

"You may say that, if you wish. I would not." She turned away, unable to bear the anger keen as steel in eyes that had once looked at her as though she was all of beauty and desire. She understood that anger and the hurt it masked, but still resented both. What had she done but all she knew to do? Knowledge was ever imperfect and incomplete. She had known how to be Atreides but not, it seemed, how to be the woman Royce wanted.

"What brings you up here?" she asked because it was something to say while yet her mind reeled from the chasm at her feet. What would life be without him? How would she manage with only memory?

"Marcellus mentioned it. We have an observatory at Hawkforte, the legacy of an ancestor who refused to be deterred by our oft cloudy climes."

"Persistence in the face of adversity is to be admired."

"So is a realistic assessment of the chances for success."

He was speaking of them, she realized, and her heart tightened a little further. Even so, she was determined to ask while yet she could, "Why didn't you kill Deilos?"

The question made him draw back slightly. He was a little time answering. "I dreamt of killing him," Royce said slowly into the night. "For a time, I seemed to think of little else. Even more recently, there scarcely has been a day when I did not imagine his death."

"Yet he lives."

"Don't ask me to explain it, I can't."

Perhaps not but she could, that well did she know the man. "You are too honorable to kill a foe who can no longer do harm."

His laugh was hard. "I merely find disgust a poor goad to vengeance."

"He is a craven husk. In some ways, to leave him alive is the crueler punishment."

"Perhaps, but whether he lives or dies is no longer my decision." With a hint of surprise, he added, "I'm glad of that."

Her spirit lifted. If she could not be joyful with him, she could at least rejoice for him. "You are free now."

Her perception prompted a quick, sharp look. "I suppose I am, as much as any man can ever be. Life tangles us in itself."

He was right, life did that, weaving its endless skeins of dreams and disappointments, joy and sorrow, all to some unknown yet certain purpose.

Dare she nurture any hope that it might yet weave them together?

Dawn crept closer, casting a pale gray light over the horizon.

"Royce . . . ?"

"Atreides?"

It was too much, this cool dismissal in a name that carried with it the reminder of all that lay between them. It stabbed right through her fragile composure and wrung a snarl from her. Better that than yet more tears.

"There was a time when you called me Kassandra." As he could damn well remember, considering how he had whispered it against her heated skin in the depths of the night, cried it out when pleasure was upon them both, and murmured it even in his sleep. Oh, yes, he could remember!

"I know who you are," he claimed.

"I think not. Indeed, I think you never had the slightest glimmer, nor I of you."

She waited, silently daring him to dispute her and for a moment it appeared he might do so. But just then his attention was diverted. Out over the brightening sea, a ship had appeared. As they both watched, it moved swiftly and steadily toward Ilius. On its sail, glowing in the rays of the rising sun, shone the bull's head emblem of the royal house of Akora.

Alex had come home.

The Prince of Akora raised his goblet. Firelight born in the copper braziers filled with glowing charcoal and in the iron candelabras holding slender tapers of beeswax shone through the golden liquid within the balloon of glass.

Alex was freshly if swiftly shaved. His skin was bronzed by sun and sea, his dark hair slightly long, very thick and stubbornly untamed. He wore the unbridled happiness of one who is, at least temporarily, in the home of his heart.

"A toast," he said. Kassandra looked at him expectantly and saw the others do the same. They were gathered around the table in the family dining hall. Outside, the first stars reclaimed the sky. A day that had raced past was almost done.

Joanna sat beside her husband. She looked both dazed and delighted, as though she could scarcely fathom that he was truly present and feared he might vanish at any moment. Her eyes on him were fiercely tender and the smile with which she returned his own was filled with love.

They had, Kassandra knew, enjoyed only a very brief private reunion before the demands of state drew Alex away. Seemingly endless meetings had gone on as Alex sought to grasp quickly all that had transpired on Akora since the attack during the Games. He met first with

441

Atreus, then with Kassandra herself and finally with the Council. In between, she knew he had spoken several times with Royce.

It was only now, when they were all finally able to sit down together, that Alex could turn his mind to other matters.

"To the Americans," he said, and grinned at their surprise. But his smile came and went swiftly as, with due solemnity, he continued, "And to their President, Mr. James Madison, for at his behest, on the eighteenth of June of this year, the Congress of the United States saw fit in its wisdom to declare war on Great Britain."

"Damn if they didn't!" Andrew exclaimed. He looked quite pleased at this confirmation of his own prediction.

"Word reached London just as I was preparing to embark," Alex continued. "Prinny is in his glory. Here is his chance to do what his father could not, crush the rebels and restore them to the Empire once and for all. Of course, he also has to defeat Napoleon, and managing both will not leave men or matériel for anything else. Anyone fool enough to promote an invasion of Akora now would find himself trotted off to Bedlam."

He raised the glass again with a cold and fierce light in his eyes. "We are, and I say this with the greatest pleasure, no longer of interest as a potential conquest. At least not for the moment. God willing, we will find a way to make this state of blessed disinterest permanent."

There was laughter at this, as well as obviously profound relief, until Phaedra said, "We have friends in America. I hope matters will not go too hard on them."

"Oh, I wouldn't be too worried about that," her husband replied. "They surprised us once at Yorktown when they won what they are pleased to call their Revolution. When our forces marched onto the field there to surrender, our soldiers played a little tune called 'The World Turned Upside Down.' It expressed rather well what had happened. I wouldn't put it past the Americans to turn the world upside down a time or two again. They seem to have a genuine genius for surprising, themselves above all."

"Then let us bid Fortune's favor for them," Atreus said quietly. He was, despite his objections, lying on a settee set beside the low table. Had he his druthers, he would have been sitting upright, a foolish proposition for a man only lately returned to consciousness. That he was there at all was the source of great rejoicing. Kassandra thought him weary but resolute, and feared he would overdo.

But perhaps he would not have the opportunity, for both Phaedra and Elena were keeping a close eye on him. Brianna was also there but she remained off to one side. From time to time, her gaze slipped to Atreus. She looked . . . concerned to be sure, but something more Kassandra could not quite identify. Bewildered?

There was no time to think of it, for Royce was saying, "This is good news indeed, Alex, but tell us, with Perceval dead were you able to get any sense of who was actually behind the British plan to invade Akora?"

"I wasn't," Alex said with regret. "That remains a task yet to be done." He looked to Royce. "When the time is right, of course."

Royce nodded. "Better sooner rather than later, I think. Invasion remains a temptation while there are those in England who can presume it would succeed."

"Presume?" Atreus asked. He spoke mildly enough, but anger flashed in his eyes.

Alex nodded. "Those in positions of influence have no more knowledge of Akora than does the next man beyond these shores. Left in ignorance, guided only by greed and ambition, how difficult do you think it would be for them to convince themselves that we would be overcome readily?"

The Vanax nodded slowly. "I see . . . Perhaps it is time for me to consider a trip to England."

"Perhaps it is time first for you to heal," Phaedra said. She spoke gently but with unmistakable determination.

The Chosen ruler of Akora, the anointed one, ruthless in conflict, wise in council, the leader to whom thousands of people looked for strength and determination, knew better than to pick that particular battle.

"As you say, Mother." He turned to Alex. "I have read the letter you brought from the Prince Regent." They both looked to Royce. "His Majesty requests that I expedite your immediate return to England," Atreus said. "It seems in the present crisis he cannot continue to do without your services."

Kassandra inhaled sharply. She stared at Royce. His gaze met hers for but an instant before he looked away. Without apparent expression, he said, "Then I had best go."

It was chilly on the roof, much more so than the night before. But she had not been alone then. She had been with Royce.

She was alone now, sitting with her back propped against the dome of the observatory. So tired was she that her eyes burned, yet she had no thought of sleep. To lie alone in her bed, thinking of Royce . . . that was unbearable.

Better here on the roof, nearer the stars, alone with her thoughts.

He would go. Of that, she had absolutely no doubt. With day would come the bustle to ready a ship and, too quickly, the turning of the tide. He would go. Back to England. Away from her.

"*Oh, God . . .*" The cry broke from her softly but even so she feared someone would hear. Pride was only a tattered garment compared to love, but it might be all she had. She would protect it.

The stars whirled overhead, turning . . . turning. The sky began to lighten. Too soon. Too soon!

People would come to tend the roof garden, to make use of the paths that offered shortcuts through and round the vast labyrinth of the palace, or simply to enjoy the view. She could not stay where she was.

Aching in mind and body, she rose and went back downstairs. Mercifully, Sida slept, or at least there was no evidence of her. Kassandra had almost gained her apartment when she looked down the long corridor of the family quarters and noticed the faint light beneath Atreus's doors.

He must be asleep . . . surely? And if he was or not, someone would be with him. Unless he had sent them away, preferring as she did to conceal weakness.

She would just take a quick look and make sure he wanted for nothing.

Her brother was alone and sitting up in bed, reading from a sheaf of documents piled at his side.

"What is this?" Kassandra asked as she entered. "I thought you were resting."

"I'm just catching up on a bit of reading. Shouldn't you be in bed?"

"Probably, but I'm not. Look, really, you've only just begun to recover. You know you can't overdo."

He set aside the report he'd been studying

and gestured her closer. When she sat on the bed beside him, he said, "I do know that but I also know I am going to recover. Elena has assured me of it but I knew that even before she said so."

"That's good . . . but even so, you came very close . . ."

He nodded. "Very close, although I can't say it was unpleasant. I think I dreamed a great deal."

He was distracting her from worry over him; she knew that full well. All the same it worked. Her interest was caught. "Do you remember any of the dreams?"

"Not really . . . well, one . . . I think toward the end, just before I woke up. I was standing on a road that ran through forests near the sea. It wasn't actually a road I know but it seemed familiar all the same. There was a fork in the road. It seemed to appear suddenly and I was surprised because it hadn't been there a moment before. You know how it is in dreams, you understand things without there being any particular reason to do so? Standing there, I knew that if I took the fork, I'd come back here and I did want to do that very much. But if I simply stayed on the road I'd been on, I'd go someplace else that was concealed from me but about which I felt a great sense of excitement and longing."

"You made a choice?"

He nodded. "It wasn't hard really. I realized

that other road will still be there and someday I'll walk it again to wherever it leads. But not just now. Now there are things to do right here."

"There are . . . so many things and I want to help. I've been thinking, there must be a way to reach out to the people in Helios, to make them realize you are open to their concerns and that they can join in making Akora an even better place. It would be hard, of course, because we only know who some of them are, but it could be done and . . ."

"Kassandra —"

"Or if you don't like that idea, there are other things I can do . . ."

"It's an excellent idea but you've already done so much." His gaze narrowed for all that it remained loving and she knew that eventually they would discuss her vision of her own death, and her decision to tell no one of it. But for now, he asked, "Don't you think it's time you did something for yourself?"

"For myself?"

Patiently, he explained, "For your own happiness."

"Oh, that. I don't know, Atreus. It seems to me that happiness doesn't come to all of us."

"Of course it doesn't. Happiness doesn't come to *any* of us. You have to go after it. Don't those Americans have an expression for that? The pursuit of happiness? What an extraordinary notion that people have a right to at least try to be happy, but it's a good notion all the same."

"That's the sort of thing those in Helios need to hear."

"Don't change the subject. We're talking about you."

"You're talking about me. I'm going to bed."

"Kassandra . . ."

She heeded the note in his voice, gentle reminder that he was ruler here, and stayed where she was. Her brother reached out to take her hand. "It would please me greatly if you were happy."

Her eyes burned. She looked away. Softly, on a whisper of sound, she said, "Atreus, I am in a world where I never thought to be. Glad though I am of that, I cannot find my way. I don't know what to do."

"Our mother would tell you to listen to your heart."

"And she would be right, up to a point. But I am not just heart. I am mind and spirit as well." She looked to him, seeing brother and Vanax, man and Chosen, feeling yet again the uplifting of joy in her that he lived. "What do you say?"

His smile was wry. "Allowing for the fact that I have no personal expertise in such matters?"

She laughed a little, surprised that she did so. "And we both know what mother has to say about that. She is pure eagerness for you to wed."

"We were talking about you," he said quickly.

Her smile deepened. "You won't be able to evade it forever."

"I suppose not, but for the moment, I say this: Have faith. It sounds so simple and it is often so hard. Have faith the Creator loves us. Here on Akora we know that to the essence of our being. We even take it for granted to a certain extent. But I wonder how often we really think about it. The Creator loves us. Love lies at the center of creation itself. There is no greater power."

He was right, of course. She knew it, as he said, to her essence. All the same, the reminder was light cast into darkness.

Royce would leave. As she had been called to do her duty, so he was called to his.

She had hurt him but, truth be told, his refusal to forgive her hurt her as well.

Time heals, people said.

They'd see about that.

Chapter
TWENTY-ONE

The wind was freshening and very soon now the tide would turn.

Royce remained where he was until finally there was no reason for him not to board. About to step up the gangway, he hesitated and looked back down the length of the quay.

There was no sign of Kassandra. Their paths had crossed briefly during the morning. She had smiled, wished him fair sailing, and gone her way.

He tried to tell himself it was for the best.

Joanna and Alex had come down to the harbor, bringing little Amelia with them. His sister and brother-in-law looked very happy and content, as well they might. Amelia looked solemn until she grinned at him, prompting him to smile back.

He chucked her lightly under the chin, which made her frown, then waggled his fingers, which restored her good humor.

"We'll miss you," Joanna said.

"As I will miss all of you." He looked to Alex. "Do you have any idea when you may return to England?"

His sister and brother-in-law exchanged a glance. After a moment, Alex said, "Hard to say precisely, what with the situation and all."

Royce nodded. There was really very little else to say. He embraced his sister, shook hands with Alex and dropped a light kiss on Amelia's forehead. "Take care of these two," he told Alex.

"Be assured, I will."

"A few months then, perhaps?"

"Christmas at Hawkforte," Joanna said, and smiled though her eyes glistened.

One more long look down the quay, up along the flower-draped roads to the palace gleaming in the sun. One more moment to wonder . . .

She was not coming. He really had to accept that. Fine, then.

He went up the gangplank swiftly. It was pulled up behind him as the captain shouted the order to raise anchor. Swiftly, too swiftly, the wind took them.

He waved to Alex and Joanna standing on the dock until they were no more than small, dark blurs fast fading from sight. Only then did he go below where he found the cabin allotted to him. It was comfortable and spacious, even luxurious. He took scant notice of it, stowed his gear and returned to the deck where he remained while the ship sailed through the northern inlet and met the ocean swell.

Ten days to England. Ten days to remember and reflect.

Ten damnably long, frustrating days. And added to them, ten nights shadowed by taunting memories and a sense of loss that left him feeling hollowed out, as though he had become no more than the husk of the man he had been, but lately filled with life and love.

It did not help that he had with him the drawing of Kassandra that he had purchased from Rudolph Ackermann. As many times as he resolved to leave the sketch in the drawer where he had placed it when he unpacked, it seemed to find its way to the table beside his bunk. At the first gray light of morning, he woke to the sight of the same face that haunted his dreams.

No, that did not help at all.

Straight upon docking, Royce went to Carlton House. He would have gone to his own residence but after ten days in which to contemplate frustration and folly he was in a foul mood, unfit company for the loyal servants who were among the very few of his acquaintance in the capital he respected. The Prince Regent was in London rather than in Brighton where he would normally have been at that time of year, in recognition of the martial state of his kingdom now fighting on two fronts. The city itself looked much the same, a jumble of the old and the new, the decrepit and the elegant. It also looked different — more crowded, more haphazard, dirtier than he remembered. He supposed that was because he still had Ilius in his mind. And in his heart.

Prinny was with his tailors, being fitted for a new satin waistcoat. In the midst of an intense discussion about the merits of gold embroidery rather than silver, he spied Royce.

"Hawkforte! Damn, man, it's good to see you!"

The habit of loyalty, refined through the ages, drew from Royce the proper response. "Thank you, Sire. I trust you are well?"

"Tolerable, better than I was at any rate. War's a rare tonic, don't you think?"

Royce did not but he refrained from saying so. As servants scurried to remove the piles of garments awaiting fittings and the tailors departed, the Prince Regent availed himself of a restoring brandy. Royce joined him, as etiquette demanded, but did not drink.

"You've actually been there," the Prince said, unable to contain his excitement. "Been to Akora? You've seen it?"

"I have, Sire. It is a formidable land. Everything we've always believed, a true Fortress Kingdom."

"And the Vanax, what is he like?"

"Well . . . he lacks Your Majesty's sophistication, of course." God would forgive him such perfidy for it was in a good cause.

Prinny puffed himself up. "Can't hold that against him, wouldn't expect anything else. But you've taken the measure of the man. What more can you tell me?"

Not that Atreus had almost been killed and was still recovering. Never that.

"He is a warrior, Sire, born and bred to it, and a leader of warriors. But he is also a thinker. He understands that Akora cannot remain isolated."

"Excellent! Precisely what I hoped. Someone we can work with, would you say?"

"Definitely, Sire. In fact, I am charged with a message from the Vanax. He would like to visit England."

Prinny could not have looked more pleased. Entertainment was his element. His inventive mind, agile still despite the sodden and self-indulgent years, sprang ahead to all the balls, musicales, receptions, masquerades, phantasmagoria and all the rest that would be required to entertain so August a personage as the Vanax of Akora. "And we would be delighted to receive him, damn if we wouldn't. Show him a fine time. I trust you to arrange it, Royce, all of it, good man that you are. Knew it, of course. Always can count on Hawkforte."

"You are too kind, Sire."

"Not at all, absolutely not. Now tell me, what about that lovely Princess Kassandra? How is she faring these days?"

Royce flinched, but inwardly. He eyed the brandy and set it aside. "Well enough, I assume."

"Shouldn't assume with women," the Prince

advised. He spoke from personal experience, all of it sorry. "Never do that."

"As you say, Sire."

"Damn glad you're back. No place like old England, is there?"

"No, Sire, definitely not."

"That fellow Liverpool who's taken over for Perceval seems to think I ought to plod through reams of documents every week. It's not enough that there's a war on — well, two wars actually — I'm supposed to know every twist and turn in intimate detail along with all the usual balderdash from Parliament, Tories and Whigs still at it. Still hoping you can do something about that, don't you know. Has me quite at a loss."

"Perhaps it would be a better use of Your Majesty's time to receive a summary of the more important developments."

"Just what I thought. Much better use. If you would be so good —" He gestured to the desk near the windows and the extremely large pile of documents covering it.

"Delighted," Royce murmured and reminded himself that what he did, he did for England.

It did not make the doing easier but it did make it bearable. The sheer, mind-numbing weight of the material through which he slogged, coupled with the occasional discovery of bright nuggets of information within it, offered some measure of distraction. He worked late into each night and rose with the dawn, alternating long hours at his desk with hard rides beyond London. He slept little and had no appetite, despite Mulridge's best efforts to bludgeon him into eating.

Shortly, those he encountered on his forays to Carlton House regarded him with even more than the usual caution. The Lord of Hawkforte, he who had always epitomized the virtues of strength and honor all the more notable for being so extremely rare, had acquired a dangerous edge. He moved through the gilded halls and gaudy chambers of the Royal Court like a predator prowling a landscape in which he found no sustenance.

A week after Royce's return to England, at about the time even his own servants were tending to give him wide berth, Bolkum brought in the mail. The smithy, who was also a faithful friend, had chosen to stay on in London along with Mulridge but he carried the aura of the countryside with him in his bushy brows, luxuriant beard and matter-of-fact manner.

"Something in there you won't like," he said as he offered the collection of letters to Royce.

The Hawk Lord looked up briefly from the pile of documents he was perusing and snarled. "If it's yet more invitations, toss them in the fire like all the rest."

Bolkum held his ground, undeterred. "Fair enough, but it's from the Spider. Third she's sent. Footman brought it. Poor chap looks gray around the gills. Says he'll be camping out here next if she don't get an answer."

"Damn woman." Royce sighed, cast one more glance at the low fire in the grate, and reached for the envelope. Lady Melbourne liked her own way in the same sense mountains were tall; it was her nature. But she was not known for pursuing anyone so foolish as to decline her favor.

He read the brief missive twice before crumpling it in his hand. "It appears I will be going out this evening."

Bolkum made a low sound of sympathy and went to warn Mulridge. Over his shoulder, the fellow who could not get a comb through his own impressive tresses said, "Might want to get that hair trimmed a bit before you do."

Royce's response, vivid as it was, was muffled by the door Bolkum hastily closed behind him.

Melbourne house was ablaze with lights when Royce approached it shortly after sunset. The center rotunda was already crowded with many more guests spilling into the surrounding reception rooms. As usual, the noise, heat and odors were intense. Nothing fazed the latter two, but the wave of sound diminished noticeably the moment he stepped inside.

Very quickly, he stood at the center of ever-widening ripples of attentive silence. While his appearances at Carlton House were occasions for caution, his presence in the Spider's Lair was a source of wonderment and, very swiftly, of calculation.

Why was he there, this man who so stubbornly refused to align himself with one faction or the other? This lord of ancient lineage so trusted by the Prince Regent. This champion of England who seemed to carry with him whispers of long-ago battles and battles yet to be.

For what purpose had he come?

If only they knew, he thought, and was glad they could not. There was little dignity in paying with his presence for the so-clever Lady Melbourne to explain what she had hinted at in her note:

"Does the Earl of Hawkforte wish to know who met with a gentleman of Akora at Brighton last year?"

He found his hostess holding court in the main reception room just as she had been weeks before when he accompanied Joanna, Alex and Kassandra. And just as then, Byron was with her. The poet of the age was chatting with his hostess's niece, Annabella Milbanke, but broke off when he spied Royce.

"My lord, how fortuitous! I heard you had returned from Akora, indeed I think all England has heard, so great has your fame become. But you have accepted no invitations, not even my own." Byron waved a hand languidly in what Royce supposed was an expres-

459

sion of astonishment at so great an oversight.

"I have little inclination for society," he said through gritted teeth and sketched a bow in Lady Melbourne's direction. "Madame, you have drawn me out. I trust the effort will prove worthwhile."

The lady smiled, quite prettily to give her credit. But then, she had the equivalent of several lifetimes' experience in the fine art of manipulating men. "It already has, my lord, at least for me. Your presence assures the evening's success."

"Madame, shame if you think me so prone to flattery. We both know every evening at Melbourne House is guaranteed a success by your own presence. Surely, nothing more is required."

He was rewarded with a look of surprise, quickly concealed to be sure but satisfying all the same.

"Why, my lord," Lady Melbourne said, "I had no idea you could dispose yourself so charmingly. Come, sit beside me. You have lately returned from Akora, so I hear. Will you indulge our vast interest in that mysterious land?"

"Do not refuse," Byron entreated, even as others gathered closer around them. "Ignorance is the bane of all existence, don't you agree, my lord? To have visited a place of such fascination and not share what you have learned would be an act of . . ."

The poet rattled on but Royce did not attend him. He had meant to make clear to Lady Melbourne that his patience was limited in the extreme. But Byron had, all inadvertently, used the one word certain to capture Royce's notice.

Ignorance.

Was it not to remedy ignorance that Atreus was contemplating a visit to England? Perhaps it would be just as well to begin laying the ground for him, as it were.

He glanced round at the men gathering close. Without exception, they were Whigs denied high office by the whim of the Prince Regent they had spent so many years cultivating all to no end. However, such disappointment did not mean they were lacking in power, to the contrary. Among them, they controlled much of the wealth of the kingdom. Their influence reached into every sector, but most particularly into the military, where even officers of the highest rank were grateful for a wealthy patron.

"Akora," he said deliberately, "is a fortress. This is true geographically, as we already knew, but it is true in every other way as well. Virtually every Akoran male is a warrior, superbly trained, magnificently disciplined and devoted to the defense of his country. But their martial nature does not end there. The women are also trained to fight and from what I have seen, are quite adept at it."

"The women are?" Lady Melbourne exclaimed. "I thought Akoran women existed

461

only to serve." Her tone left no doubt as to her opinion of that.

"It's rather more complicated. Suffice to say, while I believe the Akorans make excellent friends, I would never wish them as enemies."

"But then you would not under any circumstances, would you, my lord?" The speaker was a tall, slender man whose pleasant, rather bland features did not entirely conceal his keen and agile mind. Charles, Second Earl of Grey, ignored the avid stirrings of the crowd and nodded to Royce. "Welcome home, Hawkforte. It is good to see you can still find your way here."

"There's no trick to finding England, my lord," Royce replied, though he knew full well that was not Grey's meaning. The man who had thought to take the helm at the Foreign Office in a Whig government was pleased to see him at Melbourne House, headquarters of the disgruntled former friends of Prinny.

"You had more difficulty doing so last year, my lord," Grey said, "when the Akorans saw fit to hold you in what I understand was a quite unpleasant captivity."

Grey was clever indeed. The circumstances of Royce's imprisonment on Akora had not been explained in England because to do so would be to reveal that there was division and discord within the Fortress Kingdom, making it all the more vulnerable to anyone considering it for possible conquest.

"That," Royce said dismissively, "was a misunderstanding. It is no longer of any consequence."

"Apparently not, since you raised no objection to your sister's marriage to a prince of Akora who has, it seems, become your very good friend."

"I am honored to count the Marquess of Boswick — let us not forget Alex also holds British titles — as my friend."

"I've often wondered how awkward it must be to have ties to two kingdoms. How does one avoid the problem of conflicting loyalties?"

"Are you asking that of me, my lord?" Royce inquired with deceptive quiet. No slur against his honor could be greater than a suggestion that he was less than completely loyal to England. No insult would be better guaranteed to cause shots to ring out or rapiers flash on Wimbledown Common, the preferred location for such encounters.

As sharks are drawn to the scent of blood in the water, the crowd stirred. The Spider looked torn. Was a challenge about to be issued . . . and accepted? The potential for scandal was vast if such an encounter had its origins beneath her roof. Yet the possibility of all the frantic, delicious gossip that would result was enticing just the same.

Lady Melbourne cleared her throat. The sound was loud enough in the expectant silence to momentarily draw Royce's attention. Their eyes met. She looked at him, looked at Grey, and looked back again. Very deliberately, with a tilting of her head in the renowned Whig's direction, Lady Melbourne nodded.

Royce stared at her even as his mind turned swiftly from surprise to summon memory. Grey? Could it be? Grey had been in Brighton the previous summer. Royce had encountered him there and been surprised, for the Earl was said to despise Brighton. What had he said when Royce remarked on his presence? Something about a man not always being able to choose his circumstances?

Grey wanted to be Foreign Minister, was said to be intensely frustrated that he was not. Grey wanted to make peace with Napoleon and might see a British conquest elsewhere as making that task more palatable. But Grey was also a reformer who seemed to genuinely believe it wrong that only a tiny fraction of Englishmen could vote and have any say in their government.

Deilos had been in Brighton at the same time. Deilos who should have died there but who lived yet.

He looked again. Lady Melbourne widened her eyes slightly and arched one brow in Grey's direction.

There was, of course, the possibility that she was mistaken or simply dissembling. But there could be no benefit to her in either, and indeed, peril lay in such error whatever its cause.

No, she must be very sure. Because Grey had let drop some word or she had overheard something elsewhere or someone had brought her the tidbit as she sat at the center of the web she had spent decades spinning.

Besides, there was scarcely a handful of men in England who could have conspired to bring about an invasion of Akora. Perceval, as Prime Minister, had been one of them but he was dead. Royce himself was another by virtue of his power, wealth and the deep respect accorded his name. And Grey, oh, yes. Grey . . . brilliant, impatient, superbly well connected for all that he was Whig . . . Grey, driven by unbearable disappointment, succumbing to the notion that the ends would justify the means however brutal they might be.

Damn, he might have known. But then hindsight rivaled the sun's own brilliance.

Grey smiled. "We all know Hawkforte's proud history. 'The Shield of the Throne,' isn't that what you were called in medieval days?"

"We still are a shield, my lord. A shield against danger, treachery and, when necessary, the folly of ambitious men."

And just then, quite clearly, he knew the plan he had devised during those ten long days and nights would succeed.

He leaned forward and said for Grey's ear only, "Meet me at Wimbledown Common, my lord, on the morrow. Not for the purpose these

fools would like but for your own enlightenment."

Grey took a step back, regarding him. His
brow was knit, his manner on guard. Stiffly, he
nodded.

The invitation having been quietly uttered
with the intent being to keep it secret, it was, of
course, only a matter of hours before word
spread among the *ton*. Hawkforte and Grey had
argued. Lord Grey had issued the challenge . . . or Lord Hawkforte had. The matter
seemed confirmed when a tweenie in Lord
Grey's kitchen told the butcher boy who
stepped out with her that a maid had heard the
butler claim that Lord Grey's valet had been
told to take special care with his master's en-
semble for the following day. The obvious conclusion was that if wounded — or worse — his
lordship wished at least to maintain his elegance. This news spread swiftly below stairs,
hopping from one great house to another,
across adjoining fences and through garden
gates.

It was carried upward by suitably solemn
butlers, valets and lady's maids who whispered
it into the ears of their masters and mistresses,
adding it to the vast, delightful sea of conjec-
ture swirling through London that summer
night.

Royce was aware of none of this. He left Melbourne House shortly after learning what he

had gone there to discover, spent the remainder of the evening reading documents and went to bed where, for a change, he slept relatively well if only for a few hours.

Bolkum woke him an hour before dawn. Royce bathed and shaved, with a stray thought for the pleasures of a warm shower. He paid no more than the bare minimum of attention to what he wore, but even Mulridge was satisfied when he emerged in buff trousers, a shirt of finely woven linen, a dark brown frock coat of summer weight wool, and boots of impressive sheen. He had not suffered his hair to be trimmed and it brushed the collar of the frock coat even as it glowed in the faint light like beaten gold.

"You'll be back for breakfast," Mulridge instructed. Royce grinned, easier in his mind than he had been in some time, and nodded. "I will, and a pair of those eggs Cook makes — coddled, are they? — wouldn't go amiss."

"All right then, off with you." But before he went, Mulridge hugged him fiercely. "You're a good lad. Be careful."

"She worries," Bolkum announced as he accompanied Royce around the back to the stables where his mount was being saddled. "All the same, she's got a point. Why did you pick Wimbledown Common, if you don't mind my asking? Got a nasty reputation, that place does."

"That's why I picked it. It's nice and isolated,

467

far from prying eyes." Mounted, Royce reached down and accepted the sturdy box Bolkum handed to him. With care, he placed it in a saddlebag already filled with thick wads of cotton wool.

"Mind how you ride," Bolkum said.

Royce nodded, gave his very old friend a grin, and set off toward the river. A few minutes later, he rode past Alex and Joanna's London residence. Glancing through the wrought-iron gates, he thought he saw lights on in the house. That surprised him as he assumed Alex had sent the servants back to his manor at Boswick before embarking for Akora, but perhaps not.

A short while later, he crossed the Thames and turned southwest. The heath called Wimbledown Common lay sufficiently removed from London proper to be frequented only by shepherds, the stray idler and noblemen inclined to kill each other. Much of the ground there had been cleared long ago and given over to pigs and sheep. But here and there, ancient oak trees cast their gnarled branches into the sky, creating pockets of darkness where ravens gathered and shadows whispered.

It had rained during the night and the ground was wet, which suited Royce well. He dropped his horse's reins through the low cleft of a tree and walked out into the wide field where so many encounters of what passed for honor had occurred.

Grey was already there. He turned and observed Royce as he came. The mists of early morning rose between them, swirling like so much spectral fog.

"I thought perhaps I had misunderstood you, my lord," Grey said.

"Not at all."

"Then I did not err in failing to bring a second?"

"You have erred but not in that regard. As I said, the purpose here is enlightenment."

Grey looked at once relieved and mildly amused. The brief motion of his hand encompassed their surroundings. "And that requires . . . this drama?"

"Oh, I would not call this drama, my lord. We have a far way to go before that." As he spoke, Royce set down carefully the saddlebag he had brought, and opened it. He straightened with the wooden box in his hands. "I understand you to be a man of learning."

"So I have been told," Grey said modestly.

"Then you will comprehend what I am about to show you."

Royce opened the box. For a moment, he did nothing more than look at the plain clay receptacle within. Atreus had given it to him before Royce's departure from Akora. It was, he knew, the ultimate symbol of the Vanax's trust in a *xenos* who was also a son of the very land that marched through Kassandra's vision of invasion.

Trust Royce would die before betraying.

He lifted the clay pot, hefted it lightly and faced the far end of the field. His arm was strong, his aim true. The pot landed several dozen yards away and broke immediately. For an instant, no more than a heartbeat, nothing happened. Grey had just that long to begin to look at Royce questioningly.

Fire exploded. Where there had been only wet grass and gently rolling earth, flames stretched a dozen feet in either direction and almost as high into the sky.

The flames roared. Even at such a distance, Royce could hear them. The smell was equally intense, being both acrid and cloying.

"What have you done?" Grey asked. He was startled, to be sure, and even somewhat shaken. But he still did not truly understand.

"I threw a pot," Royce said quietly.

"You must have lit whatever was in it first."

"No, you saw I did not."

It was true, Grey had. Staring at the flames, he said, "The ground is wet."

"Very wet but water will not put out this fire. You could throw a veritable lake on it and it wouldn't make any difference. It will burn out eventually, of course, when the fuel is consumed. But this was only one small pot and there could be very many more."

He stepped in front of Grey, commanding his attention. "Hurled against an invading navy, the substance in that pot will turn the proudest vessel into a funeral pyre. No man can survive it. If you doubt that, think of what happened to the Arab fleet that attacked Constantinople in 673."

The color went out of Grey's face. He was indeed an educated man and he knew exactly what Royce meant. Staring at the still-burning fire, he said, "My God, the Akorans have Greek Fire."

"That's right."

"But you . . ." Grey whirled, looking at him. "You got it away from them! You brought it back here. We can analyze it, determine its components, find the formula —"

"Alas, that was my only sample."

"Your only . . . ? What do you mean? You couldn't possibly have —"

Royce moved closer, blocking Grey's view of the still-smoldering fire. The sun was rising above the trees and the morning mists were evaporating. It promised to be a beautiful day. He was suddenly very eager to be in it.

"A conquest of Akora would do nothing but send good men to a hideous death and make of your own name a curse to resound on English tongues down through the ages."

Grey was sweating. He patted his brow absently with one end of what had been an impeccably tied cravat. "I don't know what you —"

"A man named Deilos met with you in Brighton last summer. That's why you were there when otherwise you never would have

471

been. He told you Akora was ripe for invasion. He'd sniffed you out quite well, guessing at your discontent. You'd already been casting an eye in Akora's direction, wondering if it would suit your purposes."

"You can't possibly know this —" Grey looked ill, caught between shock and bewilderment. As might he be, this man who had no glimmer of the terrible "gift" that had given warning of Akora's peril.

"Deilos sought to use you. He believed a British invasion of Akora would be defeated readily." With a nod toward the flames, Royce added, "He had good reason to think so. He also anticipated that he could use such a threat to turn Akora away from the outside world and catapult himself into power."

Shocked Grey undoubtedly was, but his native shrewdness remained. Slowly, he asked, "It was Deilos who kept you captive?"

Royce nodded. "But Deilos is finished. He is imprisoned and will stand trial. His followers, such as remained, are dead or also captured."

"I gather you had a hand in that."

"You could say so. Listen to me. I think I understand what drove you to contemplate such an act but you must see now that it would have led only to disaster. You have some genuinely solid ideas about reform. *Bide your time.* If Fortune favors you, the opportunity may come to do genuine good rather than unspeakable evil."

The mask of imperturbability Grey usually wore was gone. In its place was the man he truly was, filled with noble dreams contesting with all-too-human flaws. "It is my most fervent belief that this country has something good and lasting to give to the world, but to achieve that we must have strength. We lost the damned Colonies and we may or may not get them back. We're battling Napoleon, who wants to swallow the world. We have a mad king and a drunken Regent. Discontent stirs our people and revolt threatens. We are standing on the edge!"

"No," Royce said with calm conviction, "the ground of this scepter'd isle is firmer than you know. It is rooted in the very men and women you claim to want to help. But strength without honor is a weakness waiting to devour us. The Akorans will be our friends. Let that be enough."

Grey took a breath and another. Slowly, the urgency went out of him. He had seen and, more importantly, he had accepted. The road to the future of the red serpent was closed.

There was nothing more to be said. Royce turned away. Very suddenly, he felt hollow inside.

"My lord."

On the fire-charred field, Grey looked smaller than he did in elegant drawing rooms but his color was improving and as Royce watched, he straightened his shoulders.

"It is true what they say, Hawkforte is the Shield of the Throne."

Royce sketched a weary smile. "It was a king who first said that. He made it up to flatter one of my ancestors, but he was wrong. We are England's Shield and that we will always be."

The last of the mist blew away just then, revealing the silver ribbon of the River Thames winding through verdant fields. A yearning too long resisted rose in Royce.

He would go back to London. He would eat coddled eggs.

And then he would go home.

Chapter
TWENTY-TWO

Ten days. Of long baths in oil-scented water that cooled slowly in the evening air. Of long nights gazing at the stars. Of mornings welcomed because they meant one more day had passed.

She read Austen again and Chaucer, dwelling on his description of the "verray, parfit gentil knight" until that reminded her too much of Royce and she put the tales of pilgrims en route to Canterbury aside.

She played with Amelia and chatted with Joanna. She argued with Alex about the best way to make *marinos* and persuaded him to show her how to play euchre.

She did needlework, which she could manage quite credibly although she seldom had the patience for it. When that paled, she sketched, giving that up when she found herself with page after page of drawings of a certain golden-haired warrior.

She brushed her hair, braided it, and undid the braids. She paced. A time or two . . . or twenty, she wept. The tears always came without warning and made her angry at herself.

She slept poorly and her dreams were often disturbing. The golden-haired warrior again.

On the eighth day, cautiously and in what she decided was merely an experiment, Kassandra sought vision.

Nothing happened. Absolutely nothing. Not only did she receive no glimmer of any possible future, neither did she suffer any of the consequences so familiar in the past. No headache, no nausea or dizziness, nothing.

The next day, she tried again with identical results and dared to hope she might never again see the twisting, twining pathways of the future.

By the tenth day, it was colder and the sky was wreathed in clouds. Even so, she woke eagerly and peered at the day.

She was there yet again hours later, looking out the porthole of the bull-masted ship as the spires of London appeared on the evening tide.

Someone was banging on the door. The sound reverberated through Kassandra's dreams and drew her from a sleep of pure exhaustion.

Bang . . . bang . . . bang.

What was that? Rising through layers of consciousness, she sought the cause.

She was no longer at sea. They had reached London . . . finally. She was in Alex and Joanna's house.

Bang . . . bang . . . bang.

Royce! It could be Royce. He might know somehow that they had returned. Heedless of all thought, driven only by her desperate longing to be with him, she sprang from the bed and dashed across the room toward the door, remembering at the last moment that she was scarcely garbed. With a muttered exclamation, she seized a wrapper from a nearby chair and tugged it on as she raced down the corridor, her hair flowing untamed behind her.

The English servants were still at Boswick, where Alex had sent them before departing when word reached him of the attack on Atreus. Only Akorans were in the house, including the half-dozen warriors on guard. Two of them were in the entry hall, confronting the early caller.

Who stood framed within the just-opened door, looking caught between trepidation and stunned, delighted fascination.

"Odysseus!" he exclaimed as he observed the tunic-clad men, swords belted at their waists. "Hector and Achilles! The legions of the Greeks and Trojans returned to life. I am transported!"

Byron. Disappointment filled her and hard upon it, annoyance. The poet was flushed, ecstatic, all but dancing with excitement. His avid gaze fastened on the guards who shared a puzzled glance.

In another moment, he would see her. Bad

enough the caller was not Royce, but Byron before breakfast was not to be borne.

"Go back to bed," Alex advised. He had appeared on the landing behind her, stuffing a shirt into his trousers. "I'll deal with him."

She nodded gratefully yet lingered, just out of sight.

"My lord," Byron called when he saw Alex. "How fortunate to find you at home."

"And why would that be?" Alex asked as he nodded to the guards, who withdrew but not very far. "It is hardly an hour to expect to be received."

"Certainly not and normally I would not dream of intruding. But when I heard you had returned, I thought is it possible —"

"How did you hear that?" Alex interjected.

"The night watch noted the activity hereabouts . . . the carriages, lights and the like. But as I was saying —"

"And saw fit to spread word of it? How reassuring to know London enjoys such peace that the watchmen have time for idle gossip."

"Oh, well, as to that, they've the habit of it. Much more enjoyable than chasing down wrongdoers, don't you think? But I was saying, I wondered at first how it was you had not intervened. Then it occurred to me quite in a flash that possibly *you did not know.* I thought it only proper to assure that was not the case."

With strained patience, Alex asked, "Did not know what?"

"Why, about the events at Wimbledown Common, of course." When still this failed to rouse any acknowledgment, Byron blurted out, "The disagreement between Lord Hawkforte and Lord Grey? I was there, at Melbourne House, standing right beside them when it happened. No one's been speaking of anything else. They engaged to meet this morning. Did you *truly* not know?"

Kassandra's strangled cry was muffled behind her hand. She staggered against the wall, staring at the man who had brought such devastating news. Surely, she had misunderstood him? Byron had a flair for the dramatic, to say the very least. He might have meant anything . . . or nothing.

"Are you telling me," Alex said, very low, "that my brother-in-law and Lord Grey are dueling today?"

"Rather have done, I would think. Generally get an early start for that sort of thing, don't they? As there's been no word of the outcome and everyone is on tenterhooks —"

The poet paused delicately, as he well might. His avid appetite for scandal had not found a warm reception.

"Get out," Alex said and raised a hand, summoning a guard.

"But my lord," Byron protested even as he stared with alarm at the man advancing on him. "I meant no harm! I hold Lord Hawkforte in the highest possible esteem, as I do you all, most especially Her Highness, the Princess Kassandra. It was only with thought for her tender concern and wishing to prevent her from hearing this from a source less *simpatico* that I —"

It would never occur to Alex to repeat an order nor would there be any reason for him to do so. The door was opened and Byron was through it, his legs tangling in the air as he was unceremoniously ejected.

Scarcely had he gone than Kassandra was in the hall, beseeching her brother. "I must go with you! For pity's sake, do not say otherwise. I cannot sit here waiting to know —"

He looked at her just a touch oddly. "Of course you can't. I'll get a carriage brought round while you dress. Only hurry."

A few months before, he would have insisted she remain where she was while he handled the matter. But between then and now lay a world of change. She had ceased to be the protected princess of the royal house and emerged instead as a woman of maturity and grace.

She would need both as she rushed upstairs and began pulling on the first gown that came to hand. Fortunately, it was a simple day dress and she was able to manage the buttons down the back without great difficulty. She had just finished the last when Joanna hurried in. She, too, had dressed hastily. Brianna, who had accompanied them back to England, came right behind, holding Amelia.

"You're ready?" Joanna asked. She was pale but composed.

Kassandra nodded. "You know?"

"I woke when Alex went to see what was happening. Should we thank Byron or throttle him? He is hardly the most reliable source yet if there is anything to what he says —"

"We will find out for ourselves," Kassandra concluded. She mustered a quick smile for Brianna, dropped a kiss on Amelia's forehead and hurried out along with Joanna.

Alex was standing by the carriage drawn up before the front door. He assisted each woman inside, then quickly joined them. A rap of his cane on the roof and the wheels turned.

They reached Royce's residence within minutes, entering through the broad gates that gave way to a drive framed in ancient oaks. The London property had been in the family for more generations than most knew, although the family itself had the records to date possession precisely. It had evolved over the years from a stone fortress to a gracious manor to the present elegant mansion completed scarcely half-a-century before. Broad windows reflected the early morning light at regular intervals across the limestone façade interrupted by a colonnaded porch in front of the main entrance.

Alex's knock was answered promptly by no less a personage than Bolkum himself.

"Thought you might come by," the smithy

said. "The baker's boy came round with the bread and said you were back. Missed him, you did. His lordship, that is, not the boy."

"Royce is all right?" Joanna asked as they stepped into the hall.

"Right as rain," Bolkum said. He looked surprised. "Any reason he shouldn't be?"

"Damn Byron," Alex muttered.

"The poet fellow?" Bolkum inquired. "Well, as to that, no accounting for taste, is there? At any rate, our chap is fine. Gone off to Hawkforte, he has."

Joanna sighed with relief. "Hawkforte? He isn't even here. I might have known. All that nonsense about Grey . . ."

"Seemed to go well with him," the smithy said. "Leastways, his lordship had no complaint."

"They met?" Kassandra asked. "Royce and Lord Grey?"

"They did," Bolkum confirmed. "This morning at Wimbledown Common. But not for the usual reason. You didn't think that, did you?" When their expressions revealed that they had indeed, the smithy shook his head. "Lord Royce has a parcel more sense than that. He had another purpose in mind altogether. Took that pot he brought back from Akora with him."

"Pot?" Under other circumstances, Alex's surprise might have been comical. "It was Grey, was it? Good lord, should have thought of that. Any idea how Royce found out?"

"From the Spider, would be my guess," Bolkum said. "Heard there's a great burned patch on the Common. Folk have been out to see it but no one has any explanation for how it could have come to be. Leastways, not anyone who's talking."

Alex nodded, satisfied that all was as it should be. "And he's gone to Hawkforte."

"Had his breakfast," Mulridge said, appearing over Bolkum's shoulder. "Said he couldn't bear London a moment longer. Knew he'd have to be back but needed a few days away." She looked at Kassandra rather pointedly. "Has too much on his mind, that lad does."

"Hawkforte," Kassandra murmured, and all her longing sang in the single word.

It was nightfall before Royce reached the strand beneath his ancestral home. He would have been there a good deal sooner were it not for the frantic message from the Prince Regent that found him on the quay just as he was about to depart.

Prinny had heard about the encounter with Grey, or at least a badly garbled version of it. He was overcome at the thought that so trusted a friend and adviser would have risked himself so needlessly. He was in urgent need of reassurance that Royce remained alive and whole. He expected the Earl of Hawkforte to call at Carlton House *posthaste.*

Royce did, entering by a private door adjacent to the servants' quarters. He found the Regent lying down with a cold compress on his head and the bedcurtains drawn against the light.

"Migraine," Prinny moaned. "How I suffer. The throne is a rack! I vow I would sooner have been born a simple farmer asking nothing more of life than decent weather and the occasional pint."

As it was utterly impossible to imagine the Regent in such circumstances or anything remotely approaching them, Royce did not comment directly. He took a seat beside the bed and spoke to calm.

"I gather there's been a misunderstanding, Sire. As you will recall, you asked me to use my good offices to see if there might be some easing of the disagreement between Whigs and Tories. I thought it useful to meet with Lord Grey who, I am confident, understood me very well."

This was misdirection of a sort, but Royce felt perfectly justified in it. With the possibility of an invasion of Akora eliminated, Grey would have no choice but to school himself to patience. If he managed it — and Royce rather thought he would — the tide of history would reward him. In the meantime, there would at least be an end to the most overt hostilities between Whigs and Tories.

The Prince picked his head up from the pillows without evident difficulty. "Good, good, glad to hear it. Grey's not a bad fellow, just misguided. All the same, when I heard Wimbledown Common . . ."

"I was seeking privacy, Sire." Royce smiled apologetically. "Rather naïve of me, I suppose."

"Not at all, I see your intent was good." The Prince sat up, swinging his plump legs over the side of the bed. "Privacy . . . it's not to be had, of course. Eyes everywhere and ears. Oh, well, price to be paid, I suppose." He sighed deeply and made a visible effort to gather himself. "I do appreciate your work, Hawkforte. You've a knack for making sense of things."

"Thank you, Sire. I hope my efforts assist in some small way."

In a rare burst of genuine gratitude, the Prince said, "Don't really know what I'd do without you. Still and all, don't want to wear you out. You're looking a bit peaked, if you don't mind my saying."

"Not at all, Sire. You are, of course, correct. As a matter of fact, I was thinking of taking a few days . . ."

His concerns eased and his vanity soothed, the Prince waved a hand magnanimously. "By all means, take whatever you need. I'll tell Liverpool to hold on to everything. It will be there when you get back."

Royce hid a rueful smile and stood, inclining his head. "Thank you, Sire. I do appreciate that."

"Before you go, there are just one or two matters . . ."

Or ten or twenty, all apparently of pressing urgency. The day trickled by as Royce dealt with them. He sealed himself away in a small office near the royal apartments to which the footmen admitted only those favored few Royce himself summoned. Anyone else wishing a word with the man of the hour was disappointed. By such ruthless attention to duty, he managed to plod his way through the tangle of the Prince's "one or two matters" and emerged from Carlton House in mid-afternoon.

To discover that the weather had changed. The pleasant day was gone and in its place was steady rain. It did not matter. A driving need to put London behind him, even temporarily, spurred him on. Just then he needed Hawkforte as he needed air. It was the touchstone of his being, the one place he truly felt at home and to which he turned at times of trial.

Ordinarily, he enjoyed the sail home, the freedom of sea and wind, the interlude apart from the concerns of the world. This time he merely endured it. Prudence suggested he should make anchor before nightfall, short of his goal. But just at sunset, the sky cleared. Very shortly thereafter, the moon rose.

By its light, he sailed on until he came at last to the strand beneath the proud towers of Hawkforte. Buoyed by the sight of them, Royce made quick work of securing his boat. He climbed the steep path to the road agilely and was soon at his own door.

Bolkum answered it. He looked just as he had when Royce last saw him that morning in London, showing no weariness from a journey that must have been swiftly made.

"I didn't expect you here so quickly," Royce said.

The smithy shrugged. "Nothing wrong with being unexpected, is there?"

"No, of course not. Did you have any trouble coming?"

"Not a bit," Mulridge assured him. "Never do."

Royce shook the dank drops from his cloak and looked gratefully to the fire. From the heart, he said, "It's always good to be here."

Bolkum nodded. "Rain's coming down from the north. Going to be a nasty night."

"Poke up the fire," Mulridge advised.

Bolkum gave the logs a tweak that sent sparks shooting up the huge stone chimney.

To Royce, she said, "Don't sit up too late."

"I don't plan to," he assured her, but they had already gone. He looked back to the flames, thinking he would sleep when he could, when he was finally so tired that thoughts of Kassandra lost their bitter bite.

She would have died.

Constant repetition, drumming over and over in his mind, had robbed the words of much of their sting. As they faded, what was truly im-

487

portant emerged: She had not died. Kassandra lived. Apart from him, to be sure, but she still lived. And for that he was quite desperately grateful.

She was a woman of courage and honor, truly the Atreides, but she was also Kassandra twirling in jonquil-yellow as he first saw her, as though round the maypole in the giddy flush of fairest spring. It was high summer now for all that the weather mimicked autumn, and his feelings for her were beyond any hope of ever rooting out.

God, how he missed her! Missed the warmth of her skin against his, the heat of her desire, the sound of her laughter, her quicksilver smile, the light in her eyes, on and on until he thought the world was defined by what was missing from it.

He should have stayed. Should have remained in Akora and fought through to some understanding between them. And so he might have were it not for duty, the selfsame duty that had led Kassandra to do as she had.

They were both creatures of duty. It was one of the many facets of their beings that joined them together.

What was she doing right then? Sleeping, perhaps? Dreaming of a future that did not include him?

His fist slammed against the ancient oak mantel. Was he not a man and a Hawkforte in the bargain? Never had his forebears shied from taking what they rightly viewed as theirs.

The wind sucked up the chimney, drawing fire. He stared into it, seeing not present flame but ancient shadow, the unbroken line of proud lords and valiant ladies who had made Hawkforte their own. What would they say to him if they could? Indeed, what did they say to him? For truth be told, they seemed to linger in the place where they had lived and loved, a gentle presence, to be sure, but as real as the very stone and mortar.

"Royce . . ."

He turned, startled, but saw no one. Yet he could have sworn he heard his name.

Weariness made for an overly active imagination, he supposed, yet he didn't feel weary. On the contrary, he felt suffused with strength as though the doubts that had weighed on him too long were suddenly lifted.

"Royce . . ."

He lifted his head, looking toward the top of the staircase wreathed in darkness from which the voice seemed to come. A spirit? If so, an oddly plaintive one.

"It's rather cold, don't you think?" the spirit said.

"Kassandra . . . ?" It couldn't be. He was tired, filled with longing, and he had conjured her in some strange way.

He'd also done a damn good job of it. She was wearing some sort of filmy white thing, a nightrobe perhaps, and her ebony hair tumbled over her shoulders. She looked young and very uncertain. Not the Atreides at all but most definitely Kassandra.

He was moving, quick strides devouring the distance between them, the power of ages surging. He was Hawkforte, always and eternal, and she was the woman he had waited for all his life.

"Is it often cold like this?" she asked. "Even in the summer?"

"Yes, sometimes," he spoke, walking toward the stairs and mounting them quickly. As he climbed, she became clearer. Her teeth worried her lower lip.

"It's an English summer," he explained gently though he was bursting with relief, joy and utter, absolute certainty. "Good for the roses."

"Are there roses here?" She was very close, not more than an arm's length away. He reached out, schooling himself to care lest he startle or, God forbid, hurt her in any way, and did not breathe again until his hand caught hers.

Then, only then, did he relax just the smallest degree. "Yes, quite a few. I'll show them to you, if you like. In the morning."

"Yes," she said and stepped nearer, coming within the circle of his arms. They closed around her and she trembled, giddy relief and heartfelt pleasure tumbling one over the other. She was here, at Hawkforte, with Royce, in the place and the life she had scarcely dared to dream of. No dream now but the reality where she belonged so completely every step she had ever taken from her very first seemed intended to bring her to this incandescent moment.

He was warm and hard against her, his strength her refuge, his love her glory. Tears blurred her vision but her smile rivaled the radiance of the sun.

"In the morning," she said.

"My God, Kassandra," he murmured and gathered her closer still. They clung together. "Are you truly here?"

She laughed shakily. "Oh, yes, finally. Eighteen days have never been so long! Before you even left Akora, I knew I could not bear to say goodbye. No matter how hurt or angry you are, we are meant to be together, I am absolutely certain of that. I would have knocked together a raft and rowed it myself to get here so do not tell me I should not have come, for I will not listen. You are what brought me to England in the first place though I did not know it. You were the purpose of my being here, so that we two could accomplish what neither one of us could do alone."

Struggling with the miracle of her presence, Royce was hard-pressed to follow her quicksilver speech, but he caught the gist of it.

"I would never be so great a fool as to send you away," he vowed. "But how did you get here?"

"Atreus is doing marvelously well and has fully resumed his duties. Deilos's trial is being arranged. Many of those in Helios have been released, they clearly had no notion of what Deilos plotted. But a few are still being held pending clarification of what role they played, if any. With all so well in hand, Atreus agreed that Alex and Joanna should return to England without delay. I came along."

Royce stiffened slightly. The intimacy of their embrace was a bit more than he thought a brother should be called upon to witness. "Alex is here?"

Kassandra leaned back a little, the better to drink him in with eyes overflowing with love. "He is in London but he sent a message. I don't quite understand it but here it is all the same: He said he and Joanna will come to Hawkforte on the morrow and that he trusts you will behave as well as he himself did."

Thinking of the circumstances in which Alex had proposed to Joanna the year before there in the great hall of Hawkforte, Royce grinned. "He said that, did he?"

"He did. Do you intend to be as mysterious?"

"Oh, no," Royce assured her. "I promise to explain fully . . . tomorrow, after I show you the roses."

His arms tightened around her. Gruffly, the man who had faced down demons said, "I feared losing you."

"You, fear?" she asked.

"Far too much," he said, breathing in the scent of her. "It made me forget what matters most."

"This moment," said the former prophetess, "and all the moments that follow one after another down through all the years. Every surprising, precious one of them."

His laughter, born of vast relief and even vaster love, echoed up the curving stone steps to the top of the ancient tower. He carried her there, swiftly and surely, and laid her on the wide bed that looked out past broad windows to the moon-washed sea.

And there, in the place where so many lovers had wrought their magic, the Lord of Hawkforte and his princess pledged themselves to the future that was theirs to make together.

Later . . .

. . . so late the world seemed wreathed in slumber, a solitary figure slipped into the library of the London house. Brianna shut the door quietly and checked to be sure it was closed before striking flint to tinder to light one of the oil lamps. By its glow, she scanned the library shelves. When she found the book she sought, she took it down carefully and set it on a nearby table.

The binding was tooled Moroccan leather embossed with the title: A History of Essex. *She knew the book, having found it shortly after she first arrived in England months before. Then she had accompanied her aunt to assist at the birth of*

Alex and Joanna's child. Now she had returned for her own sake . . . and because of the book.

Slowly, she opened it. It was a weighty tome thick with kings, queens, battles, and the like dating all the way back to the time of Alfred the Great. It had much to say about Hawkforte and the mighty family that ruled there. But it also spoke of other places, including one called Holyhood.

There was a picture of the manor of Holyhood, a simple line drawing depicting a graceful house. Brianna stared at it as fragments of memory stirred. She had been there. She had been in that house, somewhere in the lost time before the terrible storm that took her parents' lives and left her a nameless orphan washed up on Akoran shores.

If she shut her eyes and thought of the house, she heard the distant sound of voices calling.

She was suddenly very cold but the chill rooted within her heart held a tiny spark of light. Her spirit yearned toward it, feeling the spark grow and warmth turn to heat. Her arms were wrapped around herself but they felt strangely like another's arms, far stronger, drawing her powerfully.

In that embrace was protection and so much more, but in the house . . . the house held a secret, the key to a mystery that both terrified and tempted her. She stared again at the drawing and felt within herself the hardening of resolve . . .

. . . He could sense her again almost as he had on the road between this world and the next. She was the woman who had hovered near him, calling

*his name, slowing his journey into death and be-
yond.*

*He had recognized her. She had been with him
before, deep in the caves during the trial of selection
when so much had been revealed to him. Then he
had only the briefest glimpse of her, but he had
never forgotten.*

*He knew her, knew her face and her voice, knew
the scent and touch of her, knew how she felt even
now almost as though he already held her safe
within his arms.*

*But he had not known her name. Until he woke
and saw the silver glisten of her tears and the fiery
glory of her hair.*

*She was his. Of that, he was entirely certain. But
she did not know it . . . not yet.*

*She would, he promised himself, and very soon.
On the roof of the palace, beneath the stars, the
Vanax of Akora turned his eyes to the north and
saw with his warrior's heart the prize awaiting him
there.*

About the Author

Josie Litton lives in New England, where she is happily at work on a new trilogy of historical romances. She is also at home at *www.josielitton.com.*